A NOTE ON THE AUTHOR

Rorie Smith is a former journalist. He is the author of four novels: *Tombola; Counterpart; One Million Euro;* and *Bordeaux, Private Eye (*all published by Tan Tan Books). He lives in Bordeaux, France but also calls the Rame Peninsular in Cornwall home.

The Wonderful World of Jane & Oliver Bloke

Rorie Smith

write side left

ISBN: TPB: 978-1-7396993-8-3
ISBN:eBook: 978-1-7396993-9-0

Compilation & Cover Design by S A Harrison
Published by WriteSideLeft UK
https://www.writesideleft.com

The essential detail of Lillian Alling's long walk was taken from *Lillian Alling: The Journey Home* by Susan Smith-Josephy. With thanks.

The Wonderful World of Jane & Oliver Bloke

Rorie Smith

For Jeanne

I beg you do something.
Learn a dance step, something to justify your existence,
something that gives you the right to live in your own skin.
Learn to walk and to laugh.
Because it would be too senseless, after so many have died,
for you to do nothing with your life.

Charlotte Delbo, Auschwitz survivor

CHAPTER ONE

Roughly told Tirana, when he came home from work one evening and was settled into an armchair with a bottle of beer, that he planned to write a book.

Tirana looked up and asked, 'What's it about, then?' and Roughly replied, 'It starts with first memories, when I am a nipper with Alfred and Rita in Hounslow. Then it recounts my life as a policeman in London and North Wales. After that I'm going to turn it into a spy thriller like James Bond. I've already asked my cousin Otis in Jamaica to check out a hotel where we can spring a honey-trap, because all spy thrillers need a honey-trap.'

Then he stopped and asked Tirana what she thought about that.

Tirana stood up and walked into the kitchen to check on the dinner. Otherwise she would have to tell Roughly that it sounded like a pile of old nonsense. She worked in the Wales Flower Shop in Colwyn Bay where the owner was a fellow with a front tooth missing who had also started to write a memoir. So he was at the same game as Roughly.

One afternoon the fellow had told Tirana the story of how he was vice-president of the Wales Flower Club in 1973 and they were playing a golf tournament in Llandrindod Wells which he won and afterwards they were having drinks and dinner to celebrate. But, because he had drunk so much, when he stood up to make his speech his trousers fell down. Even though that was many years ago he was still laughing about it today. So that is certainly a story he will put in the memoir.

After dinner Tirana told Roughly, 'You need to take a course in book writing before you start. If not, people will say that it's a good idea to write a book but behind your back they'll say you don't know what you're talking about.'

So the next day Roughly walked into the University of Colwyn Bay and went up to the wooden counter until he was opposite a Wales Chapel Lady who was a dried-up and stick-thin party. He told her he had come to sign up for the course on book writing.

When she heard that she took a step back as if Roughly had said he'd stopped believing in God. Then she picked up the phone and was talking quickly in Welsh. At the same time she looked at Roughly slyly out of the corner of her eye. Then she put down the phone and did a great big sneeze into a handkerchief that was tucked up her sleeve. After that she opened a ledger and studied it. Roughly could see that it was an old-style ledger with all the entries in fountain pen. Finally she told Roughly, in her Wales Chapel Voice, 'Climb the stairs to the top of the building and knock on a door marked Dr Heinz Williams-Jones, Writing Professor.' Then she closed up the ledger and turned away.

Roughly climbed to the top of building, which was six floors up. It was really the attic, all musty and dusty. To the side was a wooden door with a brass plaque with 'Dr Heinz Williams-Jones, Writing Professor' written on it.

When he was at home Roughly was mild-mannered, but like all policemen he had only one way to knock on a door. So he gave a sharp copper-style rat-a-tat-tat, which would normally paralyse whoever was on the other side. But this time Roughly was the one who got the surprise because a loud voice, in an accent Roughly had never heard before, called out, 'Come in before you break the bloody door down.'

Roughly opened the door to see Dr Heinz Williams-Jones.

Now we need to give a description of him. We can start by saying that there is a similarity to Albert Einstein in the famous photograph where he has his mouth open and is giving the manic stare. The difference is that Einstein is a diminutive shape while Heinz is the size of an angry bear. Heinz is also wearing a bright red sweater. He is seated in a wooden swivel chair. In front of him there is a wooden desk covered in papers and letters. An easel is set up facing the window and there is a paintbrush on a stand next to it.

He looked at Roughly, who was still standing in the doorway.

'You got to be a copper. No one else is knocking in a door like that.'

Roughly laughed.

'Well, I am certainly a copper but I am not investigating a crime. I have come about the book writing course.'

When he heard this, Heinz leant back in his chair and ran his hands through his unruly hair. After that he gave a slow belly-laugh and Roughly could see tears of laughter forming at the corners of his eyes. Soon they were running down the sides of his face as his whole frame shook. Then Heinz opened a drawer in the desk and brought out a bottle of Wales Brandy and a couple of glasses and told Roughly to sit down. Then he poured a tot for them both.

Roughly took that as a sign to open up the file he had brought with him and to start to read the first chapter, which recounted his earliest memories when he was kicking a football round the streets of Hounslow with the other nippers. Then he described how Alfred, his dad, got a watch from British Rail and how he was always consulting it, which is incidentally how Roughly received his name. But then Heinz put up his hand and cried, 'Stop! All that is all very interesting but we need to talk first.'

They sipped their Wales Brandies and Heinz told Roughly he came to Colwyn Bay thirty years ago from Germany.

'To begin with I was working in a bookshop in Prestatyn. But I always wanted to be a writer and because the damn bookshop was a bit slow I'd got time to do the writing. So I am clack-clack on the old typewriter in between serving the customers, who are mainly little old ladies looking for books by Agatha Christie and other people like that.'

Heinz told Roughly that he put the story of his life into the book.

'I described how I grew up in a valley in the country in Bavaria, milking the cows morning and evening, and bringing in the harvest at the end of summer and frolicking with the maidens. Then I got a break when I heard that Wales was the land of milk and honey. So I left Germany and came to Prestatyn, where I fell in love with a Wales girl. She was called Williams-Jones and I am called Pumpernickel and because I wanted to be like the Wales guys we decided to turn tradition around. So when we became married I took the name Williams-Jones and I am putting that story in the book as well.

'Now I am banging away on the typewriter and starting to get the swollen head. I am telling everybody coming into the bookshop that I will soon be a big-shot writer. When it is finished I am packaging it up and sending it to a publisher. And, oh boys, I am getting the clip round the ear because it comes back a few weeks later with a neat typewritten note which is reading, "This book is a load of old Wales Sheep Poo and we has got no intention of publishing it."'

But, Heinz tells Roughly, he keeps on till in the end he's sent it to every publisher in Wales and they have all sent it back.

'Then my wife, who has a bit of money of her own, gives me some Wales Dollars, which is the currency they are using then, and a local printer prints the damn thing.

'Now I am holding the first copy in my hand and I'm proud as punch. I've forgotten that every publisher in Wales has called it a load of old Wales Sheep Poo.'

Heinz describes how he hands out signed copies to friends.

'They say, "Thank you very much, Heinz," and put it on top of the fridge with all the other bits and bobs. But when I call back a week later to ask what they think about it, they stand there like goldfish with their mouths open because they have forgotten all about it. Then I discover I have less friends than I used to have because when I ping on a doorbell with a copy of the book there is no reply. A lot of the local Wales citizens are hiding behind the curtains till I have gone back up the garden path.'

In the end, Heinz said, his Wales wife told him that most people had got better things to do with their lives than read his book.

'Then she is asking around and finding that a lot of other wives are in the same boat. They have got the spare room filled up with copies of their husband's memoirs which detail how they were the first people in Caernarvon to put in central heating. Some of them are even turning that into a thriller as well.'

For a moment, Heinz says, he went into a quite a depression. Then he woke up one morning and it all came to him in a flash. He turned up at the University of Colwyn Bay and spoke to the guy who set up the courses. The guy mulled it over and then he said it was actually a good idea because he had been hit by a neighbour who was at the same scam.

'He gave me this attic room where we are now. Anyone who comes into the university to ask about writing a book is sent to see me and I try to discourage them.'

Heinz filled up Roughly's glass and pointed to a picture set up on his easel and said, 'What you need to do is take up painting, like this.' He took the painting off the easel and Roughly saw that it was a Wales landscape with a flock of sheep standing on a hillside in the rain. Then he put the picture back on the easel and opened a drawer and pulled out a tray full of objects. Roughly could see a small dog made out of matchsticks.

'If you paint a picture or make a matchstick model your neighbours will be happy as anything,' Heinz said. 'They will put the picture on the wall and the matchstick dog on the sideboard and they will say Roughly did that and everyone will say well I never.'

After that Roughly drank up his tot of Wales Brandy and then went down the stairs and out past the Wales Chapel Lady. When he arrived home he asked Tirana if they had a big box of matches in the house because he intends to start making matchstick models.

Over the next few weeks Roughly made a whole series of matchstick animals – foxes, rabbits, chickens – till in the end he had the whole damn farmyard. He gave them to friends and neighbours, who were pleased to receive them, though some of them complained that their sideboards were getting cluttered up with this stuff and that they had run out of wall space for the pictures he was turning out as well.

Then one day he was handing out a matchstick sheep to a fellow policeman for his daughter's birthday when the guy said, 'Hold on, Roughly, why are you handing out all this nonsense? You were planning to be a big-shot writer but all you do is make damn models. All the while we are waiting for you to produce your damn book.'

That night Roughly went home and had a big old think and after that he threw all the matchstick animals in the bin.

The next day he went in to the university and he was

past the Wales Chapel Lady and up to the top floor two at a time and rapping on the attic door. Then he was inside and sharing a tot of Wales Brandy with Heinz and telling him that he was fed up with making matchstick models and that he wanted to be a writer.

Heinz ran his hands through his wild hair and shook his head in surprise.

'Well you are the first guy who ever came back.'

Then he took down his art easel and put it away and told Roughly that really he was a well-known book writer in Germany, under another name. Then he agreed to teach Roughly about book writing. But he also told him, 'I am going to be tough with you and tell you if you are writing a load of old Wales Sheep Poo.'

And that is how Roughly O'Reilly set out to learn about book writing

CHAPTER TWO

The next week Roughly is opposite Heinz in his attic room at the university. In front of them on the desk are two tots of Wales Brandy. Heinz had told him that before he started the course he needed to set out his stall, so one evening Roughly had sat down at the kitchen table at home and made some notes. He read them out now.

'My father came to the UK after the war from Kingston, Jamaica. He was called Alfred. When he arrived he started as a porter with British Railways but in the end he was promoted to station-master and everyone said how well Alfred O'Reilly had done.

'My mother, who was called Rita, arrived by another route. She came from Czechoslovakia, where the Communist Party was making life hell for everyone. They listened in to phone conversations and ordered people around all the time. So one day Rita's father lost his temper and started to yell down the phone at a man in a government department. He called him an interfering "S-o-B" and threatened to visit the office where he worked and twist his head off his shoulders. After that it was too dangerous to stay and the family was smuggled out of Prague in the back of a truck and that's how they ended up in London.

'Then one day Rita was on a train and she got off at the station where Alfred was working. She asked him the time of the next train for Hounslow and they had a bit of a chat and that was the start of that. At the time Rita had a job in a shop in Hounslow but then she joined Oddbins. In the end she was made up to be a shop manager there. That's why in gratitude she gave me my second name of Oddbins.'

Roughly stops reading and looks up to see that Heinz has turned to gaze out of the window, where the wind and the rain are rattling the windowpanes hard.

'Don't worry, Mr Oddbins, I is taking it all in,' he says, without turning his head back. Roughly frowns for a moment. Then he continues his story.

'Not long after Alfred started work at the station, a passenger asked when the next train due was due. Alfred said, "About ten minutes, roughly," and everyone had a good laugh at that. But when he did it again there was a complaint and the station-master told him that he needed to be precise when he was in the UK. So that was a good lesson learnt. And it's why I have the first name Roughly, to remind me to be punctual. Our family name is O'Reilly because of all the Irish immigrants who went to Jamaica. So that is the story of how I got the full mouthful of Roughly Oddbins O'Reilly and there are not too many people with a set of names like that.' Heinz swivels back slowly in his chair and stares at him.

'Well I'll be damned. Roughly Oddbins O'Reilly. That's quite a name. You are even more of a mongrel than I am.'

Roughly laughs at that and continues.

'I grew up in Hounslow, hearing a mishmash of

different voices. I spoke Czech with Rita but at the same time I picked up the accent of the Caribbean crowd who were always in the house. There was also family turning up from Prague and they have a way of murdering the English language that is all their own. Rita never got rid of her East European accent and Alfred always had that beautiful Calypso way of speaking. Rita was a beauty when she was younger but she put on a few pounds when she was older. They were always the odd couple but they were never apart.

'Then I caused the big bloody upset with the announcement I was joining the police. No one in Hounslow, East Europe or the Caribbean had much time for the police. Rita was only converted when she saw me in uniform, I can still recall the tear coming to her eye. Then she told me, when Alfred had gone out of the room, that she was proud of me.

'So now we are coming to Tirana, who started out from Albania. She came into my life when I was at home on police force leave. She was part of the East European group that drifted in and out of the house. She was a real beauty too, slim as a stick with raven-dark hair. Everyone in her family back home in Albania was surprised when they heard she had become a copper's wife. But she has got all the smarts, no one puts anything over on Tirana O'Reilly. At the moment she works in the Wales Flower Shop but in the evenings she's studying computer and accounting courses.

'We also have two young nippers who are stars of the Colwyn Bay under-11s soccer team and when I'm finished here I'm due to take them to soccer practice. I also like to do the cooking. All the coppers in Colwyn Bay are happy to get an invitation to our house. They know they'll get a damn good Caribbean meal.

'Tirana always says I should have been an actor. She laughs when I do the police in different voices. But I'm always careful with the Wales guys in Colwyn Bay. If they hear a guy with my skin colour pitching into the Wales accent they will think I am taking the pee.

'The final thing to say is I am a detective inspector with the Colwyn Bay force and I've just been handed a cold case review, but I am not allowed to talk about that.'

After that he stops. Heinz pulls a face.

'That's a damn shame. Everyone is interested in cold case reviews. They are the staple of the TV programmes. That would have been a good place to start with your first story.'

Roughly shakes his head.

'If I talked now, the powers that be would haul me over the coals.'

So Heinz thinks for a moment. Then he says, 'In that case, Roughly Oddbins O'Reilly, your first writing assignment is to invent two characters, a man and a woman. Later you can place them in a story.'

§

Roughly walks down the stairs and out of the university building, deep in thought about the characters he needs to invent for the following week. The rain has stopped so there's no need to put up his umbrella. As he crosses the square in front of the university he sees a fellow copper from the Colwyn Bay force. He's standing side-on, half looking into a shop window. His collar's up and he's wearing a baseball cap pulled down over his eyes.

This copper is called Idris, which is both a Wales name and an Arab name, so to avoid confusion he is called Jimmy. Roughly comes up to him and says hello Jimmy what are you doing skulking round here. This is the way the coppers talk when they are joshing with each other.

Jimmy turns round suddenly, looking startled. Roughly has been so preoccupied with his writing assignment for the following week he's not realised that Jimmy is on a case and doing surveillance.

Jimmy relaxes, though he still keeps an eye on the university while they talk. He asks Roughly what he is doing there and Roughly replies he is taking a course. Then Jimmy says, strictly on the QT like, but has he seen this guy and he takes out of his pocket a photo which he passes over to Roughly, who looks at it and replies that is Dr Heinz Williams-Jones, né Pumpernickel, my professor of creative writing.

Roughly laughs. What the hell are you going to charge him with, Jimmy, bad grammar and other offences against the English language?

CHAPTER THREE

Roughly and Tirana discuss the assignment over the weekend. They make a list of the people they know in Hounslow and Colwyn Bay and build up a composite picture.

When Roughly arrives at the university, he folds up his umbrella, walks past the Wales Chapel Lady and climbs the stairs to the attic office. Heinz, who is wearing a bright yellow sweater, pours the tots of Wales Brandy.

They raise their glasses. Heinz looks out of the window at the rain that is beginning to fall more heavily. He shakes his head and laughs.

'If this weather continues we'll all be drowned ducks.'

Then he sits back.

'So what have you got for me today, Roughly O'Reilly?'

'Well,' Roughly says, 'I've invented two characters. They're called Jane Jones and Oliver Bloke,' and he opens his notebook to read to Heinz.

Jane Jones left school and her parents, Sheila and Morris, were on her back. They were concerned about her future and told her she needed to knuckle down. So then Jane Jones was working through what are called the dry thickets of the law. But where she was studying was a low-grade factory turning out run-of-the-mill lawyers. So Jane Jones put her head down and treated it like an illness she had to see through.

That evening she was on her second pint at The Nutmeg. Oliver Bloke was at a table nearby with his friend Nebs. They were discoursing on the best type of Moroccan weed. He had the long hair which was the style then and he was wearing the Russian greatcoat as well. Oliver and Nebs were both studying business accounting. But then everyone looked up because Nebs was just announcing in a loud voice, 'I am packing in the course and heading for France to join the Foreign Legion.' Jane, who was at a table with two girls from Cox's Bazaar in Burma, caught Oliver's eye for the first time. Later they both said it was love at first sight.

When Jane left the pub that night she had the first inkling she was not going to make it in the law. She lay in bed and wondered about Oliver. She was unable to sleep because the full horror of life in a lawyer's office was slowly dawning on her. The highlight of the day, she imagines, will be when an old lady in a flowered hat changes her will to leave £5,000 to her cat. She arranges that and they have a coffee and a chocolate biscuit to celebrate. After that it's all downhill. A thin guy claims his neighbour's fence blocks his view. Then a hatchet-faced woman wants a divorce and she has to stick the knife in, legally speaking, until the blood flows.

After that there are the property guys who want to talk about partition walls and how many garages they are allowed to put up. There are other guys who think their business is so damn important it's worth her time to talk about it. By the end of the day it's all running round in her head and she thinks they're people any other time she will cross the road to avoid. She takes a swig from a bottle she keeps in the desk drawer and on the way out she stuffs all the papers down the toilet and says goodbye to all that.

But we have got ahead of ourselves in the story here.

Jane Jones is still at the learning stage. The evenings in The Nutmeg with Oliver and Nebs are her Oxford education, though they are minus the punts and the cream teas. Instead she is learning the different types of Moroccan weed and how to cross the Sahara desert on a camel.

Jane Jones rented a room on Lees Hall Crescent where the landlady was called Edna Skull. No, that's not right. In a legal sense it's probably even a libel because she was really called Edna Schull but the two names are pronounced the same.

One night Edna Schull walked into the kitchen to make a cup of cocoa and found Jane Jones slumped over a chair and singing a lullaby, following an evening in The Nutmeg with Oliver. The next morning she said in a stern voice, 'Jane Jones, you got to shape up or ship out – and you a law student and all that.'

In time Jane became good friends with Edna Schull, who told Jane over fireside chats that she was a widow.

'When we first arrived from Ireland thirty years ago we didn't have two pennies between us. Joe started as a porter at Exchange Street station. I began as a dinner lady. Then I joined M&S and they promoted me till I was in charge of a floor.'

Edna introduced Jane to her twin girls, who were called Freddie and Ginger after Fred Astaire and Ginger Rogers. Jane noted how they were slinky and beautiful. Then Edna explained that Joe was from Shanghai and he was a merchant seaman who washed up in Ireland. When he put in his papers to become an Irish citizen he changed his name to Schull, which was the town where they were living. That is why Edna, whose maiden name is Smith, is called Schull.

Freddie and Ginger invited Jane to go dancing with them at weekends. Edna often joined them as well. The girls, who both worked at M&S, were on the lookout for husbands and they tried to fix up Jane as well. She went out first with a builder and then a plumber but really she had her eye on Oliver. One evening she persuaded him to come along and soon he was in with the Schull family also. When Jane and Oliver got married, Freddie and Ginger were invited with their builder bloke husbands. Edna arrived with a Greek guy who had a reputation but Edna could deal with him so there was no worry about that.

One Friday afternoon, with the weekend coming up, Oliver was off with Nebs, and Edna and the girls were also away so Jane was on her own. She got up on a chair and took down a rucksack from the top of the wardrobe. She put a sleeping bag and a few warm clothes into the rucksack. Then she studied a map, tracing a line with her finger, before she put on a warm coat and a hat and stepped outside and pulled the door closed behind her. She took the bus into the city centre then a bus out the other side. Soon she was standing by the side of the road and the light was beginning to go because it was late afternoon towards the end of the year. Finally a truck drew up and she climbed into the cab and they were heading north on the A6 past Preston, Lancaster, Kendal, then they were grinding up Shap in low gear. She changed trucks at a stop near Carlisle and then she was over the border into Scotland and approaching Glasgow.

Later, in her sleeping bag, she looked up at the moon going in and out behind the clouds. She woke an hour later, the cold nipping at her feet. She walked round the building site flapping her arms to get warm. The half-built houses and the cement mixers and a couple of trees to one side were all bathed in the silvery light of the moon.

It was too cold to stand out for long but Jane had the feeling time had expanded, so that ten minutes felt like ten hours. The silvery light of the moon had created a new world more scary than the daytime world: reversed, like a photographic negative, it was pulling her in. Jane thought if she could stand the cold for an hour the secret of the universe would be revealed to her, but she was starting to shiver badly so she dived back into the sleeping bag. She woke again to see a sliver of grey light and to hear a bus and then a truck go by. Then she was out of her sleeping bag and rolling everything up and on her way before anyone discovered her.

In the morning she got a lift out of Glasgow and recalled later that she had walked by the side of a loch. Then she was back on the road waiting for a lift. The noise and the warmth of the cab made her relax and her eyes started to close. She got down from the cab on the edge of the city and yawned and took the night bus home.

Other people were doing the same thing. They were levering open the space and never saying a word about it. So at Monday morning legal classes Jane kept quiet about her weekend. But the scene with the silvery light of the moon was imprinted on her memory. She only mentioned it to Oliver years later, when they were living on the lighthouse. But Oliver is one of those guys who never wants to get topped on a story. So when Jane was finished he said he had a story of his own which followed a similar theme.

'I am going tell you about my Auntie Dolly,' he said. 'Every Saturday morning she took the train from Manchester, where she lived, to Weston-super-Mare, which is a journey of about three and a half hours. She changed at Bristol Temple Meads and she had her lunch in the station buffet.

'Everyone is teasing Auntie Dolly and saying she'd found a boyfriend in Weston because she never married. But the only explanation she ever gave was that she liked the smell of the sand and sea at Weston. But then she let on that she bought her supply of cigarettes for the week when she was there. She bought them from the same tobacconist by the pier and they always had a chat about the government and the weather and so on. She smoked the first cigarette in a shelter on the pier looking out to sea and she said that was the best cigarette she ever smoked. After that she caught the train home.

'Then one day – and this was the only time she ever did it – she bought a lottery ticket from the tobacconist.

Her number came up and she won £10,000 which she divided up between her three great-nieces, who at that time were Hazel, Laura and Isabelle.

'But after that she never went back to Weston and soon after she stopped smoking altogether. Then a year later she's dead from the lung cancer and at the funeral everybody says how she was a nice lady and a pity she never married. But nobody ever mentioned her going to Weston every Saturday. She was about sixty years old when she died.'

Roughly stops reading and looks up. Heinz has turned to listen to the wind, which is still knocking hard at the windowpanes. Roughly wonders why Jimmy is investigating him.

Heinz runs his hands through his hair.

'Well, Mr Cold Case Review of the Colwyn Bay force, you have the imagination, I am allowing you that. But you have forgotten to give a description of Jane or Oliver, which is a bit amiss. Though there are some writers recommending to give hints rather than coming out with the full description. The reader is filling in the rest. If that is what you are intending, then I see Oliver as a skinny guy whose hair will recede when he is older. Jane has got a square frame already and she'll need to be careful for the future otherwise she'll bulk out.'

Roughly laughs at that.

'Don't worry about Jane. She keeps active so she will be okay.'

Then Roughly says that Jane is based on an Irish girl who visited the house in Hounslow when he was young.

Everyone was surprised when she took off for Rome, where she developed a crush on a Jesuit priest. So that is how the next story is starting.

Heinz nods his head and sits back to listen and Roughly reads out the next instalment.

Jane Jones finally abandoned the law. For the time being she'd also given Oliver Bloke the heave-ho and was travelling north from Rome in a blue VW Beetle with a Jesuit priest who was on papal business.

They were outside Salzburg in Austria finishing up their lunch at a roadside taverna. The Jesuit priest, originally from California, looked at his watch and said, 'It's time we were pushing on.' He walked out to the car and Jane followed on a moment later. As she crunched over the gravel she saw the Jesuit priest, who was a tall guy with a bushy beard, squashed up in the front seat and fiddling with the radio dial. He called out, 'Hey listen to this.' Jane leant in to the car to hear an announcer on the Voice of America saying in an excited voice, because this was 1968, that Russian troops had entered Prague and there was shooting in the streets.

The Jesuit priest spun the radio dial and they picked up the same news from Swiss and German stations. Then they got out the maps and saw they were only a couple of hours' drive from the Czech border. The Jesuit priest thumped his hands against the steering wheel and said, 'Goddam, goddam.' Because everyone knows the Jesuit priests love a good barney.

This made Jane think of the spy Kim Philby and his

father who was St John Philby, the Arabist. The date was 1933. Kim had just come down from university and his father had given him £50 to buy a motorbike. But Kim had used the money to buy a railway ticket to Vienna, where the Dollfuss government was in a vicious crackdown on the socialists.

Soon Kim was in the thick of the action, fighting mano a mano in the streets. He had classically levered open some space and he was having the time of his life, the socialist flame burning in his belly. At the same time he was meeting a gorgeous young revolutionary and after the usual heart-stopping adventures they escaped back to London and got married. After that he was approached by the Soviet spy service and was on his way to becoming a master spy and a bloodstained traitor.

In a couple of hours Jane and the Jesuit priest arrived at the Czech border. They stopped the car and walked up to the top of an incline overlooking the border post. There, Jane took out a pair of binoculars the Jesuit priest always carried in the car and looked down at the border post. Then she said, 'Well if you ask me there's no one there at all.'

They drove on through the deserted border post and found themselves in a village where they parked up and it was as quiet as hell. They were discussing if they should wing it and drive straight through to Prague, telling anyone who asked they were papal observers, but it was getting dark and the rain was starting to come down hard. Then they were surprised by a tap on the window and a little old guy was standing there. The Jesuit priest rolled down the window and the little old guy stuck his head in and said in Italian, because he'd seen the Italian plates, 'What the fuck are you guys doing here? You need to get the hell out. The Russians and God knows who else are coming up the road and you are in danger of getting your arses canned, 'specially if they see the Italian plates.'

The Jesuit priest looked back at him and replied in Italian, 'We are here as papal observers to monitor what is going on with the fighting in Prague.' The little old guy, who had now covered his head with a piece of sacking to keep off the rain, took a step back. 'Well that is the craziest thing I ever heard,' he said. Then he shook his head and said they had better come with him.

They ended up staying the night with the little old guy and his wife. When the Jesuit priest opened the briefcase with the papal insignia and showed the letters signed by the Pope they were all over him. Then they were eating dinner and the little old guy and his wife told them they were keeping fingers crossed and saying prayers that the lads up in Prague could turn the tide.

As they were finishing dinner they heard a rumbling in the distance and soon the whole street was lit up. The house even felt like it was moving. They peeped out and saw that a line of Russian tanks was passing. Then someone on the other side of the street lifted an upstairs window and threw a homemade bomb at a tank which caused the column to halt and the officers got down for a brief parley.

Then the senior officer barked an order and one of the tanks backed up and lowered its gun and aimed at the house. After that there was a hell of a bang which left Jane Jones temporarily deaf.

When they looked again, the house the guy threw the bomb from had disappeared. It was just a pile of dust and rubble. Then the column of tanks was on the move again.

The next morning they listened on the radio and heard that it was all over, that the Russians had won. The leaders of the government, including Alexander Dubček, had all been arrested. But as they were getting back into the blue VW Beetle the little old guy said, 'The Russian troops got control of the border post now. So you are in danger of getting arrested as spies never mind you got a letter from the Pope.'

So they waited till it was dark again and then they drove slowly up a back road without lights and inched across the border on a cattle track, scraping the bottom of the car, until they were finally back in Austria.

They were shocked by what they had seen. The Jesuit priest told Jane, 'I need a day to write up a papal observer's report before we go on to London and then to Ireland.' The Jesuit priest was on a mission to find out what was happening with the priests in Ireland. There was a strong rumour going around that they had been messing with the kids and it was a scandal waiting to blow.

They were finishing up lunch in another roadside taverna. They were having a couple of brandies to calm their nerves before they drove on towards the hotel (which was recommended in the guide because it had a swimming pool and a jacuzzi). Jane Jones was spinning the radio dial while the Jesuit priest was driving and suddenly she was hearing the BBC from London. They had put the aerial up so they were getting an unexpectedly good reception.

They caught the news and it was Alvar Lidell reading it so they knew it was being read properly. It gave the detail about the street fighting, mano a mano, in Prague and a provisional death count. There was the usual breathless eyewitness reporter like there always has to be in a war situation. She added in the dashes of colour. Then there was a bit of home news and some sports news and then at the end of the bulletin, like they always used to have in those days, there were a couple of police messages. One of them made Jane Jones sit straight up in her seat because old Alvar was reading out, 'This is a message for a Miss Jane Jones, believed to be travelling on the Continent, to say that her father Morris is dangerously ill. She is asked to contact her family immediately.'

They abandoned the night in the smart hotel and, not finding a pay phone to connect them to the UK, they pushed on across Switzerland and France and caught the first ferry and arrived in Dover. But when Jane Jones finally arrived home she found it was only a bad case of indigestion. Morris was fine and propped up on a sofa in front of the TV but Sheila said better safe than sorry.

Everything got a bit delayed after that. But finally they set off again across England in the blue VW Beetle with the Jesuit priest at the wheel. They drove up through North Wales going south of Colwyn Bay and then across the Menai Straits and up to Holyhead, where they took the night boat over to Dun Laoghaire and on into Dublin.

Now we are coming to the bit about Ireland.

In Dublin they were received kind of leerily. The priests they met told them, 'No need to worry here, boss.'

Finally they were shown in to see the archbishop and the Jesuit priest gave him the papal letter, which he held like it was too hot for his fingers. At first he didn't say anything. He just shot glances at Jane and then at the Jesuit priest who was sitting there like butter wouldn't melt in his mouth even though he'd just handed the guy a primed grenade.

Finally the archbishop got the situation weighed up. The leathery face cracked open.

'Tell the Holy Father he ain't got no cause for concern. The place is clean as a whistle. Everything's under control.'

Then he stood up and walked out, banging the door hard behind him. Jane Jones said later, 'Well I don't know about you but he scared the jumping Jesus out of me.' The Jesuit priest responded with a laugh. 'He's not the sort of guy to meet in a dark alley late at night.'

But after that they were not getting any word out of the other priests. They had all been struck dumb because the message had come down from the top to zip the lip. But people came up to them on the sly in pubs and whispered into their ears. They picked up a confirmation that the priests were up to all sorts of high jinks and some of the nuns were even worse.

Now they decided to widen their enquiry so they took a trip to the west. They stayed a night with two priests who had not got the word from Dublin about buttoning the lip. They chatted about this and that and the Jesuit priest omitted to give the real reason they were in Ireland. Jane Jones said they were just travelling through and wasn't Ireland a grand place.

After a few wines and a good dinner one of the priests leant out of his armchair in front of the warming fire and said in a low voice so Jane Jones couldn't hear, 'The choir's practising at the moment. If you want to cast your eye over the young 'uns for a bit of a root about later then go ahead.' The Jesuit priest pretended he was a bit deaf and had not got the drift of the conversation but afterwards he noted it down in his report.

They ended up on the west coast at the palace of the Bishop of Galway. The bishop was a rum cove and when the Jesuit priest showed him the papal letter he got in a muddle and asked the Jesuit priest if he was from the police. Jane Jones noted his hand trembling so much he could barely hold his glass of whiskey.

When they were leaving, the Jesuit priest asked Jane Jones what she thought. She said, 'Well, the bishop is certainly a scallywag with something to hide. But he's not hiding it that well because when I went upstairs to take a wee I saw baby's clothes hanging up to dry alongside ladies' tights and undergarments and they did not look like the sort of undergarments that nuns wear.'

In the end the Jesuit priest wrote a stinking report saying a scandal was brewing in Ireland that would blow the Catholic church out of the water. But the Pope laughed when he read it because the day before he had received a letter from the archbishop in Dublin saying everything was clean as a whistle and no need to worry. So the Pope used the Jesuit priest's report to light up one of the cigars he smoked in the evening.

When it all came out years later the Jesuit priest was

dead on right because the priests had abused thousands of children. They'd even got pictures in the newspapers of priests being led away in handcuffs and everyone told the joke that a special wing in Mountjoy Prison, Dublin had been set aside to house the jailed priests and not forgetting the cemetery in Gortahork, County Donegal, where there are a total of eight men who killed themselves after they were abused by the priests.

The Jesuit priest returned to California, where he did some teaching in a college, but at the same time he was writing letters to Jane Jones saying his heart was not in it anymore and he was about to pack it in. Jane Jones realised, in fact she had known it all along, that the Jesuit priest was sweet on her. But by then it was too late because she was married to Oliver and they had got the garden centre and their two strapping boys.

Roughly stops reading and for a moment they listen to the wind, which is still rattling the window panes. Then Heinz pours out two more tots of Wales Brandy. Then he tugs at his sweater.

'Well, it is a bit rough round the edges and of course the Irish priests has been kicked by other writers but the story from Czechoslovakia is quite original, I am giving you that. However we are still waiting to hear about Oliver Bloke.'

Roughly picks up a page and tells Heinz, 'Well I am about to rectify that now.'

When he was young, Oliver Bloke stayed with cousins in Harrogate. While there, he did what all young people do. He told his family in Bury St Edmunds he would be back on the Thursday but he informed his cousins in Harrogate that he would be leaving on the Wednesday. That way he levered open twenty-four hours free and easy.

He was on the train to London when he flipped a coin and decided to get off at the next station. This turned out to be Leicester, which was a town he had never visited before.

So he was in the centre of Leicester and he walked around until he found himself in front of a concert hall. He bought a ticket and went inside and sat down to wait for the start of the show. He thought if everyone had a million guesses they would never work out that he was in a concert hall in Leicester. Then the show began and the main singer was a guy called Roy Orbison who was a big name then but is forgotten now.

'And oh boy,' Oliver said to Jane when they were living in the lighthouse years later, 'that guy had the whole box of tricks in his sweet voice. He did the melancholy at the same time he drove it along with an excitement you aren't going to believe unless you were there.'

Jane replied, 'What you were hearing for the first time, like a sharp knife levering you open, was life starting up. Everyone has got that moment and they are never forgetting it.'

They were in the pub after the show. Two guys from the supporting group, who were called the Small Faces, were next to them at the bar. They were big names then but they are also forgotten now. So they were exchanging some chit-chat. But a few years later one of them, he was called Steve Marriott, went to sleep in a thatched cottage he owned in the countryside in Essex after he had drunk too much. A lighted cigarette caught fire on the sheets and soon the whole cottage was ablaze. One of the firemen, who was a Small Faces fan himself, found Steve Marriott's body in the morning curled up by the side of the bed. He was burnt to a cinder. But that is for the future.

Oliver ordered a pint for himself and a glass of cider for the girl who had been sitting next to him at the show. In the future if he ever smelled the perfume she wore that night he was back with her in the pub.

In the middle of the night Oliver woke to find he was in a cheap lodging-house. The beds around him were full of drunks and tramps. He felt under his pillow to make sure he still had his wallet. The next morning he got up and looked in the mirror and saw there were traces of blood around the side of his mouth. There was some bruising as well but he could never recall where that came from.

'And that is a story about Oliver Bloke,' Roughly says. He picks up a last sheet of paper. 'There is one more story about Jane Jones and then we are done.'

Before Jane Jones settled down with Oliver Bloke and they opened the garden centre in Devonshire and had their two strapping boys called Jackson and Pollock she was always ducking and diving and doing strange things like going off with the Jesuit priest.

In this last story she was in Sweden doing the old hitch-hiking, or autostop as they call it on the Continent, when she arrived at the town of Gothenburg. And that was another strange thing because she found that the locals pronounced it Jottaburi. She looked round for someone to ask about that but instead ran into a woman called Petra who said she was from Scotland and who was also moving about Europe. They put out their sleeping bags on the beach outside the city and in the morning they cooked up tomatoes and bacon on a camping stove. When Jane looked back years later she thought with the sea air it was the best meal she had ever eaten.

Later in the day she was by the side of a road, thumb out, looking for a lift. But it was a small country road with not too many people around. There were just a few sheep. She thought she would have to spend the rest of her life there and they would end up burying her by the side of the road. They would put up a sign on the grave which read, 'Jane Jones lived here a long time'.

Then a car came along with a woman at the wheel and with two kiddies in the back. She stopped and leant out of the window and said, 'Hey, where are you going?' She had the long hair and the natural open look like they all had in Sweden at that time.

Jane Jones replied, 'Well, I am heading for Stockholm,' and the woman said, 'Well, you'd better get in then.'

They were doing a bit of chit-chat and the next thing she was inviting Jane Jones to come home and eat dinner en famille and stay the night. They sat round the table drinking glasses of Swedish beer and eating meatballs, which the husband had cooked and which were delicious. He asked about England and it turned out that, though currently he had a regular office job, his plan was to open a record store because he was a fan of the Beatles.

When they were done with the supper the husband switched on the TV and said, 'We are going to watch this programme because it is a historic moment and you will always remember where you were when you saw it.'

It was those guys in the space suits, they were still in black and white then, they didn't get the colour till later. They were doing the landing and they had climbed down on to the surface of the Moon and then one of them said the words everyone can recall. They were quiet as they watched but Jane Jones looked round out of the corner of her eye and she was mighty impressed with Sweden and the Swedish people. But they suffered their own tragedy a few years later and people said that is when they lost their innocence. The PM was Olof Palme so we have fast-forwarded to 1986. One evening he and his wife were sauntering home from the cinema in central Stockholm, that was the sort of country it was then, when a lone gunman leapt out of a dark alley and dropped him stone dead with a shot to the back and his wife got a wound too.

The police investigated, even arresting the wrong man and throwing him in jug and then having to let him go. Then the thriller writer Stieg Larsson who was a very bright guy started his own investigation. He filled his garage with files and talked to everyone. At the time of his death he was following a trail that was leading to the South African spy service as being the responsible party. So that is another cold case review for the Swedish equivalent of a Roughly Oddbins O'Reilly to take up.

The next day Jane Jones said goodbye to the family and arrived in Stockholm and took a ferry over to Helsinki, where she planned to spend the summer. But sadly because there is a limit on space that is not part of this story.

Roughly has turned the last page now. He looks up. Heinz has got his head forward and his mouth open. Then he is laughing.

'Well, Mr Wales out of Jamaica out of Prague copper, I will say you are like the racing driver who travels at 100mph. A bit of a daredevil and showing off, but you are needing the brake as well. And absolutely, and sad to say, the publishers will pass because you are not following the normal tramlines the readers expect. Everybody will nod their heads and be confused. The amount of copies the publisher will sell is not even paying for the printer's ink.'

Roughly looks downcast at that but Heinz says it is a good lesson because writers should realise that publishers are running a business not a charity.

After that he tells Roughly that for next week he wants him to put Jane and Oliver in their own story and see how that develops.

Then he looks out of the window and sees that the rain has stopped.

'Now there is a short break in the weather I need to get out and do some shopping and I have to meet someone as well.'

§

Jimmy hesitates and says he is not supposed to talk about it but if Roughly is seeing this guy he could be useful. So he says let's go over to the Wales Coffee Bar. There I will explain to you what is happening. After that you can be our inside man but you are not allowed to breathe a word to anyone especially to Tirana because she works in the Wales Flower Shop and everybody knows that place is a hotbed for the gossip.

They put up their collars against the rain which has started to come down again and cross the street and enter the Wales Coffee Bar, which has not altered its décor since the first espresso machines came over to Wales from Italy in the 1960s. It is not a welcoming place. In fact it is cold and the tables all have chipped Formica tops and they are the only customers. But even so they head for a table in the corner and talk in quiet voices.

Finally their coffees are served which are all frothy and steaming. Then Jimmy leans forward across the table in the way coppers do when they are beginning an interrogation. He asks Roughly what he is really doing there with Heinz Williams-Jones, né Pumpernickel, and what information is passing between them because it is not the first time he has been observed going into the university.

Roughly is annoyed when he hears this hostile tone so he replies if you want me to be part of this investigation you need to level with me. Jimmy nods in agreement with this. Roughly reaches into his bag and takes out the story he has just read out to Heinz about Jane Jones and Oliver Bloke. He pushes it over the table to Jimmy saying that is what we get up to.

Jimmy reads it through and then pushes it back across the table and says with a smile my ten-year-old boy can write better than that. After that the temperature gets dialled down a notch.

CHAPTER FOUR

Heinz has told Roughly to build a story around his two characters, Jane Jones and Oliver Bloke. Roughly discusses it with Tirana but they struggle to come up with a good idea. Then along comes the Covid and Tirana says well that is an interesting subject. Roughly nods his head in agreement and every night for the following week, after they have had their supper, he settles down at the kitchen table to write.

Then he is climbing the stairs to the attic office and Heinz pours out the tots of Wales Brandy. They are having some general chit-chat and Roughly casts a sly glance over the papers on Heinz's desk but he is still not seeing anything that will interest Jimmy. So he says, 'I have written a story for Jane Jones and Oliver Bloke.'

Heinz leans back and smiles.

'Well fire away then, Sir Oddbins,' he says, and Roughly obliges.

A year before the Covid arrived, Oliver Bloke's father sadly turned up his toes and died. But he was 92 years old and the end was quick. He was living in Bury St Edmunds and was walking to the newsagent to buy his morning paper but he had to cross a busy main road and that morning he lost his footing and stumbled and was knocked down by a speeding car. But the doctor told Oliver and his brother Ralph it all happened so quick he would not have felt a thing.

But everyone was still sad because that's the way it is when someone dies. There was a good turnout at the funeral and Oliver and Ralph came out with the kind words which are all merited because their father, who was called Vivian, had been a Christian sort of guy. He had worked abroad in places like Uganda and Kenya as an international development engineer.

At the wake Jane, who was now married to Oliver, and Suzie, who was married to Ralph, organised the refreshments. When everyone was gone Oliver and Ralph read through the will.

Because their mother Jill died a dozen years before it was a straight 50/50 split. Once the house was sold there would be money to invest in pension pots. Ralph was an accountant living in Sussex and Oliver and Jane ran the small garden centre in Devonshire.

They were wrapping it up when in the bottom of a drawer in the filing cabinet Ralph found a last file. It had lain unnoticed because it was the same metallic colour as the filing cabinet. When they opened it they discovered to their surprise bank statements and letters and notes and postcards that showed Vivian had been leading a double life. They found a passport which had Vivian's photo in it but the name was different and there were entry stamps for countries all over the Middle East.

Ralph went through the bank statements and in half an hour he had pieced it all together. Now he'd got a bloody great grin on his face as he said to Oliver, 'Well, our father is not an international development engineer at all. That is just a cover he is using. He is really an international arms dealer and he has £5 million squirrelled away in Swiss bank accounts, which now belongs to us.'

Once they were over the shock Ralph and Oliver thought that the cover Vivian and Jill used was perfect. They were the sort of couple who said grace before meals and family holidays were a caravan park in North Wales. Everyone said they were church-mouse poor but happy, so nobody was suspicious. Their neighbours said if there were more people like Vivian and Jill the world would be a better place. A friend who worked in London heard that Vivian was in line for an MBE but that never happened.

Oliver and Ralph figured out that Jill was also involved in the scam. She certainly handled the paperwork for the deals. They recalled that sometimes she flew out to Africa to meet up with Vivian when he was on a project there. That was certainly when they levered open the space to do a bit of the high living.

The only odd moment Oliver and Ralph recalled from their childhood was one time they all jetted off to Jamaica to stay in a five star hotel in Montego Bay for a week. Vivian and Jill sat on the hotel terrace in colourful beach shirts drinking fancy cocktails and one evening they even visited a casino. Jill told them it was paid for by a legacy from an aunt who had died.

It took six months to deal with the paperwork but finally Oliver and Jane Bloke got the confirmation from the bank that they were richer by two and a half million pounds. They had already decided to keep the garden centre in Devonshire. They had spoken to a lottery winner who advised them to keep their life as normal as possible.

But then along came 'events' which turned 'lives' upside down.

They were watching the TV news and the pictures came up of the empty streets in China. The reporter explained that everyone had to stay home because there was a new flu. Then it spread over to Europe and a week later they were staring at pictures of bodies piled up in mortuaries in Italy.

Then Jane got a toothache and was at the dentist. She was in the waiting room leafing through a magazine when her eye fell on an advertisement which read Lighthouse for Sale.

At dinner that night Jane told Oliver and the boys about the advertisement. She told them, 'It might be a good investment in case we need a place to shelter from the Covid.' Jackson and Pollock were enthusiastic but Oliver was not sure. However he said it was worth an enquiry.

The next day Jane telephoned the number on the advertisement and left a message but there was no reply and for the moment they forgot about the lighthouse. The Covid had now arrived in England and Jane and Oliver had to make preparations because they might have to close up their business. Then a week later a message appeared on her phone which read, 'Are you the lady who was interested in the lighthouse?'

Jane poured a coffee and went outside. She lit a cigarette and her hands were trembling. The lady was called Mrs Kernow and she confirmed that the lighthouse was still for sale. The price was half a million pounds and it was situated off the coast of Cornwall.

A moment later pictures of the lighthouse clicked on to Jane's phone and she said, 'Oh my!' because it looked so beautiful.

Jane and Oliver and the boys made the two-hour drive down from the garden centre to the coastal town which was the jumping off point for the lighthouse. There they met Mrs Kernow.

'Victor has been gone two years now and both my boys are grown up,' she told them, her silver hair glinting in the sunlight. 'So when my youngest and his wife asked me to go and live with them in Falmouth, where they both work as dentists, it was an offer I couldn't refuse.'

She took them out in a motor boat. As they approached the lighthouse it grew in size until it towered over them. Then they saw it was constructed on a small island about the size of a football pitch.

Then they were ashore and looking round. When Jane and Oliver looked back years later they both said it was a turning point in their lives. They recalled that as soon as they landed a soft wind sprang up to ruffle their hair and the sun appeared from behind the clouds to warm their faces. At the same time all around them they could hear the soft murmur of the sea on the rocks. The shore from which they had come was covered by a soft heat haze and the buildings of the coastal town looked like miniatures in the distance.

Mrs Kernow showed them around and they discovered a small flock of sheep and goats along with a dozen chickens. They were quite tame and crowded around Mrs Kernow. She explained, 'They were Victor's pride and joy when he was alive. In good weather they are fine outside but when a storm hits they need to go into the shelter otherwise the poor things will be washed away.'

Then she took them into the ground floor of the lighthouse, which had been turned into the shelter. 'They eat dried seaweed when they are in here, but it has to be collected regularly. That was always a job for my boys.'

She looked at Jackson and Pollock when she said that. She pointed out the racks for drying the seaweed and explained the technique of how it was done. She also showed them the small sailing boat at the back of the shelter they could use to reach the shore in an emergency.

Next they looked up at the outside of the lighthouse. Mrs Kernow told them it was built with blocks of granite but when a storm blew up it did sway round a bit. But then she added with a smile, 'Don't worry it's not going to fall down on your head.'

Then she pointed up to the top of the lighthouse where they could see solar panels were attached. 'When Victor installed those we got the heat and light all the time. It was tough before when we had to rely on the generator. Sometimes it didn't work for days in the winter.'

Inside the lighthouse they started to climb the winding stairs. Mrs Kernow explained that the lighthouse was six storeys high and that there were a total of 103 steps from bottom to top. Oliver and Jane noted that Mrs Kernow climbed up them like she was still a youngster so that was another indication that life on the island would be good for the health. As they went up she pointed out how each floor had got a different function, kitchen, bedrooms, bathroom and so on.

When they arrived at the top floor Mrs Kernow said, 'We call this the Light Room.' Jane and Oliver looked round. The regular light, in place when it was a working lighthouse, had been taken out so what was left was a large circular space. Because it was a sunny afternoon a brilliant light poured in from all sides.

But what caught the attention of Jane and Oliver was that half the space was taken up by a colourful kitchen garden. Herbs and salads and root veg had been carefully planted in pots. Mrs Kernow explained they used a mix of sea weed and fish oil as fertiliser and with the light coming in all day everything was growing easily. Jane noted there were flowers and bulbs growing as well.

'Now you need to look up,' Mrs Kernow said.

Jane and Oliver did that and gave out a big old laugh because strong green vines were spreading out and twisting over each over on a wooden trellis which was attached to the ceiling. Mrs Kernow added with a smile, 'Don't worry, I will show you how we make the wine as well.'

The other half of the room had wooden chairs and a table and a large telescope which gave a 360-degree view out to sea and then back to the shore. Mrs Kernow said she lived in the Light Room in the summer but in the winter she moved down to the kitchen area.

Finally she showed them the water tank, which

collected the rain water that drained down from the roof. She said she'd never known them to be short of water but they were still always careful.

Then Jane and Oliver told Mrs Kernow they were in love with Light Island and they would certainly take it. They settled it over a glass of Chateau Oceanic which Jane said was not bad at all.

Then Mrs Kernow gave Jackson and Pollock half a dozen gaily coloured kites. Neither Jane nor Oliver nor the boys had ever seen kites like them before. Mrs Kernow explained, 'I made them for my boys. But I would like them to stay on the island for the next generation.'

Jackson and Pollock descended to the open ground and ran up and down with the kites, dodging the sheep and the goats and chickens as they went. Mrs Kernow looked down and Oliver saw a tear forming in her eye.

'That's the way it was when Victor was alive and our two boys were young,' she said.

When they first arrived on Light Island they spent time on the telescope looking towards the shore, trying to figure out was happening there. In the evening they discussed whether the Covid was advancing or retreating and when it would be safe to return. But as the weeks and months passed they talked less about life on the shore and concentrated more on daily life on Light Island. This was the first indication that their perception of the way time passes was changing.

The family divided up the jobs between them. The boys collected and dried and stored the seaweed until there was enough to see the animals through the winter. Jane did the fishing, catching mackerel and sea bass. She also took over responsibility for the plants. Oliver found he was a natural at the cooking. He also shared the care of the animals with the boys. So there was a natural division of labour happening there. One day when they were exploring the far side of the island they discovered a large bed of mussels in a break in the rocks so that was another supplement to their diet.

When the grapes were ripe they all pitched in to make the wine and bottle it and lay it down. Then they prepared jams and conserves and chutneys. But they had a problem with the butchery. They had no idea how to do that at all. But luckily along with the school books for the boys they have brought a collection of encyclopaedias. Oliver looked up the section on how to butcher a sheep. Jane said there was no point in hiding away from it so they were all present when Oliver killed the first lamb. It gave a squeal when the knife went in but they packed it away so they had meat for the winter. Then Oliver said, 'We need to put the old ram up on the ewes so they will have lambs for the spring,' and that was another lesson learnt.

So the days passed. The boys had their school time in the Light Room in the morning. In the afternoons they were out collecting seaweed. They also organised races up and down the island on the back of the sheep.

In the evening Jane and Oliver enjoyed a glass of Chateau Oceanic with their supper. Oliver called it a rough old plonk but Jane said that was a bit unkind. Then one day they were exploring a store room off where the animals sheltered and they found dozens of bottles of Chateau Oceanic from different years. They laughed about that and said, 'Now we are drinking vintage plonk.'

When the weather was good they set up a table in the lee of the lighthouse and ate their meals there. There was also a small shingly beach where they could swim but they were careful to attach themselves by a safety line before they went in because the currents were strong.

When they looked back on that first summer on Light Island, when the sky was blue and the boys flew their kites and raced up and down on the island on the backs of the sheep and the breeze was soft on the cheek, they thought they were the best months of their lives.

On midsummer's day Jane told Oliver she wanted to eat out under the stars. Jackson and Pollock laid the table with a white cloth and Jane picked wild flowers and made little crowns for everyone to wear. Then the three of them were seated at the table under the stars and the bright light of the silvery moon. Then Oliver approached from the lighthouse carrying a pot of steaming mussels and soon they were feasting on the mussels. As they ate they laughed and told stories. Then they fell silent. They looked up at the starry night and listened to the background music of the sea hitting the rocks. They always remembered that moment, especially Jane who recalled the night she slept out under the stars in Glasgow when she was a student.

After that the days began to shorten. They drew the protective cover over the Light Room at night and let in a bit of heat from the solar panels. Jackson and Pollock brought the animals in at night. Then one morning they woke to their first storm. In the Light Room they could feel the lighthouse sway and when they looked down waves were crashing onto the base of the lighthouse. They recalled how Mrs Kernow said that in winter Light Island was a different world.

The lives of this small family were now governed by the seasons. In summer they were outside most of the day. They even launched the small boat and sailed round the island. At night they watched the constellations moving across the heavens. In autumn there were the first of the storms. Then in winter they could be locked inside for days gazing down at the raging sea. The animals only emerged to nibble at the stubbly grass on days when the sea had temporarily abated.

The boys learnt to interpret the sky and the sea. When the sea birds altered their patterns of flight it was an indication that a change in the weather was coming up. They kept a daily log where they recorded information on water temperature and wind and current direction and so on. They also described the vividness of sunsets and sunrises alongside other detail such as the number of mackerel and bass caught. Jackson illustrated the log with miniature paintings of the sunsets. All this would be useful when they left the island and Pollock became a sea captain and Jackson an artist.

The boys also logged the vapour trails of the planes flying overhead. When there were no trails they knew the Covid was bad and that flights had been grounded. When the trails resumed they noted their direction so they could work out which countries had opened up. Using the telescope, Jane also noted the numbers of boats coming in and out from the shore. She also followed the movement of the bigger ships on the horizon.

The occasional pieces of debris that washed up on Light Island were another tool they used to figure out what was happening in the outside world.

One day the sea pushed a waterlogged pram up onto the beach. Inside they were surprised to discover a label reading, *Made in Scotland – a proud product of Pollokshields*. From that Jane figured out that Scotland had gone independent. She laughed and said, 'The quality of the material shows that Scotland is making a bid for the high class goods market.' After that Jackson and Pollock turned the pram into a trailer for carrying sea weed up from the beach.

The discovery of the pram made them think. Even though they'd got the sky and the seas and the stars to study, their world had shrunk from the hills and fields of Devonshire to a small island the size of a football pitch. So they wondered if time was also passing at a different rate.

One day in early spring, when the days were beginning to warm, they received their first big surprise. Jane was looking through the scope when she spotted an object in the sea. She called out to Oliver, who was in the Light Room with her. He squinted through the scope and then straightened up and said, 'Well how about that.' Then they both checked the scope again and confirmed that it was the periscope of a submarine. So now they knew that as well as observing they were also being observed. They discussed it at dinner that night but they didn't come to any conclusions.

A month after that Oliver was in the Light Room by himself. He looked up and he did not need the scope that time because he could see four warships not that far away. They were steaming out from the shore past Light Island. He called out to the others and they came up to join him. The ships had pennants flying but even though they got the encyclopaedias out they were not able to figure out what the pennants indicated. Oliver tracked them over the horizon on a course south-west out into the Atlantic until they were lost from sight.

A week after that the sea was rising and the wind was strengthening so they had brought the animals inside as a precaution. They were all in the Light Room. Jackson and Pollock were at the table doing their homework and Oliver was asking everyone what they wanted for their supper because he had found a new way to cook the mackerel. Jane had straightened up – she had been watering the plants – and she was looking to where the sun was dipping down.

Suddenly there was a bright flash on the horizon. Oliver reacted immediately.

'Down on the floor, quick!' he shouted. 'Don't look up. The light will blind you.'

But even as they got down the sun seemed to stop its descent and start to climb up again. This was a picture they would all remember for the rest of their lives. Jackson drew it over and over. A minute later there was a bang which left their ears ringing for hours. When they looked again the sky had gone a red that was turning to black. Then Jane said in a shocked voice, 'Thank God we brought the animals in.' She was right there because a few hours after the explosion a mini tidal wave swept over the island.

A day later the wind changed to the south and brought up something which didn't smell too good. It left them with sore throats and coughs.

A week after that the ships steamed back past them again in the direction of the shore. The pennants were flying still. But when Oliver turned the scope on them he could see they had all sustained damage. One even had a big hole in the side. But the sailors were all on deck and their arms were raised and they were cheering like they were celebrating a great victory. That night the family saw fireworks coming up from the shore.

They kept the scope turned on the shore for the next few days. They picked up twinkling lights and fireworks rising into the night sky. They even heard the faint strains of music floating out. One day a ferry boat left the port in the direction of France and they could see the people out on the deck.

But a week after that it went quiet. Then in January they observed a chimney to the west of the town. It released a dense cloud of black smoke four days in a row. The wind was from the north and it blew a dark gritty dust towards them, leaving a trace over the whole island.

Oliver and Jane discussed it but they did not share their fears with the boys. They were relieved when a few days later a storm hit Light Island and everywhere was washed clean. After that there were several weeks of spring weather. They were busy with the animals and put the gritty dust cloud out of their minds.

Now we need to move on a season.

It was an August night when it had been hot and unusually close and Oliver woke because he'd heard a noise. At first he thought it was just the sound of the sea on the rocks. But then he was sitting up because what he could hear was a ship's engine and it was not too far away.

He got quietly out of bed. He did not want to disturb Jane, whose face he could see lit up by the moonlight. He thought, as he always did, that with everyday that passed she looked more beautiful. Then he realised the noise was not one but several ship's engines.

He climbed quietly up the stairs. He stepped into the Light Room and his mouth fell open. Because in front of him there were more than fifty boats and they were close by.

He was on the scope swinging it round in the moonlight. His eye confirmed that it was a fleet of fishing boats. Some were halfway towards the horizon while others were no more than few hundred metres off Light Island. He went in close on the scope until he could see the fishermen on the decks pulling on the lines.

Then Oliver heard a noise behind him which made him jump. But when he turned round quickly round it was only Jane who had come up after him. They were soon joined by Jackson and Pollock who had also been sleeping lightly because of the heat.

The light came up on a grey day with a sea running and the wind picking up. The fishing fleet had moved further out but the boats were still going up and down. It was as if they were cutting the grass with a lawnmower. Jackson and Pollock put the scope on them looking for indications as to who they were, but there was nothing. By the following morning the strange fleet had gone.

That afternoon Jackson and Pollock noted the clouds were building. The way the sea birds were moving was an indication that a storm was approaching from the Atlantic. So they had no time to worry about the strange fishing fleet. They put the sheep and goats and chickens inside. Then they were snug in the kitchen, listening as the wind built around them.

When it had blown out a few days later and they had emerged to let out the animals, Jackson and Pollock discovered a small boat overturned on the beach. They turned it upright and dragged it up. Jane and Oliver, who had been watching from the Light Room, came down to join them. There was no sign of a sail or a motor so it looked like it was just a rowing boat. They pulled the boat inside the base of the lighthouse next to where they kept their own boat.

When they examined it they found a locker with a bag of clothes and a bag with packets of food and a plastic bottle with fresh water. They concluded that one of the fishermen had got fed up with life on board and had launched the row boat hoping to make it to the shore.

Jane took the clothes and the packets of food upstairs to the kitchen to dry them out. Jackson and Pollock continued their examination and found lettering at the stern of the boat which had a strange circular form.

Jane laid the clothing and the packets of food out on the kitchen table.

'The clothing is certainly good quality,' she said.

Then she found a label on a sweater which read, *Made in Scotland — another proud product of Pollokshields* and underneath the same strange circular writing. She turned to Oliver and laughed.

'I think we have found our Rosetta Stone here.'

That evening after supper the boys went through the pages on scripts and languages in their encyclopaedias. Finally Pollock turned a page and Oliver who was looking over his shoulder said, 'Well what have we got here, then?'

Pollock did a double check on the rounded script and replied, 'I think what we have here is the Burmese language.'

Jane laughed. 'So now we know that Scotland has gone independent and is supplying high class knitwear to Asian fishing fleets.'

But why the Burmese should come all this way to do their fishing was a puzzle they were unable to solve even though they discussed it late into the night. They also thought of the cheering sailors on the decks on the warships when they returned to the port. At the same time the body of the guy in the rowing boat never washed up.

One summer morning Oliver was up in the Light Room pruning a vine. At the same time he was watching Pollock, who was glued to the telescope pointed at the shore. Oliver said to Jane that night, 'Those boys are getting restless, we need to think about returning to the mainland.'

For the next week they watched the shore carefully. They noted that the town was lit up at night and ferries were leaving regularly. On a still evening they even heard the faint sound of music floating across the water. Then one day a plastic bag drifted ashore with a magazine inside and they saw the writing was Burmese which confirmed their suspicions.

The boys studied the faces of the pretty girls in the magazine and Oliver said to Jane, 'That is another indication that we need to be getting back.'

They waited for a break in the weather. Jackson and Pollock studied the sky and the way the sea was running and then finally pronounced, 'We've got a clear few days coming up.' So they knew it was safe to leave the animals outside. Then they dragged the boat out and launched it and put up the sail and headed for the shore. As the shore got bigger and Light Island became smaller they stopped their excited chatter. Jane looked back at the island and said in an anxious voice, 'Maybe it's still too early to leave.' But finally they reached the port.

As they entered the harbour they saw the fishing fleet tied up, so that was one mystery solved.

When they put their feet on the shore the first thing they discovered was that the Covid had been gone a long time. People were not talking about it anymore. Their suspicion that the Burmese had done a takeover was also correct.

They noted Burmese restaurants and Burmese bars and Burmese grocery stores. Oliver looked perplexed and said to Jane, 'So how long have we been away?'

Jane looked at the boys.

'They were nippers when we went so maybe we have been gone longer than we thought.'

They observed the people on the terraces of the bars

and cafes enjoying the sunshine. They noted that a lot of their faces were now a light brown colour. The faces also seemed to be rounder. Jane said she thought it was an improvement but Oliver was not so sure.

As they walked down the street, people stared at them as if they had come from another planet. And in a sense they were right because they had stepped from the old world into the new.

There were so many differences. The first was that their hair was cut short. This made sense on an island where water was at a premium, especially if there was a dry spell in the summer. Jane had fashioned them hats out of warm material for when it was cold in the winter. But the style on the shore was to let the hair grow long and then tie it up in a knot on top of the head. They called this the Burmese Style and there were hairdressers offering variations for both men and women. Their old-style trousers and jackets got stares as well because most people now wore sarongs and colourful tops.

The other thing they didn't realise, because they had been on Light Island for so long, and because they were eating a lot of fish and often having a quick dip in sea water for a wash, was that they had developed what you could call a rich body smell. They had noted that the fashion on the shore was for everyone, even the men, to wear a good quality perfume. So people were walking past them in the street holding their noses and making stinky gestures with their hands.

When they got to the hotel they washed with regular soap and dabbed on the new perfume which they admitted was a great improvement. They also noted, when they talked to the staff in the hotel, that the way people spoke had also changed. The accent was rounder and softer and they even dropped in some Burmese words which left Jane and Oliver all at sea.

Down a side street they discovered an English pub where Jane and Oliver enjoyed a pint of English beer. They were offered fish and chips to eat but they refused because they'd been eating fish every day on Light Island. Instead they went for the Cornish pasties and they all agreed they were delicious.

Jane and Oliver discovered that while the people were polite they were not forthcoming. Jane asked an old couple on a table next to them, 'How did it happen then? How did the Burmese arrive and do their takeover?' The old couple looked startled. 'Mustn't grumble,' they replied in a low voice, keeping their heads down. 'All for the best, really.' Then they got up abruptly and left.

Oliver and Jane also noted that the people never enquired about them. This led Oliver to say, 'With the takeover it looks like everyone has gone a bit sheeplike.'

The next night they decided to eat at a Burmese restaurant but they were turned away by a guy on the door who said this restaurant was reserved for Burmese only, which left them quite uncomfortable. But they didn't complain because they were still finding their feet.

They ordered a Burmese meal at the hotel instead. They enjoyed it and it was certainly tasty enough but in the night they were all as sick as dogs because they were not used to such rich food.

Then at six o'clock in the morning there was a bang on the door of their room and when Oliver opened it there were two Burmese policemen standing there. They asked where they had come from and why they had been asking questions in the pub. When Oliver answered, 'Well, we have been sheltering on Light Island because of the Covid,' the two policemen look unbelieving. But for the time being they left them alone.

After a few days Jane and Oliver wanted to return to Light Island but Jackson and Pollock looked at the sky and said it would stay clear a few more days and they were having fun talking to the girls. So they decided to stay. The boys wanted to grow their hair so they could have top knots and they were already dropping Burmese words into the conversation.

One afternoon, while Jackson and Pollock were chatting with some girls, Jane and Oliver took a walk. They left the town centre, passing the churches – which had been converted into Buddhist temples. They found to their surprise that the town ended sooner than they remembered when they visited before going out to Light Island. When they did a calculation they realised that there must be far fewer people than before.

In the pub that evening they are asked some of the older guys where all the people had gone. They got a blank look in return. Then people started to shuffle away from them. When they left the pub to go back to the hotel Oliver looked over his shoulder and saw that the landlord had come out onto the street and was staring hard at them.

In the middle of the night Oliver woke Jane up and said, 'You remember the smoke coming up from the chimney and the cloud of grit drifting over us?'

Jane nodded her head grimly and replied, 'I hope you are not coming to the same conclusion as me.'

The next afternoon they turned down a street they had not seen before and Jane pointed out a sign above a shopfront which read 'Embassy of Scotland – Pollokshields is our Capital,' But when they peered in through the window they saw a pile of unopened mail on the floor. Then they took a step back to see it is was all closed up.

Oliver asked an old guy standing nearby, 'So has Scotland gone independent then?'

The guy rolled his eyes and replied, 'They've been gone donkey's years, mate.'

'So why is the embassy all closed up?' Jane said and the old guy gave them a startled look. Then Jane said to herself in for a penny in for a pound. She took a deep breath.

'A few years ago there was an explosion in the sky to the south. We watched it from a lighthouse where we were sheltering from the Covid and we are wondering what it was all about.'

The old guy looked even more startled now. He said in a shaky voice. 'Sorry, but I need to be moving on. I got an appointment with my dentist.' He touched the front of his mouth. Then he turned and walked quickly down the street and did not look back.

The next morning at six o' clock – they were almost expecting it – there was another bang at the door. This time it was a Burmese man on his own. He was dressed in a well-cut lounge suit. He was followed by a waiter pushing a trolley with coffee and cakes.

He said, 'I was just passing and thought to come in and introduce myself.'

A few minutes later they were all seated drinking the coffee and eating the cakes.

'We have been following your life on Light Island with interest,' he said. His voice was soft and polite. 'We all liked the idea of you having a flock of sheep and goats and doing the fishing.'

Then he took out from his jacket pocket a photograph that showed Jackson sitting on the back of a sheep soon after they arrived on Light Island. He smiled as he passed it round. They all looked at it. Then he put the photograph back in his pocket.

'When I retire from government I could imagine having a small farm and living the natural life like you.'

He leant forward and his voice became sharper.

'But for now I will give you a word of warning. You are going to get into a lot of trouble if you keep asking questions about things that happened in the past. There are already people upset with you, but for the moment I have got your back.'

Then he turned to Jackson.

'We have heard that you are a good artist and we are certainly not wanting to see that upset.'

After that he stood up and gave a polite smile, and a nod of his head, and left. When he had gone they all breathed a sigh of relief and Jane said, 'That guy's eyes were as cold as steel.'

The visit gave them all a shock. On the surface everything looked like it was working well but underneath there were some dark currents. Then Jane and Oliver said they wanted to get back to Light Island, even if they were under observation there. Jackson and Pollock argued to stay on the shore a bit longer. So that is how it happened for the next while. They were to and fro. The boys even brought out friends to visit. They all looked round and said what a cool place to live.

Now we are going to fast forward a bit towards the end.

Jackson and Pollock settled on the shore and Jane and Oliver found it too much on their own. They put out an advertisement and there was an interest from a young couple who they took out to Light Island in the boat. They showed them around and they agreed to take it. So Jane and Oliver found themselves back on the mainland. Then Jackson was married with a nipper on the way. So the period of the Bloke family on Light Island ended.

Doctors and researchers studied Jackson and Pollock. They found that their powers of observation were first class and that their memory was also excellent and that on the whole they were in not bad shape. But truth to tell, the doctors said, they will never to adapt to regular urban life.

They were right on that. Jackson always stayed close to the water. He also made a name for himself as a painter. The experts said the way he captured the sky was not far off the way painters like Turner and Constable did it. He was able to make a living as a painter.

His wife had a lot of patience so the marriage lasted. She told Jane, 'Jackson is fine provided no one talks to him when he is painting and provided he has always got the sea in front of him.'

She recounted the time they went to London to visit the galleries and study the Constables and the Turners. They also went to the theatre and to restaurants. When they returned home Jackson stayed in his room for a week. Their nipper is completely normal with no interest in the sea and when he grows up he wants to be a dentist.

Pollock became a sea captain and took boats around Cape Horn. His crews always had confidence in him. They watched him when he was up on the bridge studying the way the birds were circling and the sea was running and they said, 'The old man is reading the elements.'

But he found it difficult to settle. He did a couple of years on shore with a woman in Rio de Janeiro which turned into a bit of a crazy time when he started drinking and getting into fights. Then one morning he woke up and looked around and said he'd had enough of that. So he packed his bag and went down to the port and signed back on with a ship.

Roughly puts down the last page, looks at Heinz and says, 'That is the story of Jane and Oliver Bloke on Light Island.'

Heinz runs his fingers through his unruly hair.

'As I said before, Mr Oddbins O'Reilly, you got the imagination, even if it is running at a 100mph. I was enjoying the story while you were reading it but at the same time I was also thinking of my brother, Frederick.'

Heinz leans back into his wooden chair and tugs at the bright red sweater which is covering his tummy.

'We are sharing a room together in the valley in Bavaria. On summer nights when the moon is shining we are speculating about our future. I have the first inkling that I am destined for North Wales, but one night Frederick announces out of the blue that he intends to be a lighthouse keeper. Our parents laugh at this because the valley where we were living is already pretty remote.

'Then Frederick is forgetting about the lighthouse and he tells everyone he plans to become a priest. But a few years after that he falls in love with a girl and moves to Hamburg, where he now runs a dental practice and they have two fine nippers as well. In fact the elder one, Cedric, is staying with me in Colwyn Bay right at the moment.'

Then he stares hard at Roughly.

'Actually you has taken the story off at a bloody queer angle, Señor Oddbins. You are going along nicely with the Robinson Crusoe stuff and we are all following you and then suddenly you introduce a crazy Burmese angle. The publishers will not like that because the readers will be confused.'

Roughly laughs.

'I thought when you are a writer you are supposed to hide your hand and keep a surprise for later on in the book?'

This makes Heinz give one of his great big belly laughs. He slaps his hand on the wooden desk.

'Okay, Roughly, you is original I will give you that. Whether you got the technique to pull it off we will be seeing.'

After that he raises his tot of Wales Brandy to his

lips and swallows it and Roughly notes that his hand is shaking badly.

§

After that there is a bit more sparring; then Jimmy says the police have information that someone is spilling Wales government secrets to the Germans. A spy we have got over there has seen opened envelopes lying on a desk with the postmark of the University of Colwyn Bay, he says.

When they are making enquiries they are discovering that the only German citizen at the university is Heinz Pumpernickel who has also taken the name Williams-Jones, which is suspicious by itself. They are putting two and two together and reckoning he is the spy. That is why he is standing outside the university doing surveillance. He is hoping to see Heinz come out and then he plans to follow him.

Roughly looks puzzled now. He asks why the Germans are interested in Wales government secrets? Then he adds and how on earth is Heinz stuck up there in his attic room at the university going to discover them? Jimmy asks him if he has seen the paper this morning and Roughly replies he has not got time for that so Jimmy pushes the paper over the Formica table and points to a story.

CHAPTER FIVE

The next time they meet, Heinz is wearing a vivid green sweater. He is standing at the window looking out towards the rising sea on the front. Roughly wonders if the colour of the sweater he wears is a way of passing a message to a handler.

Heinz turns to Roughly.

'We are parking Jane and Oliver for a minute because on this course we also need to consider other types of writing.'

Then he asks if Roughly ever had a stab at writing poetry.

Roughly snorts.

'Coppers are not generally known as poets.'

But Heinz is already rummaging round in a drawer in his desk and he comes up with a little book called Words and Phrases that Poets Use. He hands it to Roughly saying he can study it if he is stuck and Roughly puts it in his pocket and takes it home.

That evening he tells Tirana his next assignment is to write a poem and she says when she was at school in Albania everyone had to write a poem about Enver Hoxha and they all enjoyed doing that.

Then they watch a programme on TV about an old guy who is a poet. He walks round his garden looking at the flowers and he wears a wide-brimmed felt hat and he smokes a Sherlock Holmes-style pipe. The film also shows him at his desk writing away and there is always a tot of something beside him. Every so often his wife puts her head round the door and asks if he wants anything, a sandwich or another tot of this or that, and he replies by nodding or shaking his head. All the critics say the poetry he composed is like music, it brings a tear to the eye. Then he dies and all the critics come to the church for the funeral. It's only after the funeral is over they discover that he has been levering open company pension funds and that is the point of the programme.

Tirana says that despite the ending the programme still gives a good idea of how to become a poet. Roughly thinks Tirana is pulling his leg but when he comes home the next evening he finds that she has bought him a surprise present.

He unwraps the present, which is a Sherlock Holmes-style pipe, the same sort the poet smoked. The nippers have also clubbed together to buy him a wide-brimmed felt hat. Then Roughly looks at Words and Phrases that Poets Use and notes it is a private printing by the Colwyn Bay Printing Company. The name of the author is not recorded so Roughly thinks it is probably Heinz.

But when Roughly reads it through he is puzzled, because he has not heard of a lot of the words before. So he thinks that Heinz, if he is the author, has made a mistake and they are really German words. But then Tirana, who has a good idea on old words, looks at them and says they are okay. After that Roughly starts to roll the words round on his tongue. One night he even dreams about them, which Tirana says is an inspiration.

In the morning, before he leaves for work, and wearing the wide-brimmed felt hat and with the Sherlock Holmes-style pipe in his mouth, he prowls round the garden searching for inspiration. He looks up at the sky and listens to the birds. At the weekend they go for a walk on the beach at Rhos on Sea. Roughly stares out at the cold, grey waves that are rolling in.

On the TV news in the evening they are still talking about the Covid. Then a reporter interviews an old Wales guy who was trapped abroad and he describes how a tear came to his eye when he finally returned to his home in Caernarvon and this makes Roughly think.

He tells Tirana and the nippers to give him bit of silence and he sits down at the kitchen table and composes a poem which he calls An Ode to People Missing their Wales Homeland. When he has finished he reads it back to Tirana and the two nippers and they all say it is not bad at all.

Two days later he is past the Wales Chapel Lady, who looks like she has never had a tear in her eye in her life except on a Sunday morning in chapel. Then he's up the stairs to the attic office. Then Heinz pours out two tots of the Wales Brandy and says, 'Fire away, Poet Roughly.'

Roughly reads the poem in the Richard Burton-style voice he'd practised in front of the bathroom mirror last night. He looks up every so often to see if there is a tear forming in Heinz's eye. He notes one eye has gone a little red but that could be just the attic dust.

When Roughly has finished, Heinz takes a sip of his Wales Brandy and moves some of the papers around on his desk.

'I already made it clear at the beginning I will be speaking out if the writing is not up to snuff. And writing poetry is damn difficult and a lot of people are falling on their ass.'

Then he cites the American poet Robert Frost, who said that writing free verse was like playing tennis with the net down. Then he gestures to Roughly to hand over the poem, opens a desk drawer marked 'Wales Sheep Poo', and drops the poem in there.

Then he looks at Roughly and his face is serious. 'If you are planning to be a writer, Roughly Oddbins O'Reilly, you need to take the rough with the smooth.'

After that he stands up and puts on his coat over his yellow sweater. He buttons it up and reaches for his umbrella and looks at his watch. 'Sorry, Mr O, but I have to leave you now because I need to meet someone in town.'

Roughly has a bit of a showdown with Heinz on the telephone the next day. Tirana says he had been too harsh and it is a good poem. She even reminds Roughly of the cruelties the Germans inflicted on the Albanians during the war. But Heinz stands firm. He tells Roughly over the phone there is all sorts of writing and no one is good at them all. They have already done adventure. Other categories they need to cover are comedy, historical and satire. If they have time maybe they will also touch on the future.

After that there is another phone call, which Tirana picks up and it is Roughly's cousin Otis, who has just returned to Jamaica from a business trip to Detroit. Tirana passes the phone to Roughly and for a while the cousins are gasbagging about the trip and then Otis tells Roughly a story that makes him laugh. So he works that up into a story, which he reads to Heinz the following week. He puts it under the heading of comedy.

My cousin Otis is just finishing up a business trip to Detroit. He is at the bus station waiting for a bus out when a panhandler comes up to him. The guy is slopping along in dirty trousers with a red felt hat on his head, with ear flaps. He has a dog on a lead by his side. Otis reaches into his pocket to give him a dollar but the guy opens his mouth and leans in towards him. He says, 'I need to get to Toledo urgent because my sister is ill there and I ain't got the fare so can you help me out?' His voice is whiny and Otis isn't having any of it.

But the guy isn't going away. He can see that Otis is checking out the dog, which looks like a small greyhound. He says, 'You know what this dog is called?' When Otis doesn't reply the panhandler says, 'He's called Obama.' Then he looks at Otis and says, 'You give me the money for the fare, you can keep the dog.' But Otis can see a mark on the dog's side so he says, 'Hold on there, buddy; your dog is diseased. You can't go round trying to offload a diseased dog.' But the panhandler replies, 'The dog's not sick, that's a birth mark. The dog has a pedigree.' He reaches into his pocket and pulls out a piece of paper and Otis sees it is a clipping from a newspaper. The panhandler hands it to him. It is an account of how the Obama family obtained a new dog. There is also a photo of President Obama and his wife Michelle and their two daughters. And there in the middle of the family grouping is the damn dog, though in the article it is called Washington.

The panhandler says, 'Check out the picture.' Otis holds the paper up and checks it against the dog and sure enough the birthmark is identical so there is no doubt it is the same dog. Then the panhandler says, 'I changed the name from Washington to Obama.'

Otis looks at the dog and says, 'Hi, Obama,' but the dog doesn't move so the panhandler says, 'You need to show more respect than that.' So Otis says, 'Good to meet you, Mr President,' and the goddam dog stands up and starts to wag its tail. Then Otis looks at the panhandler and says, 'How come you've got President Obama's dog?'

'Well, it's a long story,' the panhandler replies, 'and I ain't got time to tell it now because the bus is leaving soon.'

Otis is intrigued by this so he goes over to the ticket counter and he asks the man there the price of a ticket to Toledo and the man replies, 'Fifteen dollars.' Otis thinks for a moment and then says, 'Okay,' and he buys the ticket and he gives it to the panhandler and the panhandler hands over the dog and the clipping from the paper. The next thing Otis is seeing him off on the bus to Toledo. As the bus leaves the station he waves out of the window and he looks happy as hell. So Otis is left in Detroit bus station with a dog called President Obama. People are staring at him as if he has been played for a sucker. But Otis is tickled by it, he is that sort of a guy.

To cut a long story short, six weeks later Otis arrives back in Jamaica with the dog. It has got all its shots and it has cost Otis a small fortune. But he still has the clipping from the paper, which shows who the previous owner was. Now Otis has a bit of a party trick. Whenever he is invited out he tells people how friendly the Americans are, and how everyone is on the same level, and to prove it he says, he even has President Obama staying with him right now.

Roughly stops and looks up at Heinz who pulls a face.

'Well, Roughly, you have found a way of telling a comic story that is making me chuckle even if I am not yet giving the full-throated laugh that is needed if it's going to be a success. But if you got any more stories like that I will listen to them.'

Roughly is pleased to hear this because he has been working on getting the punchline right. So he says, 'I have a couple of other short pieces if you got the time to hear them.'

'Don't worry,' Heinz replies. 'I got the time.'

'So this is the next story,' says Roughly. 'Again it comes from Cousin Otis when he was in Detroit, and it concerns Donald Trump. But it begins with a man called Ronald Rump, who was a former patient at the Bellevue psychiatric hospital in New York.'

Ronald Rump emigrated to the USA with his parents when he was a nipper, so Otis heard. The parents were Nell and Archie Rump and they previously lived on a housing scheme in Pollokshields in Glasgow. It was sometime in the 1950s and Ronald's five-year-old sister Dottie was with them too, so they were a family of four when they arrived. The Rumps settled in the Queens district of New York and took straight away to the new life in America. Archie Rump found a job as a school janitor and Nell worked behind the counter in a Jewish deli.

Ronald Rump and his sister Dottie soon forgot about the old life in Pollokshields. They became proper American kids, though they still kept a trace of the old Glasgow accent. Then one day Ronald Rump's high school teacher in Queens scratched her head and said, 'Goddamit, Ronald Rump is the cleverest kid I ever taught. His ability with figures is outstanding. I predict a great future for him in finance or computers.'

At the same time Ronald Rump had become friendly with the young Donald Trump who was also living in Queens. Donald Trump had his eye on Dottie Rump who was beginning to fill out nicely. For a moment in high school they were even an item. At the same time Ronald Rump was starting to fill out and people said they could be brothers they were so similar.

Then Donald Trump went off to join his father's property company and Ronald Rump – and it can happen with the clever guys – turned the other way. He became part of the New York drug scene and a few years later he was sent to Bellevue for burning down a Post Office when he was high on cocaine.

Ronald Rump did five years there, with impeccable behaviour and top scores in all his assessment tests. He was judged 'minimal risk' and was let out on day release.

He found a job as an auto mechanic at a garage and it looked as if the story would have a happy ending. But then he woke up one morning and something had changed – maybe the wind had moved in the wrong direction – but he didn't come back to the garage after the lunch break and absconded.

A couple of weeks later Ronald Rump was driving along a remote highway in the north of the state. It was a real forested area near the border with Canada. By chance he was just behind his old friend Donald Trump who was in a big convertible. For a moment Donald Trump took his eye off the road as he tuned the radio looking for a country music station. At the same time a big old moose crossed the road in front of him. Donald Trump, going at full speed, crashed right into the moose and that was the end of Donald Trump.

Ronald Rump drew up behind Donald Trump's wrecked car and there was no one else around, the road was deserted. So he leant into the car and swapped his ID with the dead Donald Trump and drove off. The police thought it was Ronald Rump who was dead in the car crash and so he was away scot-free.

The two were so alike, all Ronald Rump had to do was gain a few pounds by eating Donald Trump's favourite food and he was able to fool even close family. He continued the property business and the casinos. Then he went into politics and became President of the United States and the rest, as they say, is history.

The only man who ever rumbled Ronald Rump was Kim Jong-un of North Korea who said to an aide, as his train pulled back into the station at Pyongyang after one of those summits, 'That guy is even crazier than I am.'

Roughly looks up and Heinz is pulling a long face.

'I said it before Señor Oddbins, you have got the imagination. But you need a stronger punchline there.'

But Roughly has already drawn another paper from his bag.

'There's just one more and then I am done with the comedy.'

'Okay,' Heinz sighs. 'But I hope it is short because I am ready for my lunch.'

Roughly begins by saying, 'Otis heard this story from his nephew who works in a pub in Dublin.'

It concerns a guy called Liam O'Bama who runs a pub in the Liberties area of the city, which at the time is not the best part of town. There is a slaughterhouse just across the road from the pub so when the wind is in the wrong direction the smell is not too agreeable. At the same time the pub is only a stone's throw from the Guinness brewery in the other direction. So the smell from the brewery drifts over from that way as well.

In the pub, Liam always keeps an ear open because a group of the IRA boys are regulars and he never knows what they are planning. One day the IRA boys are sitting in a corner and Liam overhears them planning a big action. Then he sees they are totalling up the numbers and realising they are a man short. So they turn to Liam and ask him if he wants to step in. So that's how Liam joins an Active Service Unit preparing to blow up Nelson's Column in Trafalgar Square in London.

The other thing you need to remember about Liam is that he has been bald as a coot since he was a young man but he wants to keep that a secret so he always wears a syrup. Sometimes the syrup slips but nobody ever brings the subject up.

A few weeks later they take the boat over to Holyhead and the train down to London. Then in the middle of the night they arrive in Trafalgar Square with a backpack full of dynamite. Liam is bending over to take the dynamite out of the bag when a big gust of wind comes up and blows off his syrup. At the same time a couple of coppers come round the corner and spot them. Then all hell breaks loose and the gang has to dump everything and leg it. They are lucky to get the boat train back from Holyhead to arrive safely in Dublin.

Liam gets another break when the police in London put out a description saying one of the bombers is bald as a coot. That is good news for Liam because everyone thinks he has got a full head of hair because he always wears his syrup.

But the heat is still on, the coppers in London and Dublin are not happy at all, and the guys running the IRA reckon the net is closing in. So Liam is smuggled out of the country to America. He works in a bar in New York and after a couple of years he gets his papers and is legal.

Then the owner of the bar says they are getting too busy so he brings in this svelte looking black girl to help.

Liam is smitten straight away, in fact he is totally head over heels and soon they are an item. But Liam makes sure he has her properly hooked before he tells her he is really bald as a coot.

They are talking about getting married but she says he has to drop the apostrophe from his name before that can happen because she cannot imagine being called by a name that had got an apostrophe in it. So that is all arranged and they get married and in the fullness of time they have a son. And the rest as they say is history.

Otis's nephew heard this story from a manager at the Guinness brewery who drank in his pub. He said that every month when Obama was president the brewery received an order to send out a crate of Guinness to the White House and the label was always marked, 'Private: for the Attention of the President'. This made him curious so he ferreted around until he dug up the story.

Roughly looks up to indicate he has finished. Heinz leans back in his chair.

He thinks for a moment and then he says, 'I already recounted that my brother Frederick is running a dental practice in Hamburg. One of the dentists working for him also considers himself a comedian so one time a week he does a stand-up sequence at a local comedy club. So one time Frederick and his wife go along to see him. Frederick told me he starts okay but then the audience becomes restless and in the end someone throws an apple core, which hits him in the face, and that is the last time he does stand-up comedy.'

Heinz pours two tots of Wales Brandy and passes one to Roughly.

'Damn difficult thing to do, Roughly. You need the hide as tough as the bloody rhino. You got to practise a lot. Miss the punchline and you get the apple core in the gob.'

That evening Roughly practises again on Tirana and the nippers. Tirana says he is coming along but at the same time she is in agreement with Heinz that he needs to sharpen up his material before he is ready for the comedy clubs at Rhos on Sea or Rhyl.

§

The story quotes an opinion poll that says forty-five per cent of people in Wales would now vote for independence from England if they were given the chance in a referendum.

Jimmy takes the paper back and says that now Roughly is in the loop he will tell him that the Wales government thinks the figure is higher than that. So they are preparing an independence plan and they have been sending people to London for talks.

He adds that the German government and the rest of the guys in Europe will certainly be interested if Wales votes for independence. They will want to know how they intend to play their hand.

Then he looks at Roughly and asks what Heinz is like. Is he a sly sort of guy who looks like he steals secrets? He also asks if he has seen any suspicious letters lying around on his desk.

Roughly laughs at this and replies that Heinz is one of the most colourful guys he has ever met and he is certainly not the sort of spy who lurks in the shadows. But he says that the next time he is up there in the attic office he will keep an eye out for any incriminating documents.

CHAPTER SIX

'The earliest memory I have is of a trilby hat and it's sitting on the head of my grandfather.'

Roughly thinks this is a good line and he reads it out to Heinz at their next lesson but then he says it is copyright Tirana O'Reilly, Colwyn Bay, because it's her line and her grandfather.

Roughly asks Heinz if he can read out the rest of what Tirana has written. Heinz replies he will be delighted to hear it, so Roughly begins.

As he got older, my grandfather took to wearing his hat indoors – and what you have to remember about my grandfather, he was the sort of guy who always needed to be the centre of attention. He would sit in his armchair and talk about whatever came into his head. When he was younger he was a big man but when he was older he thinned right down. I recall also that he had a voice that was surprisingly high-pitched. Some of the things he talked about were interesting; for instance he knew a lot about fishing. He took me down to the river with him and that is a good memory. But there were other times when he was talking so much about football or what the neighbours were up to – and remember this was when Enver Hoxha was the dictator and so it was dangerous to talk politics – that people became fed up with him. They said he was one of those guys who loved the sound of his own voice.

Then one day his brother was visiting and he was talking about how well he was doing with his farm and my grandfather could not get a word in. He took off his hat and fiddled with the band then he pulled at a thread on the old grey cardi he was wearing. Then, and he had done this before when other people were talking, he went into the bedroom and started to blow on his trumpet. My grandmother was always worried when he did this because it left him red in the face and short of breath. So we heard a few blasts, then there was a groan followed by a crash and we all ran into the bedroom to find him lying on the floor stone dead from a heart attack.

Roughly looks up. 'That is all she has written for now. Also for the moment she is not saying if she just made it up or if that is what happened.'

Heinz runs his hands through his hair and leans back in his chair.

'Tirana has an aptitude with a story, you can tell her that. It is also well known that after a certain age most people have a mind that is closed up tight. Though it can even start when they are quite young. Take the example of my nephew Cedric who is staying with me now. One evening I am opening an atlas to show him that it is still possible, provided you are careful and pick the right season, to walk from Berlin to Samarkand. But Cedric is not interested at all, his eyes are blank. So I am wasting my breath there.'

Now they are casting around for a subject for Roughly to write about next. Heinz says they have done adventure and poetry and comedy. Later they will tackle satire, romance, historical and the future. But he also says there is room for the story of the journey, which is a popular category of writing, which can also come under the heading of adventure. Sometimes it can even come under the heading of inspiration.

Tirana has been reading a life of the writer Jack London. She says old Jack went on more journeys in his lifetime than you can imagine. But when he is hunting round, Roughly finds that most of the great journeys have been done by men and they are household names, such as Lawrence of Arabia or Ernest Shackleton. So he is looking for a journey undertaken by someone, preferably a woman, who is not well known. He studies the books in the library, then he watches some documentaries on the TV. He recalls how Alfred arrived in London from Jamaica and how Rita escaped from Prague in the back of a truck. At the same time he is running ideas by Otis who has just got back to Jamaica from Detroit. Then he gets a break finding a snippet of information and following the trail, nose to the ground, like a bloodhound. He lets the idea grow for a few days while he does some more research. Then he runs it by Tirana, who says, 'That sounds interesting,' and finally he puts it all down on paper and a week later he takes it into Heinz and this is what he reads out to him.

A young woman is seated at a table in the New York Public Library. She is uneasy because this is the first time she's ever been in the New York Public Library. The painted frescoes and the high domed ceilings are intimidating her. She has blonde hair and an open face. People who have studied the photos (there are five of them that have survived), say there is a definite resemblance to Ingrid Bergman.

Then the librarian calls out, 'Lillian', and she walks up to the counter and collects the books she has ordered. She carries them over to a table and puts them down. Then she looks around at the other people who are heads down, studying. Finally she opens up the books and sets to work.

For a couple of hours she turns the pages and draws rough maps in a notebook. Then she closes up the books and hands them back in and walks out of the library into the cold air, breathing a sigh of relief. Though she is still quite young she is not too good with closed spaces.

Lillian came to America from Russia some years before. In New York she worked as a maid for a doctor and his wife but she reckoned they were not treating her right. So one morning she woke up and realised she wanted to go home. But the price of the steamer ticket was a bit of a problem.

So now she rides the subway back to the small room she rents. There she makes an inventory. She's got about twenty dollars and, for footwear, a pair of tennis shoes. She examines herself in the mirror and notes there is plenty of muscle on her legs and no fat on her belly so she is fit and still quite young so that is all on the good side. The next morning she walks out of the room, closing the door behind her.

So far she is not scared at all. She crosses into Canada at Niagara Falls on Christmas Eve, 1926. A police officer records that she is thirty years old, religion Catholic and that her last place of residence is Rochester, New York State.

Now she stands on the Canadian side of the border. For the first time the butterflies are fluttering around in her stomach. She hesitates for a moment and checks the directions she made in the library. She thinks about turning back, some snow is starting to fall, but then she gets a grip. She pulls a bag up on to her shoulder and turns her face to the west and sets off. The route she follows takes her past the city of Hamilton then on to Toronto, Sudbury and Sault Ste Marie. Then she walks round the top of Lake Superior to Kenora before finally arriving in Winnipeg.

She doesn't seek out company as she walks but people still recall her. Accounts in local papers state she is wearing a big old greatcoat, frayed at the edges. On another occasion she is reported as walking in boots that aren't matching. She tells a reporter all she has in the bag over her shoulder is a loaf of bread and a wooden stick to protect herself. She sleeps rough most of the time even though it is midwinter with snow on the ground and temperatures falling to minus twenty.

She arrives in Winnipeg at the beginning of March, which is two months after she crossed over from Niagara Falls. So she has walked about 1,300 miles and the number of people who have walked 1,300 miles in their lives at one go, even with the regular kit and the good weather, it is possible to number on the fingers of one hand but Lillian did it in midwinter with hardly a dollar in her pocket. So we can say Lillian is a remarkable person, probably one in a million.

Now Lillian rests up in Winnipeg for a few weeks to get her strength back. She works at waitressing jobs to save up money and then she sets off again. But this time she changes the direction, turning more to the north. As the weather improves she passes through the towns of Kamsack and Wakaw in Saskatchewan. This is towards the end of April. She is walking with a good swing to her pace. The sun is on her back and she is often singing. Then in mid-June there are sightings of her in the town of Grande Prairie in northern Alberta. After that the land starts to rise and soon she is high up the Rocky Mountains following the old trails used by the fur trappers and the Indians. She stands at the top of one wild mountain pass and looks slowly around. All she can see are forests and mountains. She writes in her memoir that it is the finest feeling in all the world.

At the end of summer Lillian drops out of the mountains and arrives at the town of Hazelton in British Columbia. So that is early September 1927, and she has been on the road for about ten months. But winter is coming again and that will be another test for her.

Heinz puts up his hand and Roughly stops. 'Oddbins, my friend, now is the time. We need to see the pictures of Lillian.'

Roughly finds the photographs and lays them on the desk. Heinz picks them up and squints at them. As he does so he disturbs the others papers on the desk and exposes an envelope, which Roughly can see is addressed to Heinz. But what makes his heart beat faster is that it's postmarked Berlin. He can also see peeping out of the envelope a small pile of dollar bills. This all happens very quickly and when Heinz moves again the envelope is covered up.

Heinz finishes examining the photos and puts his shoulders back. He is laughing now.

'You were certainly right when you said that Lillian has the Ingrid Bergman look. It is also happens that Ingrid Bergman is my favourite movie star.'

The laughter continues to bubble up.

'But I also think we've got our romance story right here. In my opinion you is sweet on Lillian yourself.'

Roughly admits that Tirana had the same reaction.

'She asked why I married her, because she does not look like Ingrid Bergman at all. She has even made an appointment with the hair dresser to get her hair done in the Ingrid Bergman style.'

In one of the photos Lillian is dressed in breeches and what looks like a man's shirt. Her hat brim is turned up and there is a knapsack on her back. In another photo a dog is walking beside her. She told a woman that the dog died when they were trying to cross a flooded river. In some photos Lillian has the real pioneer look. She's standing on a trail staring at the mountains in the distance. The face is wide and open with a good bone structure and the blonde hair is down to the collar. A careful study of the photos shows that she certainly has the Ingrid Bergman look.

Now Roughly continues with the story.

Lillian is in the town of Hazelton in northern British Columbia. But despite summer ending and winter approaching she is still planning to head further north on the Telegraph Trail. The locals in Hazelton tell her it is only a rough mule track that passes through real wild mountain country and on up into the Yukon. They warn her that if she is caught outside there at night in winter it is 100 per cent certain she will freeze to death.

But Lillian shares another attribute with Ingrid Bergman: they are both stubborn as mules. So she doesn't listen to the advice. In fact she gets into an argument with one woman that almost ends with fisticuffs. So now she takes off from Hazelton up the Telegraph Trail. A few days later she arrives at Kuldo, where she stumbles into the cabin of a linesmen called Bill Blackstock who stares astonished at her because she is so skinny and half frozen and half starved.

Bill Blackstock sends a message down the line to the nearest police post saying, 'You need to stop this crazy woman from travelling any further north.' When a constable finally arrives he arrests Lillian saying the iron bar she keeps in her knapsack to protect herself is a concealed weapon. Then the local magistrate in Hazelton gives her two months in jail down south in Vancouver and that saves her life, although when she hears the sentence read out in court Lillian stands up and uses what the Americans call cuss words, which is not the sort of language that Ingrid Bergman uses.

Lillian does her time at the Oakalla prison farm near Burnaby, where the staff say she is a model prisoner. When she is released she works at waitressing in Vancouver to save money. Then the spring comes – we are now in 1928 – and she hears that siren call to start travelling again. She buys a ticket on a boat going north up the coast. She arrives at the town of Stewart and the date for that is early June. Stewart is 200 miles north-west of Hazelton and is on the border between British Columbia in Canada and the town of Hyder in Alaska in the US.

And here Lillian gets a real setback. She planned to cross into Alaska but the border officers shake their heads and say her papers aren't in order. So that is her route into Alaska blocked. Now she has only one option which is to walk all the way back down to Hazelton to start over again on the Telegraph Trail that will take her north into the Yukon. We are in the summer of 1928 and the tramp down to Hazelton is a real tough old tramp too.

So now Lillian leaves Hazelton once again and is back on the Telegraph Trail heading north. But the trail is like nothing you've ever seen. It is as rough as hell, going up and down mountainsides. There are rivers she's got to cross and there are nights she is sleeping out under the stars. When there's no food she eats berries. Other times she gets a camp fire going so she can brew up a kettle of tea.

She is turning up at linesmen's cabins. The linesmen report her as stick thin and exhausted and so weather beaten and mosquito bitten that it is not clear if it is a man or a woman who just walked into their cabin. But the linesmen, despite that, all are still talking of her beauty.

They feed her and send messages up and down the line announcing 'Lillian Arrived' because by this time she has turned into a bit of a phenomenon. Whenever she arrives in a town the local reporters write stories describing her adventures. They call her the Mystery Lady and invent a whole load of nonsense about her. One time they even said she was a White Russian Princess.

On 28 August 1928 Lillian arrives at the town of Whitehorse, where she rests up a bit. But she doesn't stay long. She knows she has to make Dawson, which is 270 miles further north, before winter closes in again.

Then she discovers that the way to get around this country is by river. A look at the map shows that the towns are linked by the Yukon River. So Lillian obtains a craft which is half raft and half rowing boat – the locals call this a 'float-me-down' – and because she is travelling with the flow she just has to hang on and steer until she arrives in Dawson. Even so it is still late in the season and when she gets there the other boats are already off the river. As she steps ashore a local newspaper reporter notes, 'Fatigue showed in every line of her haggard face.'

Lillian spends that winter in Dawson. First she cooks at a dairy ranch and then she helps out at an establishment run by the nuns but she does not fit in there at all. One of the nuns recalls her as a 'troubled soul'. Other people she met on the trail said that, while she kept her distance if you got talking, she was friendly enough.

By May the ice in the river is starting to break up. Every day Lillian looks anxiously at the river because she wants to set off, but the locals tell her she needs to be patient. Finally the river is clear and she is once again aboard her crazy raft boat drifting downstream. At night she pulls into the shore sleeping in cabins abandoned by gold miners years before.

Finally she arrives at the town of Nome which is on the southern coast of Alaska. She crossed into the US by slipping past the frontier post on her raft at night. So now we are into September 1929. She stays in Nome just a few days. Then there is a report of her walking out of Nome to the west. The report says she is pulling a wheeled cart with all her possessions inside.

A few weeks later Lillian arrives on the west coast of Alaska, at the small Inuit settlement called Wales, on Cape Prince of Wales. From there, on a clear day, it is possible to see fifty miles across the Bering Strait to the coast of Siberia, which is in Russia.

Lillian talks to the local Inuit guys and they say they know the guys on the other side and a lot of them are family. They travel over in summer by boat and in winter by sledge, because it is not like the world of today, where there are barriers everywhere. This is 1929 and the Bering Strait is pretty much World's End.

Lillian asks if, the next time they are crossing over, she can ride with them and they agree to that. So then Lillian crosses the Bering Strait. She sits up in the front of the boat and watches as her homeland appears before her. A tear comes to her eye as they approach. Finally they land at the town of Provideniya in Siberia.

And that is the story of how a poor Russian girl called Lillian Alling walked across North America to get home, because she did not have the price of a steamer ticket. If you want to calculate the distance it is about 6,000 miles and it took Lillian Alling about three years to make the journey. Anyone else who is going to try that, well good luck to them, because it is near enough a hundred per cent certain you will not make it and you will die.

Heinz adjusts the navy blue sweater he is wearing.

'Actually, your story is reminding me of when I was growing up in the valley in Bavaria with my brother Frederick. We were both good runners. We used to have races up the side of the valley and we were pretty much even-stevens as to who would make it to the top first. We'd planned to enter a marathon in Munich and people in the village were taking bets as to who would finish first, but it never came about because Frederick fell in love with a girl and left for Hamburg and I came to North Wales.'

Roughly interrupts here to say that the story is not finished yet so Heinz ducks his head down, a bit embarrassed, and Roughly continues.

Lillian (the young one) has just come in from school. It's the 1960s, so it's the Soviet times. The city is Vladivostok. Lillian's grandma is in the kitchen preparing the dinner. Lillian goes in there and gives her a hug. Then Grandma tells her to take off her coat because the snow is dripping everywhere, so she goes back to the door and hangs it up.

Grandma gives her a drink and a biscuit and little Lillian sits on the sofa. Grandpa is sitting at the table where he has spread out a newspaper. He is carving a figure from a piece of wood he has found on the street. Before he retired he was a master carpenter and he still likes to work with wood.

Lillian turns the pages of a comic book. Grandpa grunts as he does his woodwork, while Grandma cooks up dinner in the kitchen. When she looks back, Lillian realises these are the best moments of her childhood.

The apartment is always warm but they are never saying very much. Later she realises they are a pair of solitaries living together. Every so often she catches Grandma, who worked thirty years as a city bus driver, staring out of the window like her head is miles away. Other times she likes to have the radio on. When she is not in the kitchen she sits down with her and they play cards together.

When her mother comes to pick her up they sometimes stay and eat dinner together. When they get home her mother always sighs and says, 'Your grandma is stubborn like an old mule.'

Lillian does not disclose that when Grandpa goes out to scavenge for wood for his carving Grandma often sings to her. It was only when she is older she realises that in the late afternoon Grandma likes to tickle her throat with a glass of vodka.

One evening Lillian's mother is working late and her grandpa is at a meeting so it is just Lillian and her grandma, sitting cosily together on the sofa. They are listening to a song on the radio. Then Grandma puts her arm around Lillian and whispers to her that she has done something when she is young that no one believed possible. She says she had an adventure to beat all adventures but that she had never told anyone about it, not even Grandpa. She says she plans to tell Lillian all about it when she is older. Sadly Lillian never heard the story, because the next winter Grandma caught a cold which went to her chest and turned into pneumonia. They took her to the hospital but she died there, before she could share her story with anyone.

A few years later, Lillian, then a teen, wanted to learn more detail of her grandma's life. Her mother recounted how she had worked as a bus driver in the city, which Lillian knew already, and how Grandpa was a master carpenter. Then Lillian repeated what Grandma had said, that she planned to tell her a story of a great adventure she'd had when she was young.

This made her mother think for a moment.

'Well I remember a strange thing happened one time when Grandma was driving her bus,' she said finally. 'I got it from a friend who rode regularly on the same bus. She said that Grandma never spoke much to the passengers. She just opened and shut the door and concentrated on the driving. But one day an American man is getting on the bus. In those days that was an event in itself. He was not speaking Russian so he addressed Grandma in English, asking if he got the right bus and Grandma, so the story goes, replied back in English and they had quite a conversation. That was the story that came back to me but when I asked about it Grandma flat out denied it ever happened.

'Grandma always said she was brought up near Moscow but then she packed up and came out here to Vladivostok. The only thing she said about her early years in the city, which always brought a smile to her face, was that one day she noticed this young guy on the bus who was looking at her in that way and she realised he was sweet on her. So she played along with it too and that is how she got together with Grandpa.'

Lillian was curious now, so she visited the bus depot. She said she wanted to discover more about her grandma for a school project. The drivers who remembered Grandma said she was tough as old boots. Anyone got on her bus and they were fooling round because they had drunk too much vodka, they soon regretted it. And every morning, even when it was colder than hell, she still walked from her apartment to the bus depot to begin her shift. A supervisor said she was the most reliable driver she ever had and that she never missed a day. But she said there were days when Grandma was friendly and you could have a chat about this and that but there were other days when you knew it was best to leave her alone.

Then Lillian got a break when a woman came out of the office and said, 'I remember your grandma. I was just starting when she was getting ready to retire so we overlapped by a couple of years. She was always on time and she never missed a day. She was also tough as hell. I still recall the time a supervisor tried to change her route and your grandma swore at her until she changed it back. Then one day I got the route wrong and I got bawled out by the supervisor and that upset me. Your grandma saw what had happened and at the end of the shift she came over to me and told me I needed to toughen up if I wanted to survive here. Then we went into a bar down the street to drink some vodka.

'There she told me the story of a crazy walk she'd done in America. She said she'd walked right across the country from New York to Alaska. Took her three years. One minute she said she was up in the mountains the next she was paddling down the river in a boat.'

Lillian was astonished when she heard this story and asked the woman if she believed it. The woman stopped to think and then said, 'Why not? I believed her. Your grandma was that sort of person. She had no reason to make it up. In those days everything was up in the air. But she never talked to me about it again.'

That evening Lillian told her mother the story and her mother shook her head and said, 'Well I certainly never heard anything about that.'

A couple of years later Lillian had left school and was applying for the university when there was a knock on the door and she went to answer it. There was a woman standing there.

'We have taken over the apartment where your grandpa and grandma lived,' the woman said. 'We were doing a bit of decorating and fixing up when we found a loose floorboard and we pulled it up.'

Then she was holding out in her hand a tin box. Lillian took it from her. On the top was written, in Grandma's hand, 'America 1926-30'.

They opened it up and found a dozen rough school exercise books. Lillian and her mother figured that she got up while Grandpa was still sleeping and sat down at the kitchen table and, using the light of a candle so as not to wake him, wrote up an account of her journey. There were a few bits and bobs to go with it in the tin. There was also a black and white photo of her with a knapsack on her back where she was turning to look at the camera. They read through the notebooks at the kitchen table. Their emotions went from marvelling at her exploits to laughing and then to crying at everything Grandma did to get back to Russia. She wrote that she wanted to go home because the people in America weren't friendly but she hadn't got the fare for the steamer. All the detail was there and the only thing she regretted was that she swore at the magistrate who put her in jail. She wrote that when she arrived at Providenya and stepped out of that Inuit boat she knelt down and kissed the soil and said she was glad she was home now.

In the years to come Lillian will make the diaries public. They will give more detail on one of the greatest journeys of all time.

After that Roughly stops reading and looks up and sees to his surprise that a tear has formed at the corner of Heinz's eye, though he brushes it away quickly like it is a piece of attic dust. Then he looks out of the window to see that the rain has stopped and a ray of sunshine has appeared. Finally he turns back to Roughly.

'Well, Señor O'Reilly,' he says, 'you has certainly captured the essential of what makes a classic story, which is a hero overcoming obstacles on a journey and making it back home, so I is obliged to say congratulations and to lift the hat to you.'

After that he pours two tots of Wales Brandy and they

drink to the success of the story. Then they discuss what Roughly is going to write next.

That evening when he arrives home Roughly tells Tirana and the nippers that Heinz liked the Lillian Alling story. The nippers high five when they hear that and Tirana tells Roughly admiringly he is certain to make it as a writer after all.

§

The Colwyn Bay Force has finally cracked the case, Jimmy tells Roughly at their next meeting at the Wales Coffee Bar.

They have received an information that the German Spy Service passed a message to Heinz that the Wales Chapel Lady, who runs the reception at the university, has a sister who is a secretary in the government offices in Cardiff where she has got access to all the private papers.

Now Heinz has received instructions from the German Spy Service to get close to the Wales Chapel Lady. But he is not doing the normal seduction routine because Heinz is still very much in love with his Wales wife. At the same time he is aware that is a hard road anyway because those Wales Chapel Ladies are tough old bags and not giving in easily.

CHAPTER SEVEN

For the next lesson Heinz asks Roughly to write a love story. Roughly composes a short piece late at night, when Tirana and the two nippers are in bed, and reads it out to Heinz.

'The first time I saw Tirana I did not fall head over heels in love with her, which is not how love stories are supposed to start. She came to the house in Hounslow with an Albanian who was a rough diamond, like a lot of those Albanians. I made some discreet enquires and learnt that he was up to all sorts of tricks that would certainly land him in trouble. So I tipped the wink to Rita and she passed the message through to Tirana and the guy got dumped but Tirana did not thank me for that at all.

'In fact for a long time we were not on speaking terms. Then Rita told me she overheard Tirana on the phone telling a girl friend that I was not that bad even if I was a bit stuck up because I was a copper. After that the warmth started to grow until we were finally walking out together and so that is how it started.

'Now I am proud as punch of my two boys and everyone says that Tirana is an excellent mother though she can blast off like a space rocket if something is not right and everyone has to live with that.

'The other thing I recall, which you could call a love

story, is a tune that Rita sang a lot when I was young. It told the story of two young lovers called Terry and Julie who met every Friday evening at Waterloo Station. They walked across Waterloo Bridge while the sun was setting and they said that together they were in paradise. Rita loved that song because on the first date with Alfred they also met under the clock at Waterloo Station. Then they walked over Waterloo Bridge as the sun was setting and Rita said they were in paradise as well. So that is another love story I can tell.'

Roughly stops and looks up.

'Is that it?' Heinz asks, surprised.

'Well what the heck do you expect from a copper? Roses strewn on the pavement?'

The next week Heinz asks Roughly to write a story which could appear under the heading of political satire. He has chosen this subject because Roughly has told him that when he and Tirana are having their supper in the evening they are often discussing politics with the two nippers.

Roughly tells the nippers how Rita had to flee the Communist government in Prague in the back of a truck and Tirana says life in Enver Hoxha's Albania was so topsy turvy nobody knew if they were on their head or their tail. The nippers are all ears when they hear this.

Roughly recounts all this to Heinz as they are drinking tots of Wales Brandy in his attic office. The rain and the wind are rattling the windows.

Heinz laughs and says, 'It's always good to cock the snook at the authorities. This is what the political satirists do. They also remind us how lucky we are to live in a place like North Wales.'

A few days later Tirana is hunting around the internet for material that would be suitable for a satire when she comes across the story of Sir Reginald Sheffield, the 8th Baronet of Normanby Hall in the county of Lincolnshire, who has become entangled with a man called Antony Wilks resulting in a trial before Grimsby Crown Court.

Roughly hands Heinz the pictures Tirana dug up. The photos show a tall guy, a bit fragile because he's over seventy, but still upright. There are also pictures of him as a younger man. He is heavier then, but that weight has gone now. The photos show him sporting the colourful bow ties the aristocrats wear. He has also got the schoolboy smile puckering the corners of his mouth. Roughly gives Heinz an account of what Tirana has discovered .

'Tirana found out on the internet that he is one of the top aristocrats. His wife is Victoria and he owns two stately homes, Sutton Park and Normanby Hall. The estates are running to about 6,000 acres and include several villages. At one time, Tirana says, the family even owned Buckingham House, which is now Buckingham Palace. Tirana has also done an estimation of his wealth and says it is about £20 million minimum. He's also got four daughters. One of them is called Samantha, who is married to David Cameron who ran the country before Stanley Johnson's son. So that is a further indication of his top class standing.'

But Heinz puts up his hand here and tells Roughly that before he can begin on political satire he needs to read Jonathan Swift and, in particular, a short pamphlet called *A Modest Proposal*, which got under everyone's skin at the time. He also tells Roughly to view the paintings of the artist William Hogarth.

Tirana takes the books out of the library and laughs out loud as she reads them. She tells Roughly, 'Jonathan Swift got a bloody sharp tongue.' They look at the Hogarth paintings online together and they appreciate his sharpness also.

But the next time they meet, Heinz warns Roughly there are dangers in writing political satire. 'It is a subject a lot of writers fail at because they think all you need to do is blast off a literary shotgun at the biggest buffoon in the room. But you have to be sharper than that.'

He lists the people to steer away from because they have been hit too often. He cites the new King and Camilla, the rest of the Royal Family, the Archbishop of Canterbury, the other bishops and the House of Lords. He also adds the crooks running the City of London because they have been done to death as well. He is not sure about an aristocrat like Sir Reginald Sheffield. Then he arrives at the political guys and in particular Stanley Johnson's son. He says that taking a swing at him is like firing a shotgun at a barn door: you ain't going to miss. He says in a few years no one will even recall who he was.

Then he is hunting round the papers on his desk. 'People lost all sense of reality with that guy,' he says. Finally he picks up an article he's clipped from the newspaper and reads out the headline, 'Why Does Everyone Pick On Stanley Johnson's Son?' The article suggests a list of alternative targets for journalists to attack. The list starts with school teachers and continues with people sleeping on the streets then it highlights illegal immigrants before it takes a sharp knock to the BBC. Then for some reason it includes road sweepers, so it looks like the writer had a bad experience there. After that it attacks artists who are doing paintings no one understands and writers who produce books that got too many long words before it finishes with the guys who climb into the trees to block motorway construction.

Heinz looks up at Roughly and asks, 'What's wrong with that list?'

Roughly replies, 'With the exception of the BBC they are the guys who are already at the bottom of the heap so it is pointless to kick them.' Heinz nods to show that Roughly understood the point.

After that and with a break in the weather Heinz looks at his watch and says he has to go into town because he has an appointment. They agree to continue the lesson in two days time.

As she is undertaking her research Tirana tells Roughly she has discovered a paradox. She says the tougher an aristocratic family is, the more they display the 'genteel' manners. She is about to expand on that when there is the clack of the letterbox and the post arrives. Among the pizza leaflets and the junk mail is a pamphlet, badly printed and on cheap paper, entitled *The Problem of Land Ownership in Modern-Day England*. The publishers are a group called Citizens Arise and it is printed by the Scottish Printing Company of Pollokshields, Glasgow.

Tirana reads it through and says she recalls the same thing happening when she was growing up in Albania: anonymous pamphlets were pushed through the door urging people to rise up against Enver Hoxha.

After that Roughly and Tirana have another big discussion about politics. They return to the situation in Albania and in Prague and attempt to draw a comparison with the case of Antony Wilks and Sir Reginald Sheffield. Then Tirana uses the pamphlet that has been pushed through the door to further analyse land ownership in England. Even the nippers put in their two pennies' worth.

That evening, as they are eating their dinner, Tirana has Roughly and the nippers in fits of laughter as she recounts some of the stories she has unearthed about Sir Reginald Sheffield and his wife Lady Victoria.

'Listen to this,' she says and reads out a post from a gossip columnist. 'Sir Reginald and his wife Victoria are on holiday in Vietnam where they are doing a bit of the old wind surfing. One day they are having lunch at a beachfront restaurant when Victoria tells Reggie, as she calls him in private, that if he wants to be up to date he needs to get a tattoo. So that afternoon Reggie sets off for the tattoo parlour.

'But when he is back at the hotel that evening Victoria is puzzled because she can't see the tattoo anywhere. It is only in bed that night she discovers that Reggie now has a six-inch Vietnamese butterfly, colour electric red, parked up on his rear end. Victoria laughs like a drain when she discovers it.'

Then Tirana finds a passage on the estate website

about an old baronet, an ancestor of Reggie's. She reads it out at breakfast.

'No matter which residence the family happened to be staying at, fresh fruit from the gardens at Normanby was sent to them. In return, the family sent hampers of dirty laundry back to Normanby for washing!'

Roughly and the nippers squeal with laughter when they hear this. They imagine the poor old estate workers out in the fields before dawn. They fill up the hamper with delicious fresh fruit which is then delivered by horse and cart to the family. In the evening the cart returns, but this time the hamper is full of the family's dirty washing. The girls who tip it out on the kitchen floor hold their noses and say, 'Hey-ho this is fun,' as they sort through the elderly baronet's smalls.

Tirana has also discovered that Robert, who is Reggie's son from his first marriage, dresses up as a drag queen. Photos in the newspapers show him in blue wig and glittery mini dress. Tirana says actually that is good cover. If they are looking like a family of harmless nitwits people are less likely to ask questions about how much money and land they have and where it all came from.

Roughly pauses here and looks at Heinz. Then he says Tirana has asked if he can include this joke. Heinz nods.

'When he's in London, Reggie dines at one of his two clubs, which are given as Whites and Pratts. Tirana says if you add the word 'only' in front of the names that is it in a nutshell. That is the punchline. It's an old joke that has been told before but provided it is not brought out too often it still works.'

Heinz pulls a face and says it is a bit lame in his opinion.

Now Roughly and Tirana's researches head the story off on a tangent. If Reggie Sheffield owns two stately homes, how many rooms does that include? Tirana has studied photos floor plans and calculated a hundred at least. With the girls gone and the boy strutting his stuff, then Reggie and Victoria must be rattling around, she said.

'So one day we are imagining,' Roughly reads out, 'Reggie opens a door to a room he has not been in for a few years and he finds to his surprise a family of Afghan refugees living there. They have made it warm and cosy. There is washing hanging up on lines and nippers running about. That night Reggie says to Victoria when they are at dinner, "Did you know we have got a family of Afghan refugees living in one of our rooms?"

'But here is the difference between the aristocrats and the middle classes. The middle classes will call the police straight away. They will say we don't want brown-skinned immigrants and if their boats are punctured and sunk in the Channel that is nothing to do with us. But Reggie and Victoria are smarter than that. They come to an arrangement with the Afghan family. Instead of rent they ask them to cook a dinner one evening a week, which he and Victoria enjoy because it turns out the family owned a restaurant in Kabul before they had to flee.

'Then Reggie becomes godfather to their first boy born here and gets the kids into local schools and fixes things with the Home Office. Soon the Afghan family are running all the cooking at the hall and visitors report it as the best dining experience they have had in a long time. Finally the family moves out and opens up a restaurant in Harrogate and of course they always remember the big guy from Normanby Hall who helped them out. This is a good example of the smart way the aristocrats work.'

Then Roughly continues, 'Tirana has discovered that even if they give the impression of being harmless nitwits these aristocrats like Reggie are actually damn sharp businessmen. The government gives Reggie a hefty wedge so he can run his farms. At one point it runs at over £30,000 a year. He also receives a wedge from the local council because they have an arrangement with him over the use of Normanby Hall. Reggie also rents out a few acres of land to a group of guys who have put up wind turbines. The amount of rent he charges them is about £350,000 a year. And by the way, Tirana points out, the tenants who are lodging in the villages he owns are not doing so for free.

'But the locals are not kicking up a fuss about this. They are not getting out their pitchforks to give him a good prod. Some of them think it is the correct order of things to have an aristocrat ruling over them. But the truth is that ninety per cent of people are not aware of the existence of Reggie and Victoria. And they certainly have no idea that his small group of aristocrats own a third of all the land in England, which we are coming to. As we have detailed above, these stately home guys, even though they sit there bold as brass in full daylight, are also the souls of discretion. You pass them in the street, you have no idea who they are. And those who do know tend to steer clear because it's better to leave alone what you are not sure about.'

Then Heinz looks at his watch and says he has to cut the lesson short as he has an appointment in town.

Roughly arrives at the university the following week. He folds his umbrella and says good morning to the Wales Chapel Lady, who blows her nose sharply in reply. Then he is up the stairs to the attic office and knocking sharply on the door and Heinz is shouting, 'Coming in, Señor Oddbins,' the same way he always does. They share a tot of Wales Brandy, then Heinz can see that Roughly is eager to begin so he sighs and says, 'Okay, Señor Oddbins I got my listening ears on.'

Roughly says as an introduction to the story of Antony Wilks and Sir Reginald Sheffield he needs to tell Heinz about the mysterious pamphlet from the Scottish Printing Company of Pollokshields, Glasgow that was pushed through their door a couple of days before. Then he takes a deep breath and asks Heinz if he can also read out a short piece he has written about land ownership in England. He says the idea, inspired by the pamphlet, came to him as he was dropping his two nippers off at school. But Heinz has been temporarily distracted by the wind and rain which is battering even harder at the windows and so does not reply. Roughly takes the plunge and starts reading anyway.

'Everyone in our lovely country – and it is a lovely country – should have the right to a place they can call their own. In town at minimum a small flat and in the country a house with a garden if that's possible. That is your right, whether you own it, rent it or whatever. The detail we are going to work out. But the main thing is nobody can put you out.

'If you have the money you can pay more for your house though there has to be a limit. A stately home guy, such as Reggie Sheffield, can have a house and a garden that is big enough for him and his family. But he's going to lose the stately home and he needs to face up to that. This is not an attack on the stately home guys because some of them are upstanding citizens who have done a lot for the community. They can still keep their titles and open the local agricultural show and sit on boards for this and that. But they will no longer have the nightmare of the upkeep of the stately home, the leaking roofs and dry rot and so on. The sense of relief they're going to feel is the same as a homeless person when they're told they've now own their own small flat.

'If you think about it, a lot of the stately homes are already being run by the National Trust and local councils so we are already half way there. So who will not vote for that?'

Roughly stops and looks up. Heinz has turned back from the window and is staring at him. He gives one of his long belly laughs. Then he says, 'Well, Mr Revolutionary O'Reilly, that comes under the heading of polemic or radical commentary, which as it happens I am not teaching this year. And also writers is advised not to throw political bombs because it blocks the flow of the story. The readers have come for a good read not a lecture. If they want a political meeting they can go to Hyde Park Corner in London. That said, your point is obviously correct. But the stately home guys are not going to like it and they still have influence with the judges. So don't be surprised if they bring forward a proposition to put you in the pokey for a spell. And you a bloody copper as well!'

As he is talking, Heinz is scrabbling round among the papers on his desk. As he moves the papers he briefly exposes a document with the Wales government crest on it and which is stamped Top Secret. That makes Roughly's heart lurch. Then the moment has passed because Heinz has found what he is after. With a triumphant gesture he holds up a copy of the pamphlet.

'So after all I am receiving the same pamphlet as Tirana. Someone has been pushing it through all the doors in the street. I recall it now because it has been printed by someone who is not that good at printing.' Heinz thumbs through the pamphlet then puts it back down on the desk. Then he looks up. 'Over to you, Comrade O' Reilly.'

Roughly begins by quoting directly from the pamphlet.

'The aristocracy, or as it is sometimes called, the nobility, which is just 25,000 people and who are making up not even one per cent of the population, own a third of all the land in England. That means if there are forty-eight counties in England the aristocrats own sixteen of them.'

Roughly can sense Heinz is suddenly alert and listening. He turns a page.

'Because the aristocracy own so much land they have got a lot of power over the way the country is run – and remember these people have never been elected to anything. So if we are talking democracy, where everyone is supposed to get a fair crack of the whip, then the system has got a damn big hole under the waterline.

'We also need to consider that most of these people never had to put their hand in their pocket or take out a mortgage. They were given the land for services rendered by this or that monarch. And this still allows them three or four centuries later to put up signs up on their land, reading Private Property and Keep Out. And they got the right to do this because they got the law on their side. The other point to note is that the ratio of one third has stayed the same for hundreds of years so their power is not fading.

'The number of people in England who know about this situation is very small.' Roughly looks up and sees Heinz staring at him with astonishment. He turns a page and ploughs on.

'The aristocrats are full of charm and they have smooth faces and they live to a good old age, well above the average, because they have got excellent healthcare. They are polite and tipping well in restaurants and giving money to charity. But if their position is threatened they are fighting as dirty as any fishwife. They also got the guys in suits on their side. They got lawyers who stifle any nonsense from the tenants before it starts and they employ top-grade accountants who know how the Island Game works. They put their money well out of the way on the Jersey Island and the Virgin Island and the Cayman Island.

'These guys are also discreet. They are like the fawns in the forest: if you shine a light on them they are dancing away. Though maybe it is more accurate to say they are like crocs hiding in a swamp. What you have got to do is not disturb them and they will leave you alone. But if you are unable to resist and you are poking them with a sharp stick they will have your leg off just like that. You are not going to believe how strong their jaws are – and they've got sharp teeth as well.'

When Roughly has finished reading the passage from the pamphlet Heinz gets up from his chair and walks over to the window, where he says some long words in German. Then he sits down again and looks straight at Roughly.

'How can these aristocrats own a third of England and nobody does anything about it? Why has the English people not risen up and driven out people like Reggie Sheffield at the end of a pitchfork? Why has there not been a revolution like in France?' Then Heinz stares at Roughly. 'In my humble opinion, Mr Oddbins, the people of England are living under an occupation.'

Roughly nods his head in agreement.

'Even Tirana was shocked when she read it. She said the first thing Enver Hoxha did when he came to power in Albania was to drive out the old landowners.'

After that, and with a break in the weather, Heinz says once again that he has to go into town because he has an appointment. They agree to continue the lesson in two days' time.

At the next lesson Roughly takes a last photo out of his stack of papers and puts it down in front of Heinz. It is a photo of Antony Wilks, who is about twenty-five years old. He has got his baseball hat cocked at a jaunty angle in the same way that Reggie Sheffield on occasion has his bow tie cocked at a similar jaunty angle. Wilks is called Buster by his mates. He lives in Grimsby but we are not going to call it the grim old town of Grimsby because that has been done a hundred times before. Tirana has pointed out that there is a strange similarity between the two men. They are both living on the margins of society, just at different ends.

Both Reggie and Buster receive wedges from the government. Reggie gets a wedge for his farms and for the stately home he is not currently living in. This is amounting to many thousands of pounds. Buster Wilks gets a wedge because he is unemployed, though some weeks that is not even making three figures. But the reaction of the people of Grimsby is different. They call Reggie an upright citizen while they think Buster is a dirty rotten scrounger. They say that Reggie has to scrabble at the coal face so that Buster can idle his days away in Grimsby's dockside boozers.

The point of everything above has been to show that while the aristocrats are happy for the public to regard them as harmless eccentrics they are really sharp as mice and know exactly what they are about.

Finally we are coming to the incident that Roughly has written down and now recounts to Heinz.

'One day Reggie is out in the family Range Rover, patrolling the grounds on the Normanby Estate, when he spots an intruder. So he stops the car and puts the binocs up. Then he sits up straight in his seat because he has seen

Buster Wilks in the distance doing wheelies and kicking up the dirt on a noisy trail bike. He drives quickly over and stops. Then he winds the car window down and starts to film Buster doing his wheelies.

'Buster Wilks always burns on a short fuse. A lot of the time he's also fuelled up on cheap beer and whacky baccy. So for Reggie to point a phone at him and film him is a real provocation.

'So Buster stops his bike from doing wheelies and digging up the dirt and stares hard at Reggie. Then he gets off the bike and walks up to the car. He put his hand through the open window and after a short tussle he grabs the phone and says – and here Tirana quotes directly from the court report – "I'll have that off ya, you daft wee c**t," which is a good line if a bit rude. But Reggie, being smart, has installed a gadget on his phone which allows it to be traced. So in a couple of hours the coppers are tapping on Buster Wilks's door and taking him away and that is how he ends up before Grimsby Crown Court.

'At the end of the trial Reggie's brief stands up on his hind legs and reads out a victim statement to the judge and that is certainly the first time anyone has referred to Reggie Sheffield as a victim. But Buster Wilks has scared the hell out of a frail old geezer and that has to be noted.

'But the point of the story, and what caught the eye of Tirana, is that Buster Wilks got eighteen months jug time, which is a lot of jug time for boosting a mobile phone, especially when it has been recovered. But the charge is not boosting a mobile phone; the charge is boosting a mobile phone belonging to Sir Reginald Sheffield 8th Baronet of

Normanby Hall in the County of Lincolnshire. And in modern day England that is a dangerous thing to do.

Roughly looks up when he has finished. Heinz tugs at his bright red sweater, pulling it down over his tummy. He leans forward.

'The story is too rambling, Comrade O. It is all over the place; anyone is going to tell you that. But I am going to criticise it because you have fallen between the two stools. You are not sure if you are writing as a comic or a political guy. I already told you about my brother Frederick in Hamburg and the dentist who is doing the stand-up. The night he gets the apple core in the gob he's doing a sketch about Angela Merkel. He's rhyming Merkel with ferkel, which is piglet in German. That is making the audience laugh. But then he's doing farmyard noises and that is finally getting up people's noses. With the satire you need to be sharp as needles. You use humour, for sure, but don't forget your purpose is to spear the guys to the heart.'

So that is another lesson Roughly learnt.

§

At the next meeting Jimmy tells Roughly he is following Heinz when he passes a tea shop and glances inside and spots the Wales Chapel Lady sitting there. He can see that she has got a slice of chocolate cake and a pot of tea in front of her. The way she is eyeing it shows she has a sweet tooth and is one for the cakes.

The next day, Jimmy says, Heinz walks into the tea shop and orders a pot of tea and a slice of the chocolate cake. He is sitting there reading the Wales Courier, pretending he hasn't got a care in the world, when the Wales Chapel Lady enters and orders her regular pot of tea and slice of chocolate cake. Then she spots Heinz and gives him a nod. Jimmy observes all this from a vantage point across the street. This is going on for a few days; then they are starting to exchange a few words and after that they are soon they are sharing the same table because they both enjoy the chocolate cake. By now Jimmy has arranged for hidden microphones to be set up under the tables.

The chocolate cake thaws out the Wales Chapel Lady. The police microphones pick up that she is becoming quite chatty. She is talking about her husband who works for the railway and their son who they are hoping will become a dentist. She even mentions that she's got a sister in Cardiff who works at the government offices.

Then Heinz recounts tales of life in Germany and he starts to pay her little compliments and she is starting to blush. Then one day when she arrives she is all jumpy and nervous. She says someone has seen them and they can't meet anymore. Her husband is a very jealous man and he is not going to believe they have just been eating chocolate cake. He will certainly speak to the rector at the Wales Chapel and she will be in trouble there as well.

CHAPTER EIGHT

When they have finished with the political satire and the romance Heinz tells Roughly to try a historical story.

For the next few evenings Roughly patrols round his garden and muses and scratches his head and thinks about history. He even puts on his felt hat and puffs away at his Sherlock Holmes-style pipe.

Tirana tells him that Enver Hoxha played fast and loose with the present. If he got it into his head to turn Monday into Tuesday no one argued. But Tirana says that Enver Hoxha also changed round the detail of the past. This makes Roughly think and the next evening when the nippers are back from school he looks through their history books to see what they are studying.

Then a light bulb comes on and he gets an idea. He hunts round the internet and on his day off takes a trip to the library, where he does some research. That evening he chews it over with Tirana. Over the next week he writes it all down and takes it to read out to Heinz. But before he starts he warns him that is it longer than the other stories. He has even given it a title: *An Alternative History of the World*.

Several centuries ago, in the town of Cox's Bazaar in Burma, an engineer invented what he called a steam engine. He placed it on iron wheels and a crowd turned up to watch as he ran it up and down a rail line outside the city. That was how the Industrial Revolution started.

This gave Burma a head start because once you've got an industrial revolution you can do all sorts of other tricks. In a few years Burma had a solid banking system and a stock market where they raised money for expeditions. They navigated doing the latitude and the longitude with a clock. They put down undersea telegraph cables and even invented their own Morse code in Burmese. Visitors declared that Cox's Bazaar was the greatest city in the world, with waterfalls and hanging gardens and so on.

When the Burmese Army invaded a new country they were followed by the missionaries who ordered the defeated people to convert to Buddhism. They told them, 'If you don't convert you will be on a path to hell. And if you keep on resisting you are in danger of having your heads chopped off.'

In a few years the Burmese had advanced as far down as the west coast of Australia, though they never went inland. They held towns on the coast as garrison ports and trading posts. Then they advanced the other way into India and the Middle East and then they were thinking about Europe.

At the time there were two controlling powers in Europe. The first was the Barbary Boys who had their base in North Africa, but who had already expanded up into Spain and what is now called Portugal. They had also got the southern half of France and the northern part of Italy.

The other controlling power was the Kippermen.

They had their base in Sweden and their capital was Gothenburg, which is pronounced Jottaburi. They had taken Scandinavia and Germany and were always disputing France with the Barbary Boys. There was always fighting going on there with armies tramping backwards and forwards.

The Burmese sent traders and missionaries along the Silk Road towards Europe. They asked sly questions and looked about and noted weaknesses they could exploit. They reported back to Cox's Bazaar on what they found: where the passes through the mountains were and which country had a strong army and which country had a weak army and so on.

Then an expedition crossed over a stretch of water to an island that the locals called Albion but the Burmese called Poki-Poki, which means in old Burmese 'Land of the People with the Big Noses'. They discovered that it was a green and pleasant land but that the people were not very bright. They did not sense the danger when the missionaries started asking sly questions. The missionaries travelled all over and made a detailed map of the whole island. They reckoned it would be a good base for the Burmese in Europe because an island is easy to defend. Their only concern was that in the north of the island the Kippermen had a hold and they had a reputation as rough fighters.

Then the leaders of the expedition travelled back to Cox's Bazaar and they were taken in to see the king. He asked a lot of questions but the Burmese were smart; they did not give all the power to the king. He had to consult with the parliament and the parliament discussed it over and over. They got out the maps and studied them. They worked out how many ships they would need. Then they assured themselves they could raise the money for the expedition on the Cox's Bazaar stock market. After that they took a vote and it passed so the decision was made to launch an invasion force.

So that is what the lookouts on the Cornish clifftops saw one fine spring morning.

And here we need to have a small diversion to talk about the Barbary Boys. For a long time they had been sending galleys over from North Africa to the Cornish coast. The sailors slipped ashore and kidnapped the locals and took them back to the Barbary Coast, which is now called North Africa. There the poor Cornish people who had been kidnapped were sold off as slaves.

An advance party for the Burmese invasion fleet went to see the Barbary Boys and did a deal with them. They borrowed a few of the Barbary Boys' galleys because they were wanting to play a trick on the Poki-Poki.

The lookouts on the Cornish cliff tops spotted the galleys on the horizon. They raised the alarm, shouting to the villagers, 'Run for the hills as fast as you can!' Then they mounted their horses and rode as fast as they could towards Plymouth to raise the alarm there.

In a couple of hours they were up to see Sir Reggie Drake, who was a cousin to Sir Francis Drake. He was on the Hoe doing a game of bowling. The lookouts said, 'The Barbary Boys are here, Sir; we have seen their galleys on the horizon.'

When he heard this news Sir Reggie finished his game of bowling, then put to sea with his fleet saying he finally planned to teach those Barbary Boys a lesson and give them a good whacking.

But as soon as they been lured far enough away from the land the Burmese Navy, which had superior guns, appeared from over the horizon and did a pincer movement and before you could say Jack Robinson all the Albion ships had been sunk or captured and Sir Reggie and all the officers of the Albion Navy were either dead or had been taken prisoner.

Sir Reggie was handed over to the Barbary Boys as a prize and was taken back to Algiers. There he was sold into slavery and ended his life cleaning out the latrines at the Imperial Palace while his cousin Sir Francis Drake spent his days quietly as Mayor of Tavistock.

Then the Burmese Navy steamed up the coast of Albion and under cover of darkness landed crack troops on the beach at Hastings. The residents were saying, 'What's going on here then,' but the Burmese were moving quickly so by morning all their stores and soldiers had been landed. A bridgehead had been formed, which the locals in Hastings couldn't get inside of.

The following day the Burmese moved out of the bridgehead but they secured their bases and supply lines as they went. Three days later they were confronted by an Albion army marching down from the city of Evesham-and-Worcester. This was the capital, where the King of the Albions, who was called Smith, had his seat.

So they had a battle but the Burmese had all the

advantages because they'd undergone an industrial revolution and the Albions were still running an agrarian economy. The Burmese had all sorts of nasty surprises for the Albions including Congreve rockets, which the Albions had never seen before. These were tubes filled with gunpowder that were attached to sharpened bamboo sticks, or in some cases metal spikes, and when they were set off and fired there was a hell of a noise and a flash of light and this bloody spike, if it hits you, will keep travelling right through you and out the other side and cause bloody havoc.

So what happened of course was that the Albion army was routed. King Smith shouted, 'Everyone fall back on the city of Evesham-and-Worcester,' because the city had got a big, thick wall. When they were inside, the Albions slammed shut the gates but the Burmese battered them down. Then they were inside the city and firing off their Congreve rockets again which caused even more mayhem and soon King Smith was forced to sign a surrender document.

Even though the fighting had now stopped, the Burmese Army was not finished yet. They knew they had to put their mark on a defeated people. They knocked down the city walls then the Burmese soldiers, who were no different from any other soldiers, got drunk on the local grog. Then they burnt down the Royal Library, which housed all the records of Albion from over the centuries. From then on the Albions were a people without history.

Before he signed the surrender document King Smith found a bit of backbone. He shouted, 'I am still the king, you got no right.' But they gave him a couple of clips around the ear, which shut him up. Eventually he was sent back to Cox's Bazaar with the other Poki-Poki leaders. He was set to work in the market and though he wasn't happy at first he eventually became a head porter and married a local girl and had some children and learnt the language and forgot about the land of the Poki-Poki.

The Burmese generals knew that when they were doing a military campaign it was important not to bite off more than they could chew. So they drew a border direct from Evesham-and-Worcester to the east coast. Then they drew another border direct from Evesham-and-Worcester to the south coast. Never mind that it went through settled communities, they were not bothered about that. They built border forts and dug trenches to defend themselves against the savage tribes who lived on the other side of the border.

Now the Burmese had to do the occupation. First they ordered everybody to convert to being a Buddhist. Workmen altered churches so they became pagodas. Anyone protesting and refusing to convert received a warning. Second time they were hung by their neck in the village square.

The Burmese knew with an occupation you had to show who was top dog. The Albions had to be broken down, so the Burmese ordered them to pay heavy tithes and tributes. They also put the Albions on low rations to weaken them physically and to make sure they bent the knee. After a couple of years they loosened the screw and increased the rations. Then they reopened the schools and introduced the Burmese language.

At the same time the first settlers came out from Burma. They were looking for a bit of adventure in a faraway country. The Poki-Poki were resentful because the settlers took the best land and were always complaining about the weather and the food. Some of the Poki-Poki even complained they were beaten up by the settlers but the Burmese governor in London investigated all these claims and found nothing had been done wrong and everything was above board.

Then the Burmese governor scrapped all the old laws of the land and took the country back to year zero so they started all over again doing things the Burmese way. Burmese was now the official language which people needed to speak if they wanted to get on. Eventually the governor reported back to Cox's Bazaar that the Poki-Poki were finally under his thumb.

So that was the end of the First Burmese Albion War.

The Second Burmese Albion War started when Burmese intelligence heard a whisper that something nasty was brewing north of the border in a town called Grantham.

They heard that a chieftain called the Thatcher, which is an old Poki-Poki word meaning 'Leader', was whipping the people up into a frenzy and telling them they needed to drive the Burmese invaders back into the sea.

The Burmese sent troops up from the new capital of London to defend the border but they arrived too late because the Thatcher had already done a surprise raid. In an early morning attack, 500 crazed Albion fighters had overrun a Burmese border post near the town of Huntingdon.

A lot of the border guards were also run over because the Thatcher had ordered the construction of a dozen wooden chariots with spikes on the wheels. These were drawn by horses going at speed and the guys driving the chariots were also slashing to the left and right with heavy swords. The others were following on behind the chariots on foot, hollering and shouting and carrying pikes and pitchforks.

After they had crashed through the border post they headed south to London, still waving their fists and shouting their heads off. But the crack Burmese regiments, bringing up the heavy armour and the Congreve rockets, had now arrived on the scene. Both the armies were camped out on opposite sides of a small valley which the historians later called Thatcher's Bottom. The Burmese soldiers dug trenches and put up fortifications while the Albions spent the night drinking mead and listening to speeches from the Thatcher.

The next morning, with the sun behind her, the Thatcher and her rebel army raced down the side of the valley towards the Burmese lines. The Thatcher was in her wooden chariot drawn by a pair of white stallions named Brown and Blair. She was waving a silver sword. She was also protected by a shield made from turtle shells, which the sun was glinting off. She had the long blonde flowing hair (though at the moment she kept that tucked up under her helmet). The Burmese soldiers, when they recounted it later, said she had the build of an Amazon, and she was beautiful too but at the same time she was also bloody scary.

Behind her in the battle line were the wooden chariots of the nobles including the Major, the Mandelson, the Corbyn and the Cameron. Their chariots were decorated in mussel and oyster shells. They had even got a specially adapted chariot for the Blind Blunkett. He was the one who uttered the bloodthirsty curses about what he was going to do to the Burmese soldiers if he captured them. Behind them were the Albion army on foot, with the pikes and pitchforks.

The Burmese soldiers and their officers were cold-eyed and calculating. They held their fire and waited till the last minute. Then the officers ordered the soldiers operating the Congreve rockets to open up and there was a bloody great bang and smoke and lighting flashes because there were more than a hundred of them. People in neighbouring villages a dozen miles away heard the rockets going off. Then the bamboo slivers were driving through the Albion soldiers and the horses were falling too, so all the chariots were crashing into each other.

After that the Burmese soldiers were quick up out of their trenches and running forward but the Albion soldiers rallied behind the Thatcher. Her chariot had turned over so now she was on her feet, fighting mano a mano. She swung her silver sword and she still had her turtle shell shield, though her helmet had been knocked off and her blonde hair was flying loose so everyone could see.

When he was talking about it afterwards, the top Burmese general said, 'The Thatcher is certainly the bravest women we ever seen and the Albion soldiers got spirit too, but they are always going to lose because we got better troops and more armour and more Congreve rockets.'

By the end of the day the Thatcher and what was left of her army were in full retreat crossing back over the border and heading into Grantham. But the Burmese decided they needed to teach the Albions a lesson so they were running up after them. They found and cornered them in Grantham. When the locals tried to close the gates the Burmese pushed in after them. They showed no mercy because if you challenge Burmese colonial authority you have to take what is coming to you.

They rounded up all the regular fighters and hanged them from the council buildings and then the ring leaders were pulled apart by wild horses. All the civilians and the women and children were transported back to Burma where they were sold as slaves in the market at Cox's Bazaar.

Then the Burmese soldiers razed Grantham to the ground, brick by brick, before ploughing salt into the surrounding fields so nothing would grow there anymore. Then the Burmese governor in London ordered the detail of what had been done to be read out in the pagodas all over Albion.

When the dust had settled the Poki-Poki finally realised that the Burmese were top dog and they needed to knuckle down. They forgot about the old days and adopted the Burmese ways and to be honest, after a bit, everyone was much happier for it.

The Thatcher escaped, even though the Burmese hunted everywhere for her. She slipped out of Grantham under cover of darkness, dressed as a milk maid. She ended up right down in the west of Cornwall, a long way from the Burmese, in fact down by Land's End past Penzance. There she spent the rest of her life fulminating and plotting but it never came to anything and then finally one day she got kicked in the head by a horse and that was the end of her.

And that was also the end of the Second Burmese Albion War.

Things started to settle down after that. The Burmese taught the Poki-Poki how to do modern farming and fishing. In a few months they reported back to Cox's Bazaar that they were coming along quite nicely. They even selected some of the young Poki-Poki, if they'd got the smarts, to study at the Royal University in Cox's Bazaar. When they came back they told everyone about the boulevards and parks and gardens and fountains. They said if there were eight wonders in the world, then four of them were in Cox's Bazaar, including the hanging gardens. When you looked at them, you wondered how in the hell they did that.

Then old Nature suddenly stepped in and decided to let off a volcano in the archipelago called Indonesia, south of Burma, and it was such a bang that it left people rubbing their ears all over Burma and the sky turned black. A few hours later there was a tidal wave and flooding, though the damage was minor in Cox's Bazaar – aside from a couple of pagodas which got their sides blown off and a palace which got some flooding in the basement. But the crops all over Burma were ruined. That left the people looking at the fields wondering what they were going to eat that year.

They were having a big debate in the parliament in Cox's Bazaar and the king joined in as well and it was decided finally that all the empire had to chip in and feed the Motherland. Orders went out over the telegraph line to Albion that all the grain, bar a small bit, needed to be transported back to Cox's Bazaar that year. The Poki-Poki were not happy about this because it was a cold and wet winter and they were getting very thin. Historians on the Albion side later talked about the Great Hunger and how it was created by the colonial power but the Burmese historians called it the Little Hunger and explained that in life you had to take the rough with the smooth.

Agitators began to stir things up and a lot of them came from the other side of the border. They were backed by the Kippermen, who were the controlling influence in the north of the country. The spark which set off the revolt was an argument between a Poki-Poki trader and a Burmese policeman in the town of Bury St Edmunds. The Poki-Poki trader got his face slapped by the Burmese policeman which was a terrible humiliation for a Poki-Poki. The people were also angry because they were hungry and soon there was rioting in the streets of Bury St Edmunds. They burst into the granaries, which were full of grain waiting to be transported back to Burma.

That started a fracas with the Burmese police, which escalated and the next thing shots had been fired and the people had scattered everywhere. When it was all over there were a total of fifty-two Albions and six Burmese dead. Most of those were settlers who were not popular with the local Poki-Poki because of the way they treated them. But when this news was reported back to Burma on the Morse code via the undersea cables, the government leaders in Cox's Bazaar were so angry they were hopping around on one foot.

The message came back on the undersea cable that they had to do a collective punishment again, so the soldiers razed the town of Bury St Edmunds, brick by brick, and salted the fields around so nothing could grow there. Then they pulled the ring leaders apart with wild horses and transported all the rest of the citizens of Bury St Edmunds back to Burma, where they were made into slaves and sold in the market at Cox's Bazaar.

Then the Burmese realised there would never be peace in Albion until they got a grip on the rest of the country. Once again they had a big debate in the parliament in Cox's Bazaar and they voted to fund a new military campaign. Thousands of crack troops were brought in to form the Burmese Expeditionary Force and supplies were built up and the best generals were put in charge. The settlers joined in as scouts and outriders because they were looking for revenge.

Because the Burmese generals were smart they were looking to train up Poki-Poki soldiers to fight alongside the Imperial troops. It was announced that any Poki-Poki joining up and fighting would be given a couple of acres of land Up North as a reward. When they heard this the young Poki-Poki men joined up because enough time had passed now and everyone understood the new situation.

They were proud to be fighting for the Empire and the Motherland and to be chasing after the terrorists and troublemakers.

Then the Burmese generals decided it would also be a good idea to find some Poki-Poki officers for the Burmese Expeditionary Force. They asked around and finally they stumbled across this guy and it turned out he was the sort of guy they were looking for because he was understanding science. The reason the Burmese had done so well and conquered the world was that they had followed the science while the Poki-Poki and the other conquered peoples still relied on the mumbo-jumbo.

This guy was from an old Poki-Poki family and he was already in the military. He was speaking not bad Burmese and he'd got the old Poki-Poki name of Major Trumpington-Bumpington-Wumpington-Smythe. But he was certainly an odd guy. When he was not doing military activities he was designing ladies clothes but everyone said he was also as tough as hell and had a mind of his own. He had a house in the New Forest and sometimes when he opened up the door to greet people he was standing there with no clothes on like it was completely normal.

But he had courage by the bucketload and he'd still got most of his smarts too. He was popular with the Poki-Poki soldiers. In fact, he was a bit of a legend with them. So the Burmese generals finally told him to put together a band of Poki-Poki soldiers because they had a special mission for him.

So Smythe picked out likely recruits to join his group and soon he had about fifty. There were a few jailbirds and adventurers and also a handful of Burmese settlers who were as tough as leather and excellent on horseback. The Burmese generals told Smythe his group would be the advance party for the raid over the border. Smythe spent weeks training up his raiders. He talked about beating them into shape at the camp in the New Forest, which on occasion he actually did. They called themselves the Bumchits, which is a corruption of an old Burmese word for Crazy Guys. When they had finished for the day and after they had eaten their dinner they lit up the long cigars which the Burmese call cheroots.

Smythe even designed a new uniform for his raiders, which everyone said was a bit tight-fitting. It also included a hat that flipped up at one side. It worked as a camouflage hat in the New Forest while at the same time it was also smart enough to be worn on parade.

Before they set off, the raiders were inspected by a Burmese general at their HQ in the New Forest. When he had finished he came out with the line that all generals use. 'I don't know about the enemy but they certainly scare the hell out of me.'

They were officially known as the Advance Raiding Party for the Burmese Expeditionary Force. So this was the start off the Third Burmese Albion War.

They were infiltrated over the border under cover of darkness. They travelled swiftly north led by Smythe, who really was as barmy as a bed bug. He didn't let his men sleep and kept driving them on.

In a few days they were in the heart of Kippermen territory but, because they had moved like silent phantoms and lived off the land, the Kippermen had no idea they were there. Soon they were outside the town of Pollokshields, which was the Scottish capital of the Kippermen.

The Burmese generals had ordered Smythe to conduct surveillance to see where the weak spots were in the town's defences, who was up on the walls and how often they opened the gates and so on. That meant that when the Burmese Expeditionary Force arrived they would be able to do a surprise attack straight away. But Smythe was so excited, because his raiders had arrived so quickly and without being spotted, that he couldn't wait. He was running around like a man desperate to take a pee. When the sun first peeked over the horizon he looked out at the walls of Pollokshields and gave a blast on his trumpet and the Bumchits charged forward. They took the local garrison by surprise and they were soon inside the town.

But because they'd gone in early the Kippermen forces in the area had time to regroup. So when the Burmese Expeditionary Force arrived the Kippermen were prepared and in full fighting form.

There was a battle south of Pollokshields and the Burmese fired off their Congreve rockets but the Kippermen, who were also pretty tough fighters, drove the Burmese slowly back. In the end the Burmese general and the Kippermen general called a truce and had a meeting. The Burmese agreed to retreat back south but they built a bloody great wall behind them, which they called the Great Wall of Burma. North of it was named Upper Albion and south of it was named Lower Albion.

Then the Burmese Expeditionary Force turned back south and in a month they had taken the rest of Albion, with the exception of Wales where they did a separate treaty so it became a protectorate. The Wales people kept their own king who was called Charles and everyone was happy with that. The other area they left alone was the extreme south-west, where a tribe called the Cornwalls lived who were known to be fierce as hell. The Burmese decided it wasn't worth the bother to take them on.

There was a big victory parade in London to celebrate the end of the Third Burmese Albion War and Smythe and his Bumchits were given a prominent role and everyone said Smythe was a hero. They covered up the fact that he had screwed up real bad in the attack on Pollokshields because it was important to have Poki-Poki heroes for the parade. After that he was made a junior minister in the government. He was in charge of designing new styles of clothing for the Poki-Poki to wear.

The new style reflected the Burmese way with the sarongs but Smythe still kept some of the old Albion fashions, particularly the baggy trousers for the older guys. He introduced a new hair style where the people grew their hair long and tied it up in a top knot. Soon all the young people were wearing that style. They were also now speaking pretty good Burmese, though the older people still spoke Poki-Poki at home.

Relations between the settlers and the Poki-Poki were still a bit bumpy and occasionally flaring up, for instance when the government announced a plan to simplify the Poki-Poki language. The settlers were making fun of that.

For example before in Poki-Poki where you could say 'go quickly', now you had to say 'go go.' If a settler asked why a Poki-Poki labourer had not turned up for work the reply now had to be, 'John got big sleep sleep this morning.'

While London was the economic capital, the administrative capital was on the Isle of Wight, now renamed Burma Island. The governor's residence was the old Poki-Poki palace called Osborne House, which had been renovated into a palace so that it almost rivalled the glories of the Royal Palace in Cox's Bazaar.

Local Albions were not allowed on the island, except for a few menial workers who were brought over from Southampton. They had to go back at night with the exception of essential workers, who stayed in a closed barracks in the middle of the island.

There were rumours among the Poki-Poki that the streets on Burma Island were paved with gold and that the Burmese were carried around in sedan chairs. There were certainly parks and gardens modelled on the gardens in Cox's Bazaar and there were peacocks and exotic animals. On the far side of Burma Island there was a quarter with brothels and bars and opium dens and later on, as the modern age dawned, a jazz club opened up.

The Burmese even developed a flying boat service called Imperial Burmese Airways. Burmese officials were sent out from Cox's Bazaar. With stops the journey could be done in seventy-two hours. Before the flying boat landed it did a slow turn over the island and the passengers looked down at the Royal Palace and the pagodas before they landed on the Solent, which had been renamed Burmese Waters.

Up to this point intermarriage between Burmese and Albions had always been frowned on with only a few soldiers marrying local girls. But then – and this was a big moment – the Burmese governor called his ministers together at Osborne House after supper one evening and announced that his eldest son planned to marry a Poki-Poki girl who could trace her lineage back to King Smith. There was quite a silence, then everyone started to applaud because they knew the place of the Poki-Poki had finally been cemented into the heart of the Burmese Empire.

Roughly stops and looks up. Heinz pauses for a moment as a gust of wind rattles the window panes. Then he runs his hands through his hair and laughs.

'Well, Comrade Oddbins, that is an admirable rewrite of history you have done. But actually, if you ask me, the story fits more into the category of political satire. There are also times when it echoed the fairytale, which is a style a lot of the satirists use. As to publishers, they might take it in Wales because they like to poke the stick at the English. But the publishers in England will steer 100 miles clear, because English readers do not like to see the empire with its leg pulled. And of course if your name is Roughly Oddbins O'Reilly and you have brown skin and you write a story like that people will think you are a bit of a cheeky chap. You are even risking a slap around the chops. So maybe you could box a bit clever and submit it under another name. Smith or Brown – or Williams-Jones, even.'

After that they have another tot of Wales Brandy and

that evening Roughly tells Tirana that Heinz liked the story.

§

Now Heinz starts to turn the screw, Jimmy tells Roughly.

The microphones pick up the conversation and the listeners hear the menace in Heinz's voice. The German accent becomes stronger and the odd German word slips through.

Heinz tells The Wales Chapel Lady that he will write a letter to her husband saying there has been some rumpy pumpy going on. She replies – and there is a tear in her eye – that her life will be ruined and she has done nothing wrong except to have a weakness for chocolate cake. Heinz smiles and says there is actually a way out for her and she is looking up at him and listening.

Heinz tells her that she needs to explain to her sister in Cardiff that she requires some help. If the sister sees any government papers to do with Wales independence she's got to photocopy them and send them to her.

Which in the end is what is happening, Jimmy says. Her sister sends the documents and she puts them in an envelope addressed to Heinz which she sends to him via the internal mail system at the university.

Then Jimmy says we are going to pick up Heinz soon. He will be charged with spying and will certainly spend a long time in jail.

CHAPTER NINE

Heinz tells Roughly now he has finished with history he wants him to write about the future.

Roughly and Tirana discuss that round the dinner table. The nippers have seen the images captured by American navy pilots on their radar screens. They show spacecraft-size objects accelerating at speeds and making turns that are not possible for man-made machines. So they are concluding the aliens have already arrived and are surveying us.

Tirana goes back to the past in Albania and says her family has already experienced the future under Enver Hoxha because everybody living there was under surveillance all the time.

'You guys in North Wales should be aware that right now you are living in the best of times,' she says. 'People in the future will look back and talk about the golden age of democracy.'

Roughly listens carefully to Tirana and the nippers. Then he asks, with a smile on his face because it has become a bit of a family joke, if anyone has seen his felt hat and his Sherlock Holmes-style pipe because he is in need of a bit of inspiration.

When Tirana and the boys are watching a film on TV, Roughly sits out in the garden observing the dying of the day and puffing on his pipe. It's there he gets the idea for a story.

But first he needs to resolve a dilemma.

Though he's not supposed to, because it's top secret, he has kept Tirana up to date on the police investigation into Heinz. He has told her that Jimmy is just about ready to arrest Heinz.

'I have built up a great affection for Heinz and even though I am a copper I do not want to see him in jail,' he says. 'So I am thinking to tip him off discreetly so he can make his escape.'

He looks at Tirana and asks what she thinks about that.

'Well,' she says, 'I have puzzled right from the beginning to understand why he betrayed the Wales people who have taken him to their hearts.'

'The story he told of growing up in the Bavarian valley is certainly only half correct,' Roughly says. 'He probably followed his brother Frederick to Hamburg and signed up for spy school there. After that he could have been sent to North Wales as a sleeper agent.'

Tirana looks doubtful. 'If you ask me he's just levering open some private space. There are guys like that. They like to have a part of them that is not on show. Others just want to kick up a little dust as they pass.'

They both agree that Heinz is not in the same league as Kim Philby, who took his revenge on the British establishment by spying for the Russians.

'A lot of people in Albania are dead because of him,' Tirana says.

'The secrets that Heinz is handing over to the Germans are so low-grade that anyone reading the newspaper and doing a bit of speculation will come to a similar conclusion,' Roughly adds.

They conclude that the only casualty is the Wales Lady Chapel who certainly got a fright and will have some explaining to do. But Roughly laughs because the last time he went past her in the university she was wearing a brightly coloured scarf around her neck and she'd also got a touch of lipstick on, so perhaps the shock had kick-started something there.

The next day Roughly arrives at the university and walks past the Wales Chapel Lady, who smiles brightly at him. Then he is up the stairs to the attic office and Heinz is pouring out the tots of Wales Brandy and it's like nothing has changed.

'The wind is up again,' Roughly says, the way he planned it with Tirana. 'I heard on Wales Radio this morning they are predicting the seas to break over the front this morning.'

They walk over to the window and look out towards the front where the waves are starting to build. Then he discreetly slips a note to Heinz, because the police certainly have the room bugged with microphones and maybe they've even installed cameras as well. Heinz doesn't blink an eye when he reads the note which says, 'Take the fire escape when I leave. There is a taxi waiting at the bottom.'

Now they are back sitting at opposite sides of the desk and Roughly is reading out the story he's written about the future.

Jane and Oliver are getting older now but they have aged not too bad. Oliver has the stiff knees and his hair is receding back and Jane has put on some weight around the middle but they are still keeping active. It is only when they look in the mirror and note the lines on the face and the hair turning grey that they realise time is passing.

Pollock has retired from the life of a sailor. He has a small house to the south of the city where he spends time working in his garden. He's also got a telescope so he can look out to sea and watch the ships. He's even found a wife that can put up with him, though she's not a great beauty and there are no children.

Jackson's marriage lasted and they have a son who's studying to be dentist. He shows no interest in the sea and when the others reminisce about the days on the lighthouse he yawns and looks away.

Jane and Oliver are celebrating Independence Day by taking a day hike out of the city. They've got a couple of light packs on their backs. They've walked through the suburbs and are beginning the slow climb up onto the moor.

Independence came a few years ago now and it seems the pendulum is swinging back in their favour. Experts say that Burma is on the down and the old colonies are on the up.

There are fewer Burmese shops and old Albion ways are starting to come back. The young are going back to the old Albion way of dressing. Some of them are even wearing the baggy trousers, which makes Oliver laugh. They have also done away with the Burmese top knot and reverted to the old Albion hair styles.

But the Burmese influence is still continuing. Jackson's wife recently took their boy to Cox's Bazaar and they came back chattering ten to the dozen about the theme parks and the food and everything else they saw there.

Now Jane and Oliver have left the road and are climbing up a path that will take them out onto the moor and the spot where they plan to picnic. They stop to take a drink of water from a bottle because the sun is starting to climb and the day is warming up. Jane says they need to put on their sun hats and rub the protective cream onto their faces.

They finally arrive at the picnic spot and Jane, who has spent weeks planning the surprise, tells Oliver to close his eyes.

When he opens them again he sees that Jackson and Pollock and their wives and his grandson have also arrived. A tear forms in his eye because now he has his whole family around him for the Independence Day picnic.

As they eat they remember their time on Light Island. They recall the first winter when the storms crashed in and the lighthouse swayed. Then they are remembering their return to the mainland and how surprised they were to see the Burmese takeover.

An hour later when they are done with the picnic and everyone is drowsy with the heat. Jane and Oliver take a walk and come to the old farm house. They've often been there before. If they had their time again they would live in a place like that. They've got all the moor all round them and it's less isolated than the lighthouse.

Oliver leans on the old wooden gate that leads up to the house. He feels the warmth of the wood beneath his arms. The farmhouse is built from granite blocks which are weathered and worn and have not changed in a hundred years. The slate roof is a faded grey.

Suddenly a shutter on the ground floor opens. Oliver takes a step back so he is in the shadow of a tree. This is the first time they have seen anyone in the house. He can see the outline of a girl tidying some papers on a desk.

Then the shutter closes again. A minute later the front door opens and the girl is standing there. Then an upstairs shutter is pushed back as well and a woman leans out.

Oliver thinks the girl has finished studying for the day and is on her way out. She has the brown skin that a lot of the young girls have these days. She also has the long dark hair and the rounded face. She is smartly dressed in the English style in trousers and a blouse top. She's wearing leather riding boots and in her hand she's holding a wide-brimmed hat.

Oliver thinks she is going out on a date. She has the dreamy smile on her face which suggests she's in love. The woman in the upstairs window leans out and Oliver notes the similar features, so she is certainly the mother.

She calls down and she speaks in the old-fashioned manner which people are using these days and which is a delight to listen to. It's long and round and rich.

'You take care, ma lovely. Make sure you is home well before the dark. Now turn and let me see you.'

The girl looks up and smiles. The mother laughs and says, 'Ma daughter you is pretty as a peach.'

Now we have to widen the shot because to the side of the house there is a wooden barn and tied up next to it, patiently waiting, is a fine roan mare. She is saddled up and behind the saddle a couple of leather bags are attached.

The girl pulls the door to behind her and walks over towards the horse. She places the wide-brimmed hat on her head and swings up in into the saddle with a practised ease. Then she turns and gives a last wave to her mother. After that she pats the pistol which is slung low on her waist and trots slowly off into the distance across the parched and dusty moor.

Roughly looks up at Heinz to indicate that the story is finished.

Normally Heinz would give an opinion on what Roughly has read out but there is no time for that today. Roughly walks quickly over to the window and looks down and sees that two police cars have drawn up. When he turns back he sees that Heinz has put on an olive green coat over a cream sweater and has got a small knapsack on his back. He gives Roughly a little Teutonic bow of farewell, which any other time would have made Roughly laugh. But then Roughly is down the stairs going as casually as he can though his heart is beating fast. As he approaches the Wales Chapel Lady half a dozen police, including Jimmy, pass by him heading up the stairs.

Roughly steps outside to find that the wind has dropped and the sun has come out. He stands for a minute, smiling. When he arrives home that evening he recounts to Tirana and the nippers everything that happened. Then they turn on the TV news and there is no mention of police arrests so they are assuming that Heinz escaped. After supper

Roughly tells Tirana that he has learnt enough from Heinz to start writing the spy thriller he had planning at the beginning of this account. Tirana smiles when she hears that.

TRANSACTIONS

OF

THE BLAVATSKY LODGE

OF THE

THEOSOPHICAL SOCIETY

———

Discussions on the Stanzas
of the First Volume of
THE SECRET DOCTRINE

———

*Reprinted Verbatim
from the Original Edition*

———

THE THEOSOPHY COMPANY
LOS ANGELES

The Theosophy Company, Los Angeles 90007
Copyright 1987 by The Theosophy Company
Printed in the United States of America
ISBN 0-938998-05-6

TRANSACTIONS OF THE BLAVATSKY LODGE
OF THE THEOSOPHICAL SOCIETY

PREFATORY NOTE
TO THE ORIGINAL EDITION

The following transactions are compiled from shorthand notes taken at the meetings of the Blavatsky Lodge of the Theosophical Society, from January 10th to June 20th, 1889, being somewhat condensed from the original discussions.

"The Secret Doctrine" being based upon the archaic stanzas of the "Book of Dzyan," and these being too abstruse for most of the new students of Exoteric philosophy, the members of the "B. L. of the T.S." agreed to devote the debates of the weekly meetings to each stanza and sundry other metaphysical subjects.

The questions were put by members who, for the most part, supported their objections and exceptions on modern scientific grounds, and assumed logical deductions based thereon. As such objections are generally the common property of students of "The Secret Doctrine," it has been judged unnecessary to incorporate them in full, so that their substance alone has been retained. The answers in all cases are based on the shorthand Reports, and are those of Esoteric Philosophy as given by H. P. B. herself.

Publishers' Notice

THE TRANSACTIONS of the Blavatsky Lodge of the Theosophical Society have long been out of print, so that the title of the Answers by H. P. Blavatsky to Questions propounded by some of her students requires explanation.

H. P. B. removed from the Continent to England in the summer of 1887. In the autumn of that year she commenced the publication of her magazine LUCIFER, which she continued to edit until her death in 1891.

Shortly after the commencement of LUCIFER some of the more ardent students of her teachings of THEOSOPHY withdrew from the London Lodge, then and thereafter under the influence of Mr. A. P. Sinnett, and established the BLAVATSKY LODGE, which soon became the centre of Theosophical activities in Britain. Many men and women of note became members of the Lodge. When the SECRET DOCTRINE was published late in 1888 it aroused intense interest, and many literary, scientific and philosophical questions were raised by the students.

H. P. B. was urged to reply to these questions and yielding to the insistencies of the students, she attended many of the meetings of the BLAVATSKY LODGE during the first half of 1889. The Questions propounded to her cover a very wide range, for they were formulated by intelligent, thoughtful, and highly educated men and women. Her Answers were given orally, but were stenographically reported and afterwards revised by her for their publication in the two TRANSACTIONS issued, No. I in 1890, and No. II in 1891.

These Transactions contain matter of great and enduring value on the subjects treated in the Secret Doctrine and, for the students of Occultism for whose instruction the Secret Doctrine was written, they are a priceless Commentary at first hand on some of the most abstruse and difficult problems of the Esoteric Philosophy.

Transaction No. 1 was reprinted in the magazine Theosophy, Volume IV, and Transaction No. II in Volume VI of the same magazine. In the intervening years there has come about a great revival of interest in the work and teachings of H. P. Blavatsky. The passage of time has but served to throw into clearer and grander relief the heroic figure of the great Messenger and the surpassing importance of her Message. Theosophists everywhere are beginning to pay more serious attention to the Source of all their inspiration, and the time seems ripe to make once more accessible to them these invaluable Transactions.

To convenience the student we have included, from the text of the Secret Doctrine, the Stanzas of Dzyan and, for the rest, the present edition of the Transactions follows faithfully the text of the Questions and Answers as they appeared in the two Numbers originally issued. It is offered, as was her Secret Doctrine itself, "to all true Theosophists, in every Country, and of every Race, for they called it forth, and for them it was recorded;"

> "*That we all labor together transmitting the same charge and*
> *   succession,*
> *Till we saturate time and eras, that the men and women of*
> *   races, ages to come, may prove brethren and lovers*
> *   as we are.*"

STANZAS FROM THE
SECRET BOOK OF DZYAN

———

Reprinted from the
Original Edition of THE SECRET DOCTRINE
By H. P. Blavatsky

THE Stanzas, therefore, give an abstract formula which can be applied, *mutatis mutandis*, to all evolution: to that of our tiny earth, to that of the chain of planets of which that earth forms one, to the solar Universe to which that chain belongs, and so on, in an ascending scale till the mind reels and is exhausted in the effort.

The seven Stanzas given in this volume represent the seven terms of this abstract formula. They refer to, and describe the seven great stages of the evolutionary process, which are spoken of in the Puranas as the "Seven Creations," and in the Bible as the "Days" of Creation.

The First Stanza describes the state of the ONE ALL during Pralaya, before the first flutter of re-awakening manifestation.

A moment's thought shows that such a state can only be symbolised; to describe it is impossible. Nor can it be symbolised except in negatives; for, since it is the state of Absoluteness *per se*, it can possess none of those specific attributes which serve us to describe objects in positive terms. Hence that state can only be suggested by the negatives of all those most abstract attributes which men feel rather than conceive, as the remotest limits attainable by their power of conception.

The stage described in Stanza II. is, to a western mind, so nearly identical with that mentioned in the first Stanza, that to express the idea of its difference would require a treatise in itself. Hence it must be left to the intuition and the higher faculties of the reader to grasp, as far as he can, the meaning of the allegorical phrases used. Indeed it must be remembered that all these Stanzas appeal to the inner faculties rather than to the ordinary comprehension of the physical brain.

Stanza III. describes the Re-awakening of the Universe to life after Pralaya. It depicts the emergence of the "Monads" from their state of absorption within the ONE; the earliest and highest stage in the formation of "Worlds," the term Monad being one which may apply equally to the vastest Solar System or the tiniest atom.

Stanza IV. shows the differentiation of the "Germ" of the Universe into the septenary hierarchy of conscious Divine Powers, who are the active manifestations of the One Supreme Energy. They are the framers, shapers, and ultimately the creators of all the manifested Universe, in the only sense in which the name "Creator" is intelligible; they inform and guide it; they are the intelligent Beings who adjust and control evolution, embodying in themselves those manifestations of the ONE LAW, which we know as "The Laws of Nature."

Generically, they are known as the Dhyan Chohans, though each of the various groups has its own designation in the Secret Doctrine.

This stage of evolution is spoken of in Hindu mythology as the "Creation" of the Gods.

In Stanza V. the process of world-formation is described:—
First, diffused Cosmic Matter, then the fiery "whirlwind," the first stage in the formation of a nebula. That nebula condenses, and after passing through various transformations, forms a Solar Universe, a planetary chain, or a single planet, as the case may be.

The subsequent stages in the formation of a "World" are indicated in Stanza VI., which brings the evolution of such a world down to its fourth great period, corresponding to the period in which we are now living.

Stanza VII. continues the history, tracing the descent of life down to the appearance of Man; and thus closes the first Book of the Secret Doctrine.

The development of "Man" from his first appearance on this earth in this Round to the state in which we now find him forms the subject of the second series of the *Stanzas*—"*Anthropogenesis.*"

The Stanzas which form the thesis of every section are given throughout in their modern translated version, as it would be worse than useless to make the subject still more difficult by introducing the archaic phraseology of the original, with its puzzling style and words. Extracts are given from the Chinese Thibetan and Sanskrit translations of the original Senzar Commentaries and Glosses on the Book of DZYAN—these being now rendered for the first time into a European language. It is almost unnecessary to state that only portions of the seven Stanzas are here given. Were they published complete they would remain incomprehensible to all save the few higher occultists. Nor is there any need to assure the reader that, no more than most of the profane, does the writer, or rather the humble recorder, understand those forbidden passages. To facilitate the reading, and to avoid the too frequent reference to foot-notes, it was thought best to blend together texts and glosses, using the Sanskrit and Tibetan proper names whenever those cannot be avoided, in preference to giving the originals. The more so as the said terms are all accepted synonyms, the former only being used between a Master and his chelas (or disciples).

Thus, were one to translate into English, using only the substantives and technical terms as employed in one of the Tibetan and Senzar versions, Verse I would read as follows: "Tho-ag in Zhi-gyu slept seven Khorlo. Zodmanas zhiba. All Nyug bosom. Konch-hog not; Thyan-Kam not; Lha-

Chohan not; Tenbrel Chugnyi not; Dharmakaya ceased; Tgenchang not become; Barnang and Ssa in Ngovonyidj; alone Tho-og Yinsin in night of Sun-chan and Yong-grub (Parinishpanna), &c., &c.," which would sound like pure *Abracadabra.*

As this work is written for the instruction of students of Occultism, and not for the benefit of philologists, we may well avoid such foreign terms wherever it is possible to do so. The untranslatable terms alone, incomprehensible unless explained in their meanings, are left, but all such terms are rendered in their Sanskrit form. Needless to remind the reader that these are, in almost every case, the late developments of the later language, and pertain to the Fifth Root-Race. Sanskrit, as now known, was not spoken by the Atlanteans, and most of the philosophical terms used in the systems of the India of the post-Mahabharatan period are not found in the Vedas, nor are they to be met with in the original Stanzas, but only their equivalents. The reader who is not a Theosophist, is once more invited to regard all that which follows as a fairy tale, if he likes; at best as one of the yet unproven speculations of *dreamers;* and, at the worst, as an additional hypothesis to the many Scientific hypotheses past, present and future, some exploded, others still lingering. It is not in any sense worse than are many of the so-called Scientific theories; and it is in every case more philosophical and probable.

Cosmic Evolution

In Seven Stanzas translated
from the Book of Dzyan.

STANZA I.

1. THE ETERNAL PARENT WRAPPED IN HER EVER INVISIBLE ROBES HAD SLUMBERED ONCE AGAIN FOR SEVEN ETERNITIES.

2. TIME WAS NOT, FOR IT LAY ASLEEP IN THE INFINITE BOSOM OF DURATION.

3. UNIVERSAL MIND WAS NOT, FOR THERE WERE NO AH-HI TO CONTAIN IT.

4. THE SEVEN WAYS TO BLISS WERE NOT. THE GREAT CAUSES OF MISERY WERE NOT, FOR THERE WAS NO ONE TO PRODUCE AND GET ENSNARED BY THEM.

5. DARKNESS ALONE FILLED THE BOUNDLESS ALL, FOR FATHER, MOTHER AND SON WERE ONCE MORE ONE, AND THE SON HAD NOT AWAKENED YET FOR THE NEW WHEEL, AND HIS PILGRIMAGE THEREON.

6. THE SEVEN SUBLIME LORDS AND THE SEVEN TRUTHS HAD CEASED TO BE, AND THE UNIVERSE, THE SON OF NECESSITY, WAS IMMERSED IN PARANISHPANNA, TO BE OUTBREATHED BY THAT WHICH IS AND YET IS NOT. NAUGHT WAS.

7. THE CAUSES OF EXISTENCE HAD BEEN DONE AWAY WITH; THE VISIBLE THAT WAS, AND THE INVISIBLE THAT IS, RESTED IN ETERNAL NON-BEING—THE ONE BEING.

8. ALONE THE ONE FORM OF EXISTENCE STRETCHED BOUNDLESS, INFINITE, CAUSELESS, IN DREAMLESS SLEEP; AND LIFE PULSATED UNCONSCIOUS IN UNIVERSAL SPACE, THROUGHOUT THAT ALL-PRESENCE WHICH IS SENSED BY THE OPENED EYE OF THE DANGMA.

9. BUT WHERE WAS THE DANGMA WHEN THE ALAYA OF THE UNIVERSE WAS IN PARAMARTHA AND THE GREAT WHEEL WAS ANUPADAKA?

STANZA II.

1. . . . WHERE WERE THE BUILDERS, THE LUMINOUS SONS OF MANVANTARIC DAWN? . . IN THE UNKNOWN DARKNESS IN THEIR AH-HI PARANISHPANNA. THE PRODUCERS OF FORM FROM NO-FORM—

THE ROOT OF THE WORLD—THE DEVAMATRI AND SVÂBHÂVAT, RESTED IN THE BLISS OF NON-BEING.

2. . . . WHERE WAS SILENCE? WHERE THE EARS TO SENSE IT? NO, THERE WAS NEITHER SILENCE NOR SOUND; NAUGHT SAVE CEASELESS ETERNAL BREATH, WHICH KNOWS ITSELF NOT.

3. THE HOUR HAD NOT YET STRUCK; THE RAY HAD NOT YET FLASHED INTO THE GERM; THE MATRIPADMA HAD NOT YET SWOLLEN.

4. HER HEART HAD NOT YET OPENED FOR THE ONE RAY TO ENTER, THENCE TO FALL, AS THREE INTO FOUR, INTO THE LAP OF MAYA.

5. THE SEVEN SONS WERE NOT YET BORN FROM THE WEB OF LIGHT. DARKNESS ALONE WAS FATHER-MOTHER, SVÂBHÂVAT; AND SVÂBHÂVAT WAS IN DARKNESS.

6. THESE TWO ARE THE GERM, AND THE GERM IS ONE. THE UNIVERSE WAS STILL CONCEALED IN THE DIVINE THOUGHT AND THE DIVINE BOSOM. . . .

STANZA III.

1. . . . THE LAST VIBRATION OF THE SEVENTH ETERNITY THRILLS THROUGH INFINITUDE. THE MOTHER SWELLS, EXPANDING FROM WITHIN WITHOUT, LIKE THE BUD OF THE LOTUS.

2. THE VIBRATION SWEEPS ALONG, TOUCHING WITH ITS SWIFT WING THE WHOLE UNIVERSE AND THE GERM THAT DWELLETH IN DARKNESS: THE DARKNESS THAT BREATHES OVER THE SLUMBERING WATERS OF LIFE. . . .

3. DARKNESS RADIATES LIGHT, AND LIGHT DROPS ONE SOLITARY RAY INTO THE MOTHER-DEEP. THE RAY SHOOTS THROUGH THE VIRGIN EGG. THE RAY CAUSES THE ETERNAL EGG TO THRILL, AND DROP THE NON-ETERNAL GERM, WHICH CONDENSES INTO THE WORLD-EGG.

4. THEN THE THREE FALL INTO THE FOUR. THE RADIANT ESSENCE BECOMES SEVEN INSIDE, SEVEN OUTSIDE. THE LUMINOUS EGG, WHICH IN ITSELF IS THREE, CURDLES AND SPREADS IN MILK-WHITE CURDS THROUGHOUT THE DEPTHS OF MOTHER, THE ROOT THAT GROWS IN THE DEPTHS OF THE OCEAN OF LIFE.

5. THE ROOT REMAINS, THE LIGHT REMAINS, THE CURDS REMAIN, AND STILL OEAOHOO IS ONE.

6. THE ROOT OF LIFE WAS IN EVERY DROP OF THE OCEAN OF IMMORTALITY, AND THE OCEAN WAS RADIANT LIGHT, WHICH WAS FIRE, AND HEAT, AND MOTION. DARKNESS VANISHED AND WAS NO MORE; IT DISAPPEARED IN ITS OWN ESSENCE, THE BODY OF FIRE AND WATER, OR FATHER AND MOTHER.

7. BEHOLD, OH LANOO! THE RADIANT CHILD OF THE TWO, THE UNPARALLELED REFULGENT GLORY: BRIGHT SPACE SON OF DARK

SPACE, WHICH EMERGES FROM THE DEPTHS OF THE GREAT DARK WATERS. IT IS OEAOHOO THE YOUNGER, THE * * * HE SHINES FORTH AS THE SON; HE IS THE BLAZING DIVINE DRAGON OF WISDOM; THE ONE IS FOUR, AND FOUR TAKES TO ITSELF THREE,* AND THE UNION PRODUCES THE SAPTA, IN WHOM ARE THE SEVEN WHICH BECOME THE TRIDASA (OR THE HOSTS AND THE MULTITUDES). BEHOLD HIM LIFTING THE VEIL AND UN-FURLING IT FROM EAST TO WEST. HE SHUTS OUT THE ABOVE, AND LEAVES THE BELOW TO BE SEEN AS THE GREAT ILLUSION. HE MARKS THE PLACES FOR THE SHINING ONES, AND TURNS THE UPPER INTO A SHORELESS SEA OF FIRE, AND THE ONE MANIFESTED INTO THE GREAT WATERS.

8.   WHERE WAS THE GERM AND WHERE WAS NOW DARKNESS? WHERE IS THE SPIRIT OF THE FLAME THAT BURNS IN THY LAMP, OH LANOO? THE GERM IS THAT, AND THAT IS LIGHT, THE WHITE BRILLIANT SON OF THE DARK HIDDEN FATHER.

9.   LIGHT IS COLD FLAME, AND FLAME IS FIRE, AND FIRE PRODUCES HEAT, WHICH YIELDS WATER: THE WATER OF LIFE IN THE GREAT MOTHER.

10.   FATHER-MOTHER SPIN A WEB WHOSE UPPER END IS FASTENED TO SPIRIT—THE LIGHT OF THE ONE DARKNESS—AND THE LOWER ONE TO ITS SHADOWY END, MATTER; AND THIS WEB IS THE UNIVERSE SPUN OUT OF THE TWO SUBSTANCES MADE IN ONE, WHICH IS SVÂBHÂVAT.

11.   IT EXPANDS WHEN THE BREATH OF FIRE IS UPON IT; IT CONTRACTS WHEN THE BREATH OF THE MOTHER TOUCHES IT. THEN THE SONS DIS-SOCIATE AND SCATTER, TO RETURN INTO THEIR MOTHER'S BOSOM AT THE END OF THE GREAT DAY, AND RE-BECOME ONE WITH HER; WHEN IT IS COOLING IT BECOMES RADIANT, AND THE SONS EXPAND AND CONTRACT THROUGH THEIR OWN SELVES AND HEARTS; THEY EMBRACE INFINITUDE.

12.   THEN SVÂBHÂVAT SENDS FOHAT TO HARDEN THE ATOMS. EACH IS A PART OF THE WEB. REFLECTING THE "SELF-EXISTENT LORD" LIKE A MIRROR, EACH BECOMES IN TURN A WORLD.

STANZA IV.

1.   .   .   .   LISTEN, YE SONS OF THE EARTH, TO YOUR INSTRUCTORS —THE SONS OF THE FIRE. LEARN, THERE IS NEITHER FIRST NOR LAST, FOR ALL IS ONE: NUMBER ISSUED FROM NO NUMBER.

2.   LEARN WHAT WE WHO DESCEND FROM THE PRIMORDIAL SEVEN, WE WHO ARE BORN FROM THE PRIMORDIAL FLAME, HAVE LEARNT FROM OUR FATHERS.   .   .   .

3.   FROM THE EFFULGENCY OF LIGHT—THE RAY OF THE EVER-DARK-NESS—SPRUNG IN SPACE THE RE-AWAKENED ENERGIES; THE ONE FROM

---

*In the English translation from the Sanskrit the numbers are given in that language, *Eka, Chatur,* etc., etc. It was thought best to give them in English.

THE EGG, THE SIX, AND THE FIVE. THEN THE THREE, THE ONE, THE FOUR, THE ONE, THE FIVE—THE TWICE SEVEN THE SUM TOTAL. AND THESE ARE THE ESSENCES, THE FLAMES, THE ELEMENTS, THE BUILDERS, THE NUMBERS, THE ARUPA, THE RUPA, AND THE FORCE OF DIVINE MAN— THE SUM TOTAL. AND FROM THE DIVINE MAN EMANATED THE FORMS, THE SPARKS, THE SACRED ANIMALS, AND THE MESSENGERS OF THE SACRED FATHERS WITHIN THE HOLY FOUR.

4. THIS WAS THE ARMY OF THE VOICE—THE DIVINE MOTHER OF THE SEVEN. THE SPARKS OF THE SEVEN ARE SUBJECT TO, AND THE SER- VANTS OF, THE FIRST, THE SECOND, THE THIRD, THE FOURTH, THE FIFTH, THE SIXTH, AND THE SEVENTH OF THE SEVEN. THESE "SPARKS" ARE CALLED SPHERES, TRIANGLES, CUBES, LINES, AND MODELLERS; FOR THUS STANDS THE ETERNAL NIDANA—THE OEAOHOO, WHICH IS:

5. "DARKNESS" THE BOUNDLESS, OR THE NO-NUMBER, ADI-NIDANA SVÂBHÂVAT:—

> I. THE ADI-SANAT, THE NUMBER, FOR HE IS ONE.
> II. THE VOICE OF THE LORD SVÂBHÂVAT, THE NUMBERS, FOR HE IS ONE AND NINE.
> III. THE "FORMLESS SQUARE."

AND THESE THREE ENCLOSED WITHIN THE ◯ ARE THE SACRED FOUR; AND THE TEN ARE THE ARUPA UNIVERSE. THEN COME THE "SONS," THE SEVEN FIGHTERS, THE ONE, THE EIGHTH LEFT OUT, AND HIS BREATH WHICH IS THE LIGHT-MAKER.

6. THEN THE SECOND SEVEN, WHO ARE THE LIPIKA, PRODUCED BY THE THREE. THE REJECTED SON IS ONE. THE "SON-SUNS" ARE COUNT- LESS.

STANZA V.

1. THE PRIMORDIAL SEVEN, THE FIRST SEVEN BREATHS OF THE DRAGON OF WISDOM, PRODUCE IN THEIR TURN FROM THEIR HOLY CIR- CUMGYRATING BREATHS THE FIERY WHIRLWIND.

2. THEY MAKE OF HIM THE MESSENGER OF THEIR WILL. THE DZYU BECOMES FOHAT, THE SWIFT SON OF THE DIVINE SONS WHOSE SONS ARE THE LIPIKA, RUNS CIRCULAR ERRANDS. FOHAT IS THE STEED AND THE THOUGHT IS THE RIDER. HE PASSES LIKE LIGHTNING THROUGH THE FIERY CLOUDS; TAKES THREE, AND FIVE, AND SEVEN STRIDES THROUGH THE SEVEN REGIONS ABOVE, AND THE SEVEN BELOW. HE LIFTS HIS VOICE, AND CALLS THE INNUMERABLE SPARKS, AND JOINS THEM.

3. HE IS THEIR GUIDING SPIRIT AND LEADER. WHEN HE COMMENCES WORK, HE SEPARATES THE SPARKS OF THE LOWER KINGDOM THAT FLOAT AND THRILL WITH JOY IN THEIR RADIANT DWELLINGS, AND FORMS THERE-

WITH THE GERMS OF WHEELS. HE PLACES THEM IN THE S X DIRECTIONS OF SPACE, AND ONE IN THE MIDDLE—THE CENTRAL WHEEL.

4. FOHAT TRACES SPIRAL LINES TO UNITE THE SIXTH TO THE SEVENTH —THE CROWN; AN ARMY OF THE SONS OF LIGHT STANDS AT EACH ANGLE, AND THE LIPIKA IN THE MIDDLE WHEEL. THEY SAY: THIS IS GOOD, THE FIRST DIVINE WORLD IS READY, THE FIRST IS NOW THE SECOND. THEN THE "DIVINE ARUPA" REFLECTS ITSELF IN CHHAYA LOKA, THE FIRST GARMENT OF THE ANUPADAKA.

5. FOHAT TAKES FIVE STRIDES AND BUILDS A WINGED WHEEL AT EACH CORNER OF THE SQUARE, FOR THE FOUR HOLY ONES AND THEIR ARMIES.

6. THE LIPIKA CIRCUMSCRIBE THE TRIANGLE, THE FIRST ONE, THE CUBE, THE SECOND ONE, AND THE PENTACLE WITHIN THE EGG. IT IS THE RING CALLED "PASS NOT" FOR THOSE WHO DESCEND AND ASCEND. ALSO FOR THOSE WHO DURING THE KALPA ARE PROGRESSING TOWARDS THE GREAT DAY "BE WITH US." THUS WERE FORMED THE RUPA AND THE ARUPA: FROM ONE LIGHT SEVEN LIGHTS; FROM EACH OF THE SEVEN, SEVEN TIMES SEVEN LIGHTS. THE WHEELS WATCH THE RING. . . .

STANZA VI.

1. BY THE POWER OF THE MOTHER OF MERCY AND KNOWLEDGE— KWAN-YIN—THE "TRIPLE" OF KWAN-SHAI-YIN, RESIDING IN KWAN-YIN-TIEN, FOHAT, THE BREATH OF THEIR PROGENY, THE SON OF THE SONS, HAVING CALLED FORTH, FROM THE LOWER ABYSS, THE ILLUSIVE FORM OF SIEN-TCHANG AND THE SEVEN ELEMENTS:*

2. THE SWIFT AND RADIANT ONE PRODUCES THE SEVEN LAYA CEN-TRES, AGAINST WHICH NONE WILL PREVAIL TO THE GREAT DAY "BE-WITH US," AND SEATS THE UNIVERSE ON THESE ETERNAL FOUNDATIONS SUR-ROUNDING TSIEN-TCHAN WITH THE ELEMENTARY GERMS.

3. OF THE SEVEN—FIRST ONE MANIFESTED, SIX CONCEALED, TWO MANIFESTED, FIVE CONCEALED; THREE MANIFESTED, FOUR CONCEALED; FOUR PRODUCED, THREE HIDDEN; FOUR AND ONE TSAN REVEALED, TWO AND ONE HALF CONCEALED; SIX TO BE MANIFESTED, ONE LAID ASIDE. LASTLY, SEVEN SMALL WHEELS REVOLVING; ONE GIVING BIRTH TO THE OTHER.

4. HE BUILDS THEM IN THE LIKENESS OF OLDER WHEELS, PLACING THEM ON THE IMPERISHABLE CENTRES.

HOW DOES FOHAT BUILD THEM? HE COLLECTS THE FIERY DUST. HE MAKES BALLS OF FIRE, RUNS THROUGH THEM, AND ROUND THEM, INFUSING LIFE THEREINTO, THEN SETS THEM INTO MOTION; SOME ONE WAY, SOME THE OTHER WAY. THEY ARE COLD, HE MAKES THEM HOT. THEY ARE

*Verse 1 of Stanza VI is of a far later date than the other Stanzas, though still very ancient. The old text of this verse, having names entirely unknown to the Orientalists would give no clue to the student.

DRY, HE MAKES THEM MOIST. THEY SHINE, HE FANS AND COOLS THEM. THUS ACTS FOHAT FROM ONE TWILIGHT TO THE OTHER, DURING SEVEN ETERNITIES.

5. AT THE FOURTH, THE SONS ARE TOLD TO CREATE THEIR IMAGES. ONE THIRD REFUSES—TWO OBEY.

THE CURSE IS PRONOUNCED; THEY WILL BE BORN ON THE FOURTH, SUFFER AND CAUSE SUFFERING; THIS IS THE FIRST WAR.

6. THE OLDER WHEELS ROTATED DOWNWARDS AND UPWARDS. . . . THE MOTHER'S SPAWN FILLED THE WHOLE. THERE WERE BATTLES FOUGHT BETWEEN THE CREATORS AND THE DESTROYERS, AND BATTLES FOUGHT FOR SPACE; THE SEED APPEARING AND RE-APPEARING CONTINUOUSLY.

7. MAKE THY CALCULATIONS, LANOO, IF THOU WOULD'ST LEARN THE CORRECT AGE OF THY SMALL WHEEL. ITS FOURTH SPOKE IS OUR MOTHER. REACH THE FOURTH "FRUIT" OF THE FOURTH PATH OF KNOWLEDGE THAT LEADS TO NIRVANA, AND THOU SHALT COMPREHEND, FOR THOU SHALT SEE. . . .

STANZA VII.

1. BEHOLD THE BEGINNING OF SENTIENT FORMLESS LIFE.

FIRST THE DIVINE, THE ONE FROM THE MOTHER-SPIRIT; THEN THE SPIRITUAL; THE THREE FROM THE ONE, THE FOUR FROM THE ONE, AND THE FIVE FROM WHICH THE THREE, THE FIVE, AND THE SEVEN. THESE ARE THE THREE-FOLD, THE FOUR-FOLD DOWNWARD; THE "MIND-BORN" SONS OF THE FIRST LORD; THE SHINING SEVEN.

IT IS THEY WHO ARE THOU, ME, HIM, OH LANOO. THEY, WHO WATCH OVER THEE, AND THY MOTHER EARTH.

2. THE ONE RAY MULTIPLIES THE SMALLER RAYS. LIFE PRECEDES FORM, AND LIFE SURVIVES THE LAST ATOM OF FORM. THROUGH THE COUNTLESS RAYS PROCEEDS THE LIFE-RAY, THE ONE, LIKE A THREAD THROUGH MANY JEWELS.

3. WHEN THE ONE BECOMES TWO, THE THREEFOLD APPEARS, AND THE THREE ARE ONE; AND IT IS OUR THREAD, OH LANOO, THE HEART OF THE MAN-PLANT CALLED SAPTAPARNA.

4. IT IS THE ROOT THAT NEVER DIES; THE THREE-TONGUED FLAME OF THE FOUR WICKS. THE WICKS ARE THE SPARKS, THAT DRAW FROM THE THREE-TONGUED FLAME SHOT OUT BY THE SEVEN—THEIR FLAME—THE BEAMS AND SPARKS OF ONE MOON REFLECTED IN THE RUNNING WAVES OF ALL THE RIVERS OF EARTH.

5. THE SPARK HANGS FROM THE FLAME BY THE FINEST THREAD OF FOHAT. IT JOURNEYS THROUGH THE SEVEN WORLDS OF MAYA. IT STOPS IN THE FIRST, AND IS A METAL AND A STONE; IT PASSES INTO THE

SECOND AND BEHOLD—A PLANT; THE PLANT WHIRLS THROUGH SEVEN CHANGES AND BECOMES A SACRED ANIMAL. FROM THE COMBINED ATTRIBUTES OF THESE, MANU, THE THINKER IS FORMED. WHO FORMS HIM? THE SEVEN LIVES, AND THE ONE LIFE. WHO COMPLETES HIM? THE FIVE-FOLD LHA. AND WHO PERFECTS THE LAST BODY? FISH, SIN, AND SOMA. . . .

6. FROM THE FIRST-BORN THE THREAD BETWEEN THE SILENT WATCHER AND HIS SHADOW BECOMES MORE STRONG AND RADIANT WITH EVERY CHANGE. THE MORNING SUN-LIGHT HAS CHANGED INTO NOON-DAY GLORY. . . .

7. THIS IS THY PRESENT WHEEL, SAID THE FLAME TO THE SPARK. THOU ART MYSELF, MY IMAGE, AND MY SHADOW. I HAVE CLOTHED MYSELF IN THEE, AND THOU ART MY VAHAN TO THE DAY, "BE WITH US," WHEN THOU SHALT RE-BECOME MYSELF AND OTHERS, THYSELF AND ME. THEN THE BUILDERS, HAVING DONNED THEIR FIRST CLOTHING, DESCEND ON RADIANT EARTH AND REIGN OVER MEN—WHO ARE THEMSELVES. . . .

Anthropogenesis
in the Secret Volume

(VERBATIM EXTRACTS*)

I.

1. THE LHA WHICH TURNS THE FOURTH IS SUBSERVIENT TO THE LHA OF THE SEVEN, THEY WHO REVOLVE DRIVING THEIR CHARIOTS AROUND THEIR LORD, THE ONE EYE. HIS BREATH GAVE LIFE TO THE SEVEN; IT GAVE LIFE TO THE FIRST.

2. SAID THE EARTH:—"LORD OF THE SHINING FACE; MY HOUSE IS EMPTY. . . . SEND THY SONS TO PEOPLE THIS WHEEL. THOU HAST SENT THY SEVEN SONS TO THE LORD OF WISDOM. SEVEN TIMES DOTH HE SEE THEE NEARER TO HIMSELF, SEVEN TIMES MORE DOTH HE FEEL THEE. THOU HAST FORBIDDEN THY SERVANTS, THE SMALL RINGS, TO CATCH THY LIGHT AND HEAT, THY GREAT BOUNTY TO INTERCEPT ON ITS PASSAGE. SEND NOW TO THY SERVANT THE SAME."

3. SAID THE "LORD OF THE SHINING FACE":—"I SHALL SEND THEE A FIRE WHEN THY WORK IS COMMENCED. RAISE THY VOICE TO OTHER LOKAS; APPLY TO THY FATHER, THE LORD OF THE LOTUS, FOR HIS SONS. . . . THY PEOPLE SHALL BE UNDER THE RULE OF THE FATHERS. THY MEN SHALL BE MORTALS. THE MEN OF THE LORD OF WISDOM, NOT THE LUNAR SONS, ARE IMMORTAL. CEASE THY COMPLAINTS. THY SEVEN SKINS ARE YET ON THEE. . . . THOU ART NOT READY. THY MEN ARE NOT READY."

4. AFTER GREAT THROES SHE CAST OFF HER OLD THREE AND PUT ON HER NEW SEVEN SKINS, AND STOOD IN HER FIRST ONE.

II.

5. THE WHEEL WHIRLED FOR THIRTY CRORES MORE. IT CONSTRUCTED RUPAS: SOFT STONES THAT HARDENED; HARD PLANTS THAT SOFTENED. VISIBLE FROM INVISIBLE, INSECTS AND SMALL LIVES. SHE SHOOK THEM OFF HER BACK WHENEVER THEY OVERRAN THE MOTHER. . . . AFTER THIRTY CRORES SHE TURNED ROUND. SHE LAY ON HER BACK; ON HER SIDE. . . . SHE WOULD CALL NO SONS OF HEAVEN,

---

*Only forty-nine Slokas out of several hundred are here given. Not every verse is translated verbatim. A periphrasis is sometimes used for the sake of clearness and intelligibility, where a literal translation would be quite unintelligible.

SHE WOULD ASK NO SONS OF WISDOM. SHE CREATED FROM HER OWN BOSOM. SHE EVOLVED WATER-MEN, TERRIBLE AND BAD.

6. THE WATER-MEN TERRIBLE AND BAD SHE HERSELF CREATED FROM THE REMAINS OF OTHERS, FROM THE DROSS AND SLIME OF HER FIRST, SECOND, AND THIRD, SHE FORMED THEM. THE DHYANI CAME AND LOOKED —THE DHYANI FROM THE BRIGHT FATHER-MOTHER, FROM THE WHITE REGIONS THEY CAME, FROM THE ABODES OF THE IMMORTAL MORTALS.

7. DISPLEASED THEY WERE. OUR FLESH IS NOT THERE. NO FIT RUPAS FOR OUR BROTHERS OF THE FIFTH. NO DWELLINGS FOR THE LIVES. PURE WATERS, NOT TURBID, THEY MUST DRINK. LET US DRY THEM.

8. THE FLAMES CAME. THE FIRES WITH THE SPARKS; THE NIGHT FIRES AND THE DAY FIRES. THEY DRIED OUT THE TURBID DARK WATERS. WITH THEIR HEAT THEY QUENCHED THEM. THE LHAS OF THE HIGH, THE LHAMAYIN OF BELOW, CAME. THEY SLEW THE FORMS WHICH WERE TWO- AND FOUR-FACED. THEY FOUGHT THE GOAT-MEN, AND THE DOG-HEADED MEN, AND THE MEN WITH FISHES' BODIES.

9. MOTHER-WATER, THE GREAT SEA, WEPT. SHE AROSE, SHE DISAPPEARED IN THE MOON WHICH HAD LIFTED HER, WHICH HAD GIVEN HER BIRTH.

10. WHEN THEY WERE DESTROYED, MOTHER-EARTH REMAINED BARE. SHE ASKED TO BE DRIED.

III.

11. THE LORD OF THE LORDS CAME. FROM HER BODY HE SEPARATED THE WATERS, AND THAT WAS HEAVEN ABOVE, THE FIRST HEAVEN.

12. THE GREAT CHOHANS CALLED THE LORDS OF THE MOON, OF THE AIRY BODIES. "BRING FORTH MEN, MEN OF YOUR NATURE. GIVE THEM THEIR FORMS WITHIN. SHE WILL BUILD COVERINGS WITHOUT. MALES-FEMALES WILL THEY BE. LORDS OF THE FLAME ALSO. . . ."

13. THEY WENT EACH ON HIS ALLOTTED LAND: SEVEN OF THEM EACH ON HIS LOT. THE LORDS OF THE FLAME REMAIN BEHIND. THEY WOULD NOT GO, THEY WOULD NOT CREATE.

IV.

14. THE SEVEN HOSTS, THE "WILL-BORN LORDS," PROPELLED BY THE SPIRIT OF LIFE-GIVING, SEPARATE MEN FROM THEMSELVES, EACH ON HIS OWN ZONE.

15. SEVEN TIMES SEVEN SHADOWS OF FUTURE MEN WERE BORN, EACH OF HIS OWN COLOUR AND KIND. EACH INFERIOR TO HIS FATHER. THE FATHERS, THE BONELESS, COULD GIVE NO LIFE TO BEINGS WITH BONES.

THEIR PROGENY WERE BHÛTA, WITH NEITHER FORM NOR MIND. THERE-
FORE THEY ARE CALLED THE CHHAYA.

16. HOW ARE THE MANUSHYA BORN? THE MANUS WITH MINDS,
HOW ARE THEY MADE? THE FATHERS CALLED TO THEIR HELP THEIR
OWN FIRE; WHICH IS THE FIRE THAT BURNS IN EARTH. THE SPIRIT
OF THE EARTH CALLED TO HIS HELP THE SOLAR FIRE. THESE THREE
PRODUCED IN THEIR JOINT EFFORTS A GOOD RUPA. IT COULD STAND,
WALK, RUN, RECLINE, OR FLY. YET IT WAS STILL BUT A CHHAYA, A
SHADOW WITH NO SENSE. . . .

17. THE BREATH NEEDED A FORM; THE FATHERS GAVE IT. THE
BREATH NEEDED A GROSS BODY; THE EARTH MOULDED IT. THE BREATH
NEEDED THE SPIRIT OF LIFE; THE SOLAR LHAS BREATHED IT INTO ITS
FORM. THE BREATH NEEDED A MIRROR OF ITS BODY; "WE GAVE IT
OUR OWN," SAID THE DHYANIS. THE BREATH NEEDED A VEHICLE OF
DESIRES; "IT HAS IT," SAID THE DRAINER OF WATERS. BUT BREATH
NEEDS A MIND TO EMBRACE THE UNIVERSE; "WE CANNOT GIVE THAT,"
SAID THE FATHERS. "I NEVER HAD IT," SAID THE SPIRIT OF THE EARTH.
"THE FORM WOULD BE CONSUMED WERE I TO GIVE IT MINE," SAID THE
GREAT FIRE. . . . MAN REMAINED AN EMPTY SENSELESS BHÛTA.
. . . THUS HAVE THE BONELESS GIVEN LIFE TO THOSE WHO BECAME
MEN WITH BONES IN THE THIRD.

V.

18. THE FIRST WERE THE SONS OF YOGA. THEIR SONS THE CHILDREN
OF THE YELLOW FATHER AND THE WHITE MOTHER.

19. THE SECOND RACE WAS THE PRODUCT BY BUDDING AND EXPAN-
SION, THE A-SEXUAL FROM THE SEXLESS.* THUS WAS, O LANOO, THE
SECOND RACE PRODUCED.

20. THEIR FATHERS WERE THE SELF-BORN. THE SELF-BORN, THE
CHHAYA FROM THE BRILLIANT BODIES OF THE LORDS, THE FATHERS,
THE SONS OF TWILIGHT.

21. WHEN THE RACE BECAME OLD, THE OLD WATERS MIXED WITH
THE FRESHER WATERS. WHEN ITS DROPS BECAME TURBID, THEY VAN-
ISHED AND DISAPPEARED IN THE NEW STREAM, IN THE HOT STREAM OF
LIFE. THE OUTER OF THE FIRST BECAME THE INNER OF THE SECOND.
THE OLD WING BECAME THE NEW SHADOW, AND THE SHADOW OF THE
WING.

VI.

22. THEN THE SECOND EVOLVED THE EGG-BORN, THE THIRD. THE
SWEAT GREW, ITS DROPS GREW, AND THE DROPS BECAME HARD AND

---

*The idea and the spirit of the sentence is here given, as a verbal translation would convey very little to the
reader.

ROUND. THE SUN WARMED IT; THE MOON COOLED AND SHAPED IT; THE WIND FED IT UNTIL ITS RIPENESS. THE WHITE SWAN FROM THE STARRY VAULT OVERSHADOWED THE BIG DROP. THE EGG OF THE FUTURE RACE, THE MAN-SWAN OF THE LATER THIRD. FIRST MALE-FEMALE, THEN MAN AND WOMAN.

23. THE SELF-BORN WERE THE CHHAYAS: THE SHADOWS FROM THE BODIES OF THE SONS OF TWILIGHT.

VII.

24. THE SONS OF WISDOM, THE SONS OF NIGHT, READY FOR REBIRTH, CAME DOWN; THEY SAW THE VILE FORMS OF THE FIRST THIRD; "WE CAN CHOOSE," SAID THE LORDS, "WE HAVE WISDOM." SOME ENTERED THE CHHAYA. SOME PROJECTED THE SPARK. SOME DEFERRED TILL THE FOURTH. FROM THEIR OWN RUPA THEY FILLED THE KAMA. THOSE WHO ENTERED BECAME ARHATS. THOSE WHO RECEIVED BUT A SPARK, REMAINED DESTITUTE OF KNOWLEDGE; THE SPARK BURNED LOW. THE THIRD REMAINED MIND-LESS. THEIR JIVAS WERE NOT READY. THESE WERE SET APART AMONG THE SEVEN. THEY BECAME NARROW-HEADED. THE THIRD WERE READY. "IN THESE SHALL WE DWELL," SAID THE LORDS OF THE FLAME.

25. HOW DID THE MANÂSA, THE SONS OF WISDOM, ACT? THEY REJECTED THE SELF-BORN. THEY ARE NOT READY. THEY SPURNED THE SWEAT-BORN. THEY ARE NOT QUITE READY. THEY WOULD NOT ENTER THE FIRST EGG-BORN.

26. WHEN THE SWEAT-BORN PRODUCED THE EGG-BORN, THE TWO-FOLD AND THE MIGHTY, THE POWERFUL WITH BONES, THE LORDS OF WISDOM SAID: "NOW SHALL WE CREATE."

27. THE THIRD RACE BECAME THE VAHAN OF THE LORDS OF WISDOM. IT CREATED "SONS OF WILL AND YOGA," BY KRIYASAKTI IT CREATED THEM, THE HOLY FATHERS, ANCESTORS OF THE ARHATS.

VIII.

28. FROM THE DROPS OF SWEAT; FROM THE RESIDUE OF THE SUBSTANCE; MATTER FROM DEAD BODIES OF MEN AND ANIMALS OF THE WHEEL BEFORE; AND FROM CAST-OFF DUST, THE FIRST ANIMALS WERE PRODUCED.

29. ANIMALS WITH BONES, DRAGONS OF THE DEEP, AND FLYING SARPAS WERE ADDED TO THE CREEPING THINGS. THEY THAT CREEP ON THE GROUND GOT WINGS. THEY OF THE LONG NECKS IN THE WATER BECAME THE PROGENITORS OF THE FOWLS OF THE AIR.

30. DURING THE THIRD RACE THE BONELESS ANIMALS GREW AND

CHANGED: THEY BECAME ANIMALS WITH BONES, THEIR CHHAYAS BECAME SOLID.

31. THE ANIMALS SEPARATED THE FIRST. THEY BEGAN TO BREED. THE TWO-FOLD MAN SEPARATED ALSO. HE SAID: "LET US AS THEY; LET US UNITE AND MAKE CREATURES." THEY DID.

32. AND THOSE WHICH HAD NO SPARK TOOK HUGE SHE-ANIMALS UNTO THEM. THEY BEGAT UPON THEM DUMB RACES. DUMB THEY WERE THEMSELVES. BUT THEIR TONGUES UNTIED. THE TONGUES OF THEIR PROGENY REMAINED STILL. MONSTERS THEY BRED. A RACE OF CROOKED RED-HAIR-COVERED MONSTERS GOING ON ALL FOURS. A DUMB RACE TO KEEP THE SHAME UNTOLD.

IX.

33. SEEING WHICH, THE LHAS WHO HAD NOT BUILT MEN, WEPT, SAYING:—

34. "THE AMANÂSA HAVE DEFILED OUR FUTURE ABODES. THIS IS KARMA. LET US DWELL IN THE OTHERS. LET US TEACH THEM BETTER, LEST WORSE SHOULD HAPPEN. THEY DID. . . .

35. THEN ALL MEN BECAME ENDOWED WITH MANAS. THEY SAW THE SIN OF THE MINDLESS.

36. THE FOURTH RACE DEVELOPED SPEECH.

37. THE ONE BECAME TWO; ALSO ALL THE LIVING AND CREEPING THINGS THAT WERE STILL ONE, GIANT FISH-BIRDS AND SERPENTS WITH SHELL-HEADS.

X.

38. THUS TWO BY TWO ON THE SEVEN ZONES, THE THIRD RACE GAVE BIRTH TO THE FOURTH-RACE MEN; THE GODS BECAME NO-GODS; THE SURA BECAME A-SURA.

39. THE FIRST, ON EVERY ZONE, WAS MOON-COLOURED; THE SECOND YELLOW LIKE GOLD; THE THIRD RED; THE FOURTH BROWN, WHICH BE-CAME BLACK WITH SIN. THE FIRST SEVEN HUMAN SHOOTS WERE ALL OF ONE COMPLEXION. THE NEXT SEVEN BEGAN MIXING.

40. THEN THE FOURTH BECAME TALL WITH PRIDE. WE ARE THE KINGS, IT WAS SAID; WE ARE THE GODS.

41. THEY TOOK WIVES FAIR TO LOOK UPON. WIVES FROM THE MINDLESS, THE NARROW-HEADED. THEY BRED MONSTERS. WICKED DEMONS, MALE AND FEMALE, ALSO KHADO (DAKINI), WITH LITTLE MINDS.

42. THEY BUILT TEMPLES FOR THE HUMAN BODY. MALE AND FEMALE THEY WORSHIPPED. THEN THE THIRD EYE ACTED NO LONGER.

XI.

43. THEY BUILT HUGE CITIES. OF RARE EARTHS AND METALS THEY BUILT, AND OUT OF THE FIRES VOMITED, OUT OF THE WHITE STONE OF THE MOUNTAINS AND OF THE BLACK STONE, THEY CUT THEIR OWN IMAGES IN THEIR SIZE AND LIKENESS, AND WORSHIPPED THEM.

44. THEY BUILT GREAT IMAGES NINE YATIS HIGH, THE SIZE OF THEIR BODIES. INNER FIRES HAD DESTROYED THE LAND OF THEIR FATHERS. THE WATER THREATENED THE FOURTH.

45. THE FIRST GREAT WATERS CAME. THEY SWALLOWED THE SEVEN GREAT ISLANDS.

46. ALL HOLY SAVED, THE UNHOLY DESTROYED. WITH THEM MOST OF THE HUGE ANIMALS, PRODUCED FROM THE SWEAT OF THE EARTH.

XII.

47. FEW MEN REMAINED: SOME YELLOW, SOME BROWN AND BLACK, AND SOME RED REMAINED. THE MOON-COLOURED WERE GONE FOREVER.

48. THE FIFTH PRODUCED FROM THE HOLY STOCK REMAINED; IT WAS RULED OVER BY THE FIRST DIVINE KINGS.

49. . . . WHO RE-DESCENDED, WHO MADE PEACE WITH THE FIFTH, WHO TAUGHT AND INSTRUCTED IT. . . .

PART I

STANZAS I AND II
(SLOKAS 1 AND 2)

I.

STANZA I.

Sloka (I). THE ETERNAL PARENT (*Space*), WRAPPED IN HER EVER INVISIBLE ROBES, HAD SLUMBERED ONCE AGAIN FOR SEVEN ETERNITIES.

Q. Space in the abstract is explained in the Proem (*pp. 8 and 9*) as follows:

". . . . Absolute unity cannot pass to infinity; for infinity presupposes the limitless extension of *something*, and the duration of that 'something'; and the One All is like Space—which is its only mental and physical representation on this Earth, or our plane of existence—neither an object of, nor a subject to, perception. If one could suppose the Eternal Infinite All, the Omnipresent Unity, instead of being in Eternity, becoming through periodical manifestation a manifold Universe, or a multiple personality, that Unity would cease to be one. Locke's idea that 'pure Space is capable of neither resistance nor motion' is incorrect. Space is neither a 'limitless void' nor a 'conditioned fulness,' but both, being on the plane of absolute abstraction, the ever-incognisable Deity, which is void only to finite minds, and on that of *mayavic* perception, the Plenum, the absolute Container of all that is, whether manifested or unmanifested; it is, therefore, that ABSOLUTE ALL. There is no difference between the Christian Apostle's 'In Him we live and move and have our being,' and the Hindu Rishi's, 'The Universe lives in, proceeds from, and will return to, Brahma (Brahmâ)'; for Brahma (neuter), the unmanifested, is that Universe *in abscondito*, and Brahmâ, the manifested, is the Logos, made male-female in the symbolical orthodox dogmas. The God of the Apostle-Initiate, and of the Rishi, being both the Unseen and the Visible SPACE. Space is called, in the esoteric symbolism, 'The Seven-Skinned Eternal Mother-Father.' It is composed from its undifferentiated to its differentiated surface of seven layers. " 'What is that which was, is, and will be, whether there is a Universe or not; whether there be gods or none?' asks the esoteric Senzar Catechism. And the answer made is—SPACE."*

*S. D., Vol. I, p. 8.

[1]

But why is the Eternal Parent, Space, spoken of as feminine?

A. Not in all cases, for in the above extract Space is called the "Eternal Mother-Father"; but when it is so spoken of the reason is that though it is impossible to define Parabrahm, yet once that we speak of that first something which *can* be conceived, it has to be treated of as a feminine principle. In all cosmogonies the first differentiation was considered feminine. It is Mulaprakriti which conceals or veils Parabrahm; Sephira the *light* that emanates first from Ain-Soph; and in Hesiod it is Gaea who springs from Chaos, preceding Eros (THEOG. IV.; 201-246). This is repeated in all subsequent and less abstract material creations, as witnessed by Eve, created from the rib of Adam, etc. It is the goddess and goddesses who come first. The first emanation becomes the immaculate Mother from whom proceeds all the gods, or the anthropomorphized creative forces. We have to adopt the masculine or the feminine gender, for we cannot use the neuter *it*. From IT, strictly speaking, nothing can proceed, neither a radiation nor an emanation.

Q. Is this first emanation identical with the Egyptian Neïth?

A. In reality it is beyond Neïth, but in one sense or in a lower aspect it is Neïth.

Q. Then the IT itself is not the "Seven-Skinned Eternal Mother-Father"?

A. Assuredly not. The IT is, in the Hindu philosophy, Parabrahm, that which is beyond Brahmâ, or, as it is now called in Europe, the "unknowable." The space of which we speak is the female aspect of Brahmâ, the male. At the first flutter of differentiation, the Subjective proceeds to emanate, or fall, like a shadow into the Objective, and becomes what was called the Mother Goddess, from whom proceeds the Logos, the Son and Father God at the same time, both unmanifested, one the Potentiality, the other the Potency. But the former must not be confounded with the manifested Logos, also called the "Son" in all cosmogonies.

Q. Is the first differentiation from the absolute IT always feminine?

A. Only as a figure of speech; in strict philosophy it is sexless; but the female aspect is the first it assumes in human conceptions, its subsequent materialisation in any philosophy depending on the degree of the spirituality of the race or nation that produced the system. For instance: in the Kabbala of the Talmudists IT is called AIN-SOPH, the endless, the boundless, the infinite (the attribute being always negative), which *absolute* Principle is yet referred to as *He!!* From it, this negative, Boundless Circle of Infinite Light, emanates the first Sephira, the Crown, which the Talmudists call "Torah," the law, explaining that she is the wife of Ain-Soph. This is anthropomorphising the Spiritual with a vengeance.

Q. Is it the same in the Hindu Philosophies?

A. Exactly the opposite. For if we turn to the Hindu cosmogonies, we find that Parabrahm is not even mentioned therein, but only Mulaprakriti. The latter is, so to speak, the lining or aspect of Parabrahm in the invisible universe. Mulaprakriti means the Root of Nature or Matter. But Parabrahm cannot be called the "Root," for it is the absolute *Rootless Root* of all. Therefore, we must begin with Mulaprakriti, or the Veil of this unknowable. Here again we see that the first is the Mother Goddess, the reflection or the subjective root, on the first plane of Substance. Then follows, issuing from, or rather residing in, this Mother Goddess, the unmanifested Logos, he who is both her Son and Husband at once, called the "concealed Father." From these proceeds the first-manifested Logos, or Spirit, and the Son from whose substance emanate the Seven Logoi, whose synthesis, viewed as one collective Force, becomes the Architect of the Visible Universe. They are the Elohim of the Jews.

Q. What aspect of Space, or the unknown deity, called in the Vedas "THAT," which is mentioned further on, is here called the "Eternal Parent"?

A. It is the Vedantic Mulaprakriti, and the Svâbhâvat of the Buddhists, or that androgynous *something* of which we have been speaking, which is both differentiated and undifferentiated. In its first principle it is a pure abstraction, which becomes differentiated only when it is transformed, in the process of time, into Prakriti. If compared with the human principles, it corresponds to Buddhi, while Atma would correspond to Parabrahm, Manas to Mahat, and so on.

Q. What, then, are the seven layers of Space, for in the "Proem" we read about the "Seven-Skinned Mother-Father"?

A. Plato and Hermes Trismegistus would have regarded this as the *Divine Thought*, and Aristotle would have viewed this "Mother-Father" as the "privation" of matter. It is that which will become the seven planes of being, commencing with the spiritual and passing through the psychic to the material plane. The seven planes of thought or the seven states of consciousness correspond to these planes. All these septenaries are symbolized by the seven "Skins."

Q. The divine ideas in the Divine Mind? But the Divine Mind is not yet.

A. The Divine Mind *is*, and must be, before differentiation takes place. It is called the divine Ideation, which is eternal in its Potentiality and periodical in its Potency, when it becomes *Mahat, Anima Mundi* or Universal Soul. But remember that, however you name it, each of these conceptions has its most metaphysical, most material, and also intermediate aspects.

[4]

Q. What is the meaning of the term "Ever invisible robes"?

A. It is, of course, as every allegory in the Eastern philosophies, a figurative expression. Perhaps it may be the hypothetical Protyle that Professor Crookes is in search of, but which can certainly never be found on this our earth or plane. It is the non-differentiated substance or spiritual matter.

Q. Is it what is called *"Laya"*?

A. "Robes" and all are in the *Laya* condition, the point from which, or at which, the primordial substance begins to differentiate and thus gives birth to the universe and all in it.

Q. Are the "invisible robes" so called because they are not objective to any differentiation of consciousness?

A. Say rather, invisible to finite consciousness, if such consciousness were possible at that stage of evolution. Even for the Logos, Mulaprakriti is a veil, the Robes in which the Absolute is enveloped. Even the Logos cannot perceive the Absolute, say the Vedantins.*

Q. Is Mulaprakriti the correct term to use?

A. The Mulaprakriti of the Vedantins is the Aditi of the Vedas. The Vedanta philosophy means literally "the end or Synthesis of all knowledge." Now there are six schools of Hindu philosophy, which, however, will be found, on strict analysis, to agree perfectly in substance. Fundamentally they are identical, but there is such a wealth of names, such a quantity of side issues, details, and ornamentations— some emanations being their own fathers, and fathers born from their own daughters—that one becomes lost as in a jungle. State anything you please from the esoteric standpoint to a Hindu, and, if he so wishes, he can, from his own particular system, contradict or refute you. Each of the

Vide Mr. Subba Row's four Lectures, *Notes on the Bhagavat Gita.*

[5]

six schools has its own peculiar views and terms. So that unless the terminology of one school is adopted and used throughout the discussion, there is great danger of misunderstanding.

Q. Then the same identical term is used in quite a different sense by different philosophies? For instance, Buddhi has one meaning in the Esoteric and quite a different sense in the Sankhya philosophy. Is not this so?

A. Precisely, and quite a different sense in the Vishnu Purana, which speaks of seven Prakritis emanating from Mahat and calls the latter Maha-Buddhi. Fundamentally, however, the ideas are the same, though the terms differ with each school, and the correct sense is lost in this maze of personifications. It would, perhaps, if possible, be best to invent for ourselves a new nomenclature. Owing, however, to the poverty of European languages, especially English, in philosophical terms, the undertaking would be somewhat difficult.

Q. Could not the term "Protyle" be employed to represent the *Laya* condition?

A. Scarcely; the Protyle of Professor Crookes is probably used to denote homogeneous matter on the most material plane of all, whereas the *substance* symbolized by the "Robes" of the "Eternal Parent" is on the seventh plane of matter counting upwards, or rather from without within. This can never be discovered on the lowest, or rather most outward and material plane.

Q. Is there, then, on each of the seven planes, matter relatively homogeneous for every plane?

A. That is so; but such matter is homogeneous only for those who are on the same plane of perception; so that if the Protyle of modern science is ever discovered, it will be homogeneous only to us. The illusion may last for some time, perhaps until the sixth race, for humanity is ever changing, physically and mentally, and let us hope spiritually too, perfecting itself more and more with every race and sub-race.

> *Q.* Would it not be a great mistake to use any term which has been used by scientists with another meaning? Protoplasm had once almost the same sense as Protyle, but its meaning has now become narrowed.

A. It would most decidedly; the *Hyle* (ὕλη) of the Greeks, however, most certainly did not apply to the matter of this plane, for they adopted it from the Chaldean cosmogony, where it was used in a highly metaphysical sense.

> *Q.* But the word *Hyle* is now used by the materialists to express very nearly the same idea as that to which we apply the term Mulaprakriti.

A. It may be so; but Dr. Lewins and his brave half-dozen of Hylo-Idealists are hardly of this opinion, for in their system the metaphysical meaning is entirely disregarded and lost sight of.

> *Q.* Then perhaps after all *Laya* is the best term to use?

A. Not so, for *Laya* does not mean any particular something or some plane or other, but denotes a state or condition. It is a Sanskrit term, conveying the idea of something in an undifferentiated and changeless state, a zero point wherein all differentiation ceases.

> *Q.* The first differentiation would represent matter on its seventh plane: must we not, therefore, suppose that Professor Crookes' Protyle is also matter on its seventh plane?

A. The ideal Protyle of Professor Crookes is matter in that state which he calls the "zero-point."

> *Q.* That is to say, the *Laya* point of this plane?

A. It is not at all clear whether Professor Crookes is occupied with other planes or admits their existence. The

[7]

object of his search is the protylic atom, which, as no one has ever seen it, is simply a new working hypothesis of Science. For what in reality is an atom?

Q. It is a convenient definition of what is supposed to be, or rather a convenient term to divide up, a molecule.

A. But surely they must have come by this time to the conclusion that the atom is no more a convenient term than the supposed seventy odd elements. It has been the custom to laugh at the four and five elements of the ancients; but now Professor Crookes has come to the conclusion that, strictly speaking, there is no such thing as a chemical element at all. In fact, so far from discovering the atom, a single simple molecule has not yet been arrived at.

Q. It should be remembered that Dalton, who first spoke on the subject, called it the "Atomic Theory."

A. Quite so; but, as shown by Sir W. Hamilton, the term is used in an erroneous sense by the modern schools of science, which, while laughing at metaphysics, apply a purely metaphysical term to physics, so that nowadays "theory" begins to usurp the prerogatives of "axiom."

Q. What are the "Seven Eternities," and how can there be such a division in Pralaya, when there is no one to be conscious of time?

A. The modern astronomer knows the "ordinances of Heaven" by no means better than his ancient brother did. If asked whether he could "bring forth Mazzaroth in his season," or if he was with "him" who "spread out the sky," he would have to answer sadly, just as Job did, in the negative. Yet this in no wise prevents him from speculating about the age of the Sun, Moon, and Earth, and "calculating" geological periods from that time when there was not a living man, with or without consciousness, on earth. Why, therefore, should not the same privilege be granted to the ancients?

Q. But why should the term "Seven Eternities" be employed?

A. The term "Seven Eternities" is employed owing to the invariable law of analogy. As Manvantara is divided into seven periods, so is Pralaya; as day is composed of twelve hours so is night. Can we say that because we are asleep during the night and lose consciousness of time, that therefore the hours do not strike? Pralaya is the "Night" after the Manvantaric "Day." There is no one by, and consciousness is asleep with the rest. But since it exists, and is in full activity during Manvantara; and since we are fully alive to the fact that the law of analogy and periodicity is immutable, and, being so, that it must act equally at both ends, why cannot the phrase be used?

Q. But how can an eternity be counted?

A. Perhaps the query arises owing to the general misunderstanding of the term "Eternity." We Westerns are foolish enough to speculate about that which has neither beginning nor end, and we imagine that the ancients must have done the same. They did not, however: no philosopher in days of old ever took "Eternity" to mean beginningless and endless duration. Neither the Æons of the Greeks nor the Naroses convey this meaning. In fact, they had no word to convey this precise sense. Parabrahm, Ain-Soph, and the *Zeruana-Akerne* of the Avesta alone represent such an Eternity; all the other periods are finite and astronomical, based on tropical years and other enormous cycles. The word Æon, which in the Bible is translated by Eternity, means not only a finite period, but also an angel and being.

Q. But is it not correct to say that in Pralaya too there is the "Great Breath"?

A. Assuredly: for the "Great Breath" is ceaseless, and is, so to speak, the universal and eternal *perpetuum mobile.*

[9]

Q. If so, it is impossible to divide it into periods, for this does away with the idea of absolute and complete nothingness. It seems somewhat incompatible that any "number" of periods should be spoken of, although one might speak of so many outbreathings and indrawings of the "Great Breath."

A. This would make away with the idea of absolute Rest, were not this absoluteness of Rest counteracted by the absoluteness of Motion. Therefore one expression is as good as the other. There is a magnificent poem on Pralaya, written by a very ancient Rishi, who compares the motion of the Great Breath during Pralaya to the rhythmical motions of the Unconscious Ocean.

Q. The difficulty is when the word "eternity" is used instead of "Æon."

A. Why should a Greek word be used when there is a more familiar expression, especially as it is fully explained in the *Secret Doctrine?* You may call it a *relative*, or a Manvantaric and Pralayic eternity, if you like.

Q. Is the relation of Pralaya and Manvantara strictly analogous to the relations between sleeping and waking?

A. In a certain sense only; during night we all exist personally, and *are* individually, though we sleep and may be unconscious of so living. But during Pralaya everything differentiated, as every unit, disappears from the phenomenal universe and is merged in, or rather transferred into, the One noumenal. Therefore, *de facto*, there is a great difference.

Q. Sleep has been called the "Shady side of life"; may Pralaya be called the shady side of Cosmic life?

A. It may in a certain way be called so. Pralaya is dissolution of the visible into the invisible, the heterogeneous into the homogeneous—a time of rest, therefore. Even cosmic matter, indestructible though it be in its essence, must have a time of rest, and return to its *Layam* state. The absoluteness of the all-containing One essence has to manifest itself equally in rest and activity.

Sloka (2). TIME WAS NOT, FOR IT LAY ASLEEP IN THE INFINITE BOSOM OF DURATION.

Q. What is the difference between Time and Duration?

A. Duration *is;* it has neither beginning nor end. How can you call that which has neither beginning nor end, Time? Duration is beginningless and endless; Time is finite.

Q. Is, then, Duration the infinite, and Time the finite conception?

A. Time can be divided; Duration—in our philosophy, at least—cannot. Time is divisible in Duration—or, as you put it, the one is something *within* Time and Space, whereas the other is outside of both.

Q. The only way one can define Time is by the motion of the earth?

A. But we can also define Time in our conceptions.

Q. Duration, rather?

A. No, Time; for as to Duration, it is impossible to divide it or set up landmarks therein. Duration with us is the one eternity, not relative, but absolute.

Q. Can it be said that the essential idea of Duration is existence?

A. No; existence has limited and definite periods, whereas Duration, having neither beginning nor end, is a perfect abstraction which contains Time. Duration is like Space, which is an abstraction too, and is equally without beginning or end. It is in its concretency and limitation only that it becomes a representation and something. Of course the distance between two points is called space; it may be enormous or it may be infinitesimal, yet it will always be space. But all such specifications are divisions in human conception. In reality Space is what the ancients called the One invisible and unknown (now unknowable) Deity.

Q. Then Time is the same as Space, being one in the abstract?

A. As two abstractions they may be one; but this would apply to Duration and Abstract Space rather than to Time and Space.

Q. Space is the objective and Time the subjective side of all manifestation. In reality they are the only attributes of the infinite; but attribute is perhaps a bad term to use, inasmuch as they are, so to speak, co-extensive with the infinite. It may, however, be objected that they are nothing but the creations of our own intellect; simply the forms in which we cannot help conceiving things.

A. That sounds like an argument of our friends the Hylo-idealists; but here we speak of the noumenal and not of the phenomenal universe. In the occult catechism (*Vide Secret Doctrine*) it is asked: "What is that which always IS, which you cannot imagine as not *being*, do what you may?" The answer is—SPACE. For there may not be a single man in the universe to think of it, not a single eye to perceive it, nor a single brain to sense it, but still Space *is, ever was, and ever will be*, and you cannot make away with it.

Q. Because we cannot help thinking of it, perhaps.

A. Our thinking of it has nothing to do with the question. Try, rather, if you can think of anything with Space excluded and you will soon find out the impossibility of such a conception. Space exists where there is nothing else, and must so exist whether the Universe is one absolute vacuum or a full Pleroma.

Q. Modern Philosophers have reduced it to this, that space and time are nothing but attributes, nothing but accidents.

A. And they would be right, were their reduction the fruit of true science instead of being the result of *Avidya* and

Maya. We find also Buddha saying that even Nirvâna, after all, is but *Maya,* or an illusion; but the Lord Buddha based what he said on *knowledge,* not *speculation.*

Q. But are eternal Space and Duration the only attributes of the Infinite?

A. Space and Duration, being eternal, cannot be called attributes, as they are only the *aspects* of that Infinite. Nor can that Infinite, if you mean by it The Absolute Principle, have any attributes whatever, as only that which is itself finite and conditioned can have any relation to something else. All this is philosophically wrong.

Q. We can conceive of no matter which is not extended, no extension which is not extension of something. Is it the same on higher planes? And if so, what is the substance which fills absolute space, and is it identical with that space?

A. If your "trained intellect" cannot conceive of any other kind of matter, perhaps one less trained but more open to spiritual perceptions can. It does not follow, because you say so, that such a conception of Space is the only one possible, even on our Earth. For even on this plane of ours there are other and various intellects, besides those of man, in creatures visible and invisible, from minds of subjective high and low Beings to objective animals and the lowest organisms, in short, "from the Deva to the elephant, from the elemental to the ant." Now, in relation to its own plane of conception and perception, the ant has as good an intellect as we have ourselves, and a better one; for though it cannot express it in words, yet, over and above instinct, the ant shows very high reasoning powers, as all of us know. Thus, finding on our own plane—if we credit the teachings of Occultism—so many and such varied states of consciousness and intelligence, we have no right to take into consideration and account only our own human consciousness, as though no other existed outside of it. And if we cannot presume to decide how far insect consciousness goes, how can we limit consciousness, of which science knows nothing, to this plane?

Q. But why not? Surely natural science can discover all that has to be discovered, even in the ant?

A. Such is your view; to the occultist, however, such confidence is misplaced, in spite of Sir John Lubbock's labours. Science may speculate, but, with its present methods, will never be able to prove the certitude of such speculations. If a scientist could become an ant for a while, and think as an ant, and remember his experience on returning to his own sphere of consciousness, then only would he know something for certain of this interesting insect. As it is, he can only speculate, making inferences from the ant's behaviour.

Q. The ant's conception of time and space are not our own, then. Is it this that you mean?

A. Precisely; the ant has conceptions of time and space which are its own, not ours; conceptions which are entirely on another plane; we have, therefore, no right to deny *a priori* the existence of other planes only because we can form no idea of them, but which exist nevertheless—planes higher and lower than our own by many degrees, as witness the ant.

Q. The difference between the animal and man from this point of view seems to be that the former is born more or less with all its faculties, and generally speaking, does not appreciably gain on this, while the latter is gradually learning and improving. Is not that really the point?

A. Just so; but you have to remember why: not because man has one "principle" more than the tiniest insect, but because man is a perfected animal, the vehicle of a fully de-

[14]

veloped *monad*, self-conscious and deliberately following its own line of progress, whereas in the insect, and even the higher animal, the higher triad of principles is absolutely dormant.

Q. Is there any consciousness, or conscious being, to cognize and make a division of time at the first flutter of manifestation? In his Lecture on the Bhagavat Gita, Mr. Subba Row, in speaking of the First Logos, seems to imply both consciousness and intelligence.

A. But he did not explain which Logos was referred to, and I believe he spoke in general. In the Esoteric Philosophy the First is the unmanifested, and the Second the manifested Logos. Iswara stands for that Second, and Nârâyana for the unmanifested Logos. Subba Row is an Adwaitee and a learned Vedantin, and explained from his standpoint. We do so from ours. In the *Secret Doctrine,* that from which the manifested Logos is born is translated by the "Eternal Mother-Father"; while in the Vishnu Purâna it is described as the Egg of the World, surrounded by seven skins, layers or zones. It is in this Golden Egg that Brahmâ, the male, is born and that Brahmâ is in reality the Second Logos or even the Third, according to the enumeration adopted; for a certainty he is not the First or highest, the point which is everywhere and nowhere. Mahat, in the Esoteric interpretations, is in reality the Third Logos or the Synthesis of the Seven creative rays, the Seven Logoi. Out of the seven so-called *Creations*, Mahat is the third, for it is the Universal and Intelligent Soul, Divine Ideation, combining the ideal plans and prototypes of all things in the manifested objective as well as subjective world. In the Sankhya and Purânic doctrines Mahat is the first product of *Pradhâna*, informed by Kshetrajna, "Spirit-Substance." In Esoteric philosophy Kshetrajna is the name given to our informing EGOS.

[15]

Q. Is it then the first manifestation in our objective universe?

A. It is the first Principle in it, made sensible or perceptible to divine though not human senses. But if we proceed from the Unknowable, we will find it to be the third, and corresponding to Manas, or rather Buddhi-Manas.

Q. Then the First Logos is the first point within the circle?

A. The point within the circle which has neither limit nor boundaries, nor can it have any name or attribute. This first, unmanifested Logos is simultaneous with the line drawn across the diameter of the Circle. The first line or diameter is the Mother-Father; from it proceeds the Second Logos, which contains in itself the Third Manifested Word. In the Purânas, for instance, it is again said that the first production of Akâsa is Sound, and Sound means in this case the "Word," the expression of the unuttered thought, the manifested Logos, that of the Greeks and Platonists and St. John. Dr. Wilson and other Orientalists speak of this conception of the Hindus as an absurdity, for according to them Akâsa and Chaos are identical. But if they knew that Akâsa and Pradhâna are but two aspects of the same thing, and remember that Mahat, the *divine ideation on our plane* —is that manifested *Sound* or Logos, they would laugh at themselves and their own ignorance.

Q. With reference to the following passage, what is the consciousness which takes cognizance of time? Is the consciousness of time limited to the plane of waking physical consciousness, or does it exist on higher planes? In the Secret Doctrine, I., 37, it is said that:—"Time is only an illusion produced by the succession of our states of consciousness as we travel through eternal duration, and it does not exist where no consciousness exists."

A. Here consciousness only on our plane is meant, not the eternal *divine* Consciousness which we call the Absolute. The consciousness of time, in the present sense of the word, does not exist even in sleep; much less, therefore, can it exist in the essentially absolute. Can the sea be said to have a conception of time in its rhythmical striking on the shore, or in the movement of its waves? The Absolute cannot be said to have a consciousness, or, at any rate, a consciousness such as we have here. It has neither consciousness, nor desire, nor wish, nor thought, because it is absolute thought, absolute desire, absolute consciousness, absolute "all."

Q. Is it what we refer to as BE-NESS, or SAT?

A. Our kind critics have found the word "Be-ness" very amusing, but there is no other way of translating the Sanskrit term, *Sat.* It is not existence, for existence can only apply to *phenomena*, never to *noumena*, the very etymology of the Latin term contradicting such assertion, as *ex* means "from" or "out of," and *sistere* "to stand"; therefore, something appearing being then where it was not before. Existence, moreover, implies something having a beginning and an end. How can the term, therefore, be applied to that which ever was, and of which it cannot be predicated that it ever issued from something else?

Q. The Hebrew Jehovah was "I am."

A. And so was Ormuzd, the Ahura-Mazda of the old Mazdeans. In this sense every man as much as every God can boast of his existence, saying "I am that I am."

Q. But surely "Be-ness" has some connection with the word "to be"?

A. Yes; but "Be-ness" is not *being*, for it is equally *non-being*. We cannot conceive it, for our intellects are finite and our language far more limited and conditioned even than our minds. How, therefore, can we express that which we can only conceive of by a series of negatives?

Q. A German could more easily express it by the word "Sein"; "das sein" would be a very good equivalent of "Be-ness"; the latter term

[17]

may sound absurd to unaccustomed English ears, but "das sein" is a perfectly familiar term and idea to a German. But we were speaking of consciousness in Space and Time.

A. This Consciousness is finite, having beginning and end. But where is the word for such finite Consciousness which still, owing to *Mâya*, believes itself infinite? Not even the Devachanee is conscious of time. All is present in Devachan; there is no past, otherwise the *Ego* would recall and regret it; no future, or it would desire to have it. Seeing, therefore, that Devachan is a state of bliss in which everything is present, the Devachanee is said to have no conception or idea of time; everything is to him as in a vivid dream, a reality.

Q. But we may dream a lifetime in half a second, being conscious of a succession of states of consciousness, events taking place one after the other.

A. After the dream only; no such consciousness exists while dreaming.

Q. May we not compare the recollection of a dream to a person giving the description of a picture, and having to mention all the parts and details because he cannot present the whole before the mind's eye of the listener?

A. That is a very good analogy.

II.

STANZA I.—*(Continued).*

Sloka (3). . . . UNIVERSAL MIND WAS NOT, FOR THERE WERE NO AH-HI (*celestial beings*) TO CONTAIN (*hence manifest*) IT.

Q. This sloka seems to imply that the Universal Mind has no existence apart from the Ah-hi; but in the Commentary it is stated that:

"During Pralaya the Universal Mind remains as a permanent possibility of mental action, or as that abstract absolute thought of which mind is the concrete relative manifestation, and that the Ah-hi are the vehicle for divine universal thought and will. They are the intelligent forces which give to nature her laws, while they themselves act according to laws imposed upon them by still higher powers, and are the hierarchy of spiritual beings through which the universal mind comes into action."*

The Commentary suggests that the Ah-hi are not themselves the Universal Mind, but only the vehicle for its manifestation.

A. The meaning of this sloka is, I think, very clear; it means that, as there are no finite differentiated minds during Pralaya, it is just as though there were no mind at all, because there is nothing *to contain or perceive it.* There is nothing to receive and reflect the ideation of the Absolute Mind; therefore, *it is not.* Everything outside of the Absolute and immutable Sat (Be-ness), is necessarily finite and conditioned, since it has beginning and end. Therefore, since the "Ah-hi were not," there was no Universal Mind as a manifestation. A distinction had to be made between the Absolute Mind, which is ever present, and its reflection and manifestation in the Ah-hi, who, being on the highest plane, reflect the universal mind collectively at the first flutter of Manvantara. After which they begin the work

*S. D., Vol. I, p. 38.

[19]

of evolution of all the lower forces throughout the seven planes, down to the lowest—our own. The Ah-hi are the primordial seven rays, or *Logoi*, emanated from the first Logos, *triple*, yet one in its essence.

Q. Then the Ah-hi and Universal Mind are necessary complements of one another?

A. Not at all: Universal or Absolute Mind always *is* during Pralaya as well as Manvantara; it is immutable. The Ah-hi are the highest Dhyanis, the Logoi as just said, those who begin the downward evolution, or emanation. During Pralaya there are no Ah-hi, because they come into being only with the first *radiation* of the Universal Mind, which, *per se*, cannot be differentiated, and the radiation from which is the first *dawn* of Manvantara. The Absolute is dormant, latent mind, and cannot be otherwise in true metaphysical perception; it is only Its shadow which becomes differentiated in the collectivity of these Dhyanis.

Q. Does this mean that it was *absolute consciousness*, but is so no longer?

A. It is *absolute consciousness* eternally, which consciousness becomes *relative consciousness* periodically, at every "Manvantaric dawn." Let us picture to ourselves this latent or potential consciousness as a kind of vacuum in a vessel. Break the vessel, and what becomes of the vacuum; where shall we look for it? It has disappeared; it is everywhere and nowhere. It is something, yet *nothing: a vacuum*, yet a *plenum*. But what in reality is a vacuum as understood by Modern Science—a homogeneous something, or what? Is not absolute Vacuum a figment of our fancy? A pure negation, a supposed Space where nothing exists? This being so, destroy the vessel, and—to our perceptions at any rate—nothing exists. Therefore, the Stanza puts it very correctly; "Universal Mind was not," because there was no vehicle to contain it.

[20]

Q. What are the higher powers which condition the Ah-hi?

A. They cannot be called powers; *power* or perhaps Potentiality would be better. The Ah-hi are conditioned by the awakening into manifestation of the periodical, universal LAW, which becomes successively active and inactive. It is by this law that they are conditioned or formed, not created. "Created" is an impossible term to use in Philosophy.

Q. Then the power or Potentiality which precedes and is higher than the Ah-hi, is the law which necessitates manifestation.

A. Just so; periodical manifestation. When the hour strikes, the law comes into action, and the Ah-hi appear on the first rung of the ladder of manifestation.

Q. But surely this is THE law and not A law?

A. Precisely, since it is absolute and "Secondless"— therefore it is not an attribute, but that Absoluteness itself.

Q. The great difficulty is to account for this law?

A. That would be trying to go beyond the first manifestation and supreme causality. It will take all our limited intellect to vaguely understand even the latter; try as we may, we can never, limited as we are, approach the Absolute, which is to us, at our present stage of mental development, merely a logical speculation, though dating back to thousands and thousands of years.

Q. With reference to the sloka under discussion, would not "cosmic mind" be a better term than "universal mind"?

A. No; cosmic mind appears at the third stage, or degree, and is confined or limited to the manifested universe. In the Purânas, Mahat (the "great" Principle of mind, or Intellect) appears only at the third of the Seven "Creations" or stages of evolution. Cosmic Mind is Mahat, or divine ideation in active (creative) operation, and thus only the periodical manifestation *in time* and *in actu* of the Eternal Universal Mind—*in potentia*.   In strict truth, Universal Mind, being only another name for the Absolute, *out of time and space*, this Cosmic Ideation, or Mind, is not an evolution at all (least of all a "creation"), but simply one of the aspects of the former, which knows no change, which ever was, which is, and will be.   Thus, I say again, the sloka implies that universal ideation was not, *i. e.*, did not exist for perception, because there were no minds to perceive it, since Cosmic Mind was still latent, or a mere potentiality.   As the stanzas speak of manifestation, we are compelled so to translate them, and not from any other standpoint.

Q.   We use the word "cosmic" as applied to the manifested universe in all its forms.   The sloka apparently does not refer to this, but to the first absolute Consciousness, or Non-consciousness, and seems to imply that the absolute consciousness could not be that universal mind because it was not, or could not be, expressed: there was, therefore, no expression for it.   But it may be objected that though there was no expression for it, still it was there.   Can we say that, like Sat, it was and was not?

A.   That will not help the interpretation.

Q.   When it is said that it was not, the idea conveyed then is that it was not in the Absolute?

A.   By no means; simply "it was not."

Q.   There seems to be a distinction, certainly; for if we could say "it was," it would be taking a very one-sided view of the idea of Sat, and equivalent to saying that Sat was BEING.   Still, someone may say that the phrase "Universal Mind was not," as it stands, suggests that it is a manifestation, but mind is not a manifestation.

A.   Mind, in the act of ideation, is a manifestation; but Universal Mind is not the same thing, as no conditioned and relative act can be predicted of that which is Absolute. Universal ideation was as soon as the Ah-hi appeared, and continues throughout the Manvantara.

Q. To what cosmic plane do the Ah-hi, here spoken of, belong?

A. They belong to the first, second, and third planes—the last plane being really the starting point of the primordial manifestation—the objective reflection of the unmanifested. Like the Pythagorean *Monas*, the first Logos, having emanated the first triad, disappears into silence and darkness.

Q. Does this mean that the three Logoi emanated from the primordial Radiation in Macrocosm correspond to Atma, Buddhi, and Manas, in the Microcosm?

A. Just so; they correspond, but must not be confounded with them. We are now speaking of the Macrocosm at the first flutter of Manvantaric dawn, when evolution begins, and not of Microcosm or Man.

Q. Are the three planes to which the three Logoi belong simultaneous emanations, or do they evolve one from another?

A. It is most misleading to apply mechanical laws to the higher metaphysics of cosmogony, or to space and time, as we know them, for neither existed then. The reflection of the triad in space and time, or the objective universe, comes later.

Q. Have the Ah-hi been men in previous Manvantaras, or will they become so?

A. Every living creature, of whatever description, was, is, or will become a human being in one or another Manvantara.

Q. But do they in this Manvantara remain permanently on the same very exalted plane during the whole period of the life-cycle?

A. If you mean by "life cycle" a duration of time which extends over fifteen figures, then my answer is most decidedly—no. The "Ah-hi" pass through all the planes, beginning to manifest on the third. Like all other Hierarchies, on the highest plane they are *arupa, i. e.,* formless, bodiless, without any substance, mere breaths. On the second plane, they first approach to Rupa, or form. On the third, they become Manasa-putras, those who become incarnated in man. With every plane they reach they are called by different names—there is a continual differentiation of their original homogeneous substance; we call it substance, although in reality it is no substance of which we can conceive. Later, they become Rupa—ethereal forms.

Q. Then the Ah-hi of this Manvantara . . . ?

A. Exist no longer; they have long ago become Planetary, Solar, Lunar, and lastly, incarnating Egos, for, as said, "they are the collective hosts of spiritual beings."

Q. But it was stated above that the Ah-hi did not become men in this Manvantara.

A. Nor do they as the formless "Ah-hi." But they do as their own transformation. The Manvantaras should not be confounded. The fifteen-figure Manvantaric cycle applies to the solar system; but there is a Manvantara which relates to the whole of the objective universe, the Mother-Father, and many minor Manvantaras. The slokas relating to the former have been generally selected, and only two or three relating to the latter given. Many slokas, therefore, have been omitted because of their difficult nature.

Q. Then, on reawakening, will the men of one Manvantara have to pass through a stage corresponding to the Ah-hi stage in the next Manvantara?

A. In some of the Manvantaras, the tail is in the mouth of the serpent. Think over this Symbolism.

Q. A man can choose what he will think about; can the analogy be be applied to the Ah-hi?

[24]

A. No; because a man has free will and the Ah-hi have none. They are obliged to act simultaneously, for the law under which they must act gives them the impulse. Free will can only exist in a Man who has both mind and consciousness, which act and make him perceive things both within and without himself. The "Ah-hi" are Forces, not human Beings.

Q. But are they not conscious agents in the work?

A. Conscious in as far as they act within the universal consciousness. But the consciousness of the Manasa-putra on the third plane is quite different. It is only then that they become *Thinkers*. Besides, Occultism, unlike modern Science, maintains that every atom of matter, when once differentiated, becomes endowed with *its own* kind of Consciousness. Every *cell* in the human body (as in every animal) is endowed with its own peculiar discrimination, instinct, and, speaking relatively, with intelligence.

Q. Can the Ah-hi be said to be enjoying bliss?

A. How can they be subject to bliss or non-bliss? Bliss can only be appreciated, and becomes such when suffering is known.

Q. But there is a distinction between happiness and bliss.

A. Granting that there may be, still there can be neither happiness nor bliss without a contrasting experience of suffering and pain.

Q. But we understand that bliss, as the state of the Absolute, was intended to be referred to.

A. This is still more illogical. How can the ABSOLUTE be said to *feel?* The Absolute can have no condition nor attribute. It is only that which is finite and differentiated which can have any feeling or attitude predicated of it.

[25]

Q. Then the Ah-hi cannot be said to be conscious intelligences, when intelligence is so complex?

A. Perhaps the term is erroneous, but owing to the poverty of European languages there seems to be no other choice.

Q. But perhaps a phrase would represent the idea more correctly? The term seems to mean a force which is a unity, not a complex action and reaction of several forces, which would be implied by the word "intelligence." The noumenal aspect of phenomenal force would perhaps better express the idea.

A. Or perhaps we may represent to ourselves the idea as a flame, a unity; the rays from this flame will be complex, each acting in its own straight line.

Q. But they only become complex when they find receptacles in lower forms.

A. Just so; still the Ah-hi are the flame from which the rays stream forth, becoming more and more differentiated as they fall deeper into matter, until they finally reach this world of ours, with its teeming millions of inhabitants and sensuous beings, and then they become truly complex.

Q. The Ah-hi, then, considered as a primary essence, would be unity? Can we regard them as such?

A. You may; but the strict truth is that they only proceed from unity, and are the first of its seven rays.

Q. Then can we call them the reflection of unity?

A. Are not the prismatic rays fundamentally one single white ray? From the one they become three; from the three, seven; from which seven primaries they fall into infinitude. Referring back to the so-called "consciousness" of the Ah-hi, that consciousness cannot be judged by the standard of human perceptions. It is on quite another plane.

Q. "During deep sleep, mind is not on the material plane"; is it therefore to be inferred that during this period mind is active on another plane? Is there any definition of the characteristics which distinguish mind in the waking state from mind during the sleep of the body?

A. There is, of course; but I do not think that a discussion upon it would be pertinent or useful now; suffice to say that often the reasoning faculty of the higher mind may be asleep, and the instinctual mind be fully awake. It is the physiological distinction between the cerebrum and the cerebellum; the one sleeps and the other is awake.

Q. What is meant by the term instinctual mind?

A. The instinctual mind finds expression through the cerebellum, and is also that of the animals. With man during sleep the functions of the cerebrum cease, and the cerebellum carries him on to the Astral plane, a still more unreal state than even the waking plane of illusion; for so we call this state which the majority of you think so real. And the Astral plane is still more deceptive, because it reflects indiscriminately the good and the bad, and is so chaotic.

Q. The fundamental conditions of the mind in the waking state are space and time: do these exist for the mind (*Manas*) during sleep of the physical body?

A. Not as we know them. Moreover, the answer depends on which *Manas* you mean—the higher or the lower. It is only the latter which is susceptible of hallucinations about space and time; for instance, a man in the dreaming state may live in a few seconds the events of a lifetime.* For the perceptions and apprehensions of the Higher Ego there is neither space nor time.

Q. *Manas* is said to be the vehicle of Buddhi, but the universal mind has been spoken of as a Maha-Buddhi. What then is the distinction between the terms *Manas* and Buddhi, employed in a universal sense, and *Manas* and Buddhi as manifested in man?

---

*See the discussion on dreams appended, p. 59.

A. Cosmic Buddhi, the emanation of the Spiritual Soul *Alaya,* is the vehicle of Mahat only when that Buddhi corresponds to Prakriti. Then it is called Maha-Buddhi. This Buddhi differentiates through seven planes, whereas the Buddhi in man is the vehicle of Atman, which vehicle is of the essence of the highest plane of Akasa and therefore does not differentiate. The difference between Manas and Buddhi in man is the same as the difference between the Manasa-Putra and the Ah-hi in Kosmos.

Q. Manas is mind, and the Ah-hi, it is said, can no more have any individual Mind, or that which we call mind, on this plane than Buddhi can. Can there be Consciousness without Mind?

A. Not on this plane of matter. But why not on some other and higher plane? Once we postulate a Universal Mind, both the brain, the mind's vehicle, and Consciousness, its faculty, must be quite different on a higher plane from what they are here. They are nearer to the *Absolute* ALL, and must therefore be represented by a substance infinitely more homogeneous; something *sui generis,* and entirely beyond the reach of our intellectual perceptions. Let us call or imagine it an incipient and incognizable state of primeval differentiation. On that higher plane, as it seems to me, Mahat—the great *Manvantaric* Principle of Intelligence— acts as a Brain, through which the Universal and Eternal Mind radiates the Ah-hi, representing the resultant Consciousness or ideation. As the shadow of this primordial *triangle* falls lower and lower through the descending planes, it becomes with every stage more material.

Q. It becomes the plane on which Consciousness perceives objective manifestations. Is it so?

A. Yes. But here we come face to face with the great problem of Consciousness, and shall have to fight Materialism. For what is Consciousness? According to modern

Science it is a faculty of the Mind like volition. We say so, too; but add that while Consciousness is not a thing *per se*, Mind is distinctly—in its Manvantaric functions at least—an Entity. Such is the opinion of all the Eastern Idealists.

Q. It is, however, the fashion nowadays to speak slightingly of the idea that the mind is an entity.

A. Nevertheless, mind is a term perfectly synonymous with Soul. Those who deny the existence of the latter will of course contend that there is no such thing as consciousness apart from brain, and at death consciousness ceases. Occultists, on the contrary, affirm that consciousness exists after death, and that then only the real consciousness and freedom of the Ego commences, when it is no longer impeded by terrestrial matter.

Q. Perhaps the former view arises from limiting the meaning of the term "consciousness" to the faculty of perception?

A. If so, occultism is entirely opposed to such a view.

Sloka (4). THE SEVEN WAYS TO BLISS (*Moksha or Nirvana*) WERE NOT.* THE GREAT CAUSES OF MISERY (*Nidâna and Maya*) WERE NOT, FOR THERE WAS NO ONE TO PRODUCE AND GET ENSNARED BY THEM.

Q. What are the seven ways to bliss?

A. They are certain faculties of which the student will know more when he goes deeper into occultism.

Q. Are the Four Truths of the Hinayâna School the same as those mentioned by Sir Edwin Arnold in "The Light of Asia"; the first of which is the Path of Sorrow; the second of Sorrow's cause; the third of Sorrow's ceasing; and the fourth is the WAY?

A. All this is theological and exoteric, and to be found in all the Buddhist scriptures; and the above seems to be taken from Singhalese or Southern Buddhism. The subject, how-

*Vide *The Voice of the Silence;* Fragment III, *The Seven Portals.*

ever, is far more fully treated of in the Aryasanga School. Still even there the four truths have one meaning for the regular priest of the Yellow Robe, and quite another for the real Mystics.

Q. Are Nidâna and Maya (the great causes of misery) aspects of the Absolute?

A. Nidâna means the concatenation of cause and effect; the twelve Nidânas are the enumeration of the chief causes which produce the severest reaction or effects under the Karmic law. Although there is no connection between the terms Nidâna and Maya in themselves, Maya being simply illusion, yet if we consider the universe as Maya or illusion, then certainly the Nidânas, as being moral agents in the universe, are included in Maya. It is Maya, illusion or ignorance, which awakens Nidânas; and the cause or causes having been produced, the effects follow according to Karmic law. To take an instance: we all regard ourselves as Units, although essentially we are one indivisible Unit, drops in the ocean of Being, not to be distinguished from other drops. Having then produced this cause, the whole discord of life follows immediately as an effect; in reality it is the endeavour of nature to restore harmony and maintain equilibrium. It is this sense of separateness which is the root of all evil.

Q. Perhaps it would therefore be better to separate the two terms, and state whether Maya is an aspect of the Absolute?

A. This can hardly be so, since Maya is the Cause, and at the same time an aspect, of differentiation, if of anything. Moreover, the Absolute can never be differentiated. Maya is a manifestation; the Absolute can have no manifestation, but only a reflection, a shadow which is radiated periodically from it—not *by* it.

Q. Yet Maya is said to be the Cause of manifestation or differentiation?

A. What of that? Certainly if there were no Maya there would be no differentiation; or, rather, no objective universe would be perceived. But this does not make of it an aspect of the Absolute, but simply something coeval and coexistent with the manifested Universe or the heterogeneous differentiation of pure Homogeneity.

Q. By a parity of reason, then, if no differentiation, no Maya? But we are speaking of Maya now as THE CAUSE of the Universe, so that the moment we get behind differentiation, we may ask ourselves—Where is Maya?

A. Maya is everywhere, and in every *thing* that has a beginning and an end; therefore, every *thing* is an *aspect* of that which is eternal, and in that sense, of course Maya itself is an aspect of SAT, or that which *is* eternally present in the universe, whether during Manvantara or Mahapralaya. Only remember that it has been said of even Nirvâna that it is only Maya when compared with the Absolute.

Q. Is then Maya a collective term for all manifestations?

A. I do not think this would explain the term. Maya is the perceptive faculty of every Ego which considers itself a Unit separate from, and independent of, the One infinite and eternal SAT, or "be-ness." Maya is explained in *exoteric* philosophy and the Purânas, as the personified active Will *of the Creative God*—the latter being but a personified *M a y a* himself—a passing deception of the senses of man, who began anthropomorphizing pure abstraction from the beginning of his speculations. Maya, in the conception of an orthodox Hindu, is quite different from the Maya of a Vedantin Idealist or an Occultist. The Vedanta states that Maya, or the deceptive influence of illusion alone, constitutes belief in the *real* existence of matter or anything differentiated. The Bhagavata Purâna identifies Maya with Prakriti (manifested nature and matter). Do not some advanced European metaphysicians, such as Kant, Schopen-hauer, and others, assert the same? Of course they got their ideas about it from the East—especially from Buddhism; yet the doctrine of the unreality of this Universe has been pretty correctly worked out by our philosophers—on general lines, at any rate. Now, although no two people can see things and objects in exactly the same way, and that each of us sees them in his own way, yet all labour more or less under illusions, and chiefly under the great illusion (Maya) that they are, as personalities, distinct beings from other beings, and that even their *Selves* or Egos will prevail in the eternity (or sempiternity, at any rate) as such; whereas not only we ourselves, but the whole visible and invisible universe, are only a temporary part of the one beginningless and endless WHOLE, or that which ever was, is, and will be.

Q. The term seems to apply to the complex points of differentiation: differentiation applying to the unit and Maya to the collection of units. But we may now put a side question.

With regard to the preceding part of the discussion, reference has been made to the cerebrum and cerebellum, and the latter described as the instinctual organ. An animal is supposed to have an instinctive mind; but the cerebellum is said to be simply the organ of vegetative life, and to control the functions of the body alone; whereas the sensual mind is the mind into which the senses open, and there can be no thought or ideation, nothing of which we predicate intellect or instinct anywhere, except in that part of the brain assigned to such functions, namely, the cerebrum.

A. However that may be, this cerebellum is the organ of instinctual animal functions, which reflect themselves in, or produce, dreams which for the most part are chaotic and inconsequent. Dreams, however, which are remembered, and present a sequence of events, are due to the vision of the higher Ego.

Q. Is not the cerebellum what we may call the organ of habit?

A. Being instinctual, it may very well be called so, I believe.

Q. Except that habit may be referred to what we may call the present stage of existence, and instinct to a past stage.

A. Whatever the name may be, the cerebellum alone— as you were already told (*vide "On Dreams," Appendix*)— functions during sleep, not the cerebrum; and the dreams, or emanations, or instinctive feelings, which we experience on waking, are the result of such activity.

Q. The consecutiveness is brought about entirely by the co-ordinating faculty. But surely the cerebrum also acts, a proof of which is that the nearer we approach the sleep-waking state the more vivid our dreams become.

A. Quite so, *when* you are waking; but not before. We may compare this state of the cerebellum to a bar of metal, or something of the same nature, which has been heated during the day and emanates or radiates heat during the night; so the energy of the brain radiates unconsciously during the night.

Q. Still we cannot say that the brain is incapable of registering impressions during sleep. A sleeping man can be awakened by a noise, and when awake will be frequently able to trace his dream to the impression caused by the noise. This fact seems to prove conclusively the brain's activity during sleep.

A. A mechanical activity certainly; if under such circumstances there is the slightest perception, or the least glimpse of the dream state, memory comes into play, and the dream can be reconstructed. In the discussion on dreams, the dream state passing into the waking state was compared to the embers of a dying fire; we may very well continue the simile, and compare the play of the memory to a current of air re-kindling them. That is to say that the waking consciousness recalls to activity the cerebellum, which was fading below the threshold of consciousness.

[33]

Q. But does the cerebellum ever cease functioning?

A. No; but it is lost in the functions of the cerebrum.

Q. That is to say that the stimuli which proceed from the cerebellum during waking life fall below the threshold of waking consciousness, the field of consciousness being entirely occupied by the cerebrum, and this continues till sleep supervenes, when the stimuli from the cerebellum begin in their turn to form the field of consciousness. It is not, therefore, correct to say that the cerebrum is the only seat of consciousness.

A. Quite so; the function of the cerebrum is to polish, perfect, or co-ordinate ideas, whereas that of the cerebellum produces conscious desires, and so on.

Q. Evidently we have to extend our idea of consciousness. For instance, there is no reason why a sensitive plant should not have consciousness. Du Prel, in his "Philosophie der Mystik," cites some very curious experiments showing a kind of local consciousness, perhaps a kind of reflex connection. He even goes further than this, demonstrating, from a large number of well authenticated cases, such as those of clairvoyants, who can perceive by the pit of the stomach, that the threshold of consciousness is capable of a very wide extension, far wider than we are accustomed to give to it, both upwards and downwards.

A. We may congratulate ourselves on the experiments of Du Prel as an antidote to the theories of Professor Huxley, which are absolutely irreconcileable with the teachings of occultism.

III.

STANZA I.—(*Continued*)

Sloka (5). DARKNESS ALONE FILLED THE BOUNDLESS ALL, FOR FATHER, MOTHER, AND SON WERE ONCE MORE ONE, AND THE SON HAD NOT AWAKENED YET FOR THE NEW WHEEL AND HIS PILGRIMAGE THEREON.

Q. Is "Darkness" the same as the "Eternal Parent Space" spoken of in Sloka (I)?

A. Not at all. Here "the boundless all" is the "Parent Space"; and Cosmic Space is something already with attributes, at least potentially. "Darkness," on the other hand, and in this instance, is that of which no attributes can be postulated: it is the Unknown Principle filling Cosmic Space.

Q. Is Darkness, then, used in the sense of the opposite pole to Light?

A. Yes, in the sense of the Unmanifested and the Unknown as the opposite pole to manifestation, and that which falls under the possibility of speculation.

Q. Darkness is not opposed to Light, then, but to differentiation; or rather, may it not be taken as the symbol of Negativeness?

A. The "Darkness" here meant can be opposed to neither Light nor Differentiation, as both are the legitimate effects of the Manvantaric evolution—the cycle of Activity. It is the "Darkness upon the face of the Deep," in *Genesis:* Deep being here "the bright son of the Dark Father"—Space.

Q. Is it that there is no Light or simply nothing to manifest and no one to perceive it?

[35]

A. Both. In the sense of objectivity, both light and darkness are illusions—*maya;* in this case, it is not Darkness as absence of Light, but as one incomprehensible primordial Principle, which, being Absoluteness itself, has for our intellectual perceptions neither form, colour, substantiality, nor anything that could be expressed by words.

Q. When does Light proceed from that Darkness?

A. Subsequently, when the first hour for manifestation strikes.

Q. Light, then, is the first manifestation?

A. It is, after differentiation has begun and at the third stage of evolution only. Bear in mind that in philosophy we use the word "light" in a dual sense: one to signify eternal, absolute light, *in potentia*, ever present in the bosom of the unknown Darkness, coexistent and coeval with the latter in Eternity, or in other words, identical with it; and the other as a Manifestation of heterogeneity and a contrast to it. For one who reads the Vishnu Purâna, for instance, understandingly, will find the difference between the two terms well expressed in Vishnu; one with Brahmâ, and yet distinct from him. There, Vishnu is the eternal x, and at the same time every term of the equation. He is Brahma (neuter) essentially matter and Spirit, which are Brahma's two primordial aspects—Spirit being the abstract light.* In the Vedas, however, we find Vishnu held in small esteem, and no mention made whatever of Brahmâ (the male).

Q. What is the meaning of the sentence, "Father, Mother and Son were once more one"?

_____

*In the second chapter of the Vishnu Purana (Wilson's translation) we read—"Parasara said: Glory to the unchangeable, holy, eternal supreme Vishnu, of one universal nature, the mighty over all: to him who is Hiranyagarbha, Hari, and Sankara, the creator, preserver, and destroyer of the world; to Vasudeva, the liberator of his worshippers; to him whose essence is both single and manifold; who is both subtile and corporeal, indiscrete and discrete; to Vishnu the cause of final emancipation. Glory to the Supreme Vishnu the cause of the creation, existence, and end of this world; who is the root of the world, and who consists of the world."

And again: "Who can describe him who is not to be apprehended by the senses: who is the best of all things; the supreme soul, self-existent: who is devoid of all the distinguishing characteristics of complexion, caste, or the like; and is exempt from birth, vicissitude, death or decay: who is always and alone: who exists everywhere, and in whom all things here exist; and who is thence named Vasudeva? He is Brahma (neuter), supreme, lord, eternal, unborn, imperishable, undecaying; of one essence; ever pure, as free from defects He, that Brahma was (is) all things; comprehending in his own nature the indiscrete and discrete.'"

A. It means that the three Logoi—the unmanifested "Father," the semi-manifested "Mother" and the Universe, which is the third *Logos* of our philosophy or Brahmâ, were during the (periodical) *pralaya* once more *one;* differentiated essence had rebecome undifferentiated. The sentence, "Father, Mother, and Son," is the antitype of the Christian type—Father, Son and Holy Ghost—the last of which was, in early Christianity and Gnosticism, the female "Sophia." It means that all creative and sensitive forces and the effects of such forces which constitute the universe had returned to their primordial state: *all* was merged into one. During the Mahapralayas naught but the Absolute is.

Q. What are the different meanings of Father, Mother and Son? In the Commentary, they are explained as (a) Spirit, Substance and Universe, (b) Spirit, Soul and Body, (c) Universe, Planetary Chain and Man.

A. I have just completed it with my extra definition, which is clear, I think. There is nothing to be added to this explanation, unless we begin to anthropomorphise abstract conceptions.

Q. Taking the last terms of the three series, do the ideas Son, Universe, Man, Body correspond with one another?

A. Of course they do.

Q. And are these terms produced from the remaining pair of terms of each trinity; for instance, the Son from the Father and Mother, the men from the Chain and the Universe, etc., etc., and finally in Pralaya is the Son merged back again into its parents?

A. Before the question is answered, you must be reminded that the period preceding so-called Creation is not spoken about; but only that when matter had begun to differentiate, but had not yet assumed form. Father-Mother is a compound term which means primordial Substance or Spirit-matter. When from Homogeneity it begins through differentiation to fall into Heterogeneity, it becomes positive and negative; thus from the "Zero-state" (or *layam*) it becomes active and passive, instead of the latter alone; and, in consequence of this differentiation (the resultant of which is evolution and the subsequent Universe),—the "Son" is produced, the Son being that same Universe, or manifested Kosmos, till a new *Mahapralaya*.

Q. Or—the ultimate state in *layam*, or in the zero point, as in the beginning before the stage of the Father, Mother and Son?

A. There is but slight reference to that which was before the Father-Mother period in the *Secret Doctrine*. If there is Father-Mother, there can, of course, be no such condition as Laya.

Q. Father, Mother are therefore later than the Laya condition?

A. Quite so; individual objects may be in Laya, but the Universe cannot be so when Father-Mother appears.

Q. Is Fohat one of the three, Father, Mother and Son?

A. Fohat is a generic term and used in many senses. He is the *light* (Daiviprakriti) of all the three *logoi*—the personified symbols of the three *spiritual stages* of Evolution. Fohat is the aggregate of all the spiritual creative ideations *above*, and of all the electro-dynamic and creative forces *below*, in Heaven and on Earth. There seems to be great confusion and misunderstanding concerning the First and Second Logos. The first is the already present yet still unmanifested potentiality in the bosom of Father-Mother; the Second is the abstract collectivity of creators called by the Greeks "Demiurgi" or the Builders of the Universe. The *third logos* is the ultimate differentiation of the Second and the individualization of Cosmic Forces, of which Fohat is the chief; for Fohat is the synthesis of the Seven Creative Rays or Dhyan Chohans which proceed from the third Logos.

Q. During Manvantara when the Son is in existence or awake, does the Father-Mother exist independently or only as manifested in the Son?

A. In using the terms Father, Mother, and Son, we should be on our guard against anthropomorphising the conception; the two former are simply centrifugal and centripetal forces and their product is the "Son"; moreover, it is impossible to exclude either of these factors from the conception in the Esoteric Philosophy.

Q. If so then comes this other point: it is possible to conceive of centripetal and centrifugal forces existing independently of the effects they produce. The effects are always regarded as secondary to the cause or causes.

A. But it is very doubtful whether such a conception can be maintained in, and applied to, our Symbology; if these forces exist they must be producing effects, and if the effects cease, the forces cease with them, for who can know of them?

Q. But they exist as separate entities for mathematical purposes, do they not?

A. That is a different thing; there is a great difference between nature and science, reality and philosophical symbolism. For the same reason we divide man into seven principles, but this does not mean that he has, as it were, seven skins, or entities, or souls. These principles are all aspects of one principle, and even this principle is but a temporary and periodical ray of the One eternal and infinite Flame or Fire.

Sloka (6). THE SEVEN SUBLIME LORDS AND THE SEVEN TRUTHS HAD CEASED TO BE, AND THE UNIVERSE, THE SON OF NECESSITY, WAS IMMERSED IN PARAN-ISHPANNA (*absolute perfection, Paranirvana, which is Yong-Grüb*), TO BE OUTBREATHED BY THAT WHICH IS AND YET IS NOT. NAUGHT WAS.

Sloka (7). THE CAUSES OF EXISTENCE HAD BEEN DONE AWAY WITH; THE VISIBLE THAT WAS, AND THE INVISIBLE THAT IS, RESTED IN ETERNAL NON-BEING, THE ONE BEING.

Q. If the "Causes of Existence" had been done away with, how did they come again into existence? It is stated in the Commentary that the chief cause of existence is "the desire to exist," but in the sloka, the universe is called the "son of necessity."

A. "The causes of existence had been done away with" refers to the last Manvantara, or age of Brahmâ, but the cause which makes the Wheel of Time and Space run into Eternity, which is out of Space and Time, has nothing to do with finite causes or what we call Nidânas. There seems to me no contradiction in the statements.

Q. There certainly is a contrast. If the causes of existence had been done away with, how did they come into existence again? But the answer removes the difficulty, for it is stated that one Manvantara had disappeared into Pralaya, and that the cause which led the previous Manvantara to exist is now behind the limits of Space and Time, and therefore causes another Manvantara to come into being.

A. Quite so. This one eternal and therefore "causeless cause" is immutable and has nothing to do with the causes on any of the planes which are concerned with finite and conditioned being. The cause can therefore by no means be a finite consciousness or desire. It is an absurdity to postulate desire or necessity of the Absolute; the striking of a clock does not suggest the desire of the clock to strike.

Q. But the clock is wound up, and needs a Winder?

A. The same may be said of the universe and this cause, the Absolute containing both clock and Winder, once it is the Absolute; the only difference is that the former is wound up in Space and Time and the latter out of Space and Time, that is to say in Eternity.

Q. The question really requests an explanation of the cause in the Absolute, of differentiation?

A. That is outside the province of legitimate speculation. Parabrahm is not a cause, neither is there any cause that can compel it to emanate or create. Strictly speaking, Parabrahm is not even the Absolute but *Absoluteness.* Parabrahm is not the cause, but the causality, or the propelling but not volitional power, in every manifesting Cause. We may have some hazy idea that there is such a thing as this eternal Causeless Cause or Causality. But to define it is impossible. In the *"Lectures on the Bhagavat Gîta,"* by Mr. Subba Row, it is stated that logically even the First Logos cannot cognize Parabrahm, but only Mulaprakriti, its veil. When, therefore, we have yet no clear idea of Mulaprakriti, the first basic aspect of Parabrahm, what can we know of that Supreme Total which is veiled by *Mulaprakriti* (the root of nature or Prakriti) even to the Logos.

Q. What is the meaning of the expression in sloka (7), "the visible that was, and the invisible that is"?

A. "The visible that was" means the universe of the past Manvantara which had passed into Eternity and was no more. "The invisible that is" signifies the eternal, ever-present and ever-invisible deity, which we call by many names, such as abstract Space, Absolute Sat, etc., and know in reality, nothing about it.

Sloka (8). ALONE THE ONE FORM OF EXISTENCE STRETCHED, BOUNDLESS, INFINITE, CAUSELESS, IN DREAMLESS SLEEP; AND LIFE PULSATED UNCONSCIOUS IN UNIVERSAL SPACE, THROUGHOUT THAT ALL-PRESENCE WHICH IS SENSED BY THE "OPENED EYE" OF THE DANGMA.

Q. Does the "Eye" open upon the Absolute: or are the "one form of existence" and the "All-Presence" other than the Absolute, or various names for the same Principle?

[41]

A. It is all one, of course; simply metaphorical expressions. Please notice that the "Eye" is not said to "*see*"; it only "sensed" the "All-Presence."

Q. It is through this "Eye" then, that we receive such sense, or feeling, or consciousness?

A. Through that "Eye," most decidedly; but then one must have such an "Eye" before he can see, or become a *Dangma*, or a Seer.

Q. The highest spiritual faculty, presumably?

A. Very well; but where, at that stage, was the happy possessor of it? There was no Dangma to sense the "All-Presence," because there were as yet no men.

Q. With reference to sloka (6), it was stated that the cause of Light was Darkness?

A. Darkness has, here again, to be read in a metaphorical sense. It is Darkness most unquestionably to our intellect, inasmuch as we can know nothing of it. I told you already that neither Darkness nor Light are to be used in the sense of opposites, as in the differentiated world. Darkness is the term which will give rise to least misconceptions. For instance, if the term "Chaos" were used, it would be liable to be confounded with chaotic matter.

Q. The term light was, of course, never used for physical light?

A. Of course not. Here light is the first potentiality awakening from its *laya* condition to become a potency; it is the first flutter in undifferentiated matter which throws it into objectivity and into a plane from which will start manifestation.

Q. Later on in the "Secret Doctrine" it is stated that light is made visible by darkness, or rather that darkness exists originally, and that that light is the result of the presence of objects to reflect it, that is of the objective world. Now if we take a globe of water and pass an electric beam through it, we shall find that this beam is invisible, unless there are opaque particles in the water, in which case, specks of light will be seen.   Is this a good analogy?

A.   It is a very fair illustration, I believe.

Q.   Is not Light a differentiation of vibration?

A.   So we are told in Science; and Sound is also.   And so we see that the senses are to a certain extent interchangeable. How would you account, for instance, for the fact that in trance a clairvoyant can read a letter, sometimes placed on the forehead, at the soles of the feet, or on the stomach-pit?

Q.   That is extra sense.

A.   Not at all; it is simply that the sense of seeing can be interchanged with the sense of touch.

Q.   But is not the sense of perception the beginning of the sixth sense?

A.   That is going beyond the present case, which is simply the interchanging of the senses of touch and sight.   Such clairvoyants, however, will not be able to tell the contents of a letter which they have not seen or been brought into contact with; this requires the exercise of the sixth sense; the former is an exercise of senses on the physical plane, the latter of a sense on a higher plane.

Q.   It seems very probable from physiology that every sense may be resolved into the sense of touch, which may be called the co-ordinating sense.   This deduction is made from embryological research, which shows that the sense of touch is the first and primary sense, and that all the rest are evolved from it.   All the senses, therefore, are more highly specialised or differentiated forms of touch.

A.   This is not the view of Eastern philosophy; in the *Anugita*, we read of a conversation between "Brahman" and his wife concerning the senses; seven are spoken of, "mind and understanding" being the other two, according to Mr.

[43]

Trimbak Telang and Professor Max Müller's translation; these terms, however, do not convey the correct meaning of the Sanskrit terms. Now, the first sense, according to the Hindus, is connected with sound. This can hardly be the the sense of touch.

Q. By touch most probably sensibility, or some sense medium, is meant?

A. In the Eastern philosophy, however, the sense of sound is first manifested, and next the sense of sight, sounds passing into colours. Clairvoyants can *see* sounds and detect every note and modulation far more distinctly than they would by the ordinary sense of sound—vibration, or hearing.

Q. Is it, then, that sound is perceived as a sort of rhythmic movement?

A. Yes; and such vibrations can be seen at a greater distance than they can be heard.

Q. But supposing the physical hearing were stopped, and a person perceived sounds clairvoyantly, could not this sensation be translated into clairaudience as well?

A. One sense must certainly merge at some point into the other. So also sound can be translated into taste. There are sounds which taste exceedingly acid in the mouths of some sensitives, while others generate the taste of sweetness, in fact, the whole scale of senses is susceptible of correlations.

Q. Then there must be the same extension of the sense of smell?

A. Very naturally, as has been already shown before. The senses are interchangeable once we admit correlation. Moreover they can all be intensified or modified very considerably. You will now understand the reference in the *Vedas* and *Upanishads*, where sounds are said to be perceived.

Q. There was a curious story in the last number of Harper's Magazine of a tribe on an island in the South Seas which have virtually lost the art and habit of speaking and conversing. Yet, they appeared to understand one another and see plainly what each other thought.

A. Such a "Palace of Truth" would hardly suit modern society. However, it was by just such means that the early races are said to have communicated with one another, thought taking an objective form, before speech developed into a distinct spoken language. If so, then there must have been a period in the evolution of the human races when the whole Humanity was composed of sensitives and clairvoyants.

IV.

Q. With reference to sloka (6), where it speaks of the "Seven Lords," since confusion is apt to arise as to the correct application of the terms, what is the distinction between Dhyan-Chohans, Planetary Spirits, Builders and Dhyani-Buddhas?

A. As an additional two volumes of the *Secret Doctrine* would be required to explain all the Hierarchies; therefore, much relating to them has been omitted from the Stanzas and Commentaries. A short definition may, however, be tried. Dhyan-Chohan is a generic term for all Devas, or celestial beings. A Planetary Spirit is a Ruler of a planet, a kind of finite or personal god. There is a marked difference, however, between the Rulers of the Sacred Planets and the Rulers of a small "chain" of worlds like our own. It is no serious objection to say that the earth has, nevertheless, six invisible companions and four different planes, as every other planet, for the difference between them is vital in many a point. Say what one may, our Earth was never numbered among the seven *sacred* planets of the ancients, though in exoteric, popular astrology it stood as a substitute for a secret planet now lost to astronomy, yet well known to initiated specialists. Nor were the Sun or the Moon in that number, though accepted in our day by modern astrology; for the Sun is a Central *Star*, and the Moon a dead planet.

Q. Were none of the six globes of the "terrene" chain numbered among the sacred planets?

A. None. The latter were all planets on *our* plane, and some of them have been discovered later.

Q. Can you tell us something of the planets for which the Sun and the Moon were substitutes?

A. There is no secret in it, though our modern astrologers are ignorant of these planets. One is an intra-Mercurial planet, which is supposed to have been discovered, and named by anticipation Vulcan, and the other a planet with a retrograde motion, sometimes visible at a certain hour of night and apparently near the moon. The occult influence of this planet is transmitted by the moon.

Q. What is it that made these planets sacred or secret?

A. Their occult influences, as far as I know.

Q. Then do the Planetary Spirits of the Seven Sacred Planets belong to another hierarchy than to that of the earth?

A. Evidently; since the terrestrial spirit of the earth is not of a very high grade. It must be remembered that the planetary spirit has nothing to do with the spiritual man, but with things of matter and cosmic beings. The gods and rulers of our Earth are cosmic Rulers; that is to say, they form into shape and fashion cosmic matter, for which they were called *Cosmocratores.* They never had any concern with spirit; the Dhyani-Buddhas, belonging to quite a different hierarchy, are especially concerned with the latter.

Q. These seven Planetary Spirits have therefore nothing really to do with the earth except incidentally?

A. On the contrary, the "Planetary"—who are not the Dhyani-Buddhas—have everything to do with the earth, physically and morally. It is they who rule its destinies and the fate of men. They are Karmic agencies.

Q. Have they anything to do with the fifth principle—the higher Manas?

A. No: they have no concern with the three higher principles; they have, however, something to do with the fourth. To recapitulate, therefore; the term "Dhyan-Chohan" is a generic name for all celestial beings. The "Dhyani-Buddhas" are concerned with the human higher triad in a mysterious way that need not be explained here. The "Builders" are a class called, as I already explained, *Cosmocratores*, or the invisible but intelligent Masons, who fashion matter according to the ideal plan ready for them in that which we call Divine and Cosmic Ideation. They were called by the early Masons the "Grand Architect of the Universe" *collectively:* but now the modern Masons make of their G. A. O. T. U. a personal and singular Deity.

Q. Are they not also Planetary Spirits?

A. In a sense they are—as the Earth is also a Planet—but of a lower order.

Q. Do they act under the guidance of the Terrestrial Planetary Spirit?

A. I have just said that they were collectively that Spirit themselves. I wish you to understand that they are not an Entity, a kind of a personal God, but Forces of nature acting under one immutable Law, on the nature of which it is certainly useless for us to speculate.

Q. But are there not Builders of Universes, and Builders of Systems, as there are Builders of our earth?

A. Assuredly there are.

Q. Then the terrestrial Builders are a Planetary "Spirit" like the rest of them, only inferior in kind?

A. I would certainly say so.

Q. Are they inferior according to the size of the planet or inferior in quality?

A. The latter, as we are taught. You see the ancients lacked our modern, and especially theological, conceit, which makes of this little speck of mud of ours something ineffably grander than any of the stars and planets known to

[49]

us. If, for instance, Esoteric Philosophy teaches that the "Spirit" (collectively again) of Jupiter is far superior to the Terrestrial Spirit, it is not because Jupiter is so many times larger than our earth, but because its substance and texture are so much finer than, and superior to, that of the earth. And it is in proportion to this quality that the Hierarchies of respective "Planetary Builders" reflect and act upon the ideations they find planned for them in the Universal Consciousness, the real great Architect of the Universe.

Q. The Soul of the World, or "Anima Mundi"?

A. Call it so, if you like. It is the Antitype of these Hierarchies, which are its differentiated types. The one *impersonal* Great Architect of the Universe is MAHAT, the Universal Mind. And Mahat is a symbol, an abstraction, an aspect which assumed a hazy entitative form in the all-materializing conceptions of men.

Q. What is the real difference between the Dhyani-Buddhas in the orthodox and the esoteric conceptions?

A. A very great one philosophically. They are—as higher Devas—called by the Buddhists, Bôdhisatvas. Exoterically they are five in number, whereas in the esoteric schools they are seven, and not single Entities but *Hierarchies.* It is stated in the *Secret Doctrine* that five Buddhas have come and that two are to come in the sixth and seventh races. Exoterically their president is Vajrasattva, the "Supreme Intelligence" or "Supreme Buddha," but more transcendant still is Vajradhara, even as Parabrahm transcends Brahmâ or Mahat. Thus the exoteric and occult significations of the Dhyani-Buddhas are entirely different. Exoterically each is a trinity, three in one, all three manifesting simultaneously in three worlds—as a human Buddha on earth, a Dhyani-Buddha in the world of astral forms, and an arupa, or formless, Buddha in the highest Nirvanic realm. Thus for a human Buddha, an incarnation of one of these Dhyanis, the stay on earth is limited from seven to seven thousand years in various bodies, since as men they are subjected to normal conditions, accidents and death. In Esoteric philosophy, on the other hand, this means that only five out of the "Seven Dhyani-Buddhas" —or, rather, the Seven Hierarchies of these Dhyanis, who, in Buddhist mysticism, are identical with the higher incarnating Intelligences, or the Kumâras of the Hindus—five only have hitherto appeared on earth in regular succession of incarnations, the last two having to come during the sixth and seventh Root-Races. This is, again, semi-allegorical, if not entirely so. For the sixth and seventh Hierarchies have been already incarnated on this earth together with the rest. But as they have reached "Buddhaship," so called, almost from the beginning of the fourth Root-Race, they are said to rest since then in conscious bliss and freedom till the beginning of the Seventh Round, when they will lead Humanity as a new race of Buddhas. These Dhyanis are connected only with Humanity, and, strictly speaking, only with the highest "principles" of men.

Q. Do the Dhyani-Buddhas and the Planetary Spirits in charge of the globes go into pralaya when their planets enter that state?

A. Only at the end of the seventh Round, and not between each round, for they have to watch over the working of the laws during these minor pralayas. Fuller details on this subject have already been written in the third volume of the *Secret Doctrine.* But all these differences in fact are merely functional, for they are all aspects of one and the same Essence.

Q. Does the hierarchy of Dhyanis, whose province it is to watch over a Round, watch during its period of activity, over the whole series of globes, or only over a particular globe?

A. There are incarnating and there are watching Dhyanis. Of the functions of the former you have just been told; the latter appear to do their work in this wise. Every class or hierarchy corresponds to one of the Rounds, the first and lowest hierarchy to the first and less developed Round, the second to the second, and so on till the seventh Round is reached, which is under the supervision of the highest Hierarchy of the Seven Dhyanis. At the last, they will appear on earth, as also will some of the Planetary, for the whole humanity will have become Bodhisatvas, their own "sons," *i. e.*, the "Sons" of their own Spirit and Essence or—themselves. Thus there is only a functional difference between the Dhyanis and the Planetary. The one are entirely divine, the other *sidereal.* The former only are called *Anupadaka*, parentless, because they radiated directly from that which is neither Father nor Mother but the unmanifested Logos. They are, in fact, the spiritual aspect of the seven Logoi; and the Planetary Spirits are in their totality, as the seven Sephiroth (the three higher being super-cosmic abstractions and *blinds* in the Kabala), and constitute the Heavenly man, or Adam Kadmon; *Dhyani* is a generic name in Buddhism, an abbreviation for all the gods. Yet it must be ever remembered that though they are "gods," still they are not to be worshipped.

Q. Why not, if they are gods?

A. Because Eastern philosophy rejects the idea of a personal and extra-cosmic deity. And to those who call this *atheism*, I would say the following. It is illogical to worship one such god, for, as said in the Bible, "There be Lords many and Gods many." Therefore, *if* worship is desirable, we have to choose either the worship of many gods, each being no better or less limited than the other, viz., polytheism and idolatry, or choose, as the Israelites have done, one tribal or racial god from among them, and while believing in the existence of many gods, ignore and show contempt for the others, regarding our own as the highest and the "God of Gods." But this is logically unwarrantable, for such a god can be neither infinite nor absolute, but must be finite, that is to say, limited and conditioned by space and time. With the Pralaya the tribal god disappears, and Brahmâ and all the other Devas, and the gods are merged into the Absolute. Therefore, occultists do not worship or offer prayers to them, because if we did, we should have either to worship many gods, or pray to the Absolute, which, having no attributes, can have no ears to hear us. The worshipper even of many gods must of necessity be unjust to all the other gods; however far he extends his worship it is simply impossible for him to worship each severally; and in his ignorance, if he choose out any one in particular, he may by no means select the most perfect. Therefore, he would do better far to remember that every man has a god within, a direct ray from the Absolute, the celestrial ray from the One; that he has his "god" *within*, not outside, of himself.

Q. Is there any name that can be applied to the planetary Hierarchy or spirit, which watches over the entire evolution of our own globe, such as Brahmâ for instance?

A. None, except the generic name, since it is a septenary and a Hierarchy; unless, indeed, we call it as some Kabalists do—"the Spirit of the Earth."

Q. It is very difficult to remember all these infinite Hierarchies of gods.

A. Not more so than to a chemist to remember the endless symbols of chemistry, if he is a Specialist. In India, alone, however, there are over 300 millions of gods and goddesses. The Manus and Rishis are also planetary gods, for they are said to have appeared at the beginning of the hu-

[53]

man races to watch over their evolution, and to have incarnated and descended on earth subsequently in order to teach mankind. Then, there are the *Sapta Rishis*, the "Seven Rishis," said exoterically to reside in the constellation of the Great Bear. There are also planetary gods.

Q. Are they higher than Brahmâ?

A. It depends in what aspect one views Brahmâ. In esoteric philosophy he is the synthesis of the seven *logoi*. In exoteric theology he is an aspect of Vishnu with the Vaishnevas, with others something else, as in the *Trimurti*, the Hindu Trinity, he is the chief creator, whereas Vishnu is the Preserver, and Siva the Destroyer. In the Kabala he is certainly Adam Kadmon—the "male-female" man of the first chapter of *Genesis*. For the Manus proceed from Brahmâ as the Sephiroth proceed from Adam Kadmon, and they are also *seven* and *ten*, as circumstances require.

But we may just as well pass on to another Sloka of the Stanzas you want explained.

Sloka (9). BUT WHERE WAS DANGMA WHEN THE ALAYA OF THE UNIVERSE (*Soul as the basis of all, Anima Mundi*) WAS IN PARAMARTHA (*Absolute Being and Consciousness which are Absolute Non-Being and Unconsciousness*) AND THE GREAT WHEEL WAS ANUPADAKA.

Q. Does "Alaya" mean that which is never manifested and dissolved, and is it derived from "a," the negative particle, and "*laya*"?

A. If it is so etymologically—and I am certainly not prepared to answer you one way or the other—it would mean the reverse, since *laya* itself is just that which is not manifested; therefore it would signify *that which is not unmanifested* if anything. Whatever may be the etymological vivisection of the word, it is simply the "Soul of the World," *Anima Mundi*. This is shown by the very wording of the

Sloka, which speaks of Alaya being in *Paramartha—i. e.*, in Absolute Non-Being and Unconsciousness, being at the same time absolute perfection or Absoluteness itself. This word, however, is the bone of contention between Yogachârya and the Madhyamika schools of Northern Buddhism. The scholasticism of the latter makes of *Paramartha (Satya)* something dependent on, and, therefore, relative to other things, thereby vitiating the whole metaphysical philosophy of the word Absoluteness. The other school very rightly denies this interpretation.

Q. Does not the Esoteric Philosophy teach the same doctrines as the Yogachârya School?

A. Not quite. But let us go on.

STANZA II.

Sloka (1). . . . WHERE WERE THE BUILDERS, THE LUMINOUS SONS OF MANVANTARIC DAWN? . . . IN THE UNKNOWN DARKNESS, IN THEIR AH-HI (*Chohanic, Dhyani-Buddhic*) PARANISHPANNA, THE PRODUCERS OF FORM (*rupa*) FROM NO-FORM (*arupa*), THE ROOT OF THE WORLD—THE DEVAMATRI AND SVABHAVAT, RESTED IN THE BLISS OF NON-BEING.

Q. Are the "luminous sons of manvantaric dawn" perfected human spirits of the last Manvantara, or are they on their way to humanity in this or a subsequent Manvantara?

A. In this case, which is that of a *Maha*-manvantara after a *Maha*-pralaya, they are the latter. They are the primordial seven rays from which will emanate in their turn all the other luminous and non-luminous lives, whether Archangels, Devils, men or apes. Some have been and some will only now become human beings. It is only after the differentiation of the seven rays and after the seven forces of nature have taken them in hand and worked upon them, that they become cornerstones, or rejected pieces of clay.

Everything, therefore, is in these seven rays, but it is impossible to say at this stage in which, because they are not yet differentiated and individualized.

Q. In the following passage:—

"The 'Builders,' the 'Sons of Manvantaric Dawn,' are the real creators of the Universe; and in this doctrine, which deals only with our Planetary System, they, as the architects of the latter, are also called the 'Watchers' of the Seven Spheres, which exoterically are the seven planets, and esoterically the seven earths or spheres (planets) or our chain also."

By planetary system is the solar system meant or the chain to which our earth belongs?

A. The Builders are those who build and fashion things into a form. The term is equally applied to the Builders of the Universe and to the small globes like those of our chain. By planetary system our solar system alone is meant.

Sloka (2). WHERE WAS SILENCE? WHERE WERE THE EARS TO SENSE IT? NO! THERE WAS NEITHER SILENCE NOR SOUND.

Q. With reference to the following passage:—

"The idea that things can cease to exist and still BE, is a fundamental one in Eastern psychology. Under the apparent contradiction in terms, there rests a fact in Nature to realize which in the mind, rather than to argue about words is the important thing. A familiar instance of a similar paradox is afforded by chemical combination. The question whether Hydrogen and Oxygen cease to exist, when they combine to form water, is still a moot one."*

Would it be correct to say that what we perceive is a different "element" of the same substance? For example, when a substance is in the gaseous state, could we say that it is the element Air which is perceived, and that when combined to form water, oxygen and hydrogen appear under the guise of the Element Water, and when in the solid state, ice, we then perceive the element Earth?

A. The ignorant judge of all things by their appearance and not by what they are in reality. On this earth, of

---

*S. D., Vol. I, p. 54.

course, water is an element quite distinct from any other element, using the latter term in the sense of different manifestations of the one element. The root elements, Earth, Water, Air, Fire, are far more comprehensive states of differentiation. Such being the case, in Occultism Transubstantiation becomes a possibility, seeing that nothing which exists is in reality that which it is supposed to be.

Q. But oxygen which is usually found in its gaseous state, may be liquified and even solidified. When oxygen, then, is found in the gaseous condition, is it the occult element Air which is perceived, and when in the liquid condition the element Water, and in the solid state the element Earth?

A. Most assuredly: we have first of all the Element Fire, not the common fire, but the Fire of the Mediæval Rosicrucians, the one flame, the fire of Life. In differentiation this becomes fire in different aspects. Occultism easily disposes of the puzzle as to whether oxygen and hydrogen cease to exist when combined to form water. Nothing that is in the Universe can disappear from it. For the time being, then, these two gases when combined to form water, are *in abscondito*, but have not ceased to *be*. For, had they been annihilated, Science, by decomposing the water again into oxygen and hydrogen, would have created something out of nothing, and would, therefore, have no quarrel with Theology. Therefore, water is an element, if we choose to call it so, on this plane only. In the same way, oxygen and hydrogen in their turn can be split up into other more subtle elements, all being differentiations of one element or universal essence.

Q. Then all substances on the physical plane are really so many correlations or combinations of these root elements, and ultimately of the one element?

A. Most assuredly. In occultism it is always best to proceed from universals to particulars.

Q. Apparently, then, the whole basis of occultism lies in this, that there is latent within every man a power which can give him true knowledge, a power of perception of truth, which enables him to deal first hand with universals if he will be strictly logical and face the facts. Thus we can proceed from universals to particulars by this innate spiritual force which is in every man.

A. Quite so: this power is inherent in all, but paralyzed by our methods of education, and especially by the Aristotelian and Baconian methods. Hypothesis now reigns triumphant.

Q. It is curious to read Schopenhauer and Hartmann and mark how, step by step, by strict logic and pure reason, they have arrived at the same bases of thought that had been centuries ago adopted in India, especially by the Vedantin System. It may, however, be objected that they have arrived at this by the inductive method. But in Schopenhauer's case at any rate it was not so. He acknowledges himself that the idea came to him like a flash; having thus got his fundamental idea he set to work to arrange his facts, so that the reader imagines that what was in reality an intuitive idea, is a logical deduction drawn from the facts.

A. This is not only true of the Schopenhauerian philosophy, but also of all the great discoveries of modern times. How, for instance, did Newton discover the law of gravity? Was it not by the simple fall of an apple, and not by an elaborate series of experiments. The time will come when the Platonic method will not be so entirely ignored and men will look with favour on methods of education which will enable them to develop this most spiritual faculty.

APPENDIX.

[The following is the Summary of the teachings during several meetings which preceded the Transactions of the "Blavatsky Lodge of the T. S." when the explanations of the *stanzas* from the "Secret Doctrine" became incorporated in a regular series of instructions.]

DREAMS.

Q. What are the "principles" which are active during dreams?

A. The "principles" active during ordinary dreams—which ought to be distinguished from real dreams, and called idle visions—are *Kama*, the seat of the personal Ego and of desire awakened into chaotic activity by the slumbering reminiscences of the lower Manas.

Q. What is the "lower Manas"?

A. It is usually called the animal soul (the *Nephesh* of the Hebrew Kabalists). It is the ray which emanates from the Higher Manas or permanent Ego, and is that "principle" which forms the human mind—in animals instinct, for animals also dream.* The combined action of Kama and the "animal soul," however, is purely mechanical. It is instinct, not reason, which is active in them. During the sleep of the body they receive and send out mechanically electric shocks to and from various nerve-centres. The brain is hardly impressed by them, and memory stores them, of course, without order or sequence. On waking these impressions gradually fade out, as does every fleeting shadow that has no basic or substantial reality underlying it. The retentive faculty of the brain, however, may register and preserve them if they are only impressed strongly enough. But, as a rule, our memory registers only the fugitive and

---

*The word dream means really "to slumber"—the latter function being called in Russian *"dreamatj."*—ED.

distorted impressions which the brain receives at the moment of awakening. This aspect of "dreams," however, has been sufficiently observed and is described correctly enough in modern physiological and biological works, as such human dreams do not differ much from those of the animals. That which is entirely *terra incognita* for Science is the real dreams and experiences of the higher EGO, which are also called dreams, but ought not to be so termed, or else the term for the other sleeping "visions" changed.

Q. How do these differ?

A. The nature and functions of real dreams cannot be understood unless we admit the existence of an immortal Ego in mortal man, independent of the physical body, for the subject becomes quite unintelligible unless we believe— that which is a fact—that during sleep there remains only an animated form of clay, whose powers of independent thinking are utterly paralyzed.

But if we admit the existence of a higher or permanent *Ego* in us—which Ego must not be confused with what we call the "Higher Self," we can comprehend that what we often regard as dreams, generally accepted as idle fancies, are, in truth, stray pages torn out from the life and experiences of the *inner* man, and the dim recollection of which at the moment of awakening becomes more or less distorted by our physical memory. The latter catches mechanically a few impressions of the thoughts, facts witnessed, and deeds performed by the *inner* man during its hours of complete freedom. For our *Ego* lives its own separate life within its prison of clay whenever it becomes free from the trammels of matter, *i. e.*, during the sleep of the physical man. This Ego it is which is the actor, the real man, the true human self. But the physical man cannot feel or be conscious during dreams; for the personality, the outer man, with its brain and thinking apparatus, are paralyzed more or less completely.

We might well compare the real Ego to a prisoner, and the physical personality to the gaoler of his prison. If the gaoler falls asleep, the prisoner escapes, or, at least, passes outside the walls of his prison. The gaoler is half asleep, and looks nodding all the time out of a window, through which he can catch only occasional glimpses of his prisoner, as he would a kind of shadow moving in front of it. But what can he perceive, and what can he know of the real actions, and especially the thoughts, of his charge?

Q. Do not the thoughts of the one impress themselves upon the other?

A. Not during sleep, at all events; for the real Ego does not think as his evanescent and temporary personality does. During the waking hours the thoughts and Voice of the Higher Ego do or do not reach his gaoler—the physical man, for they are the *Voice of his Conscience*, but during his sleep they are absolutely the "Voice in the desert." In the thoughts of the *real* man, or the immortal "Individuality," the pictures and visions of the Past and Future are as the Present; nor are his thoughts like ours, subjective pictures in our cerebration, but living acts and deeds, present actualities. They are realities, even as they were when speech expressed in sounds did not exist; when thoughts were things and men did not need to express them in speeches; for they instantly realised themselves in action by the power of *Kriya-Sakti*, that mysterious power which transforms instantaneously ideas into visible forms, and these were as objective to the "man" of the early *third* Race as objects of sight are now to us.

Q. How, then, does Esoteric Philosophy account for the transmission of even a few fragments of those thoughts of the Ego to our physical memory which it sometimes retains?

[61]

A. All such are reflected on the brain of the sleeper, like outside shadows on the canvas walls of a tent, which the occupier sees as he wakes. Then the man thinks that he has dreamed all that, and feels as though *he* had lived through something, while in reality it is the *thought-actions* of the true Ego which he has dimly perceived. As he becomes fully awake, his recollections become with every minute more distorted, and mingle with the images projected from the physical brain, under the action of the stimulus which causes the sleeper to awaken. These recollections, by the power of association, set in motion various trains of ideas.

Q. It is difficult to see how the Ego can be acting during the night things which have taken place long ago. Was it not stated that dreams are not subjective?

A. How can they be subjective when the dream state is itself for us, and on our plane, at any rate, a subjective one? To the dreamer (the Ego), on his own plane, the things on that plane are as objective to him as our acts are to us.

Q. What are the senses which act in dreams?

A. The senses of the sleeper receive occasional shocks, and are awakened into mechanical action; what he hears and sees are, as has been said, a distorted reflection of the thoughts of the Ego. The latter is highly spiritual, and is linked very closely with the higher principles, Buddhi and Atma. These higher principles are entirely inactive or our plane, and the higher Ego (*Manas*) itself is more or less dormant during the waking of the physical man. This is especially the case with persons of very materialistic mind. So dormant are the Spiritual faculties, because the Ego is so trammelled by matter, that *It* can hardly give all its attention to the man's actions, even should the latter commit sins for which that Ego—when reunited with its *lower* Manas—will have to suffer conjointly in the future. It is, as I said, the impressions projected into the physical man by this Ego which constitute what we call "conscience"; and in proportion as the Personality, the lower Soul (or *Manas*), unites itself to its higher consciousness, or EGO, does the action of the latter upon the life of mortal man become more marked.

Q. This Ego, then, is the "Higher Ego"?

A. Yes; it is the higher Manas illuminated by Buddhi; the principle of self-consciousness, the "I-am-I," in short. It is the Karana-Sarira, the immortal man, which passes from one incarnation to another.

Q. Is the "register" or "tablet of memory" for the true dream-state different from that of waking life?

A. Since dreams are in reality the actions of the Ego during physical sleep, they are, of course, recorded on their own plane and produce their appropriate effects on this one. But it must be always remembered that dreams in general, and as we know them, are simply our waking and hazy recollections of these facts.

It often happens, indeed, that we have no recollection of having dreamt at all, but later in the day the remembrance of the dream will suddenly flash upon us. Of this there are many causes. It is analogous to what sometimes happens to every one of us. Often a sensation, a smell, even a casual noise, or a sound, brings instantaneously to our mind long-forgotten events, scenes and persons. Something of what was seen, done, or thought by the "night-performer," the Ego, impressed itself at that time on the physical brain, but was not brought into the conscious, waking memory, owing to some physical condition or obstacle. This impression is registered on the brain in its appropriate cell or nerve centre, but owing to some accidental circumstance it "hangs fire," so to say, till something gives it the needed impulse. Then the brain slips it off immediately into the conscious memory of the waking man; for as soon as the conditions required are supplied, that particular centre starts forthwith into activity, and does the work which it had to do, but was hindered at the time from completing.

Q. How does this process take place?

A. There is a sort of conscious telegraphic communication going on incessantly, day and night, between the physical brain and the inner man. The brain is such a complex thing, both physically and metaphysically, that it is like a tree whose bark you can remove layer by layer, each layer being different from all the others, and each having its own special work, function, and properties.

Q. What distinguishes the "dreaming" memory and imagination from those of waking consciousness?

A. During sleep the physical memory and imagination are of course passive, because the dreamer is asleep: his brain is asleep, his memory is asleep, all his functions are dormant and at rest. It is only when they are stimulated, as I told you, that they are aroused. Thus the consciousness of the sleeper is not active, but passive. The inner man, however, the real Ego, acts independently during the sleep of the body; but it is doubtful if any of us—unless thoroughly acquainted with the physiology of occultism—could understand the nature of its action.

Q. What relation have the Astral Light and Akâsa to memory?

A. The former is the "tablet of the memory" of the animal man, the latter of the spiritual Ego. The "dreams" of the Ego, as much as the acts of the physical man, are all recorded, since both are actions based on causes and producing results. Our "dreams," being simply the waking state and actions of the true Self, must be, of course, recorded somewhere. Read "Karmic Visions" in *Lucifer,**and note

*Reprinted in "*Theosophy*" magazine for September, 1915.

the description of the real Ego, sitting as a spectator of the life of the hero, and perhaps something will strike you.

Q. What, in reality, is the Astral Light?

A. As the Esoteric Philosophy teaches us, the *Astral Light* is simply the dregs of *Akâsa* or the Universal Ideation in its metaphysical sense. Though invisible, it is yet, so to speak, the phosphorescent radiation of the latter, and is the medium between it and man's thought-faculties. It is these which pollute the Astral Light, and make it what it is —the storehouse of all human and especially psychic iniquities. In its primordial genesis, the astral light as a radiation is quite pure, though the lower it descends approaching our terrestrial sphere, the more it differentiates, and becomes as a result impure in its very constitution. But man helps considerably to this pollution, and gives it back its essence far worse than when he received it.

Q. Can you explain to us how it is related to man, and its action in dream-life?

A. Differentiation in the physical world is infinite. Universal ideation—or *Mahat*, if you like it—sends its homogeneous radiation into the heterogeneous world, and this reaches the human or *personal* mind through the Astral Light.

Q. But do not our minds receive their illuminations direct from the Higher Manas through the Lower? And is not the former the pure emanation of divine Ideation—the "*Manasa-Putras*," which incarnated in men?

A. They are. Individual *Manasa-Putras* or the Kumaras are the direct radiations of the divine Ideation—"individual" in the sense of later differentiation, owing to numberless incarnations. In sum they are the collective aggregation of that Ideation, become on our plane, or from our

[65]

point of view, *Mahat*, as the Dhyan Chohans are in their aggregate the WORD or "Logos" in the formation of the World. Were the Personalities (Lower Manas or the *physical* minds) to be inspired and illumined solely by their higher *alter Egos* there would be little sin in this world. But they are not; and getting entangled in the meshes of the Astral Light, they separate themselves more and more from their parent Egos. Read and study what Eliphas Lévi says of the Astral Light, which he calls Satan and the Great Serpent. The Astral Light has been taken too literally to mean some sort of a second blue sky. This imaginary space, however, on which are impressed the countless images of all that ever was, is, and will be, is but a too sad reality. It becomes in, and for, man—if at all psychic—and who is not?—a tempting Demon, his "evil angel," and the inspirer of all our worst deeds. It acts on the will of even the sleeping man, through visions impressed upon his slumbering brain (which visions must not be confused with the "dreams"), and these germs bear their fruit when he awakes.

Q. What is the part played by Will in dreams?

A. The will of the outer man, our volition, is of course dormant and inactive during dreams; but a certain bent can be given to the slumbering will during its inactivity, and certain after-results developed by the mutual inter-action—produced almost mechanically—through union between two or more "principles" into one, so that they will act in perfect harmony, without any friction or a single false note, when awake. But this is one of the dodges of "black magic," and when used for good purposes belongs to the training of an Occultist. One must be far advanced on the "path" to have a will which can act consciously during his physical sleep, or act on the will of another person during the sleep of the latter, *e. g.*, to control his dreams, and thus control his actions when awake.

[66]

Q. We are taught that a man can unite all his "principles" into one —what does this mean?

A. When an adept succeeds in doing this he is a *Jivan-mukta:* he is no more of this earth virtually, and becomes a Nirvanee, who can go into *Samadhi* at will. Adepts are generally classed by the number of "principles" they have under their perfect control, for that which we call will has its seat in the higher EGO, and the latter, when it is rid of its sin-laden personality, is divine and pure.

Q. What part does Karma play in dreams? In India they say that every man receives the reward or punishment of all his acts, both in the waking and the dream state.

A. If they say so, it is because they have preserved in all their purity and remembered the traditions of their forefathers. They know that the Self is the *real* Ego, and that it lives and acts, though on a different plane. The external life is a "dream" to this Ego, while the inner life, or the life on what we call the dream plane, is the real life for it. And so the Hindus (the profane, of course) say that Karma is generous, and rewards the real man in dreams as well as it does the false personality in physical life.

Q. What is the difference, "karmically," between the two?

A. The physical animal man is as little responsible as a dog or a mouse. For the bodily form all is over with the death of the body. But the real SELF, that which emanated its own shadow, or the lower thinking personality, that enacted and pulled the wires during the life of the physical automaton, will have to suffer conjointly with its *factotum and alter ego* in its next incarnation.

Q. But the two, the higher and the lower, Manas are one, are they not?

A. They are, and yet they are not—and that is the great mystery. The Higher Manas or EGO is essentially divine,

[67]

and therefore pure; no stain can pollute it, as no punishment can reach it, *per se*, the more so since it is innocent of, and takes no part in, the deliberate transactions of its Lower Ego. Yet by the very fact that, though dual and during life the Higher is distinct from the Lower, "the Father and Son" *are one*, and because that in reuniting with the parent Ego, the Lower Soul fastens upon and impresses upon it all its bad as well as good actions—both have to suffer, the Higher Ego, though innocent and without blemish, has to bear the punishment of the misdeeds committed by the *lower* Self together with it in their future incarnation. The whole doctrine of atonement is built upon this old esoteric tenet; for the Higher Ego is the antitype of that which is on this earth the type, namely the personality. It is, for those who understand it, the old Vedic story of Visvakarman over again, practically demonstrated. Visvakarman, the all-seeing Father-God, who is beyond the comprehension of mortals, ends, as son of Bhuvana, the holy Spirit, by *sacrificing himself to himself*, to save the worlds. The mystic name of the "Higher Ego" is, in the Indian philosophy, *Kshetrajna*, or "embodied Spirit," that which knows or informs *kshetra*, "the body." Etymologize the name, and you will find in it the term *aja*, "first-born," and also the "lamb." All this is very suggestive, and volumes might be written upon the pregenetic and postgenetic development of type and antitype—of Christ-*Kshetrajna*, the "God-Man," the First-born, symbolized as the "lamb." The *Secret Doctrine* shows that the Manasa-Putras or incarnating Egos have taken upon themselves, voluntarily and knowingly, the burden of all the future sins of their future personalities. Thence it is easy to see that it is neither Mr. A. nor Mr. B., nor any of the personalities that periodically clothe the Self-Sacrificing Ego, which are the real Sufferers, but verily the innocent *Christos* within us. Hence the mystic Hindus say that the Eternal Self, or the Ego (the one in three and three in one), is the "Charioteer" or driver; the personalities are the temporary and evanescent passengers; while the horses are the animal passions of man. It is, then, true to say that when we remain deaf to the Voice of our Conscience, we crucify the Christos within us. But let us return to dreams.

Q. Are so-called prophetic dreams a sign that the dreamer has strong clairvoyant faculties?

A. It may be said, in the case of persons who have truly prophetic dreams, that it is because their physical brains and memory are in closer relation and sympathy with their "Higher Ego" than in the generality of men. The Ego-Self has more facilities for impressing upon the physical shell and memory that which is of importance to such persons than it has in the case of other less gifted persons. Remember that the only God man comes in contact with is his own God, called Spirit, Soul and Mind, or Consciousness, and these three are one.

But there are weeds that must be destroyed in order that a plant may grow. We must die, said St. Paul, that we may live again. It is through destruction that we may improve, and the three powers, the preserving, the creating, and the destroying, are only so many aspects of the divine spark within man.

Q. Do Adepts dream?

A. No advanced Adept dreams. An adept is one who has obtained mastery over his four lower principles, including his body, and does not, therefore, let flesh have its own way. He simply paralyzes his lower Self during Sleep, and becomes perfectly free. A dream, as we understand it, is an illusion. Shall an adept, then, dream when he has rid himself of every other illusion? In his sleep he simply lives on another and more real plane.

[69]

Q. Are there people who have never dreamed?

A. There is no such man in the world so far as I am aware. All dream more or less; only with most, dreams vanish suddenly upon waking. This depends on the more or less receptive condition of the brain ganglia. Unspiritual men, and those who do not exercise their imaginative faculties, or those whom manual labour has exhausted, so that the ganglia do not act even mechanically during rest, dream rarely, if ever, with any coherence.

Q. What is the difference between the dreams of men and those of beasts?

A. The dream state is common not only to all men, but also to all animals, of course, from the highest mammalia to the smallest birds, and even insects. Every being endowed with a physical brain, or organs approximating thereto, must dream. Every animal, large or small, has, more or less, physical senses; and though these senses are dulled during sleep, memory will still, so to say, act mechanically, reproducing past sensations. That dogs and horses and cattle dream we all know, and so also do canaries, but such dreams are, I think, merely physiological. Like the last embers of a dying fire, with its spasmodic flare and occasional flames, so acts the brain in falling asleep. Dreams are not, as Dryden says, "interludes which fancy makes," for such can only refer to physiological dreams provoked by indigestion, or some idea or event which has impressed itself upon the active brain during waking hours.

Q. What, then, is the process of going to sleep?

A. This is partially explained by Physiology. It is said by Occultism to be the periodical and regulated exhaustion of the nervous centres, and especially of the sensory ganglia of the brain, which refuse to act any longer on this plane, and, if they would not become unfit for work, are compelled to recuperate their strength on another plane or *Upadhi*. First comes the *Svapna*, or dreaming state, and this leads to that of *Shushupti*. Now it must be remembered that our senses are all dual, and act according to the plane of consciousness on which the thinking entity energises. Physical sleep affords the greatest facility for its action on the various planes; at the same time it is a necessity, in order that the senses may recuperate and obtain a new lease of life for the *Jagrata*, or waking state, from the *Svapna* and *Shushupti*. According to *Raj Yoga*, *Turya* is the highest state. As a man exhausted by one state of the life fluid seeks another; as, for example, when exhausted by the hot air he refreshes himself with cool water; so sleep is the shady nook in the sunlit valley of life.

Sleep is a sign that waking life has become too strong for the physical organism, and that the force of the life current must be broken by changing the waking for the sleeping state. Ask a good clairvoyant to describe the aura of a person just refreshed by sleep, and that of another just before going to sleep. The former will be seen bathed in rhythmical vibrations of life currents—golden, blue, and rosy; these are the electrical waves of Life. The latter is, as it were, in a mist of intense golden-orange hue, composed of atoms whirling with an almost incredible spasmodic rapidity, showing that the person begins to be too strongly saturated with Life; the life essence is too strong for his physical organs, and he must seek relief in the shadowy side of that essence, which side is the dream element, or physical sleep, one of the states of consciousness.

Q. But what is a dream?

A. That depends on the meaning of the term. You may "dream," or, as we say, sleep visions, awake or asleep. If the Astral Light is collected in a cup or metal vessel by will-power, and the eyes fixed on some point in it with a strong will to see, a waking vision or "dream" is the result, if the person is at all sensitive. The reflections in the Astral Light are seen better with closed eyes, and, in sleep, still more distinctly. From a lucid state, vision becomes translucid; from normal organic consciousness it rises to a transcendental state of consciousness.

Q. To what causes are dreams chiefly due?

A. There are many kinds of dreams, as we all know. Leaving the "digestion dream" aside, there are brain dreams and memory dreams, mechanical and conscious visions. Dreams of warning and premonition require the active co-operation of the inner Ego. They are also often due to the conscious or unconscious co-operation of the brains of two living persons, or of their two Egos.

Q. What is it that dreams, then?

A. Generally the physical brain of the personal Ego, the seat of memory, radiating and throwing off sparks like the dying embers of a fire. The memory of the Sleeper is like an Æolian seven-stringed harp; and his state of mind may be compared to the wind that sweeps over the chords. The corresponding string of the harp will respond to that one of the seven states of mental activity in which the sleeper was before falling asleep. If it is a gentle breeze the harp will be affected but little; if a hurricane, the vibrations will be proportionately powerful. If the personal Ego is in touch with its higher principles and the veils of the higher planes are drawn aside, all is well; if on the contrary it is of a materialistic animal nature, there will be probably no dreams; or if the memory by chance catch the breath of a "wind" from a higher plane, seeing that it will be impressed through the sensory ganglia of the cerebellum, and not by the direct agency of the spiritual Ego, it will receive pictures and sounds so distorted and inharmonious that even a Deva-

chanic vision would appear a nightmare or grotesque cari-
cature. Therefore, there is no simple answer to the question "What is it that dreams?" for it depends entirely on
each individual what principle will be the chief motor in
dreams, and whether they will be remembered or forgotten.

Q. Is the apparent objectivity in a dream really objective or subjective?

A. If it is admitted to be apparent, then of course it is
subjective. The question should rather be, to whom or
what are the pictures or representations in dreams either
objective or subjective? To the physical man, the *dreamer*,
all he sees with his eyes shut, and in or through his mind, is
of course subjective. But to the *Seer* within the physical
dreamer, that Seer himself being subjective to our material
senses, all he sees is as objective as he is himself to himself
and to others like himself. Materialists will probably laugh,
and say that we make of a man a whole family of entities,
but this is not so. Occultism teaches that physical man is
one, but the thinking man septenary, thinking, acting, feeling, and living on seven different states of being or planes of
consciousness, and that for all these states and planes the
permanent Ego (not the false personality) has a distinct set
of senses.

Q. Can these different senses be distinguished?

A. Not unless you are an Adept or highly-trained Chela,
thoroughly acquainted with these different states. Sci-
ences, such as biology, physiology, and even psychology (of
the Maudsley, Bain, and Herbert Spencer schools), do not
touch on this subject. Science teaches us about the phenomena of volition, sensation, intellect, and instinct, and
says that these are all manifested through the nervous centres, the most important of which is our brain. She will
speak of the peculiar agent or substance through which these

phenomena take place as the vascular and fibrous tissues, and explain their relation to one another, dividing the ganglionic centres into motor, sensory and sympathetic, but will never breathe one word of the mysterious agency of intellect itself, or of the mind and its functions.

Now, it frequently happens that we are conscious and know that we are dreaming; this is a very good proof that man is a multiple being on the thought plane; so that not only is the Ego, or thinking man, Proteus, a multiform, ever-changing entity, but he is also, so to speak, capable of separating himself on the mind or dream plane into two or more entities; and on the plane of illusion which follows us to the threshold of Nirvâna, he is like Ain-Soph talking to Ain-Soph, holding a dialogue with himself and speaking through, about, and to himself. And this is the mystery of the inscrutable Deity in the *Zohar*, as in the Hindu philosophies; it is the same in the Kabala, Puranas, Vedantic metaphysics, or even in the so-called Christian mystery of the God-head and Trinity. Man is the microcosm of the macrocosm; the god on earth is built on the pattern of the god in nature. But the universal consciousness of the real Ego transcends a millionfold the self-consciousness of the personal or false Ego.

Q. Is that which is termed "unconscious cerebration" during sleep a mechanical process of the physical brain, or is it a conscious operation of the Ego, the result of which only is impressed on the ordinary consciousness?

A. It is the latter; for is it possible to remember in our conscious state what took place while our brain worked unconsciously? This is apparently a contradiction in terms.

Q. How does it happen that persons who have never seen mountains in nature often see them distinctly in sleep, and are able to note their features?

A. Most probably because they have seen pictures of

mountains; otherwise it is somebody or something in us which has previously seen them.

Q. What is the cause of that experience in dreams in which the dreamer seems to be ever striving after something, but never attaining it?

A. It is because the physical self and its memory are shut out of the possibility of knowing what the real Ego does. The dreamer only catches faint glimpses of the doings of the Ego, whose actions produce the so-called dream on the physical man, but is unable to follow it consecutively. A delirious patient, on recovery, bears the same relation to the nurse who watched and tended him in his illness as the physical man to his real Ego. The Ego acts as consciously within and without him as the nurse acts in tending and watching over the sick man. But neither the patient after leaving his sick bed, nor the dreamer on awaking, will be able to remember anything except in snatches and glimpses.

Q. How does sleep differ from death?

A. There is an analogy certainly, but a very great difference between the two. In sleep there is a connection, weak though it may be, between the lower and higher mind of man, and the latter is more or less reflected into the former, however much its rays may be distorted. But once the body is dead, the body of illusion, *Mayavi Rupa*, becomes Kama Rupa, or the animal soul, and is left to its own devices. Therefore, there is as much difference between the spook and man as there is between a gross material, animal but sober mortal, and a man incapably drunk and unable to distinguish the most prominent surroundings; between a person shut up in a perfectly dark room and one in a room lighted, however imperfectly, by some light or other.

The lower principles are like wild beasts, and the higher Manas is the rational man who tames or subdues them more or less successfully. But once the animal gets free from the master who held it in subjection; no sooner has it ceased to hear his voice and see him than it starts off again to the jungle and its ancient den. It takes, however, some time for an animal to return to its original and natural state, but these lower principles or "spook" return instantly, and no sooner has the higher Triad entered the Devachanic state than the lower Duad rebecomes that which it was from the beginning, a principle endued with purely animal instincts, made happier still by the great change.

Q. What is the condition of the *Linga Sarira*, or plastic body, during dreams?

A. The condition of the Plastic form is to sleep with its body, unless projected by some powerful desire generated in the higher Manas. In dreams it plays no active part, but on the contrary is entirely passive, being the involuntarily half-sleepy witness of the experiences through which the higher principles are passing.

Q. Under what circumstances is this wraith seen?

A. Sometimes, in cases of illness or very strong passion on the part of the person seen or the person who sees; the possibility is mutual. A sick person especially just before death, is very likely to see in dream, or vision, those whom he loves and is continually thinking of, and so also is a person awake, but intensely thinking of a person who is asleep at the time.

Q. Can a Magician summon such a dreaming entity and have intercourse with it?

A. In black Magic it is no rare thing to evoke the "spirit" of a sleeping person; the sorcerer may then learn from the apparition any secret he chooses, and the sleeper be quite ignorant of what is occurring. Under such circumstances that which appears is the *Mayavi rupa;* but there is always a danger that the memory of the living man will preserve the recollections of the evocation and remember it as a vivid dream. If it is not, however, at a great distance, the Double or *Linga Sarira* may be evoked, but this can neither speak nor give information, and there is always the possibility of the sleeper being killed through this forced separation. Many sudden deaths in sleep have thus occurred, and the world been no wiser.

Q. Can there be any connection between a dreamer and an entity in "*Kama Loka*"?

A. The dreamer of an entity in *Kama Loka* would probably bring upon himself a nightmare, or would run the risk of becoming "possessed" by the "spook" so attracted, if he happened to be a medium, or one who had made himself so passive during his waking hours that even his higher Self is now unable to protect him. This is why the mediumistic state of passivity is so dangerous, and in time renders the Higher Self entirely helpless to aid or even warn the sleeping or entranced person. Passivity paralyzes the connection between the lower and higher principles. It is very rare to find instances of mediums who, while remaining passive *at will*, for the purpose of communicating with some higher intelligence, some *extraneous* spirit (not disembodied), will yet preserve sufficiently their personal will so as not to break off all connection with the higher Self.

Q. Can a dreamer be "en rapport" with an entity in Devachan?

A. The only possible means of communicating with Devachanees is during sleep by a dream or vision, or in trance state. No Devachanee can descend into our plane; it is for us—or rather our *inner Self*—to ascend to his.

Q. What is the state of mind of a drunkard during sleep?

[77]

A. It is no real sleep, but a heavy stupor; no physical rest, but worse than sleeplessness, and kills the drunkard as quickly. During such stupor, as also during the waking drunken state, everything turns and whirls round in the brain, producing in the imagination and fancy horrid and grotesque shapes in continual motion and convolutions.

Q. What is the cause of nightmare, and how is it that the dreams of persons suffering from advanced consumption are often pleasant?

A. The cause of the former is simply physiological. A nightmare arises from oppression and difficulty in breathing; and difficulty in breathing will always create such a feeling of oppression and produce a sensation of impending calamity. In the second case, dreams become pleasant because the consumptive grows daily severed from his material body, and more clairvoyant in proportion. As death approaches, the body wastes away and ceases to be an impediment or barrier between the brain of the physical man and his Higher Self.

Q. Is it a good thing to cultivate dreaming?

A. It is by cultivating the power of what is called "dreaming" that clairvoyance is developed.

Q. Are there any means of interpreting dreams—for instance, the interpretations given in dream-books?

A. None but the clairvoyant faculty and the spiritual intuition of the "interpreter." Every dreaming Ego differs from every other, as our physical bodies do. If everything in the universe has seven keys to its symbolism on the physical plane, how many keys may it not have on higher planes?

Q. Is there any way in which dreams may be classified?

A. We may roughly divide dreams also into seven classes,

and subdivide these in turn. Thus, we would divide them into:

1. Prophetic dreams. These are impressed on our memory by the Higher Self, and are generally plain and clear: either a voice heard or the coming event foreseen.

2. Allegorical dreams, or hazy glimpses of realities caught by the brain and distorted by our fancy. These are generally only half true.

3. Dreams sent by adepts, good or bad, by mesmerisers, or by the thoughts of very powerful minds bent on making us do their will.

4. Retrospective; dreams of events belonging to past incarnations.

5. Warning dreams for others who are unable to be impressed themselves.

6. Confused dreams, the causes of which have been discussed above.

7. Dreams which are mere fancies and chaotic pictures, owing to digestion, some mental trouble, or such-like external cause.

PART II

STANZAS II TO IV
(SLOKAS 1 TO 5)

V.

STANZA II.—*(Continued)*.

Sloka (3). THE HOUR HAD NOT YET STRUCK; THE RAY
HAD NOT YET FLASHED INTO THE GERM; THE
MATRI-PADMA (*mother lotus*) HAD NOT YET SWOLLEN.

"The Ray of the 'ever-darkness' becomes, as it is emitted, a ray of
effulgent life, and flashes into the 'germ'—the point in the Mundane
Egg, represented by matter in its abstract sense."

Q. Is the Point in the Mundane Egg the same as the Point in the
Circle, the Unmanifested Logos?

A. Certainly not: the Point in the Circle is the Unmanifested Logos, the Manifested Logos is the Triangle. Pythagoras speaks of the never manifested Monad which lives in
solitude and darkness; when the hour strikes it radiates from
itself ONE, the first number. This number descending, produces TWO, the second number, and TWO, in its turn, produces THREE, forming a triangle, the first complete geometrical figure in the world of form. It is this ideal or abstract
triangle which is the Point in the Mundane Egg, which,
after gestation, and in the third remove, will start from the
Egg to form the Triangle. This is Brahmâ-Vâch-Virâj in
the Hindu Philosophy and Kether-Chochmah-Binah in the
Zohar. The First Manifested Logos is the Potentia, the un-
revealed Cause; the Second, the still latent Thought; the
Third, the Demiurgus, the active Will evolving from its universal Self the active effect, which, in its turn, becomes the
cause on a lower plane.

Q. What is Ever-Darkness in the sense used here?

[83]

A. Ever-Darkness means, I suppose, the ever-unknow·able mystery, behind the veil—in fact, Parabrahm. Even the Logos can see only Mulaprakriti, it cannot see that which is beyond the veil. It is that which is the "Ever-unknowable Darkness."

Q. What is the Ray in this connection?

A. I will recapitulate. We have the plane of the circle, the face being black, the point in the circle being potentially white, and this is the first possible conception in our minds of the invisible Logos. "Ever-Darkness" is eternal, the Ray periodical. Having flashed out from this central point and thrilled through the Germ, the Ray is withdrawn again within this point and the Germ developes into the Second Logos, the triangle within the Mundane Egg.

Q. What, then, are the stages of manifestation?

A. The first stage is the appearance of the potential point in the circle—the unmanifested Logos. The second stage is the shooting forth of the Ray from the potential white point, producing the first point, which is called, in the Zohar, Kether or Sephira. The third stage is the production from Kether of Chochmah, and Binah, thus constituting the first triangle, which is the Third or manifested Logos —in other words, the subjective and objective Universe. Further, from this manifested Logos will proceed the Seven Rays, which in the Zohar are called the lower Sephiroth and in Eastern occultism the primordial seven rays. Thence will proceed the innumerable series of Hierarchies.

Q. Is the Triangle here mentioned that which you refer to as the Germ in the Mundane Egg?

A. Certainly it is. But you must remember that there are both the Universal and Solar Eggs (as well as others), and that it is necessary to qualify any statement made concerning them. The Mundane Egg is an expression of Abstract Form.

Q. May Abstract Form be called the first manifestation of the eternal female principle?

A. It is the first manifestation not of the female principle, but of the Ray which proceeds from the central point which is perfectly sexless. There is no eternal female principle, for this Ray produces that which is the united potentiality of both sexes but is by no means either male or female. This latter differentiation will only appear when it falls into matter, when the Triangle becomes a Square, the first Tetraktys.

Q. Then the Mundane Egg is as sexless as the Ray?

A. The Mundane Egg is simply the first stage of manifestation, undifferentiated primordial matter, in which the vital creative Germ receives its first spiritual impulse; Potentiality becomes Potency.

Matter, by convenience of metaphor, only, is regarded as feminine, because it is receptive of the rays of the sun which fecundate it and so produce all that grows on its surface, *i. e.,* on this the lowest plane. On the other hand primordial matter should be regarded as substance, and by no means can be spoken of as having sex.

Thus the Egg, on whatever plane you speak of, means the ever-existing undifferentiated matter which strictly is not matter at all but, as we call it, the Atoms. Matter is destructible in form while the Atoms are absolutely indestructible, being the quintessence of Substances. And here, I mean by "atoms" the primordial divine Units, not the "atoms" of modern Science.

Similarly the "Germ" is a figurative expression; the germ is everywhere, even as the circle whose circumference is nowhere and whose centre is everywhere. It therefore means all germs, that is to say, unmanifested nature, or the whole

[85]

creative power which will emanate, called by the Hindus Brahmâ, though on every plane it has a different name.

Q. Is the Matri-Padma the eternal or the periodical Egg?

A. The eternal Egg; it will become periodical only when the ray from the first Logos shall have flashed from the latent Germ in the Matri-Padma which is the Egg, the Womb of the Universe which is to be. By analogy, the physical germ in the female cell could not be called eternal, though the latent spirit of the germ concealed within the male cell in nature, may be so called.

Sloka (4). HER HEART HAD NOT YET OPENED FOR THE ONE RAY TO ENTER, THENCE TO FALL AS THREE INTO FOUR IN THE LAP OF MAYA.

"But as the hour strikes and it becomes receptive of the Fohatic impress of the Divine Thought (the Logos or the male aspect of the Anima Mundi, Alaya)—its heart opens."*

Q. Does not the Fohatic impress of the Divine Thought apply to a later stage of differentiation?

A. Fohat, as a distinct force or entity, is a later development. "Fohatic" is an adjective and may be used in a more wide sense; Fohat, as a substantive, or Entity, springs from a Fohatic attribute of the Logos. Electricity cannot be generated from that which does not contain an electric principle or element. The divine principle is eternal, the gods are periodical. Fohat is the Sakti or force of the divine mind; Brahmâ and Fohat are both aspects of the divine mind.

Q. Is it not the intention in the Commentaries to this Stanza to convey some idea of the subject by speaking of correspondences in a much later stage of evolution?

A. Exactly so; it has several times been stated that the Commentaries on the First Volume are almost entirely con-

---
*S. D., Vol. I, p. 58.

cerned with the evolution of the solar system only. The beauty and wisdom of the Stanzas consist in this, that they may be interpreted on seven different planes, the last reflecting, by the universal law of correspondences and analogy, in its most differentiated, gross and physical aspect, the process which takes place on the first or purely spiritual plane. I may state here once for all that the first Stanzas treat of the awakening from Pralaya and are not concerned with the Solar system alone, while Vol. II. deals only with our Earth.

Q. Can you say what is the real meaning of the word Fohat?

A. The word is a Turanian compound and its meanings are various. In China *Pho*, or *Fo*, is the word for "animal soul," the vital *Nephesh* or the breath of life. Some say that it is derived from the Sanscrit "Bhu," meaning existence, or rather the essence of existence. Now Swayambhu means Brahmâ and Man at the same time. It means self-existence and self-existing, that which is everlasting, the eternal breath. If Sat is the potentiality of Being, Pho is the potency of Being. The meaning, however, entirely depends upon the position of the accent. Again, Fohat is related to Mahat. It is the reflection of the Universal Mind, the synthesis of the "Seven" and the intelligences of the seven creative Builders, or, as we call them, Cosmocratores. Hence, as you will understand, life and electricity are one in our philosophy. They say life is electricity, and if so, then the One Life is the essence and root of all the electric and magnetic phenomena on this manifested plane.

Q. How is it that Horus and the other "Son-Gods" are said to be born "through an immaculate Mother"?

A. On the first plane of differentiation there is no sex—to use the term for convenience' sake—but both sexes exist potentially in primordial matter. Matter is the root of the word "mother" and therefore female; but there are two kinds of matter. The undifferentiated, primordial matter is not fecundated by some act in space and time, fertility and productiveness being inherent in it. Therefore that which emanates or is *born* out of that inherent virtue is not born from, but through, it. In other words, that virtue or quality is the sole cause that this something manifests through its vehicle; whereas on the physical plane, Mother-matter is is not the active cause but the passive means and instrument of an independent cause.

In the Christian doctrine of the Immaculate Conception —a materializing of the metaphysical and spiritual conception—the mother is first fecundated by the Holy Ghost and the Child born from, and not through, her. "From" implies that there is a limited and conditioned source to start from, the act having to take place in Space and Time. "Through" is applicable to Eternity and Infinity as well as to the Finite. The Great Breath thrills through Space, which is boundless, and is *in*, not *from*, eternity.

Q. How does the Triangle become the Square, and the Square the six-faced Cube?

A. In occult and Pythagorean geometry the Tetrad is said to combine within itself all the materials from which Kosmos is produced. The Point or One, extends to a Line —the Two; a Line to a Superficies, Three; and the Superficies, Triad or Triangle, is converted into a Solid, the Tetrad or Four, by the point being placed over it. Kabalistically Kether, or Sephira, the Point, emanates Chochmah and Binah, which two, are the synonym of *Mahat*, in the Hindu Purânas, and this Triad, descending into matter, produces the Tetragrammaton, *Tetraktys*, as also the lower Tetrad. This number contains both the productive and produced numbers. The Duad doubled makes a Tetrad and the Tetrad doubled forms a Hebdomad. From another point of view it is the Spirit, Will, and Intellect animating the four lower principles.

Q. Then how does the Square become the six-faced Cube?

A. The Square becomes the Cube when each point of the triangle becomes dual, male or female. The Pythagoreans said "Once One, Twice Two, and there ariseth a Tetrad, having on its top the highest Unit; it becomes a Pyramid whose base is a plane Tetrad; divine light resting on it, makes the abstract Cube."

The surface of the Cube is composed of six squares, and the Cube unfolded gives the Cross, or the vertical Four, barred by the horizontal Three; the six thus making Seven, the seven principles or the Pythagorean seven properties in man. See the excellent explanation given of this in Mr. R. Skinner's *Source of Measures.*

"Thus is repeated on earth the mystery enacted, according to the Seers, on the divine plane. The 'Son' of the immaculate Celestial Virgin (or the undifferentiated cosmic protyle —Matter in its infinitude) is born again on Earth as the son of the terrestrial Eve—our mother Earth, and becomes Humanity as a total—past, present and future—for Jehovah or Jod-He-Vau-He is androgyne, or both male and female. Above, the 'Son' is the whole Kosmos; below, he is Mankind. The Triad or Triangle becomes the Tetraktys, the sacred Pythagorean number, the perfect Square and six-faced Cube on Earth. The Macroprosopus (the Great Face) is now Microprosopus (The Lesser Face); or, as the Kabalists have it, the 'Ancient of Days' descending on Adam Kadmon whom he uses as his vehicle to manifest through, gets transformed into Tetragrammaton. It is now in the lap of Maya, the Great Illusion, and between itself and the Reality has the Astral Light, the great deceiver of man's limited senses, unless Knowledge through Paramarthasatya comes to the rescue."*

*S. D., Vol. I, p. 60.

[89]

That is to say, the Logos becomes a Tetragrammaton; the Triangle, or the Three becomes the Four.

Q. Is the Astral Light used here in the sense of Maya?

A. Certainly. It is explained further on in the *Secret Doctrine* that practically there are only four planes belonging to the planetary chains. The three higher planes are absolutely *Arupa* and outside our comprehension.

Q. Then the Tetraktys is entirely different from Tetragrammaton?

A. The Tetraktys by which the Pythagoreans swore, was not the Tetragrammaton, but on the contrary, the higher or superior Tetraktys. In the opening chapters of *Genesis* we have a clue to the discovery of this lower Tetragrammaton. We there find Adam, Eve, and Jehovah who becomes Cain. The further extension of Humanity is symbolised in Abel, as the human conception of the higher. Abel is the daughter and not the son of Eve, and symbolises the separation of the the sexes; while the murder of Abel is symbolical of marriage. The still more human conception is found at the end of the fourth Chapter, when speaking of Seth, to whom was born a son, Enos, after which men began—not, as translated in Genesis, to "call upon the Lord"—but to be called *Jod-He-Vah*, meaning males and females.

The Tetragrammaton, therefore, is simply Malkuth; when the bridegroom comes to the bride on Earth, then it becomes Humanity. The seven lower Sephiroth must all be passed through, the Tetragrammaton becoming more and more material. The Astral Plane lies between the *Tetraktys* and Tetragammaton.

Q. Tetraktys appears to be used here in two entirely different senses?

A. The true Pythagorean Tetraktys was the Tetraktys of the invisible Monad, which produces the first Point, the second and the third and then retires into the darkness and everlasting silence; in other words the Tetraktys is the first Logos. Taken from the plane of matter, it is among other things, the lower Quaternary, the man of flesh or matter.

VI.

STANZA III.

Sloka (1). THE LAST VIBRATION OF THE SEVENTH
ETERNITY THRILLS THROUGH INFINITUDE. THE
MOTHER SWELLS, EXPANDING FROM WITHIN WITH-
OUT LIKE THE BUD OF THE LOTUS.

"The seemingly paradoxical use of the sentence 'Seventh Eternity,'
thus dividing the indivisible, is sanctified in esoteric philosophy. The
latter divides boundless duration into unconditionally eternal and
universal time, and a conditioned one (Khandakâla). One is the
abstraction or noumenon of infinite Time (Kâla), the other its phenomenon appearing periodically as the effect of MAHAT (the universal
Intelligence limited by Manvantaric duration)."*

Q. Does the commencement of Time as distinguished from Duration,
correspond to the appearance of the manifested Logos?

A. Certainly it cannot do so earlier. But "the seventh
vibration" applies to both the First, and to the manifested
Logos—the first out of Space and Time, the second, when
Time has commenced. It is only when "the mother swells"
that differentiation sets in, for when the first Logos radiates
through primordial and undifferentiated matter there is as
yet no action in Chaos. "The last vibration of the Seventh
Eternity" is the first which announces the Dawn, and is a
synonym for the First or unmanifested Logos. There is no
Time at this stage. There is neither Space nor Time when
beginning is made; but it is all in Space and Time, once that
differentiation sets in. At the time of the primordial radiation, or when the Second Logos emanates, it is Father-
Mother potentially, but when the Third or manifested Logos

*S. D., Vol. I, p. 62.

[93]

appears, it becomes the Virgin-Mother. The "Father and the Son" are one in all the world Theogonies; hence, the expression corresponds to the appearance of both the unmanifested and the manifested Logos, one at the beginning, the other at the end, of the "Seventh Eternity."

Q. Can you, then, speak of Time as existing from the appearance of the Second or Unmanifested-Manifested Logos?

A. Assuredly not, but from the appearance of the Third. It is here that the great difference between the two lies, as just shown. The "last vibration" begins outside of Time and Space, and ends with the Third Logos, when Time and Space begin, *i. e.*, periodical time. The Second Logos partaking of both the essences or natures of the first and the last. There is no differentiation with the First Logos; differentiation only begins in latent World-Thought, with the Second Logos, and receives its full expression, *i. e.*, becomes the "Word" made flesh—with the Third.

Q. How do the terms "Radiation" and "Emanation" differ in the Secret Doctrine?

A. They express, to my mind, two entirely different ideas, and are the best apologies for the original terms that could be found; but if the ordinary meanings are attached to them the idea will be missed. Radiation is, so to say, the unconscious and spontaneous shooting forth, the action of a something from which this act takes place; but emanation is something from which another thing issues in a constant efflux, and emanates consciously. An orthodox Occultist goes so far as to say that the smell of a flower emanates from it "consciously"—absurd as it may seem to the profane. Radiation *can* come from the Absolute; Emanation *cannot*. One difference exists in the idea that Radiation is sure, sooner or later, to be withdrawn again while Emanation runs into other emanations and is thoroughly separated and differentiated. Of course at the end of the cycle of time emanation will also be withdrawn into the One Absolute, but meanwhile, during the entire cycle of changes emanation will persist. One thing emanates from the other, and, in fact, from one point of view, emanation is equivalent to Evolution; while "radiation" represents to my mind—in the pre-cosmic period, of course—an instantaneous action like that of a piece of paper set on fire under a burning glass, of which act the Sun knows nothing. Both terms, of course, are used for want of better.

Q. What is meant by prototypes existing in the Astral Light?*

A. Astral Light is here used as a convenient phrase for a term very little understood, viz: "the realm of Akâsa, or primordial Light manifested through the divine Ideation." The latter must be accepted in this particular case as a generic term for the universal and divine mind reflected in the waters of Space or Chaos, which is the Astral Light proper, and a mirror reflecting and reversing a higher plane. In the ABSOLUTE or Divine Thought everything exists and there has been no time when it did not so exist; but Divine Ideation is limited by the Universal Manvantaras. The realm of Akâsa is the undifferentiated noumenal and abstract Space which will be occupied by *Chidakasam*, the field of primordial consciousness. It has several degrees, however, in Occult philosophy; in fact, "seven fields." The first is the field of latent consciousness which is coeval with the duration of the first and second unmanifested Logoi. It is the "Light which shineth in darkness and the darkness comprehended it not" of St. John's Gospel. When the hour strikes for the Third Logos to appear, then from the latent potentiality there radiates a lower field of differentiated consciousness, which is Mahat, or the entire collectivity of those Dhyan Chohans of *sentient life* of which Fohat is the repre-

*S. D., Vol I, p. 63.

sentative on the objective plane and the Manasaputras on the subjective. The Astral Light is that which mirrors the three higher planes of consciousness, and is above the lower, or terrestrial plane; therefore it does not extend beyond the fourth plane, where, one may say, the Akâsa begins.

There is one great difference between the Astral Light and the Akâsa which must be remembered. The latter is eternal, the former is periodic. The Astral Light changes not only with the Mahamanvantaras but also with every sub-period and planetary cycle or Round.

Q. Then do the prototypes exist on a plane higher than that of the Astral Light?

A. The prototypes or ideas of things exist first on the plane of Divine eternal Consciousness, and thence become reflected and reversed in the Astral Light, which also reflects on its lower individual plane the life of our Earth, recording it on its "tablets." Therefore, is the Astral Light called illusion. It is from this that we, in our turn, get our prototypes. Consequently unless the Clairvoyant or SEER can get beyond this plane of illusion, he can never see the Truth, but will be drowned in an ocean of self-deception and hallucinations.

Q. And what is the Akâsa proper?

A. The Akâsa is the eternal divine consciousness which cannot differentiate, have qualities, or act; action belongs to that which is reflected or mirrored from it. The unconditioned and infinite can have no relation with the finite and conditioned. The Astral Light is the Middle Heaven of the Gnostics, in which is Sophia Achamoth, the mother of the seven builders or Spirits of the Earth, which are not necessarily good, and among which the Gnostics placed Jehovah, whom they called Ildabaoth. (*Sophia Achamoth must not be confounded with the divine Sophia.*) We may compare the

Akâsa and the Astral Light, with regard to these prototypes, to the germ in the acorn. The latter, besides containing in itself the astral form of the future oak, conceals the germ from which grows a tree containing millions of forms. These forms are contained in the acorn potentially, yet the development of each particular acorn depends upon extraneous circumstances, physical forces, &c.

Q. But how does this account for the endless varieties of the Vegetable Kingdom?

A. The different variations of plants, &c., are the broken rays of one Ray. As the ray passes through the seven planes, it is broken on every plane into thousands and millions of rays down to the world of forms, every ray breaking into an intelligence on its own plane. So that we see every plant has an intelligence, or its own purpose of life, so to speak, and its own freewill, to a degree. This is how I, at any rate, understand it. A plant can be receptive or non-receptive, though *every plant without an exception* feels and has a consciousness of its own. But besides the latter, every plant—from the gigantic tree down to the minutest fern or blade of grass—has, Occultism teaches us, an Elemental entity of which it is the outward clothing on this plane. Hence, the Kabalists and the mediæval Rosicrucians are always found talking of Elementals. According to them, everything possessed an Elemental sprite.

Q. What is the difference between an Elemental and a Dhyan Chohan or Dhyani Buddha?

A. The difference is very great. Elementals are attached only to the four terrestrial Elements and only to the two lower kingdoms of nature—the mineral and the vegetable—in which they *inmetalize* and *inherbalize*, so to speak. The Hindu term *Deva* may be applied to them, but not that of *Dhyan Chohan.* The former have a kind of Kosmic intelli-

[97]

gence; but the latter are endowed with a supersensuous intellect, each of its kind. As to the Dhyani Buddhas, they belong to the highest Divine (or omniscient) Intelligences, answering best, perhaps, to the Roman Catholic Archangels.

Q. Is there an evolution of types through the various planes of the Astral Light?

A. You must follow out the simile of the evolution of the acorn. From the acorn will grow an oak and this oak, as a tree, may have a thousand forms, all of which vary the one from the other. All these forms are contained within the acorn, and though the form which the tree will take depends on extraneous circumstances, yet that, which Aristotle called the "privation of matter" exists beforehand, in the Astral waves. But the noumenal germ of the oak exists beyond the plane of the Astral Light; it is only the subjective picture of it that already exists in the Astral Light, and the development of the oak tree is the result of the developed prototype in the Astral Light, which development proceeds from higher to lower planes, until on the lowest plane it has its last consolidation and development of form. And here is the explanation of the curious fact according to the Vedantin assertion that each plant has its Karma and that its growth is the result of Karma. This Karma proceeds from the lower Dhyan Chohans who trace out and plan the growth of the tree.

Q. What is the real meaning of Manvantara or rather Manu-antara?

A. It means really "Between two Manus," of which there are fourteen in every "Day of Brahmâ," such a "Day" consisting of 1,000 aggregates of four ages or 1,000 "Great Ages," Mahayugas. When the word "Manu" is analysed it is found that Orientalists state that it is from the root "Man" to think, hence the thinking man. But, esoterically, every Manu, as an anthropomorphized patron of his special cycle, or Round, is but the personified idea of the "Thought Divine" (like the Hermetic Pymander). Each of the Manus, therefore, is the special god, the creator and fashioner of all that appears during his own respective cycle of being or Manvantara.

> *Q.* Is Manu a unity also of human consciousness personified, or is it the individualization of the Thought Divine for manvantaric purposes?

A. Of both, since "human consciousness" is but a Ray of the Divine. Our *Manas*, or Ego, proceeds from, and is the Son (figuratively) of Mahat. Vaivasvata Manu (the Manu of our own fifth race and Humanity in general) is the chief personified representative of the *thinking* Humanity of the fifth Root-race; and therefore he is represented as the eldest Son of the Sun and an *Agnishwatta* Ancestor. As "*Manu*" is derived from *Man*, to think, the idea is clear. Thought in its action on human brains is endless. Thus Manu is, and contains the potentiality of all the thinking forms which will be developed on earth from this particular source. In the exoteric teaching he is the beginning of this earth, and from him and his daughter Ila humanity is born; he is a unity which contains all the pluralities and their modifications. Every Manvantara has thus its own Manu and from this Manu the various Manus or rather all the *Manasa* of the Kalpas will proceed. As an analogy he may be compared to the white light which contains all the other rays, giving birth to them by passing through the prism of differentiation and evolution. But this pertains to the esoteric and metaphysical teachings.

> *Q.* Is it possible to say that Manu stands in relation to each Manvantara as does the First Logos to the Mahamanvantara?

A. It is possible to say so, if you like.

> *Q.* Is it possible to say that Manu is an individuality?

A. In the abstract sense certainly not, but it is possible to apply an analogy. Manu is the synthesis perhaps of the Manasa, and he is a single consciousness in the same sense that while all the different cells of which the human body is composed are different and varying consciousnesses there is still a unit of consciousness which is the man. But this unit, so to say, is not a single consciousness: it is a reflection of thousands and millions of consciousnesses which a man has absorbed.

But Manu is not really an individuality, it is the whole of mankind. You may say that Manu is a generic name for the Pitris, the progenitors of mankind. They come, as I have shown, from the Lunar Chain. They give birth to humanity, for, having become the first men, they give birth to others by evolving their shadows, their astral selves. They not only give birth to humanity but to animals and all other creatures. In this sense it is said in the Purânas of the great Yogis that they gave birth, one to all the serpents, another to all the birds, &c. But, as the moon receives its light from the Sun, so the descendants of the Lunar Pitris receive their higher mental light from the Sun or the "Son of the Sun." For all you know Vaivasvata Manu may be an *Avatar* or a personification of MAHAT, commissioned by the Universal Mind to lead and guide thinking Humanity onwards.

Q. We learn that the perfected humanity of one Round becomes the Dhyani-Buddhas and the guiding rulers of the next Manvantara. What bearing then has Manu on the hosts of the Dhyani-Buddhas?

A. He has no bearing at all—in exoteric teachings. But I may tell you that the Dhyani-Buddhas have nothing to do with the lower practical work of the earth-plane. To use an illustration: the Dhyani-Buddha may be compared to a great ruler of any condition of life. Suppose that it were merely that of a house: the great ruler has nothing directly to do with the dirty work of a kitchen-maid. The higher

Dhyanis evolve lower and lower hierarchies of Dhyanis more and more consolidated and more material until we arrive at this chain of Planets, some of the latter being the Manus, Pitris and Lunar Ancestors. As I show in the Second Volume of the *Secret Doctrine*, these Pitris have the task of giving birth to man. They do this by projecting their shadows and the first humanity (if indeed it can be called humanity) are the astral Chhayas of the Lunar Ancestors over which physical nature builds the physical body, which at first is formless. The Second Race is more and more formed and is sexless. In the Third Race they become bi-sexual and hermaphrodite and then finally separating, the propagation of humanity proceeds in diverse manners.

Q. Then what do you mean by the term Manvantara, or as you have explained it Manu-antara, or "between two Manus"?

A. It simply means a period of activity and is not used in any limited and definite sense. You have to gather from the context of the work you are studying what the meaning of the Manvantara is, remembering also that what is applicable to a lesser period applies also to a greater, and conversely.

Q. Is "Water" as used here purely symbolical or has it a correspondence in the evolution of the elements?*

A. It is necessary to be very careful not to confuse the universal with the terrestrial elements. Nor again do the terrestrial elements mean what is known as the chemical elements. I would call the cosmic, universal elements the noumena of the terrestrial elements, and add that cosmic is not confined to our little Solar System.

Water is the first cosmic element and the terms "darkness" and "chaos" are used to denote the same "element." There are seven states of matter of which three are generally known, viz., solid, liquid, and gaseous. It is necessary to

---

*S. D., Vol. I, p. 64.

consider everything cosmic and terrestrial as existing in variations of these seven states. But it is impossible for me to speak in terms which are unknown to you, and therefore impossible to understand. Thus "water," the "hot and moyst principle" of the philosophers, is used to denote that which is not yet solid matter, or rather that which does not yet possess the solidity of matter, as we understand it. It is rendered rather more difficult by the use of the term "water" as a subsequent "element" in the series of ether, fire and air. But ether contains in itself all the others and their properties, and it is this ether which is the hypothetical agent of physical science: moreover it is the lowest form of Akâsa, the one agent and universal element. Thus water is used here to denote matter in its precosmic state.

Q. What relation have the elements to the Elementals?

A. The same relation as the earth has to man. As physical man is the quintessence of the Earth, so Air or Fire, or Water, and Elemental (called Sylph, Salamander, Undine, etc.), is of the quintessence of its special element. Every differentiation of substance and matter, evolves a kind of intelligent Force, and it is these which the Rosicrucians called Elemental or Nature spirits. Everyone of us can believe in Elementals which we can create for ourselves. But this latter class of elemental creation has no existence outside our own imagination. It will be an intelligence, a Force, good or bad, but the form given to it and its attributes will be of our own creation, while at the same time it will have an intelligence derived also from us.

Q. Are the "Virgin-Egg" and the "Eternal Egg" the same thing, or are they different stages of differentiation?

A. The eternal egg is a pre-differentiation in a laya or zero condition; thus, before differentiation it can have neither attributes nor qualities. The "virgin egg" is already qualified and therefore differentiated, although in its essence it is the same.   No one thing can be separated from another thing, in its abstract essential nature.   But in the world of illusion, in the world of forms, of differentiation, everything, ourselves included, *seems* to be so separated.

VII.

STANZA III.—(*Continued*).

Sloka (2). THE VIBRATION SWEEPS ALONG, TOUCHING WITH ITS SWIFT WING (*simultaneously*) THE WHOLE UNIVERSE; AND THE GERM THAT DWELLETH IN DARKNESS: THE DARKNESS THAT BREATHES (*moves*) OVER THE SLUMBERING WATERS OF LIFE.

Q. How are we to understand the expression that the vibration touches the whole universe and also the germ?

A. First of all the terms used must be defined as far as possible, for the language used is purely figurative. The Universe does not mean the Kosmos or world of forms but the formless space, the future vehicle of the Universe which will be manifested. This space is synonymous with the "waters of space," with (to us) eternal darkness, in fact with Parabrahm. In short the whole Sloka refers to the "period" before there was any manifestation whatever. In the same way the Germ—the Germ is eternal, the undifferentiated atoms of future matter—is one with space, as infinite as it is indestructible, and as eternal as space itself. Similarly with "vibration," which corresponds with the Point, the unmanifested Logos.

It is necessary to add one important explanation. In using figurative language, as has been done in the *Secret Doctrine*, analogies and comparisons are very frequent. Darkness, for instance, as a rule, applies only to the unknown totality, or, Absoluteness. Contrasted with eternal darkness the first Logos is certainly, Light; contrasted with the second or third, the manifested Logoi, the first is Darkness, and the others are Light.

[105]

Sloka (3). DARKNESS RADIATES LIGHT, AND LIGHT
DROPS ONE SOLITARY RAY INTO THE WATERS, THE
MOTHER-DEEP. THE RAY SHOOTS THROUGH THE
VIRGIN EGG; THE RAY CAUSES THE ETERNAL EGG
TO THRILL, AND DROP THE NON-ETERNAL (*periodical*)
GERM, WHICH CONDENSES INTO THE WORLD-EGG.

Q. Why is Light said to drop one solitary ray into the waters and
how is this ray represented in connection with the Triangle?

A. However many the Rays may appear to be on this
plane, when brought back to their original source they will
finally be resolved into a unity, like the seven prismatic colours which all proceed from, and are resolved into the one
white ray. Thus too, this one solitary Ray expands into the
seven rays (and their innumerable sub-divisions) on the
plane of illusion only. It is represented in connection with
the Triangle because the Triangle is the first perfect geometrical figure. As stated by Pythagoras, and also in the
Stanza, the Ray (the Pythagorean Monad) descending from
"no-place" (*Aloka*), shoots like a falling star through the
planes of non-being into the first world of being, and gives
birth to Number One; then branching off, to the right, it
produces Number Two; turning again to form the base-line
it begets Number Three, and thence ascending again to
Number One, it finally disappears therefrom into the realms
of non-being as Pythagoras shows.

Q. Why should Pythagorean teachings be found in old Hindu philosophies?

A. Pythagoras derived this teaching from India and in
the old books we find him spoken of as the Yavanacharya or
Greek Teacher. Thus we see that the Triangle is the first
differentiation, its sides however all being described by the
one Ray.

Q. What is really meant by the term "planes of non-being"?

[106]

A. In using the term "planes of non-being" it is necessary to remember that these planes are only to us spheres of non-being, but those of being and matter to higher intelligences than ourselves. The highest Dhyan-Chohans of the Solar System can have no conception of that which exists in higher systems, *i. e.*, on the second "septenary" Kosmic plane, which to the Beings of the ever *invisible* Universe is entirely subjective.

> *Sloka* (4). (*Then*) THE THREE (*Triangle*) FALL INTO THE FOUR (*Quaternary*). THE RADIANT ESSENCE BECOMES SEVEN INSIDE, SEVEN OUTSIDE. THE LUMINOUS EGG (*Hiranyagharba*), WHICH IN ITSELF IS THREE (*the triple hypostases of Brahma, or Vishnu, the three Avasthas*) CURDLES AND SPREADS IN MILKWHITE CURDS THROUGHOUT THE DEPTHS OF MOTHER, THE ROOT THAT GROWS IN THE OCEAN OF LIFE.

Q. Is the Radiant Essence the same as the luminous Egg? What is the Root that grows in the ocean of life?

A. The radiant essence, luminous egg or Golden Egg of Brahmâ, or again, Hiranyagharba, are identical. The Root that grows in the ocean of life is the potentiality that transforms into objective differentiated matter the universal, subjective, ubiquitous but homogeneous germ, or the eternal essence which contains the potency of abstract nature. The Ocean of Life is, according to a term of the Vedanta philosophy—if I mistake not—the "One Life," Paramatma, when the transcendental supreme Soul is meant; and Jivatma, when we speak of the physical and animal "breath of life" or, so to speak, the differentiated soul, that life in short, which gives being to the atom and the universe, the molecule and the man, the animal, plant, and mineral.

"The Radiant Essence curdled and spread through the depths of Space." From an astronomical point of view this is easy of explanation: it is the Milky Way, the world-stuff, or primordial matter in its first form.

Q. Is the Radiant Essence, Milky Way, or world-stuff, resolvable into atoms, or is it non-atomic?

A. In its precosmic state it is of course, non-atomic, if by atoms you mean molecules; for the hypothetical atom, a mere mathematical point, is not material or applicable to matter, nor even to substance. The real atom does not exist on the material plane. The definition of a point as having position, must not, in Occultism, be taken in the ordinary sense of location; as the *real* atom is beyond space and time. The word molecular is really applicable to our globe and its plane, only: once inside of it, even on the other globes of our planetary chain, matter is in quite another condition, and non-molecular. The atom is in its eternal state, invisible even to the eye of an Archangel; and becomes visible to the latter only periodically, during the life cycle. The particle, or molecule, *is not*, but exists periodically, and is therefore regarded as an illusion.

The world-stuff informs itself through various planes and cannot be said to be resolved into stars or to have become molecular until it reaches the plane of being of the visible or objective Universe.

Q. Can ether be said to be molecular in Occultism?

A. It entirely depends upon what is meant by the term. In its lowest strata, where it merges with the astral light, it may be called molecular on its own plane; but not for us. But the ether of which science has a suspicion, is the grossest manifestation of Akâsa, though on our plane, for us mortals, it is the seventh principle of the astral light, and three degrees higher than "radiant matter." When it penetrates, or informs something, it may be molecular because it takes on the form of the latter, and its atoms inform the particles of that "something." We may perhaps call matter "crystallised ether."

Q. But what is an atom, in fact?

A. An atom may be compared to (and is for the Occultist) the seventh principle of a body or rather of a molecule. The physical or chemical molecule is composed of an infinity of finer molecules and these in their turn of innumerable and still finer molecules. Take for instance a molecule of iron and so resolve it that it becomes non-molecular; it is then, at once transformed into one of its seven principles, *viz.*, its astral body; the seventh of these is the atom. The analogy between a molecule of iron, before it is broken up, and this same molecule after resolution, is the same as that between a physical body before and after death. The principles remain *minus* the body. Of course this is occult alchemy, not modern chemistry.

> *Q.* What is the meaning of the allegorical "churning of the ocean" and "cow of plenty" of the Hindus, and what correspondence is there between them and the "war in heaven"?

A. A process which begins in the state of "non-being," and ends with the close of Maha-Pralaya, can hardly be given in a few words or even volumes. It is simply an allegorical representation of the unseen and unknown primeval intelligences, the atoms of occult science, Brahmâ himself being called *Anu* or the Atom, fashioning and differentiating the shoreless ocean of the primordial radiant essence. The relation and correspondence between the "churning of the ocean" and the "war in heaven" is a very long and abstruse subject to handle. To give it in its lowest symbolical aspect, this "war in heaven" is going on eternally. Differentiation is contrast, the equilibrium of contraries: and so long as this exists there will be "war" or fighting. There are, of course, different stages and aspects of this war: such for instance as the astronomical and physical. For everyone and everything that is born in a Manvantara, there is "war in heaven" and also on the earth: for the fourteen Root and

Seed-Manus who preside over our Manvantaric cycle, and for the countless *Forces*, human or otherwise, that proceed from them. There is a perpetual struggle of adjustment, for everything tends to harmonise and equilibrate; in fact it must do so before it can assume any shape. The elements of which we are formed, the particles of our bodies, are in a continual war, one crowding out the other and changing with every moment. At the "Churning of the Ocean" by the gods, the Nagas came and some stole of the Amrita—the water of Immortality,—and thence arose war between the gods and the Asuras, the *no*-gods, and the gods were worsted. This refers to the formation of the Universe and the differentiation of the primordial primeval matter. But you must remember, that this is only the cosmogonical aspect,—one out of the seven meanings. The war in heaven had also immediate reference to the evolution of the intellectual principle in mankind. This is the metaphysical key.

Q. Why are numbers so much used in the Stanzas; and what is really the secret of their being so freely used in the World-Scriptures—in the Bible and in the Purânas, by Pythagoras and by the Aryan Sages?

A. Balzac, the unconscious occultist of French literature, says somewhere, "the Number is to Mind the same as it is to matter, an incomprehensible agent." But I would answer—perhaps so to the profane, never to the initiated mind. Number is, as the great writer thought, an Entity, and at the same time, a Breath emanating from what he called God and what we call the ALL; the breath which alone could organise the physical Kosmos, "where nought obtains its form but through the Deity, which is an effort of Number."* "God geometrizes" says Plato.

Q. In what sense can numbers be called Entities?

A. When intelligent Entities are meant; when they are

---

*S. D., Vol. I, p. 66.

regarded simply as digits they are, of course, not Entities but symbolical signs.

Q. Why is the radiant essence said to become seven inside and seven outside?

A. Because it has seven principles on the plane of the manifested and seven on that of the unmanifested. Always argue on analogy and apply the old occult axiom, "As above so below."

Q. But are the planes of "non-being" also Septenary?

A. Most undeniably. That which in the *Secret Doctrine* is referred to as the unmanifested planes, are unmanifested or planes of non-being only from the point of view of the finite intellect; to higher intelligences they would be manifested planes and so on to infinity, analogy always holding good.

VIII.

THE ROOT REMAINS, THE LIGHT REMAINS, THE CURDS REMAIN, AND STILL OEAOHOO IS ONE.

Q. What is meant by saying that these remain?

A. It means simply that whatever the plurality of manifestation may be, still it is all one. In other words these are all different aspects of the one element; it does not mean that they remain without differentiation.

"The curds are the first differentiation and probably refer to that cosmic matter which is supposed to be the origin of the 'Milky Way'—the matter we know. This 'matter,' which, according to the revelation received from the primeval Dhyani-Buddhas, is, during the periodical sleep of the universe, of the ultimate tenuity conceivable to the eye of the perfect Bodhisatva—this matter, radiant and cool, becomes at the first reawakening of cosmic motion, scattered through space, appearing when seen from the earth, in clusters and lumps, like curds in thin milk. These are the seeds of future worlds, the 'star-stuff.' "*

Q. Is it to be supposed that the Milky Way is composed of matter in a state of differentiation other than that with which we are acquainted?

A. I thoroughly believe so. It is the store-house of the materials from which the stars, planets and other celestial bodies are produced. Matter in this state does not exist on earth; but that which is already differentiated and found on earth is also found on other planets and *vice-versâ*. But, as I

*S. D., Vol. I, p. 69.

understand, before reaching the planets from its condition in the Milky Way, matter has first to pass through many stages of differentiation. The matter, for instance, within the Solar system is in an entirely different state from that which is outside or beyond the system.

Q. Is there a difference between the Nebulæ and the Milky Way?

A. The same, I should say, that there is between a highway road and the stones and mud upon that road. There must be, of course, a difference between the matter of the Milky Way and that of the various Nebulæ, and these again must differ among themselves. But in all your scientific calculations and measurements it is necessary to consider that the light by which the objects are seen is a *reflected* light, and the optical illusion caused by the atmosphere of the earth renders it impossible that calculations of distances, &c., should be absolutely correct, in addition to the fact that it entirely alters observations of the matter of which the celestial bodies are composed, as it is liable to impose upon us a constitution similar to that of the earth. This is, at any rate, what the MASTERS teach us.

Sloka (6). THE ROOT OF LIFE WAS IN EVERY DROP OF THE OCEAN OF IMMORTALITY (*Amrita*) AND THE OCEAN WAS RADIANT LIGHT, WHICH WAS FIRE AND HEAT AND MOTION. DARKNESS VANISHED AND WAS NO MORE. IT DISAPPEARED IN ITS OWN ESSENCE, THE BODY OF FIRE AND WATER, OF FATHER AND MOTHER.

Q. What are the various meanings of the term "fire" on the different planes of Kosmos?

A. Fire is the most mystic of all the five elements, as also the most divine. Therefore to give an explanation of its various meanings on our plane alone, leaving all the other planes entirely out of the question, would be much too arduous, in addition to its being entirely incomprehensible for the vast majority. Fire is the father of light, light the parent of heat and air (vital air). If the absolute deity can be referred to as Darkness or the Dark Fire, the light, its first progeny, is truly the first self-conscious god. For what is light in its primordial root but the world-illuminating and life-giving deity? Light is that, which from an abstraction has become a reality. No one has ever seen real or primordial light; what we see is only its broken rays or reflections, which become denser and less luminous as they descend into form and matter. Fire, therefore, is a term which comprehends ALL. Fire is the invisible deity, "the Father," and the manifesting light is God "the Son," and also the Sun. Fire—in the occult sense—is æther, and æther is born of motion, and motion is the eternal dark, invisible Fire. Light sets in motion and controls all in nature, from that highest primordial æther down to the tiniest molecule in Space. MOTION is eternal *per se*, and in the manifested Kosmos it is the Alpha and Omega of that which is called electricity, galvanism, magnetism, sensation—moral and physical—thought, and even life, on this plane. Thus fire, on our plane, is simply the manifestation of motion, or life.

All cosmic phenomena were referred to by the Rosicrucians as "animated geometry." Every polar function is only a repetition of primeval polarity, said the Fire-Philosophers. For motion begets heat, and æther in motion is heat. When it slackens its motion, then cold is generated, for "cold is æther, in a latent condition." Thus the principal states of nature are three positive and three negative, synthesized by the primeval light. The three negative states are (1) Darkness; (2) Cold; (3) Vacuum or Voidness. The three positive are (1) Light (on our plane); (2) Heat; (3) All nature. Thus Fire may be called the unity of the Universe.

Pure cosmic fire (without, so to speak, fuel) is Deity in its universality; for cosmic fire, or heat which it calls forth, is every atom of matter in manifested nature. There is not a thing or a particle in the Universe which does not contain in it latent fire.

Q. Fire, then, may be regarded as the first Element?

A. When we say that fire is the first of the Elements, it is the first only in the visible universe, the fire that we commonly know. Even on the highest plane of our universe, the plane of Globe A or G, fire is in one respect only the fourth. For the Occultist, the Rosecroix of the Middle Ages, and even the mediæval Kabalists, said that to our human perception and even to that of the highest "angels," the universal Deity is darkness, and from this Darkness issues the Logos in the following aspects, (1) Weight (Chaos which becomes æther in its primordial state); (2) Light; (3) Heat; (4) Fire.

Q. In what relation does the Sun, the highest form of Fire we can recognise, stand to Fire as you have explained it?

A. The Sun, as on our plane, is not even "Solar" fire. The Sun we see, gives nothing of itself, because it is a reflection; a bundle of electro-magnetic forces, one of the countless milliards of "Knots of Fohat." Fohat is called the "Thread of primeval Light," the "Ball of thread" of Ariadne, indeed, in this labyrinth of chaotic matter. This thread runs through the seven planes tying itself into knots. Every plane being septenary, there are thus forty-nine mystical and physical forces, larger knots forming stars, suns and systems, the smaller planets, and so on.

Q. In what respect is the Sun an illusion?

A. The electro-magnetic knot of our Sun is neither tangible nor dimensional, nor even as molecular as the electricity we know. The Sun absorbs, "psychisizes" and vampirizes its subjects within its system. Further than this it gives out nothing of itself. It is an absurdity, therefore, to say that the solar fires are being consumed and gradually extinguished. The Sun has but one distinct function; it gives the impulse of life to all that breathes and lives under its light. The sun is the throbbing heart of the system; each throb being an impulse. But this heart is invisible: no astronomer will ever see it. That which is concealed in this heart and that which we feel and see, its apparent flame and fires, to use a simile, are the nerves governing the muscles of the solar system, and nerves, moreover, outside of the body. This impulse is not mechanical but a purely spiritual, nervous impulse.

Q. What connection has "weight," as you use it, with gravity?

A. By weight, gravity in the occult sense of attraction and repulsion is meant. It is one of the attributes of differentiation, and is a universal property. By attraction and repulsion between matter in various states it is possible, in most cases, to explain (whereas the "law of gravitation" is insufficient to do so) the relation which the tails of the comets assume when nearing the sun; seeing that they manifestly act contrary to this hypothesis.

Q. What is the meaning of water in this connection?

A. As Water, according to its atomic weight, is composed of one-ninth of Hydrogen (a very inflammable gas, as you know, and without which no organic body is found), and of eight-ninths of Oxygen (which produces combustion when too rapidly combined with any body), what can it be but one of the forms of primordial force or fire, in a cold or latent and fluidic form? Fire bears the same relation to Water as Spirit to Matter.

[117]

Sloka (7). BEHOLD, O LANOO, THE RADIANT CHILD OF THE TWO, THE UNPARALLELED REFULGENT GLORY, BRIGHT SPACE, SON OF DARK SPACE, WHO EMERGES FROM THE DEPTHS OF THE GREAT DARK WATERS. IT IS OEAOHOO, THE YOUNGER, THE * * * (*whom thou knowest now as Kwan-Shai-Yin*). HE SHINES FORTH AS THE SUN. HE IS THE BLAZING DIVINE DRAGON OF WISDOM. THE EKA IS CHATUR (*four*), AND CHATUR TAKES TO ITSELF THREE, AND THE UNION PRODUCES THE SAPTA, (*seven*) IN WHOM ARE THE SEVEN WHICH BECOME THE TRIDASA (*the thrice ten*), THE HOSTS AND THE MULTITUDES. BEHOLD HIM LIFTING THE VEIL, AND UNFURLING IT FROM EAST TO WEST. HE SHUTS OUT THE ABOVE AND LEAVES THE BELOW TO BE SEEN AS THE GREAT ILLUSION. HE MARKS THE PLACES FOR THE SHINING ONES (*stars*) AND TURNS THE UPPER SPACE INTO A SHORELESS SEA OF FIRE, AND THE ONE MANIFESTED (*element*) INTO THE GREAT WATERS.

Kwan-Shai-Yin and Kwan-Yin are synonymous with fire and water. The two deities in their primordial manifestation are the dyadic or dual god, bi-sexual nature, Purusha and Prakriti.

Q. What are the terms corresponding to the three Logoi among the words of Oeaohoo, the younger, Kwan-Shai-Yin, Kwan-Yin, Father-Mother, Fire and Water, Bright Space and Dark Space?

A. Everyone must work this out for himself, "Kwan-Shai-Yin marks the places for the shining ones, the stars, and turns the upper space into a shoreless sea of fire, and the one manifested into the great Waters." Think well over this. Fire here stands for the concealed Spirit, Water is its progeny, or moisture, or the creative elements here on earth, the outer crust, and the evolving or creative principles within, or the innermost principles. Illusionists would probably say "above."

Q. What is the veil which Oeaohoo, the younger, lifts from East to West?

A. The veil of reality. It is the curtain which disappears in order to show the spectator the illusions on the stage of Being, the scenery and actors, in short, the universe of MAYA.

Q. What is the "upper space" and "shoreless sea of fire"?

A. The "upper space" is the space "within," however paradoxical it may seem, for there is no *above* as no *below* in the infinitude; but the planes follow each other and solidify *from within without.* It is in fact, the universe as it first appears from its *laya* or "zero" state, a shoreless expanse of spirit, or "sea of fire."

Q. Are the "Great Waters" the same as those on which the Darkness moved?

A. It is incorrect in this case, to speak of Darkness "moving." Absolute Darkness, or the Eternal Unknown, cannot be active, and moving *is* action. Even in *Genesis* it is stated that Darkness *was* upon the face of the deep, but that which moved upon the face of the waters, was the "Spirit of God." This means esoterically that in the beginning, when the Infinitude was without form, and Chaos, or the outer Space, was still void, Darkness (*i. e., Kalahansa Parabrahm*) alone *was*. Then, at the first radiation of Dawn, the "Spirit of God" (after the First and Second Logos were radiated, the Third Logos, or Narayan) began to move on the face of the Great Waters of the "Deep." Therefore the question to be correct, if not clear, should be, "Are the Great Waters the same as the Darkness spoken of?" The answer would then be in the affirmative. Kalahansa has a dual meaning. Exoterically it is Brahmâ who is the Swan, the "Great Bird," the vehicle in which Darkness manifests itself to human comprehension as light, and this Universe. But esoterically, it is Darkness itself, the unknowable Absolute which is the Source, firstly of the radiation called the First Logos, then of its reflection, the Dawn, or the Second Logos, and finally of Brahmâ, the manifested Light, or the Third Logos. Let us remember, that under this illusion of manifestation, which we see and feel, and which, as we imagine, comes under our sensuous perceptions, is simply and in sober reality, that which we neither hear, see, feel, taste nor touch at all. It is a gross illusion and nothing else.

Q. To return to an early question, in what sense can electricity be called an "entity"?

A. Only when we refer to it as Fohat, its primordial Force. In reality there is only one force, which on the manifested plane appears to us in millions and millions of forms. As said, all proceeds from the one universal primordial fire, and electricity is on our plane one of the most comprehensive aspects of this fire. All contains, and is, electricity, from the nettle which stings to the lightning which kills, from the spark in the pebble to the blood in the body. But the electricity which is seen, for instance, in an electric lamp, is quite another thing from Fohat. Electricity is the cause of the molecular motion in the physical universe, and hence also here, on earth. It is one of the "principles" of matter; for generated as it is in every disturbance of equilibrium, it becomes, so to say, the Kamic element of the object in which this disturbance takes place. Thus Fohat, the primeval cause of this force in its millions of aspects, and as the sum total of universal cosmic electricity, is an "entity."

Q. But what do you mean by this term? Is not electricity an entity also?

A. I would not call it so. The word Entity comes from the Latin root *ens*, "being," of *esse*, "to be;" therefore everything independent of any other thing, is an entity, from a grain of sand up to God. But in our case Fohat is alone an entity, electricity having only a relative significance, if taken in the usual, scientific sense.

Q. Is not cosmic electricity a son of Fohat, and are not his "Seven Sons" Entities?

A. I am afraid not. Speaking of the Sun, we may call it an Entity but we would hardly call a sunbeam that dazzles our eyes, also an Entity. The "Sons of Fohat" are the various Forces having fohatic, or cosmic electric life in their essence or being, and in their various effects. An example: rub amber—a Fohatic Entity—and it will give birth to a "Son" who will attract straws: an apparently inanimate and inorganic object thus manifesting life! But rub a nettle between your thumb and finger and you will also generate a Son of Fohat, in the shape of a blister. In these cases, the blister is an Entity, but the attraction which draws the straw, is hardly one.

Q. Then Fohat is cosmic electricity and the "Son" is also electricity?

A. Electricity is the work of Fohat, but as I have just said, Fohat is *not* electricity. From an occult standpoint, electric phenomena are very often produced by the abnormal state of the molecules of an object or of bodies in space: electricity is life and it is death: the first being produced by harmony, the second by disharmony. Vital electricity is under the same laws as Cosmic electricity. The combination of molecules into new forms, and the bringing about of new correlations and disturbance of molecular equilibrium is, in general, the work of, and generates, Fohat. The synthesized principle, or the emanation of the seven cosmic Logoi is beneficent only there where harmony prevails.

Sloka (8). WHERE WAS THE GERM, AND WHERE WAS NOW DARKNESS? WHERE IS THE SPIRIT OF THE FLAME THAT BURNS IN THY LAMP, O LANOO? THE

GERM IS THAT, AND THAT IS LIGHT; THE WHITE
BRILLIANT SON OF THE DARK HIDDEN FATHER.

Q. Is this spirit of the flame that burns in the lamp of every one of
us, our Heavenly Father, or Higher Self?

A. Neither one nor the other; the sentence quoted is
merely an analogy and refers to a real lamp which the dis-
ciple may be supposed to be using.

Q. Are the elements the bodies of the Dhyan-Chohans, and are
Hydrogen, Oxygen, Ozone and Nitrogen, the primordial elements on
this plane of matter?

A. The answer to the first part of this question will be
found by studying the symbolism of the *Secret Doctrine.*
With regard to the four elements named it is the case; but
bear in mind that on a higher plane even volatile ether would
appear to be as gross as mud. Every plane has its own
denseness of substance or matter, its own colours, sounds,
dimensions of space, etc., which are quite unknown to us on
this plane; and as we have on earth intermediary beings, the
ant for instance, a kind of transitional entity between two
planes, so on the plane above us there are creatures endowed
with senses and faculties unknown to the inhabitants of
that plane.

There is a remarkable illustration of Elihu Vedder to the
Quatrains of Omar Khayyam, which suggests the idea of the
Knots of Fohat. It is the ordinary Japanese representation
of clouds, single lines running into knots both in drawings
and carvings. It is Fohat the "knot-tier," and from one
point of view it is the "world-stuff."

Q. If the Milky Way is a manifestation of this "world-stuff" how
is it that it is not seen over the whole sky?

A. Why should it not be the more contracted, and therefore, its condensed part which alone is seen. This forms
into "knots" and passes through the sun-stage, the cometary

and planetary stages, until finally it becomes a dead body, or a moon. There are also various kinds of suns. The sun of the solar system is a reflection. At the end of the solar manvantara, it will begin to get less and less radiant, giving less and less heat, owing to a change in the real sun, of which the visible sun is the reflection. After the solar Pralaya, the present sun will, in a future Manvantara, become a cometary body, but certainly not during the life of our little planetary chain. The argument drawn from spectrum star-analysis is not solid, because no account is taken of the passage of light through cosmic dust. This does not mean to say that there is no real difference in the spectra of stars, but that the proclaimed presence of iron or sodium in any particular star may be owing to the modification of the rays of such a star by the cosmic dust with which the earth is surrounded.

Q. Does not the perceptive power of the ant—for instance, the way in which its perceptive faculties differ from our perceptive powers of colour—simply depend upon physiological conditions?

A. The ant can certainly appreciate the sounds that we do, and it can also appreciate sounds that we can never hear, therefore evidently, physiology has nothing whatever to do with the matter. The ant and ourselves possess different degrees of perception. We are on a higher scale of evolution than the ant, but, comparatively speaking, we are the ants to the plane above.

Q. When electricity is excited by rubbing amber, is there anything corresponding to an emanation from amber?

A. There is: the electricity which is latent in the amber, exists in everything else, and will be found there if given the appropriate conditions necessary for its liberation. There is one error which is commonly made, than which there can be no greater error in the views of an occultist. A division is made between what you call animate and inanimate objects, as if there could be such a thing as a perfectly inanimate object on earth!

In reality, even that which you call a dead man is more alive than ever. From one point of view, the distinguishing mark between what is called the organic and the inorganic is the function of nutrition, but if there were no nutrition how could those bodies which are called inorganic undergo change? Even crystals undergo a process of accretion, which for them answers the function of nutrition. In reality, as Occult philosophy teaches us, everything which changes is organic; it has the life principle in it, and it has all the potentiality of the higher lives. If, as we say, all in nature is an aspect of the one element, and life is universal, how can there be such a thing as an inorganic atom!

IX.

Sloka (10). FATHER-MOTHER SPIN A WEB WHOSE UP-
PER END IS FASTENED TO SPIRIT (*Purusha*), THE
LIGHT OF THE ONE DARKNESS, AND THE LOWER
ONE TO MATTER (*Prakriti*), ITS (*the Spirit's*) SHADOWY
END; AND THIS WEB IS THE UNIVERSE SPUN OUT OF
TWO SUBSTANCES MADE IN ONE, WHICH IS SVABHA-
VAT.*

Q. Spirit and matter are the opposite ends of the same web; light
and darkness, heat and cold, void or space and fulness of all that exists are also opposites. In what sense are these three pairs of opposites associated with Spirit and Matter?

A. In the sense in which everything in the universe is
associated with either Spirit or Matter, one of these being
taken as the permanent element or both. Pure Matter is
pure Spirit and cannot be understood even if admitted by
our finite intellects. Neither light nor darkness as optical
effects, are matter, nor are they spirit, but they are the qualities of the former (matter).

Q. In what relation does Ether stand to Spirit and Matter?

A. Make a difference between Æther and Ether, the
former being divine, the latter physical and *infernal*. Ether
is the lowest of the septenate division of Akâsa-Pradhâna,
primordial Fire-Substance. Æther-Akâsa is the fifth and
sixth principles of the body of Kosmos—thus corresponding
to Buddhi-Manas, in Man; *Ether* is its Kosmic sediment
mingling with the highest layer of the Astral Light. Beginning with the fifth root-race, it will develop fully only at the
beginning of the fifth round. Æther is Akâsa in its higher
aspect, and *Ether* Akâsa, in its lowest. In one sense it is

*S. D., Vol. I, p. 83.

equivalent to the Father-Creator, Zeus, Pater Ether; on the other to the infernal Serpent-Tempter, the Astral Light of the Kabalists. In the latter case it is fully differentiated matter, in the former only rudimentally differentiated. In other words, Spirit becomes objective matter; and objective matter rebecomes subjective Spirit, when it eludes our metaphysical senses. Ether has the same relation to the Cosmos and our little Earth, as Manas to the Monad and body. Therefore, Ether has naught to do with Spirit, but a good deal, with subjective matter and our Earth.

Q. "Brahmâ, as the 'germ of unknown Darkness,' is the material form which all evolves and developes." It is one of the axioms of logic that it is impossible for the mind to believe anything of that of which it comprehends nothing. Now if this "material" which is Brahmâ be formless, then no idea concerning it can enter the mind for the mind can conceive nothing where there is no form. It is the garment or manifestation in the form of "God" which we can perceive, and it is by this and this alone that we can know anything of him. What, therefore, is the first form of this material which human consciousness can recognise?

A. Your axioms of logic can be applied to the *lower* Manas only and it is from the perceptions of *Kama Manas* alone that you argue. But Occultism teaches only that which it derives from the cognition of the Higher Ego or the *Buddhi Manas*. But, I will try to answer you on your own familiar lines. The first and only form of the *prima materia* our brain-consciousness can cognise, is a circle. Train your thought first of all to a thorough acquaintance with a limited circle, and expand it gradually. You will soon come to a point when without its ceasing to be a circle in thought, it yet becomes infinite and limitless even to the inner perceptions. It is this circle which we call Brahmâ, the germ, atom or *anu:* a latent atom embracing infinitude and boundless Eternity during Pralaya, an active one during the life-cycles; but one which has neither circumference nor plane, only limitless expansion. Therefore the Circle is the first geometrical figure and symbol in the subjective world, and it becomes a Triangle in the objective. The Triangle is the next figure after the Circle. The first figure, the Circle with the Point, is really no figure; it is simply a primeval germ, the first thing you can imagine at the beginning of differentiation; the Triangle must be conceived of once that matter has passed the zero point, or *Layam*. Brahmâ is called an atom, because we have to imagine it as a mathematical point, which, however, can be extended into absoluteness. *Nota Bene*, it is the divine germ and not the atom of the chemists. But beware of the illusion of form. Once you drag down your Deity into human form you limit and condition it, and behold, you have created an anthropomorphic god.

> *Sloka* (11). IT (*the Web*) EXPANDS WHEN THE BREATH OF FIRE (*the Father*) IS UPON IT; IT CONTRACTS WHEN THE BREATH OF THE MOTHER (*the root of Matter*) TOUCHES IT. THEN THE SONS (*the elements with their respective powers or intelligences*) DISSOCIATE AND SCATTER, TO RETURN INTO THEIR MOTHER'S BOSOM AT THE END OF THE "GREAT DAY" AND REBECOME ONE WITH HER. WHEN IT (*the Web*) IS COOLING, IT BECOMES RADIANT, ITS SONS EXPAND AND CONTRACT THROUGH THEIR OWN SELVES AND HEARTS; THEY EMBRACE INFINITUDE.*

Q. Is the word "expand" here used in the sense of differentiating or evolving, and "contract" in that of involution, or do these terms refer to Manvantara and Pralaya; or again to a constant vibrating motion of the world-stuff or atoms? Is this expansion and contraction simultaneous or successive?

A. The Web is the ever-existent primordial substance— pure spirit to our conception—the material from which objective universe or universes are evolved. When the breath of fire or Father, is upon it, it expands; that is to say, as sub-

_____
S. D., Vol. I, p. 83.

jective material it is limitless, eternal, indestructible. When the breath of the Mother touches it, that is, when the time of manifestation arrives and it has to come into objectivity of form, it contracts, for there is no such thing as an objective material form which is limitless. Though Newton's proposition that every particle of matter has the property of of attraction for every other particle, is on the whole correct; and though Leibnitz's proposition that every atom is a universe in itself, and acts through its own inherent force, is also true; yet both are incomplete. For man is also an atom, possessing attraction and repulsion, and is the Microcosm of the Macrocosm. But would it be also true to say that because of the force and intelligence in him he moves independently of every other human unit, or could act and move, unless there were a greater force and intelligence than his own to allow him to live and move in that higher element of Force and Intelligence?

One of the objects of the *Secret Doctrine* is to prove that planetary movements cannot be satisfactorily accounted for by the theory of gravitation alone. Besides the force acting *in* matter there is also a force acting *on* matter.

When we speak of the modified conditions of Spirit-Matter (which is in reality Force), and call them by various names such as heat, cold, light and darkness, attraction and repulsion, electricity and magnetism, &c., &c., to the occultist they are simple names, expressions of difference in manifestations of one and the same Force (always dual in differentiation), but not any specific difference of forces. For all such differences in the objective world result only from the peculiarities of differentiation of matter on which the one free force acts, helped in this by that portion of its essence which we call imprisoned force, or material molecules. The worker within, the inherent force, ever tends to unite with its parent essence without; and thus, the Mother acting within, causes the Web to contract; and the Father acting without, to expand. Science calls this gravitation; Occultists, the work of the universal Life-Force, which radiates from that Absolute and Unknowable FORCE which is outside of all Space and Time. This is the work of Eternal evolution and involution, or expansion and contraction.

Q. What is the meaning of the phrase "the Web cooling," and when does this take place?

A. Evidently it is itself which is cooling, and not anything outside of itself. When? We are told that it begins when the imprisoned force and intelligence inherent in every atom of differentiated as well as of homogeneous matter arrives at a point when both become the slaves of a higher intelligent Force whose mission it is to guide and shape it. It is the Force which we call the divine Free-Will, represented by the Dhyani-Buddhas. When the centripetal and centrifugal forces of life and being are subjected by the one nameless Force which brings order in disorder, and establishes harmony in Chaos—then it begins cooling. It is impossible to give the exact time in a process the duration of which is unknown.

Q. Is form the result of the interaction of the centrifugal and centripetal forces in matter and nature?

A. Every form, we are told, is built in accordance with the model traced for it in the Eternity and reflected in the DIVINE MIND. There are hierarchies of "Builders of form," and series of forms and degrees, from the highest to the lowest. While the former are shaped under the guidance of the "Builders," the gods, "Cosmocratores;" the latter are fashioned by the Elementals or Nature Spirits. As an example of this, look at the strange insects and at some reptiles and non-vertebrate creatures, which so closely imitate, not only in their colour but by their outward shape, leaves, flowers, moss-covered branches and other so-called "inanimate" things. Shall we take "natural selection" and the explanations of Darwinists as a solution? I trust not. The theory of natural selection is not only utterly inadequate to explain this mysterious faculty of imitation in the realm of being, but gives also an entirely false conception of the importance of such imitative faculty, as a "potent weapon in the struggle for life." And if this imitative faculty is once proved— as it can easily be—an absolute *misfit* for the Darwinian frame; *i. e.*, if its alleged use, in connection with the so-called "survival of the fittest" is shown to be a speculation which cannot stand close analysis, to what then can the fact of this faculty be attributed? All of you have seen insects which copy with almost a mirror-like fidelity the colour and even outward form of plants, leaves, flowers, pieces of dead twigs, etc. Nor is this a law but rather a frequent exception. What then but an invisible intelligence *outside* the insect can copy with such accuracy from larger originals?

Q. But does not Mr. Wallace show that such imitation has its object in nature? That it is just this which proves the "natural selection" theory, and the innate instinct in the weaker creatures to seek security behind the borrowed garb of certain objects? The insectivora which do not feed upon plants and leaves, will thus leave a leaf-like or moss-like insect safe from attack. This seems very plausible.

A. Very plausible, indeed, if, besides negative facts, there were no very positive evidence to show the unfitness of the natural selection theory to account for the phenomena of imitation. A fact to hold good, must be shown to apply if not universally, then, at any rate, always under the same conditions, *e. g.*, the correspondence and identity of colour between the animals of one and the same locality and the soil of that region would be a general manifestation. But how about the camel of the desert with his coat of the same "protecting" colour as the plains he lives in, and the zebra whose intense, dark stripes *cannot* protect him on the open plains of South Africa, as Mr. Darwin himself admitted. We are assured by Science that this imitation of the colour of the soil is invariably found in the weaker animals, and yet we find the lion—who need fear no stronger enemies than himself in the desert—with a coat that can hardly be distinguished from the rocks and sandy plains he inhabits! We are asked to believe that this "imitation of protecting colours is caused by the use and *benefit* it offers the imitator," as a "potent weapon in the struggle for life"; and yet, daily experience shows to us quite the reverse. Thus, it points to a number of animals in which the most pronounced forms of the imitative faculty are entirely useless, or, worse than that, pernicious and often self-destructive. What good, I ask, is the imitation of human speech to the magpie and parrot—except leading them to be shut up in a cage? Of what use to the monkey its mimicking faculty which brings so many of them to grief and occasionally to great bodily harm and self-destruction; or to a herd of idiotic sheep, in blindly following their leader, even if he happens to tumble down a precipice? This irrepressible desire, also (of *imitating* their leaders) has led more than one unlucky Darwinist, while seeking to prove his favourite hobby, into the most absurdly incongruous statements. Thus, our Hæckelian friend, Mr. Grant Allen, in his work upon the subject under discussion, speaks of a certain Indian lizard blessed with three large parasites of different kinds. Each of these three imitates to perfection the colour of the scales of that part of the body it dwells on: the parasite on the stomach of the creature, is yellow like its stomach; the second parasite having chosen its abode on the back, is as variegated in colour as the dorsal scales; while the third having selected its hermitage on the lizard's brown head, is almost undistinguishable from it in colour. This careful copy of the respective colours, we are told by Mr. G.

Allen, is for the purpose of preserving the parasites from the lizard itself. But surely this doughty champion of natural selection does not mean to tell his public that the lizard can see the parasite *on its own head!* Finally, of what use is its brilliant red colour to the fish which lives amidst coral reefs, or to the tiny Birds of Paradise, *colibri*, the rainbow hues of their plumage, imitating all the radiant colours of the tropical fauna and flora—except to make them the more noticeable?

Q. To what causes would Occultism attribute this imitative faculty?

A. To several things. In the case of such rare tropical birds and leaf-like insects to early intermediate links, in the former case between the lizard and the *colibri*, and in the latter between certain vegetations and the insect kind. There was a time, millions of years ago, when such "missing links" were numerous, and on every point of the globe where life was. But now they are becoming with every cycle and generation more rare; they are found at present, only in a limited number of localities, as all such links are relics of the Past.

Q. Will you give us some explanation from the occult standpoint of what is called the "Law of Gravitation"?

A. Science insists that between bodies attraction is directly as the mass and inversely as the square of the distance. Occultists, however, doubt whether this law holds good with regard to the entirety of planetary rotation. Take the first and second laws of Kepler included in the Newtonian law as given by Herschel. "Under the influence of such attractive force mutually urging two spherical gravitating bodies toward one another, they will each, when moving in each other's neighbourhood, be deflected into an orbit concave toward each other, and describe one about the other, regarded as fixed, or both around their common centre of gravity, curves whose forms are limited as those figures known in geometry by the general name of Conic Sections. It will depend upon the particular circumstances or velocity, distance and direction, which of these curves shall be described, whether an ellipse, a circle, a parabola, or an hyperbola, but one or the other it must be. . . . . &c., &c."

Science says that the phenomena of planetary motion result from the action of two forces, one centripetal, the other centrifugal, and that a body falling to the ground in a line perpendicular to still water does so owing to the law of gravity or of centripetal force. Among others, the following objections brought forward by a learned occultist, may be stated.

[1] That the path of a circle is impossible in planetary motion.

[2] That the argument in the third law of Kepler, namely that "the squares of the periodic times of any two planets are to each other, in the same proportion as the cubes of their mean distances from the Sun," gives rise to the curious result of a permitted libration in the eccentricities of planets. Now the said forces remaining unchanged in their nature, this can only arise, as he says, "from the interference of an extraneous cause."

[3] That the phenomenon of gravitation or "falling" does not exist, except as the result of a conflict of forces. It can only be considered as an isolated force by way of mental analysis or separation. He asserts, moreover, that the planets, atoms, or particles of matter are not *attracted* towards each other in the direction of right lines connecting their centres, but are forced towards each other in the curves of spirals closing upon the centre of each other. Also that the tidal wave is not the result of attraction. All this, as he shows, results from the conflict of imprisoned and free force; antagonism apparently, but really affinity and harmony.

[133]

"Fohat, gathering a few of the clusters of cosmic matter (nebulæ) will, by giving it an impulse, set it in motion anew, develope the required heat, and then leave it to follow its own new growth."*

Q. Is Fohat to be understood as synonymous with force, or that which causes the changing manifestation of matter? If so, how can Fohat be said to "leave it to follow its own new growth," when all growth depends upon the indwelling force?

A. All growth depends upon the indwelling force, because on this plane of ours it is this force alone which acts consciously. The universal force cannot be regarded as a conscious force as we understand the word consciousness, because it would immediately become a personal god. It is only that which is enclosed in form, a limitation of matter, which is conscious of itself on this plane. This Free Force or Will, which is limitless and absolute, cannot be said to act understandingly, but it is the one and sole immutable Law of Life and Being.

Fohat, therefore, is spoken of as the synthetic motor power of all the imprisoned life-forces and the medium between the absolute and conditioned Force. It is a link, just as Manas is the connecting link between the gross matter of the physical body and the divine Monad which animates it, but is powerless to act upon the former directly.

Q. If Force is a unity or One, manifesting in an unlimited variety of ways, it is difficult to understand the statement in the Commentary that: "There is heat internal and external in every atom"; *i. e.*, latent and active heat or dynamic and kinetic heat. Heat is the phenomenon of a perception of matter actuated by force in a peculiar manner. Heat, therefore, on the physical plane is simply matter in motion. If there is heat in a more interior and occult sense than physical heat, it must be perceived by some higher and more interior senses by virtue of its activities on whatever plane it manifests. For this perception three conditions are necessary, an actuating force, a

*S. D., Vol. I, p. 84.

form which is actuated and that which perceives the form in motion. The terms "latent," "potential" or "dynamic" heat are misnomers, because heat, whether on the first or the seventh plane of consciousness, is the perception of matter or substance in motion.

Is the discrepancy between the above statement and the teaching of the "Secret Doctrine" apparent or real?

A. Why should heat on any other plane than ours be the perception of matter or substance in motion? Why should an occultist accept the condition of [1] the actuating force; [2] the form which is actuated; [3] that which perceives the form in motion, as those of heat?

As with every ascending plane heterogeneity tends more and more to homogeneity, so on the seventh plane the form will disappear, there being nothing to be actuated, the acting Force will remain in solitary grandeur, to perceive but itself; or in Spencer's phraseology, it will have become both "subject and object, the perceiver and the perceived." The terms used are not contradictory, but symbols borrowed from physical science in order to render occult action and processes more clear to the minds of those who are trained in that science. In fact, each of these specifications of heat and force, corresponds to one of the principles in man.

The "heat centres," from the physical standpoint, would be the zero-point, because they are spiritual.

The word "perceived" is somewhat erroneous, it should rather be "sensed." Fohat is the agent of the law, its representative, the representative of the Manasa-putras, whose collectivity is—the eternal mind.

Q. In the passage of a globe into Pralaya does it remain *in situ, i. e.,* still forming part of a planetary chain and maintaining its proper position in relation to the other globes? Does the dissociation by means of heat play any part in the passage of a globe into Pralaya?

A. This is explained in "Esoteric Buddhism." When a globe of a planetary chain goes into "obscuration" every quality, including heat, retires from it and it remains *in statu quo*, like the "sleeping Beauty," until Fohat, the "Prince Charmant," awakens it with a kiss.

Q. The sons are spoken of as dissociating and scattering. This appears to be opposed to the action of returning to their "mother's bosom" at the end of the "Great Day." Does the dissociating and scattering refer to the formation of the globe from the universally diffused world-stuff, in other words emerging from Pralaya?

A. The dissociating and scattering refers to Nitya Pralaya. This is an eternal and perpetual Pralaya which is taking place ever since there were globes and differentiated matter. It is simply atomic change.

Q. What is meant by the expression expanding and contracting through their own "selves and hearts" and how is this connected with the last line of the sloka, "They embrace Infinitude"?

A. This has already been explained. Through their own inherent and imprisoned force they strive collectively to join the one universal or free force, that is to say, embrace infinitude, this free force being infinite.

Q. What is the relation between electricity and physical or animal magnetism and hypnotism?

A. If by electricity, you mean the science which unfolds on this plane, and under a dozen various qualifications the phenomena and laws of the electric fluid—then I answer, none at all. But if you refer to the electricity we call *Fohatic*, or *intra*-cosmic, then I will say that all these forms of phenomena are based on it.

X.

STANZA IV.

Sloka (1). LISTEN, YE SONS OF THE EARTH, TO YOUR IN-
STRUCTORS—THE SONS OF THE FIRE. LEARN THERE
IS NEITHER FIRST NOR LAST; FOR ALL IS ONE NUM-
BER, ISSUED FROM NO NUMBER.

Q. Are the sons of the Fire, the Rays of the Third Logos?

A. The "Rays" are the "Sons of the Fire-Mist," produced by the *Third Creation*, or Logos. The actual "Sons
of the Fire" of the Fifth Race and Sub-races are so called
simply because they by their wisdom belong, or are nearer
to, the hierarchy of the divine "Sons of the Fire-Mist," the
highest of the planetary Chohans or Angels. But the Sons
of the Fire here spoken of as addressing the Sons of the
Earth are, in this case, the King-Instructors who incarnated
on this earth to teach nascent Humanity. As "Kings" they
belong to the divine dynasties of which every nation, India,
Chaldea, Egypt, Homeric Greece, &c., has preserved a tradition or record in some form or other. The name "Sons of
the Fire-Mist" was also given to the Hierophants of old.
They are certainly subdivisions of the Third Logos. They
are the Fire-Chohans or Angels, the Ether Angels, the Air
and Water Angels, and the Angels of the Earth. The seven
lower Sephiroth are the earthly angels and correspond to the
seven hierarchies of the seven elements, five of which are
known, and two unknown.

Q. Do they, then, correspond to the Races?

A. They do. Otherwise where would be the intellectual

[137]

Races with brains and thought, if it was not for these hierarchies that incarnated in them?

Q. What is the distinction between these various Hierarchies?

A. In reality these fires are not separate, any more than are the souls or monads to him who sees beyond the veil of matter or illusion.

He who would be an occultist must not separate either himself or anything else from the rest of creation or *noncreation.* For, the moment he distinguishes himself from even a vessel of dishonour, he will not be able to join himself to any vessel of honour. He must think of himself as an infinitesimal something, not even as an individual atom, but as a part of the world-atoms as a whole, or become an illusion, a nobody, and vanish like a breath leaving no trace behind. As illusions, we are separate distinct bodies, living in masks furnished by Maya. Can we claim one single atom in our body as distinctly our own? Everything, from spirit to the tiniest particle, is part of the whole, at best a link. Break a single link and all passes into annihilation; but this is impossible. There is a series of vehicles becoming more and more gross, from spirit to the densest matter, so that with each step downward and outward we get more and more the sense of separateness developed in us. Yet this is illusory, for if there were a real and complete separation between any two human beings, they could not communicate with, or understand each other in any way.

Thus with these hierarchies. Why should we separate their classes in our mind, except for purposes of distinction in *practical* Occultism, which is but the lowest form of applied Metaphysics. But if you seek to separate them on this plane of illusion, then all I can say is, that there exists between these Hierarchies the same abysses of distinction as between the "principles" of the Universe or those of man, if you like, and the same "principles" in a bacillus.

There is a passage in the Bhagavad-Gita (ch. viii.) wherein Krishna, speaking symbolically and esoterically, says: "I will state the times (conditions) . . . . at which devotees departing (from this life) do so never to return (be reborn). The Fire, the Flame, the day, the bright (lucky) fortnight, the six months of the Northern solstice, (dying) in these, those who know the Brahman (Yogis) go to the Brahman. Smoke, Night, the dark (unlucky) fortnight, the six months of the southern solstice, (dying) in these, the devotee goes to the lunar light (or mansion, the astral light also) and returns (is reborn)."*

Q. What is the explanation of this passage?

A. It means that the devotees are divided into two classes, those who reach Nirvana on Earth, and either accept or refuse it (though never to be born again, in this *Mahakalpa*, or age of Brahmâ); and those who do not reach this state of bliss as Buddha and others did.

"The Fire, the Flame, the day, the bright fortnight of the moon," are all symbols of the highest absolute deity. Those who die in such a state of absolute purity, go to Brahman, *i. e.*, have a right to Moksha or Nirvana. On the other hand "Smoke, night, the dark fortnight, &c.," are all symbolical of matter, the darkness of ignorance. Those who die in such a state of incomplete purification, must of course be reborn. Only the homogeneous, the absolutely purified unalloyed spirit, can be re-united to the Deity or go to Brahma.

Sloka (2). LEARN WHAT WE, WHO DESCEND FROM THE PRIMORDIAL SEVEN, WE WHO ARE BORN FROM THE PRIMORDIAL FLAME, HAVE LEARNED FROM OUR FATHERS.

"The first 'Primordial' are the highest beings on the scale of existence. The 'Primordial' proceed from 'Father-Mother.' "†

---
*S. D., Vol. I, p. 86.
†S. D., Vol. I, p. 88.

Q. Is Father-Mother here synonymous with the Third Logos?

A. The first primordial seven are born from the Third Logos. This is before it is differentiated into the Mother, when it becomes pure primordial matter in its first primitive essence, Father-Mother potentially. Mother becomes the immaculate mother only when the differentiation of spirit and matter is complete. Otherwise there would exist no such qualification. No one would speak of pure spirit as immaculate, for it cannot be otherwise. The mother is, therefore, the immaculate matter before it is differentiated under the breath of the pre-cosmic Fohat, when it becomes the "immaculate mother" of the "Son" or the manifested Universe, in form. It is the latter which begins the hierarchy that will end with Humanity or man.

Sloka (3). FROM THE EFFULGENCY OF LIGHT—THE RAY OF THE EVER-DARKNESS—SPRING IN SPACE THE RE-AWAKENED ENERGIES (*Dhyan-Chohans*): THE ONE FROM THE EGG, THE SIX AND THE FIVE; THEN THE THREE, THE ONE, THE FOUR, THE ONE, THE FIVE, THE TWICE SEVEN, THE SUM TOTAL. AND THESE ARE: THE ESSENCES, THE FLAMES, THE ELE- MENTS, THE BUILDERS, THE NUMBERS, THE ARUPA, (*formless*), THE RUPA (*with bodies*), AND THE FORCE OF DIVINE MAN—THE SUM TOTAL. AND FROM THE DIVINE MAN EMANATED THE FORMS, THE SPARKS, THE SACRED ANIMALS, AND THE MESSENGERS OF THE SACRED FATHERS (*the Pitris*) WITHIN THE HOLY FOUR.

Q. Can you explain these numbers and give their meaning?

A. As said in the Commentary, we are not at present con- cerned in the process, that is to say, it cannot at present be made public. Some few hints, however, may be given. The Rabbins call the Circle (or as some say, the first Point in it) Echod, the ONE or Ain-Soph. On a lower plane, the fourth, it becomes Adam Kadmon, the manifested seven and the unmanifested ten, or the complete Sephirothal Tree. The Sephiroth, therefore, are the same as the Elohim. Now the name of the latter written in Hebrew, Alhim, is composed of five letters; and these letters in their values in numerals, being placed round a circle can be transmuted at will, as they could not be were they applied to any other geometrical figure. The circle is endless, that is to say, has neither beginning nor end. Now the literal Kabala is divided into three parts or methods, the third of which is called Temura or permutation. According to certain rules one letter or numeral is substituted for another. The Kabalistic alphabet is divided into two equal parts, each letter or numeral of one part corresponding to a like number or letter in the other part. By changing the letters alternately, twenty-two permutations or combinations are produced, which process is called Tziruph.

The footnote on pages 90 and 91 (Vol. I, *Secret Doctrine*), makes my meaning quite clear.

> *Sloka* (4). THIS WAS THE ARMY OF THE VOICE—THE DIVINE SEPTENARY. THE SPARKS OF THE SEVEN ARE SUBJECT TO, AND THE SERVANTS OF, THE FIRST, THE SECOND, THIRD, FOURTH, FIFTH, SIXTH AND THE SEVENTH OF THE SEVEN. THESE ("*Sparks*") ARE CALLED SPHERES, TRIANGLES, CUBES, LINES, AND MODELLERS: FOR THUS STANDS THE ETERNAL NIDANA—THE OI-HA-HOU (*the permutation of Oeaohoo*).

Q. What are the "Life-Winds" in the commentary [page 96]?

A. The Life-winds are the various modes of out-breathing and in-breathing, changing thereby the polarity of the body and states of consciousness. It is Yoga practice, but beware of taking the exoteric works on Yoga literally. They all require a key.

Q. What is the meaning of the sentence beginning "The Sparks, etc." (*vide supra*)?

A. The sparks mean the Rays as well to the lower intelligence as to the human sparks or Monads. It relates to the circle and the digits, and is equivalent to saying that the figures 31415 as given on pages 90 and 91, are all subject to the circumference and diameter of the circle.

Q. Why is Sarasvati (the goddess of speech) also called the goddess of esoteric wisdom? If the explanation lies in the meaning of the word Logos, why is there a distinction between the immovable mind and movable speech? Is mind equivalent to Mahat, or to the Higher and Lower Manas?

A. The question is rather a complicated one. Sarasvati, the Hindu goddess, is the same as Vâch, whose name means Speech and who is the female Logos, esoterically. The second question seems rather involved. I believe it is because the Logos or Word is called the incarnate wisdom, "Light shining in darkness." The distinction lies between the immovable or eternal immutable ALL, and the movable Speech or Logos, *i. e.*, the periodical and the manifested. It can relate to the Universal, and to the individual mind, to Mahat, or to the Higher Manas, or even to the lower, the Kama Manas or Brain-Mind. Because that which is desire, instinctive impulse in the lower, becomes thought in the Higher. The former finds expression in acts, the latter in words. Esoterically, thought is more responsible and punishable than act. But exoterically it is the reverse. Therefore, in ordinary human law, an assault is more severely punished than the thought or intention, *i. e.*, the threat, whereas *Karmically* it is the contrary.

Q. "God geometrizes," says Plato, but seeing that there is no personal God, how is it that the process of formation is by Dots, Lines, Triangles, Cubes, Circles, and finally Spheres? And how when the sphere leaves the static state, does the inherent force of Breath set it whirling?

A. The term "God"—unless referring to the Unknown

Deity or *Absoluteness*, which can hardly be supposed *acting* in any way—has always meant in ancient philosophies the collectivity of the working and intelligent Forces in nature. The word "Forest" is singular, yet it is the term to express the idea of thousands or even millions of trees of different kinds. Materialists have the option of saying "Nature," or still better—"Law geometrizes" if they so prefer. But in the days of Plato, the average reader would hardly have understood the metaphysical · distinction and real meaning. The truth, however, of Nature ever "geometrizing" is easily ascertained. Here is an instance: Heat is the modification of the motions or particles of matter. Now, it is a physical and mechanical law that particles or bodies in motion on themselves, assume a spheroidal form—this, from a globular planet down to a drop of rain. Observe the snowflakes, which along with crystals exhibit to you all the geometrical forms existing in nature. As soon as motion ceases, the spheroidal shape alters; or, as Tyndall tells us, it becomes a flat drop, then the drop forms an equilateral triangle, a hexagon and so on. In observing the breaking up of ice-particles in a large mass, through which he passed heat rays, he observed that the first shape the particles assumed, was triangular or pyramidal, then cubical and finally hexagonal, &c. Thus, even modern physical science, corroborates Plato and justifies his proposition.

Q. When Tyndall took a large block of ice and threw a powerful ray upon it and thence on to a screen, there were to be seen the forms of ferns and plants in it. What is the reason of this?

A. This question ought really to be addressed first to Professor Tyndall, who would give a scientific explanation of it—and perhaps he has already done so. But Occultism would explain it by saying either that the ray helped to show the astral shapes which were preparing to form future ferns and plants, or that the ice had preserved the reflection of actual ferns and plants that had been reflected in it.   Ice is a great magician, whose occult properties are as little known as those of Ether.   It is occultly connected with the astral light, and may under certain conditions, reflect certain images from the invisible astral region, just as light and a sensitised plate may be made to reflect stars that cannot be perceived even by the telescope.   This is well known to learned Yogis who dwell on the eternal ice of Bodrinath and the Himalayas.   At any rate, ice has certainly the property of retaining images of things impressed on its surface under certain conditions of light, images which it preserves invisibly until it is melted.   Fine steel has the same property, though it is of a less occult nature.   Were you to observe the ice from the surface, these forms would not be seen.   But once that in decomposing the ice with heat you deal with the forces and the things that were impressed on it, then you find that it throws off these images and the forms appear. It is but one link leading to another link.   All this is not modern science of course, yet it is fact and truth.

Q. Do numbers and geometrical figures represent to human consciousness the laws of action in the Divine Mind?

A. They do, most assuredly.   There is no chance evolution or formation, nor is any so-called abnormal appearance or cosmic phenomenon due to haphazard circumstances.

Sloka (5). "DARKNESS," THE BOUNDLESS OR THE NO-NUMBER, ADI-NIDANA SVABHAVAT: THE O (*for x, unknown quantity*).
I.   THE ADI-SANAT, THE NUMBER, FOR HE IS ONE.
II.   THE VOICE OF THE WORD, SVABHAVAT, THE NUMBERS, FOR HE IS ONE AND NINE.
III. THE "FORMLESS SQUARE" (*Arupa*).
AND THESE ENCLOSED WITHIN THE O (*Boundless Circle*), ARE THE SACRED FOUR, AND THE TEN ARE THE ARUPA (*subjective, formless*) UNIVERSE; THEN COME THE

"SONS," THE SEVEN FIGHTERS, THE ONE, THE EIGHTH LEFT OUT, AND HIS BREATH WHICH IS THE LIGHT-MAKER (*Bhâskara*).

Q. The "One Rejected" is the sun of our system. Astronomically is there any explanation of Mârttanda's rejection?

A. The sun is older than any of its planets—though younger than the moon. Its "rejection" means that when bodies or planets began to form, helped by its rays, magnetic radiance or heat, and especially by its magnetic attraction, it had to be stopped, otherwise it would have swallowed all the younger bodies like as Saturn is fabled to have treated his progeny. This does not mean that all the planets are thrown out from the sun, as modern Science teaches, but simply that under the Rays of the sun they acquire their growth. Aditi is the ever-equilibrizing mother-nature on the purely spiritual and subjective plane. She is the Sakti, the female power or potency of the fecundating spirit; and it is for her to regulate the behaviour of the sons born in her bosom. The Vedic allegory is very suggestive.

Q. Were all the planets in our solar system first comets and then suns?

A. They were not suns in our, or their present solar systems, but comets in space. All began life as wanderers over the face of the infinite Kosmos. They detached themselves from the common storehouse of already prepared material, the Milky Way (which is nothing more or less than the quite developed world-stuff, all the rest in space being the crude material, as yet invisible to us); then, starting on their long journey they first settled in life where conditions were prepared for them by Fohat, and gradually became suns. Then each sun, when its Pralaya arrived, was resolved into millions and millions of fragments. Each of these fragments moved to and fro in space collecting fresh materials, as it rolled on, like an avalanche, until it came to a stop through the laws of attraction and repulsion, and became a planet in our own, as in other systems, beyond our telescopes. The sun's fragments will become just such planets after the Solar pralaya. It was a comet once upon a time, in the beginning of Brahmâ's Age. Then it came to its present position, whence it will burst asunder, and its atoms will be whirled into space for æons, and æons, like all other comets and meteors, until each, guided by Karma, is caught in the vortex of the two forces, and fixed in some higher and better system.

Thus the Sun will live in his children as a portion of the parents lives in their offspring. When that day comes, the semblance or reflection of the Sun which we see, will first fall off like a veil from the face of the true Sun. No mortal will see it, for no mortal eye could bear its radiance. Were this veil once removed for even a second, all the planets of its system would be instantaneously reduced to ashes, as the sixty thousand of King Sagara's Sons *were destroyed by a glance of Kapila's eye.*

Sloka (6). THEN THE SECOND SEVEN, WHO ARE THE LIPIKA, PRODUCED BY THE THREE (*Word, Voice and Spirit*). THE REJECTED SUN IS ONE, THE "SONS-SUNS" ARE COUNTLESS.

Q. What is the relation of the Lipika, the "Second Seven" to the "Primordial Seven" and to the first "Sacred Four"?

A. If you believe that any, save the highest Initiates, can explain this to your satisfaction, then you are greatly mistaken. The relation can be better understood, or rather, shown to be above all understanding, by first studying the Gnostic systems of the early centuries of Christianity, from that of Simon Magus down to the highest and noblest of them, the so-called PISTIS-SOPHIA. All these systems are derived from the East. That which we call the "Primordial Seven" and the "Second Seven" are called by Simon Magus the Æons, the primeval, the second and the third series of Syzygies. They are the graduated emanations, ever descending lower and lower into matter, from that primordial principle which he calls Fire, and we, Svâbhâvat. Behind that Fire, the manifested but silent Deity, stands with him as it does with us, that "which is, was, and ever will be." Let us compare his system with ours.

In a passage quoted from his works by the author of *Philosophumena*, we read:—"From this permanent Stability and Immortality of this first manifested principle 'Fire' (the third Logos) which immutability does not preclude activity, as the second from it is endowed with intelligence and reason (Mahat), it (the Fire) passed from the potentiality of action to action itself. From this series of evolutions were formed six beings, or the emanation from the infinite potency; they were formed in Syzygies, *i. e.*, they radiated out of the flame two by two, one being active, the other the passive principle." These Simon named Nous and Epinoia, or Spirit and Thought, Phône and Onoma, Voice and Name, and Logismos and Euthumêsis, Reasoning and Reflection. And again —"In each of these six primitive Beings the Infinite Potency was in its totality; but it was there in potentiality and not in act. It had to be established therein through an image (that of the paradigm), in order that it should appear in all its essence, virtue, grandeur and effects; for only then could it become like unto the Parent Potency infinite and eternal. If, on the contrary, it was not conformed by or through the Image, that Potentiality could never become Potency or pass into action, but was lost for lack of use, as it happens to a man who having an aptitude for grammar or geometry does not exercise it; it gets lost for him just as if he never had it" (*Philosophumena*, p. 250).

He shows that whether these Æons belong to the superior,

middle or lower world, they are all one, except in material density, which determines their outward manifestations and the result produced, not their real essence which is one, or their mutual relations which, as he says, are established from eternity by immutable laws.

Now the first, the second, third or primordial seven or Lipika, are all one. When they emanate from one plane to another, it is a repetition of—"as above, so below." They are all differentiated in matter or density, not in qualities; the same qualities descend on to the last plane, our own, where man is endowed with the same potentiality, if he but knew how to develop it, as the highest Dhyan-Chohans.

In the hierarchies of Æons, Simon gives three pairs of two each, the seventh being the fourth which descends from one plane to another.

The Lipika proceed from Mahat and are called in the Kabala the four Recording Angels; in India, the four Maharajahs, those who record every thought and deed of man; they are called by St. John in the Revelation, the Book of Life. They are directly connected with Karma and what the Christians call the Day of Judgment; in the East it was called the Day after Mahamanvantara, or the "Day-Be-With-Us." Then everything becomes one, all individualities are merged into one, yet each knowing itself, a mysterious teaching indeed. But then, that which to us now is non-consciousness or the unconscious, will then be absolute consciousness.

Q. What relation have the Lipika to Mahat?

A. They are a division, four taken from one of the Septenates that emanates from Mahat. Mahat corresponds with the Fire of Simon Magus, the secret and the manifested Divine Ideation, made to witness to itself in this objective Universe through the intelligent forms we see around us, in what is called creation. Like all other emanations, they are

"Wheels within Wheels." The Lipika are on the plane corresponding to the highest plane of our chain of globes.

Q. What is the difference between Spirit, Voice and Word?

A. The same as between Atma, Buddhi and Manas, in one sense. Spirit emanates from the unknown Darkness, the mystery into which none of us can penetrate. That Spirit—call it the "Spirit of God" or Primordial Substance—mirrors itself in the Waters of Space—or the still undifferentiated matter of the future Universe—and produces thereby the first flutter of differentiation in the homogeneity of primordial matter. This is the Voice, pioneer of the "Word" or the first manifestation; and from that Voice emanates the Word or Logos, that is to say, the definite and objective expression of that which has hitherto remained in the depths of the Concealed Thought. That which mirrors itself in Space is the Third Logos. We may express this Trinity also by the terms Colour, Sound, and Numbers.